Wakefield Press

Datsunland

Stephen Orr is the author of six previous novels. He contributes essays and features to several magazines, journals and newspapers. His short fiction has been published widely over the last ten years, and a selection is gathered here for the first time. Stephen Orr lives in Adelaide.

Praise for *The Hands*

'Orr writes with a skilful lightness of touch, punctuating his quietly subdued prose with understated humour and restrained emotion ... There was something about this book – the all-encompassing portrait of one family living in rural isolation – that transfixed me from start to finish, almost as if I had accompanied them on this emotional journey, perhaps sitting in the farm truck as it made its rounds fixing fences or checking on cattle.' – *Reading Matters*

'The Hands has the scope of a Greek tragedy – not only in its focus on the violence underlying familial relationships. Ineluctable fate seems to press on a family forced into painful reflection. The encroaching desert is, like the Greek Moirai, remorseless: "It didn't like him, it didn't hate him; it refused to know anyone or anything." Catharsis is evoked, but its form is not predictable. Orr is a restrained writer when it counts.' – *Australian Book Review*

'The Hands is a raw, honest and absorbing portrait of pastoral life from Orr ... he eloquently captures the practical trials and emotional angst experienced by farmers torn between a generations-long connection to country and the reality of a fragile future dependent on nature's whims. The pastoral portrait he paints is so vivid you can almost taste the suffocating dust ... A true Australian story – and one well worth reading.' – *InDaily*

'The triumphant culmination of a five-book fascination with the dynamics of (family) groups as they function in extreme and often liminal situations ... Orr slides seamlessly in and out of his different characters' heads ... always moving the story efficiently along ... and always making the reader effortlessly, endlessly, insistently aware of the breadth and rigour of the landscape, the dominance and dryness.' – *Advertiser*

'Orr creates great atmosphere in the setting and portrays each character beautifully.' – *Good Reading*

'This is at times a heartbreaking read, but the story is told with elegant, beautiful prose ... It is hard not to be drawn into this family's life.' – *Weekly Times*

Praise for *One Boy Missing*

'Stephen Orr's detective is sunnier than Kurt Wallander, but his talkative characters and bitter realism stands comparison with Henning Mankell. He's a sincere storyteller with a flinty eye for the landscape and the sadness that drives good stories forward.' – *Weekend Press*

Praise for *Dissonance*

'Stephen Orr writes a story with great tension and momentum. The emotional and psychological layers of *Dissonance* prompt us to ponder the deep nature of familial relationships ...' – *Good Reading*

'Orr brings us a cast of characters that are wholly believable. The first hundred pages alone would make a fine novella. As it stands, the entire novel is an accomplished work.' – *InDaily*

'This is an intelligent, beautifully-wrought novel. Its finely nuanced characters intrigue and move because of the complexity of their motivations and identities.' – *Australian Book Review*

'Orr is a no-nonsense, vivid storyteller. He punches out exchanges between his characters in a pragmatic way that transmits jealousy and heartbreak without sentiment.' – *Australian*

Praise for *Time's Long Ruin*

'*Time's Long Ruin* is Orr's eloquent, unusual, bold but responsible retelling of a veritable urban nightmare that still haunts the Australian imagination.' – *Sydney Morning Herald*

'The writing is accomplished, the imagery beautifully evocative ... despite the distressing subject matter at its core, this is a deeply affectionate novel.' – *Age*

'It is Orr's cleaving of the ordinary to the unspeakable that gives the novel its potency and brings it within the margins of the Australian Gothic.' – *Big Issue*

'Every now and again, you open a book that is so richly evocative, so poignant and haunting that the characters leach into your subconscious and you are caught in an intricately spun web of emotion, scent and feeling.' – *Sunday Tasmanian*

Datsunland

Stephen Orr

Wakefield
Press

Wakefield Press
16 Rose Street
Mile End
South Australia 5031
www.wakefieldpress.com.au

First published 2017

Cover designed by Liz Nicholson, designBITE
Edited by Emily Hart, Wakefield Press
Typeset by Michael Deves, Wakefield Press

National Library of Australia Cataloguing-in-Publication entry

Creator: Orr, Stephen, 1967– , author.
Title: Datsunland / Stephen Orr.
ISBN: 978 1 74305 475 8 (paperback).
Subjects: Short stories, Australian.

CORIOLE
McLAREN VALE

Contents

Dr Singh's Despair
1

The Shot-put
25

The One-Eyed Merchant
50

A Descriptive List of the Birds Native to Shearwater, Australia
60

The Keeping of Miss Mary
71

Guarding the Pageant
85

Akdal Ghost
98

The Barmera Drive-in
107

The Confirmation
115

The Adult World Opera
122

The Syphilis Museum
142

The Shack
161

The Photographer's Son
170

Datsunland
181

Dr Singh's Despair

Dr Sevanand Singh
Anandpur Sahib Rd
Nangal 140124
Punjab

SA Health Commission
Citi Centre Building
11 Hindmarsh Square
Adelaide South of Australia

Dear Sir or Madam

Let me make it clear – I have no intention of repaying the $7328. My reasons for returning to India are set out in my last two letters. Still, I have more to add. My address has changed so there is no point sending more correspondence. I no longer live beside the Nangal Fertiliser and Heavy Water Factory but have found a small home in the country. Here I can recover and lick my wounds (if that is how it is said). I can talk to pandits and thank God I realised my mistake before it was too late – before I brought my wife and son to Australia, to your outback, to Coober Pedy. You say I only worked three days – true. You say you paid my airfares – true. Also, I thank you for paying for my motel in Adelaide. But you did not pay for my taxi, accommodation or meals in CP. In fact, nothing was paid for or arranged as promised. And now I will tell you more of the story of my not repaying.

Dr Sevanand Singh stared out of the football-shaped window. The landscape had changed from brown to red to off-Fanta. As the small jet descended, sheds, petrol stations and even shrubs gained definition.

There was a road, and a small white car, and you could see sand ridges that stretched towards the horizon. As he waited, he thought without thinking. About why God had made so much nothing. What was the point of creating a void? No dams or powerhouses, no towns or shops, or apartment buildings. No forests. No petrol tankers. No animals. No ants. No bacteria. Had God abandoned this place? Was He displeased with it or was it an experiment of some kind? Or was He just resting, and yet to cover the sand with trees, rivers and animals, or pine trees, or anything?

No, he thought. This is it. God has finished. Maybe there's an order, a system, a hierarchy of animals and plants that can't be seen from ten thousand feet.

He looked at the brochure in his lap and remembered. Flicked through the photos of polished opal and thought, So what? Remembered his wife saying, 'These are the eyes of Buddha, or a cat, or snake.'

'But snakes' eyes are black,' he'd said.

'No, turquoise, with runs of red and silver.'

Yes, perhaps it is God's work, he guessed. Hiding beauty in the most inaccessible places. Challenging pale-skinned, bow-legged men to find it. He could even hear God's voice: Come and get it, boys. But you'll need to dig through sand, clay and rocks. What, you want to look into my eyes? Not likely!

As Sevanand studied his brochure he saw images of life in the outback. Hawker Gate – one small opening in an eight-thousand-mile-long fence – an attempt to keep dingoes out of God's nothingness, and a sign threatening six months' imprisonment for not shutting the gate. A man in overalls peeling the skin off a dead kangaroo. Alice Springs, its homes lined up like overcooked cupcakes. Quonset huts full of tractor parts and fence posts, a deserted railway siding called 'Nevertire', and the Tibooburra Post Office with its promise of a radio trunk line to all states. A hundred and one pictures of nothingness, in the place he'd chosen to live. To bring his family, to make their future. Australia – a picture of two men asleep in a swag as a lamb licked chop grease from their lips.

They were descending, and he could feel the engines slowing. As they banked he saw thousands of peach-white pockmarks on the landscape. Each had its own slag-pile and there were small iron huts, trucks with drilling rigs and even a few people wandering between the shafts. Faint tracks connecting the mines like a dot-to-dot. Reminding him of his mother's lace tablecloth, laid out across their particleboard table whenever a rich uncle came to visit.

They landed, and taxied, and the jet stopped in front of a cream-brick terminal with the words 'COOB R P DY' in cracked plastic. He thanked the cabin assistant, gathered his briefcase and climbed out. Stepped onto the tarmac and stopped to get his breath. Sweat on his forehead. Shirt and pants sticking to his body. 'Hot?' he said to another man, who had fat red cheeks and three or four days' stubble.

'Warm.' Pulling his underwear out of his arse.

Sevanand could feel the heat through his rubber soles. He put down his briefcase, took off his jacket and draped it across his arm. An Aboriginal man wearing shorts and steel-capped boots removed bags from the luggage compartment and threw them onto a trolley. He stopped to finish a cigarette, step on it and say, 'You're a funny sort of black fella.'

Sevanand was unsure. 'I'm the new doctor.'

'Good for you. We just lost one. Pommy fella. He lasted a few weeks ... or was it that long?'

'A few weeks?'

'Yeah.' The man ran his tongue over his yellow teeth, spat and motioned for him to come closer. 'See, problem was, he couldn't see the funny side of things.'

'No?'

'Next thing you know, a bloke goes crazy. That's what started happening to him.'

'How's that?'

He tapped his nose. 'That'd be telling tales.'

Sevanand raised his head and tried to straighten his sore neck. The short, balding black man fought with a heavy case. 'You got a sense of humour, Doctor?'

'Yes.'

'You'll need it. You like beer?'

'Sometimes.'

'All the time, mate. And what about sex?'

'Pardon?'

'You know, fuckin'. Plenty of it here. TV reception's shithouse.' He smiled slyly. 'Listen, mate, you don't need to be married. We're pretty open-minded up here.' And he laughed.

'I must get along.'

'Go on then. If you stay, we'll make you an honorary black fella.'

As Sevanand walked towards the terminal he heard the man say, 'Fuckin' coon.' He went into a hot shed choked with fumes, the smell of antiseptic and the cries of a pudding-faced baby. On one side, the shed opened to the desert, the other, tarmac. There were a few plastic seats, a ticket desk, a Coke machine and a brochure stand with one brochure: Ian and Judy's Shell House, with a picture of Uluru and the Opera House made from cowries. Flies made a meal of dog biscuits, shit scrolls and urine in the pet bay before mingling with the tourists. Neil Diamond's 'Sweet Caroline' played on an ancient PA as a television flickered on the wall with grainy images of men in fake beards panning for gold as they explained the history of mining in Australia (although they never mentioned Coober Pedy).

He sat on a loose seat, took a freshly ironed handkerchief from his pocket and wiped his forehead. He remembered the brochures the Health Commission had sent him: Barossa Valley vineyards, fishing off white beaches on the Eyre Peninsula and marvelling at the Naracoorte Caves.

Yes, some of this please, he'd written back. He was tired of living in the most densely populated place on the planet. A swarm of humans that just kept coming, filling his waiting room, his days, his nights, his dreams with broken bodies, malaria, typhoid and TB, floating through the small, hot room he worked in for sixteen hours a day.

Yes, some of this please.

But then came the next letter. We have shortages in remote locations. Very considerable financial incentives are involved.

Yes, some of that too.

So, sign here, Dr Singh, and we'll pay your airfare, accommodation – the whole lot.

Almost.

He approached the ticket desk. A pimply girl picked the orange laminate until a biscuit-sized piece snapped off. The ticket clerk looked at her.

'Oops.' Grinning.

He looked at her loose, tie-dyed top with tassels. Pants – purple, silk, ballooning, tied off at the knees. Leather slippers. Unwashed dreadlocks – as if she, and the boyfriend, busy arguing over tickets, had just come off of the Shiva Ashram.

Cardboard people, he thought. Phonies! Hardly Indian.

Finally, he approached a tall, crisp meringue-looking woman behind the counter. 'My name is Dr Sevanand Singh.' He waited, assuming she'd know who he was.

'Dr Singh?'

'Yes, I've just been appointed by your Health Commission. I was told someone would pick me up.'

'Who?'

'Someone.'

They looked around the terminal, which by now was almost empty.

'Anyone for Dr Singh?' she called, but there was no reply.

'Was a car sent?' he asked.

She shrugged. 'I wasn't told.'

'This is most upsetting. If someone says they'll do something …'

'That's the government,' she explained. 'I wouldn't expect too much. They don't know anything exists outside of Adelaide.'

He took a deep breath. 'Is there someone we can call?'

'A taxi?'

He waited. 'Yes … that please.'

> Despite the fact that I had been forgotten I arranged my own lift, at my own expense. I waited for ninety minutes in the shed before I was asked to move outside (the airport was closing for the day). There was very little shade. You probably think I complain, but no. A thermometer in my bag read 54 degrees. Sir, I am a doctor. Six years of education earned as a scholarship from the Rupnagar Council. Two years as a junior doctor. So, in India I am respected. Cars are sent for me and rooms prepared in hotels. But CP? No wonder the man before me shifted to the Gold Coast, or (someone said) returned to Leeds.

He'd never known a straight road. Nangal drivers were catfish, navigating their asphalt rivers: the Satluj River Road, the road to the dam and Hydel Channel. The highway south, which led all the way to New Delhi, with never more than a hundred straight metres. Roads wrapped around hills, along valleys, fighting their way through towns, forests and tea plantations.

But this was different. A bamboo stake, a metre-rule, a million miles of English iron floating a foot (or so) above the sand. A road from and to nowhere. Grey tar and white paint rolling on and on towards a horizon that kept tumbling towards infinity, as far, as remote, as unthinkable as his lost Punjab.

The taxi driver was studying him in the rear-vision mirror. 'I couldn't have been no quicker, mate,' he said, winding down his window. 'When she called I had the carby in pieces.'

'Carby?'

'*Car-bu-rettor*. Petrol, Air!'

'Well, how far is it?'

'Another fifteen clicks.' He narrowed his eyes to size up the small Indian. 'What, you pissed off, fella?'

'Not with you. But they were meant to pick me up.'

'Who?'

'Someone from the hospital.'

Silence. He studied the landscape. The small shrubs and groundcovers, something green growing in the cracks in the road, a few pine trees struggling beside a rest stop. He was acclimatising to the outback, to the small things. It was a geography of oxygen, dust, the wind exciting the sand like so many sine waves. He wondered how much Punjab could be squeezed into a single line of longitude beyond his tinted window.

'Where to?' the driver asked.

'The hospital.'

More silence. Rubber rolling across road. The growl of five-and-a-half cylinders. Cold, stale air. Johnny Cash.

The driver was still looking at him. 'Where you from?'

'Nangal. The Punjab.'

'India?'

'Yes.'

'Bet this is a bit of a shock, eh?'

He didn't know what to say. Shock? 'Perhaps I will get used to it?'

But the driver just grinned back at him.

Sevanand asked, 'Have you lived here long?'

'Long enough.' He cleared his throat and spat out the window. Most of it came back. 'So, you seen plenty of dead bodies?'

'Many.'

'They sorta ... spook you out?'

Sevanand stopped to picture a dead body: an old man with sunken cheeks and prominent eyebrows. 'It's nothing, until the colour goes out of them.'

'What then ... like a leg o' lamb?' Half-grinned, half-grimaced.

'The skin is surprisingly tough to cut ... like leather.'

'Christ, that'll be us one day, eh?'

Sevanand imagined his own lifeless body sitting up in bed in a motel room, his tongue protruding from his mouth, his left hand clutching his Coober Pedy brochures. Or spread across the highway, his stomach cavity exposed, his intestines sizzling on the hot tar. He looked across the desert, then at his hands. 'The Lord said, *As a man casts off worn out garments and takes on new ones.*'

He looked up at the driver, who smiled and asked, 'You a Bible basher?'

'Hindu. The Sankhya Yoga.'

'Ah ...'

'The *Bhagavad Gita*.'

'Fuck!' He pumped the accelerator as the car lost power. They drifted to a stop.

'This would be the carburettor?'

'This would be, mate.'

They popped the bonnet and got out to look. The driver, Trevor (he could see his name badge), showed him the small metal part sitting loose in its cradle. 'That's what you get for rushing a job,' he said, glaring at him.

'I didn't realise.'

Trevor kicked the front bumper. 'Fuck!'

'Perhaps, if it wasn't ready you shouldn't have used it.'

Trevor's face turned redder as his hair follicles formed their own pockmarked landscape. 'Perhaps you shouldn't have fuckin' called me.'

'I don't appreciate your tone.'

'I don't appreciate your ...'

Attitude, colour, smugness, smell, race? He could just guess what Trevor was thinking.

Trevor took a deep breath. Stared at his passenger. Shot forward and attempted to wave down an old Dodge truck.

'Can I help?' Sevanand asked, but his voice was drowned by the truck's engine, and a loud stereo. He fanned fine dust, coughed, wiped his eyes and spat the outback from his mouth.

Trevor approached the driver and said, 'I need a lift.'

'Get in,' the man replied.

Trevor looked back at Sevanand. 'I'll be back in a minute.'

'Can I come?'

He indicated the truck's load of scaffold and replied, 'Just a few minutes ... maybe an hour.'

'What should I do?'

But he was already in the cab, waving, and the old truck was pulling onto the road.

Sir, in CP people do as they want. There is no such thing as punctuality, an appointment, deadlines, promises – the simplest bits of courtesy. No, the driver did not return that night so I tried to sleep in the taxi. It was very cold and I put on four or five layers of clothing. There were lights, and tooting, but no one stopped. I understood the outback was a place where people helped each other. Not the case. As trucks passed they rocked the vehicle. So, at two or three in the morning I decided it was safer to sleep on the grass beside the road. I gathered my bags and found a hollow in the ground.

Sevanand stood surrounded by a soup of stars, high cloud and the distant light of what he assumed was Coober Pedy. He turned on the spot, searching the desert, and after two complete orbits looked down to find himself buried up to his ankles in sand. He pulled himself free, sat down, took off his shoes and emptied them.

Found himself placing them neatly together, taking out his wallet and arranging it beside them, removing his watch and placing it in his left shoe and finally, opening out his handkerchief and using it to cover his effects. 'Lord Krishna,' he called, but there was no echo, sound, companionship. Just a dampening, a deadening – of noise, movement and thought.

'Coober Pedy!'

A car sliced through the night.

'Thank you very much,' he whispered. '*Mate*.'

Then, his wife appeared before him. She was smiling, and laughing, and said, You'll always remember your first night in the outback.

He wasn't laughing. And last.

Come on, think of why you're doing this.

Why?

For us.

And he could hear the voices of his children in the distance.

We can't continue in this flat, she said. There's a whole new life itn the West. We'd be mad stay here.

He could see the desert full of people: Buddhist monks, drink sellers, lepers, children, a taxi navigating the crush of bodies and police chasing a gang of child thieves. Millions of bodies crowding his world of nothing. The din of conversation, singing, prayer, ads for Pepsi blaring from a speaker, floating in the cold air and settling on the warm, hi-vis sand. There were five, ten, maybe fifteen million people, but no one person. Just numbers, like ibis crowding an estuary, or pigs waiting in a slaughterhouse yard.

Would you forgive me? If this didn't work? he asked his wife, but she just turned, and walked towards a spice seller.

Sevanand rolled his jumper and used it as a pillow. He laid back and looked at the millions of stars and eventually whispered, '*All beings are in Me, I am not in them*.'

> Later, I discovered that when Trevor returned in the morning, he'd called for me, and looked, but mustn't have looked far. He fixed his carburettor and returned to CP. Meanwhile, it seems, I was in a deep sleep.

Sevanand stirred slowly. He could feel the sun on his skin. He sat up and started removing clothing. Looking towards the road, he noticed the taxi had gone.

He stood and studied the area. 'Trevor?' Ran to the side of the road and looked left and right. Perhaps the car had been stolen? Maybe someone had retrieved it for Trevor without knowing he was asleep? If so, he would just have to wait and they would come back for him. Then he thought, Maybe Trevor couldn't find me ... but he mustn't have seen me walking into town. Perhaps he thought I'm returning to the airport and he's checking there?

Either way, I just have to wait.

He repacked his clothes and returned to sit beside the road. Every time a car or truck went by he stood and tried to hitch a lift. People slowed, looked at him strangely and continued.

By nine am it was hot again. He used his jacket for shade. By ten he was soaked with sweat and could smell himself. Out of desperation, he emptied his case again, set it up as a sort of tent and slid under it. By lunchtime he'd given up. Repacked his belongings and started walking towards Coober Pedy.

Not long after, a police car passed, slowed, completed a U-turn and drove up behind him. He put down his bags and turned to face the constable as she approached him.

'Dr Sevanand Singh,' he said, extending his hand.

She was unsure, but shook it. 'Should I ask?'

Yes, it was a town, he guessed, but barely. Someone or some people had avoided resurfacing the highway that ran into town, paved as few footpaths as possible, abstained from fixing gutters or installing stoplights and put off replacing the plywood police station. When he saw children playing on the primary school's old monkey bars and kicking balls on the dusty oval he wondered if he had come all that far from Nangal.

Beyond the dry-cleaners, delis, supermarkets and newsagents of Hutchison Street, there were openings in the earth where suburbs should have been.

'These are the famous underground homes?' he asked the constable.

'Yes,' she replied. 'This is no place for human beings.'

'But people adapt?'

'Apparently … until they escape.'

She slowed, stopped, got out and moved a shopping trolley from the middle of the road. When she got back in she said, 'Some of these wog miners, they've been here for sixty years. They're the ones go and dig out these homes. But if you ask me' – and she drove off as she looked across at him – 'some of their circuits have fried.'

She stopped in front of the hospital and helped him with his bags. 'Well, Dr Singh,' she half-sang, 'I'm sure we'll be in contact.'

'You'll keep me in work?'

'Long as you've got a good supply of stomach pumps.'

He thought of the baggage handler – humour, beer and sex – although he was unsure of the order.

He climbed a few stairs littered with cigarette butts and walked into a terrazzo foyer with an almost life-size portrait of the Queen. A faintly reassuring antiseptic smell, the sound of plates being thrown onto a metal trolley, guttural moans and a distant cricket match on a tinny-sounding radio. An old Aboriginal man with a bandage around his throat approached him and asked, 'Are you a doctor?'

'Yes.' Proudly.

The man started undoing his bandage.

'I can't look at you now,' Sevanand explained, holding the man's arm.

'Why not?'

'I haven't started work yet.'

'When do you start?'

'A few days.'

The man was confused. 'So I gotta see that other fella?'

'Yes.' For the first time in weeks he felt like a doctor. 'Now, return to your room. Do you know the way?'

The man shrugged, and indicated. 'That way, isn't it?'

'Is it?'

'Is it?'

'I'm asking. Do you remember?'

And then he turned and walked off.

Under a sign that read 'Dial 9 for Assistance' (which somebody had changed to 'Arse-istance') he found an old touch-phone and called for help. An irritated voice answered and he explained who he was. 'I'm very tired. Could someone please come rapidly?'

'Hold your horses, Doctor.' The line disconnected.

As he waited he read the names on an honour roll. 'Directors of the Coober Pedy Area Hospital'. Starting with 1928: 'Dr HV Kimber'. He noticed there was a new name nearly every year. Dr White had lasted for five years in the fifties, but apart from that.

A tall man in his early thirties, wearing jeans, sneakers and a T-shirt, entered the foyer through a swinging door. '*Nice*,' he said, staring at him. 'You're our next fella, eh?'

Sevanand looked surprised. 'Next?'

'But I'm sure you're the one ... are you?'

'Which one?'

The young man shook his hand. 'We weren't expecting you until next week.'

'I arrived yesterday, but I've slept in the desert.'

'The desert?'

Sevanand explained and the man said, 'I'm sorry, I was going to come and get you.'

'It's done now.' Thinking of his wife and his promise.

The man introduced himself as Mark Ash, Director of Nursing, and took him into a small room. Made him watery coffee, sat down and said, 'You should've called.'

'I didn't think, but I'm here now. If you can show me my room I'll shower.' He noticed the look on Ash's face. 'Is there a problem?'

'The thing is, the last fella left it in a bit of a mess. So we've had the painters in.'

'Are they finished?'

'Started.'

'I was promised a room.'

Ash tried to smile. 'Yes, we've got one … Might even be able to arrange some new curtains.'

Sevanand tried the coffee and the taste made him madder still. 'I really do need a rest and a shower. Someone should've told you when I was coming.'

'You see, there's your problem. You never assume anything with the government. If you want something done you gotta do it yerself.'

'It's been a long few days.'

And with these few words Mark Ash knew that Sevanand was not the one. He could already guess how long he'd last – four, five, maybe six months.

'Listen, Dr Singh, Sevanand,' he said, 'up here you gotta take things as they come. It's bush time. You know? Outback time. Like the black fellas. Doesn't bother them if it takes six months to change a tyre. A year, ten years, so what? Get what I mean?'

Sevanand tried to smile. 'And people enjoy their sex?'

Ash slapped his knee and laughed. 'Yeah, that's it, that's how you wanna be.'

'Flexible?'

'That's one way, eh?' And he broke up laughing.

'Beer?'

'Plenty of beer.'

'And humour?'

Ash stopped. 'That, my friend, is the most important thing of all.'

'So, I wait for my room? In the meantime?'

And smiled. 'A few nights' kip? I've got the perfect place.'

Yes, I agreed to be flexible, and I tried, but a professional man must maintain some dignity. The following night I stayed in a backpackers' hostel run by one of Mr Ash's friends. When I first met the landlord (Mr Bruce Grierson) I thought that things were looking up. He wore a business shirt and tie and the carpeted foyer within the underground bunker was clean, well lit and decorated with posters of German castles and Greek islands. But then I discovered that Mr Grierson had just returned from a funeral (a Swiss man who'd fallen down a mineshaft and broken his back, waiting nine days for help that never came). So, looks are deceiving. Very much so.

Mark Ash said his goodbyes and climbed the carpeted steps to the surface. Meanwhile, Bruce Grierson pulled off his tie and started to unbutton his shirt. 'Punjab, eh? We don't get many Indians. Mainly Brits and Germans. Germans seem to love underground bunkers, eh?'

Grierson removed his shirt to reveal a landscape of saltbush, and a pair of nipples that had hardened in the cold air. 'Should be able to squeeze you in,' he said, before pulling on a T-shirt ('If you've got the shaft, I've got the drill'). He led Sevanand through double doors into a classroom-sized chasm lit with half a dozen bare globes hanging from a ceiling of chicken wire over red rock. 'We're pretty full up, but there's always people coming and going.'

There were nine or ten triple bunks against each wall and three more rows extending across the room. Someone lazing on each bed, or a backpack and clothes as a claim. The entire floor was covered in sleeping bags, piles of washing and food and maps and books, more bodies (some wearing nothing more than bathers and shorts, one girl in a bra and undies), beer and spirit bottles scattered everywhere (although Grierson had said alcohol was banned), a pair lying on a bunk kissing and someone's pet rat in a cage on top of an old fridge. A school group, perhaps nine or ten boys, throwing a basketball to each other while singing a riff on some sort of hymn:

> The blessed saint,
> A sacred start,
> The Lindisfarne Creed,
> A holy fart …

'Here we go,' Grierson said, creating a space on the floor. 'Got a sleeping bag?'

'No.'

'I've got some spares. Make yourself at home. Gratis, too, eh? Mark said the hospital will pay yer bill.'

Sevanand searched for a suitable response. He'd learnt something about sarcasm (No, that'd be far too generous) and a lot about incredulity (Exactly how much do you charge for half a square metre of beer-soaked shag pile?). There was always aggression (Do you know who I am? Do you know who'll be removing your appendix when it bursts?), bile (You wouldn't house animals like this!) or acceptance (Here? Yes, that'll do nicely).

Still, what was the point? He could see his wife smiling down at him, her face highlighted by hot, yellow globes. At least it's shag pile, she said.

'Thank you, Mr Grierson, and if I could borrow a sleeping bag?'

Half an hour later he was stretched out on a Camp-Masta 690. He'd showered, combed his hair and doused himself in powder before dressing in a pair of light summer pyjamas and returning to his square of carpet to rest.

Strange, he thought, as he closed his eyes. So much emptiness. So few people. And here I am back in my apartment building. Then he drifted off, his children's voices mingling with muffled AC/DC.

'Oi, mate, you're on me jocks.'

Sevanand opened his eyes to see a caramel-coloured Aussie towering above him. Apart from a towel around his neck, he was naked. Sevanand studied bulging, steel girder legs that led up to a tight, dimpled scrotum frosted with grey hairs, a lopped cock dangling like overstretched taffy, a sixpack like the gorilla in Mumbai Zoo.

'Me undies?'

Sevanand felt under his sleeping bag and found the underpants. Handed them over, and the giant put his legs through the holes, eventually gathering his tackle and packing it away in a manner that left nothing to the imagination. Then he pulled on some shorts and a singlet and said, 'You sleepin' next to me?'

'Do you mind?'

He sniffed the air. 'What you got on?'

'Powder.'

'Fuck, I've got some Old Spice if you want it.'

'What sort?'

'Old fuckin' Spice!'

'No thank you.' He extended his hand.

The giant shook it, combed his hair and said, 'My name's Rob Foster, from Broome.'

'Dr Singh.'

'Doctor?'

'Yes.'

Foster smiled at him. 'What you doin' here? Did yer kill someone?'

Sevanand sat up and crossed his legs. 'My room at the hospital is being painted.'

'Doctor, eh?'

'Yes.'

'Some of the fellas are goin' down the pub. You wanna come?'

Sevanand stopped to think. Yes, he had to make an effort to fit in, but no, these weren't locals. 'Thank you anyway, but I've just arrived.'

'Suit yerself.'

And with this Foster slipped on a pair of thongs and headed for the big double doors. Sevanand returned to his resting position, interlocking his fingers across his stomach, crossing his legs at the ankles and breathing deeply.

It was late, and dark, when he woke. The only light came from the fridge, the door having been left ajar. He could hear movement and a guttural moan, and he froze. A girl's voice, laughing, and Foster's, whispering. He kept his eyes closed and tried to control his breathing.

The voices stopped and he could hear lips and tongues and slurping and sucking. It wasn't subtle. Bodies moving and clothes and sleeping bags rustling and then, an even longer silence. A few moments later the rustling became regular – a slow, acrylic whoosh getting faster and faster. He dared open his eyes just a few millimetres and made out the giant's frame moving on top of the girl. He could see his monstrous buttocks rise and fall in the Kelvinator's dim light. Before long the movement became forceful and louder and the girl started to moan. Foster soldiered on, grunting as if he was shovelling a pile of dolomite. And then there was a sort of frenzy of clothes and skin and oohs and ahs and, 'Just there … don't stop now.'

He heard them fall apart, and laugh and whisper, and then Foster burped and said, 'Ssh, careful, you'll wake the Paki.'

'He's probably been listening,' she replied.

'Oi, Paki, you awake?'

They laughed again.

Sevanand was petrified. He'd gained his own erection and feared they'd be able to see it through his light summer pyjamas. He improvised a roll to the right and they laughed again.

Over the next hour she returned to her giant three times. After this they stood, walked through the minefield of bodies and made their way to the showers. When Sevanand guessed it was safe he jumped up, pulled on some clothes over his pyjamas, gathered his bags and made for the foyer.

Twenty minutes later he was heading back to the hospital. With his briefcase in one hand and bag in the other he tried to balance, occasionally tripping on a gutter, slipping on gravel or stumbling on an old beer bottle. He could hear the grunting, and the baggage handler's words: one of three things. Not because of any sense of sloth, laziness or stupidity (he supposed, as he passed the Chicago Motor Repairs with a herd of white utes parked out front) but out of necessity, a lack of alternatives, an acceptance of a life composed of imperfect things. Maybe, he guessed, as he looked up at the stars in the bruised, black sky, this was a sort of alcoholic perfection, a utopia sparkling with veins of red and green. Yes, colour. That's what it was all about. Finding the perfect in the imperfect. But still, he mused, it was the life of a gambler. Sixty years of body odour, lung disease and frozen food for a few small stones. But if that's what people wanted.

Three small consolations.

Or the story of the man who'd come from Russia. Three weeks later he was a millionaire. First shaft he'd ever put down.

A car slowed and pulled up beside him. A few young men stuck out their heads and said, 'I'll have a vindaloo, please,' and, 'How hot's your masala?' They all laughed.

'Do you do butter chicken?'

'I'll have a fuckin' laksa.'

And his mate. 'That's not fuckin' Indian, y' prick.'

The driver planted his foot and they disappeared in a cloud of dust.

Would you forgive me? Sevanand asked his wife, as he stood collapsing under the weight of his bags. As I sat listening to that pair, I was thinking how I could arrange it.

How? she asked.

He put down his bags. I could write a letter to the Health Commission explaining how the heat has triggered my asthma. Or maybe depression … or something like heart disease?

Or you could tell the truth?

Yes, I could write it all in a letter, couldn't I?

And with this realisation, that the world wasn't about to end just yet, he found the strength to pick up his bags and keep walking.

He passed what seemed to be a spaceship, a blocky, beyond-this-galaxy Nebula Class cruiser (yes, he could remember, sitting in his uncle's lounge room, watching a grainy *Star Trek*) that promised an escape from one hostile planet to another. This led to a fish shop where he ordered whiting and chips and sat in front of a 60-minute dry cleaner to eat his meal. The fish was flavourless, full of bones and speckled with scales, cold in the middle, tasting of old cooking oil. The chips were undercooked and flaccid, soaked in vinegar and sprinkled with pepper (he'd seen the girl pick up the wrong shaker, but thought perhaps that this was the way the locals liked their chips).

He passed the Commercial Hotel, and for a moment thought about going in for a drink. He too could succumb, adapting to local conditions, joining the choir of teenagers vomiting on the weary Digger in the car park across the road. He watched as one of them flashed his arse at the traffic, held up his bottle and chanted, 'Lindy, Lindy, Lindy, oi oi oi.' But why should he? He needed order, routine, structure – a hierarchy of people in their places. He wanted to hear the words appendectomy, sclerosis, staphylococcus and peritoneal. To be around people who knew what CCF, ESR and FRC meant. He'd never be able to make conversation with people who were proud of their genitals.

His plan had been to walk to the hospital and find a bed – a treatment room, a spare mattress, anything. But he'd run out of puff. Up ahead he saw a motel sign, so he quickened his pace.

He entered the office and a man with cracked glasses greeted him. 'Good evening, sir.'

'Good evening. A standard room, please.'

As he filled in the register the clerk asked, 'Come far?'

'India.'

He smiled. 'Best cricket team money can buy.'

Sevanand shrugged. 'How much?'

'The team?'

'No, a room.'

'One twenty, my friend.'

He searched his wallet but could only find eighty dollars in cash. 'Will this do until the morning?'

'You have a credit card?'

'No.'

'Well ...' He pointed to a sign on the wall. 'All rooms must be paid for in advance'.

Sevanand shook his head. 'Do you know who I am?'

'Tell me.'

'The new doctor in your hospital. Apparently they couldn't get an Australian to work here.'

The clerk just stared at him.

'I take it you don't plan on getting sick.'

'No need to get nasty.'

'Well?'

And then he slid a key across the desk.

Before you start saying this Singh was a lazy fellow, let me tell you, I have always been a hard worker. I was supporting my family at age twelve – washing windows, serving in a bread shop and c. Then to school, or university. Never more than six hours sleep, ever. Even on that third day I was at the hospital by 8 am, and Mr Ash showed me where to fetch a coat and eat lunch and who to ask for cultures, or referrals, or discharge planning. So, as you wave your finger at me, remember, I was only ever eager to please.

Mark Ash and Sevanand Singh stood at the door to the medical ward. Someone was watching *Songs of Praise*, someone else coughing sputum into a cup as a falsetto cursed Aunt Velma for having never married the surveyor from Hervey Bay.

'What are my shifts?' Sevanand asked.

'Sixteen hours on, eight hours off. That's over four days. Then y' get two days off. Of course …' He smiled.

'Yes?'

'You might be on-call for those two days.'

'Might be?'

'Well, you are. I mean, if Dr Lindsay is busy in surgery.'

Sevanand lifted his head and rubbed his eyes. 'Exactly how many doctors are there?'

Ash waited. 'Two.'

'And me?'

'Including you.'

'For the whole town?'

'Of course, there's Dr Brooks, but he's on extended leave.'

'A holiday?'

'You could call it that. And Dr Carey's gone back to Adelaide. He's on WorkCover, with his shoulder. So it's just you and Brett Lindsay.'

Sevanand couldn't believe it. 'So when do we get some proper time off?'

Ash just stared at him, and grinned. 'Listen, Sevanand … you've gotta get your head around this place. Yes, the shifts seem long, but some days you may sit there for hours with nothing to do.'

'Doctor!' a voice called from the far end of the ward.

Ash raised his eyebrows. 'Well, shall we get started?'

Lung disease. A seventy-eight-year-old miner with a cup of phlegm in his hand. Sevanand checked his chart, sat him forward, listened to his chest and asked, 'Are the antibiotics helping?'

The old man looked at him and replied, 'You tell me, you're the doctor … aren't you?'

'Are you having trouble with your breathing?'

The miner looked at Ash. 'Where's Dr Lindsay?'

'Don't worry about Dr Lindsay, this is Dr Singh. He's just arrived from India.'

Dr Singh's first patient stared at him with fierce, red eyes. 'Well, you mob make pretty good doctors,' he said.

Sevanand smiled. 'Us mob?' He looked at Ash, who grinned and repeated, 'You mob.'

Sevanand told the miner he had to stop smoking.

'Fuck, that's what me mum told me sixty years ago. You know, Doctor, this isn't from the fags.'

'Nonetheless …'

'I'm seventy-eight, Dr Singh. I haven't found a decent bit of opal for thirty-five years, my wife's dead and my son won't talk to me. And you're tellin' me to stop smoking?'

Sevanand draped his stethoscope around his neck. 'Maybe we can give you some oxygen, Mr Ball.'

'Yeah.' As he closed his eyes.

They moved on to the next bed. 'This is Mr Elliot,' Ash explained. 'Again, lungs, isn't it, Mr Elliot?'

But Mr Elliot looked confused. He retreated under his covers. Sevanand went to take his wrist but he moved his hand away. 'I need your pulse,' he said, but Mr Elliot drew his hand over his chest.

'Come on, don't be silly, Mr Elliot,' Ash urged.

'I pay my taxes,' the man explained, studying Sevanand's chocolate skin.

'Mr Elliot!' Ash scolded.

'Has he cleaned his hands?'

> But that wasn't the worst of it. Then came the following Sunday, when I went for a walk around the town. I stopped outside the Commercial Hotel and looked in the dining-room window. And there, seated having lunch, was Mark Ash, Dr Lindsay, other nurses and administrators, and people who I supposed were their husbands and wives and children – all of them laughing, patting each other on the back.

Sevanand sat on the bench outside the CWA hall. Inside he heard more voices and the smell of cooking food.

Now do I have your permission? he asked his wife.

Yes.

I've been terribly lonely, he explained. I've already checked the bus timetable (over and over, as he sat in his motel room) and the next service leaves at four.

> To whom it may concern – sirs, madams. Save yourself the stamps. I am home. In a way, back where I started, minus the money (you owe me) and many weeks of family life, sanity, work. Although I am disappointed, I am at least happy. To know that every infection I cure, is curable. Every word I speak, valued. Every hand I shake, of blood and tissue and bone. For a while this was not so. People not what they seemed. And so I sit, remembering the desert. Taken there (not in a pleasant way) in my own transporter. So much of value, hidden in the ground, never to be revealed.

The Shot-put

Spring 1919

YANDA HAD SETTLED IN A VALLEY. It was surrounded by honey-brown paddocks that had given up on wheat, resigning themselves to bony sheep that slipped on moss-covered granite as they searched for anything green, or living. The old bluestone cottage was hemmed in by bare hills that cast long shadows across Sam Lancaster's front garden of burnt clivias and wireweed. It was quiet all day on the front porch. Silent, still, except for when Barbara, Sam's wife, played piano, or Sam brought the sheep down for shearing or drenching. His yards would fill with dust, and fences would crack and splinter where Barb allowed the mob to bunch.

Yanda was marginal country. Goyder's Line passed through their backyard. It was only a line on a map but apparently it meant something. It was the northern-most limit of cropping in South Australia, but everyone agreed it should've been drawn a hundred miles south.

But it was there. People had trusted it – including Sam's grandfather, who believed he was onto a bargain because of the cheap price of this northern land. But it didn't last. By the 1880s he'd sold off three thousand acres to nearby Yarrara. Now they had four thousand acres, but that was low-yielding country. Once Barb said, 'We should sue the government.'

'Why?' Sam asked.

'They drew the line.'

But he just looked at her, shaking his head.

On a clear day you could see the Southern Flinders Ranges to the west, and when you went to town you passed the old Merinee goldmine. Sam often wondered about the sanity of men who'd tried to extract gold from the granite hills. Or grow wheat in this soil. Despite this he'd once spent an afternoon sifting through an old mullock heap. He did find gold – flecks nearly as big as sugar crystals. But how would you ever get it out?

In 1919 the winter lasted until October. Dry, as usual. A meteorologist in the *Northern Argus* said it was because of a rain shadow, caused by the nearby ranges. More stuff the government hadn't told them. Anyway, it was probably bullshit, Sam guessed. If it didn't rain it didn't rain. Who cared why?

It was a Sunday, but Sam had been working, pulling an old boiler over land covered with woody weeds. He'd filled it with heavy rocks and bolted chains to each end. Hitched these to his horses, Harry and Albert. Led them across the paddocks in overlapping rows, and now the weeds were gone. But not before they'd set seed and blown everywhere.

My fault, Sam guessed, for not getting to them earlier. He could still hear his dad in his ear: Don't put off until tomorrow … But so what, he thought, he was just another part of the problem.

He went into his shed, opened a louvred window and sat down on his old toolbox. He leaned back on the wall but felt the iron coming away from the wood. Took a towel, smelling of turps and tool oil, and wiped his forehead. 'Barb,' he called, but then heard her inside, singing to herself, probably mumbling prayers. A rat appeared in the doorway, looked at him and scampered behind his old stripper. It had been ten years since he'd used it. Most of the paint had peeled off but you could still read 'Morton and Heading' on the side. He'd covered it with a canvas, but even this was spotted with mould from where the roof leaked its little bit of rain.

Behind the stripper was an old stump-jump plough. Half of the tynes had come off, but they were all blunted and rusting anyway.

Sam reached into a barrel and produced a handful of almonds. He used alligator pliers to crack them. Knew how to place the shells in the bronze teeth so they shattered first time, every time. Soon he had a pile of nuts on the box. When he was finished he replaced the pliers, brushed himself off and started eating. Chewed as thoroughly as he could, until he could feel the muscles in his jaw. It was at this point during his evening meal that Barb would usually say, 'Stop masticating your food, you sound like cow.'

As he ate he studied a collection of trophies, medallions and ribbons on a shoulder-high shelf. They were polished, arranged on a doily he'd stolen from Barb. Set up in rows so that each could be seen through the gap in front of it. He'd made small wooden receptacles for the medallions, so they sat at an angle of almost ninety degrees. He stood, stepped towards the shelf. There was a dead moth on the lace doily, and he flicked it off. Then he started reading, as he did a dozen times a day.

Presented to Thomas Lancaster

Field and Track Champion

1912

Lindisfarne College

The words never changed, but the achievement never diminished, he guessed. He could still remember his visits to town, to Lindisfarne College, for their annual sports day. Standing under the same pepper tree, eating the same pork sausages with bread, watching his son throw javelins, run, spin in circles as he launched a discus on a perfect parabola, grunting as he put his every ounce of energy behind a shot-put.

Lindisfarne College

1913 Athletics

School Record for Shot-put

Tom Lancaster

There'd been shouting, and jumping around, and the sports master had been called to verify the measurement. But Tom had done it. Beaten boys three and four years older. And the record still stood, as far as he knew.

They'd got to bring home the shot-put – all nine pounds of it, sitting proudly beside the trophy. Sam kept polishing it, but it was still dull, dented, dropping on the ground when a mouse brushed past. Or perhaps it was because he'd never fixed the shelf evenly.

'Sam.'

He stepped back and looked out the door. She had her head out of the window. 'What?'

'Lunch.'

He looked at the trophies again. Blew dust from them, but there was none. Ran his rust-coloured hand through the collection of ribbons he'd nailed up with tacks. There was even a newspaper report (*Northern Argus*, May 1913). 'Local Boy Makes Good at Lindisfarne'. A grainy picture of father and son standing in front of the pepper tree. Sam had his arm around Tom's shoulder as Barb stood in the background. He was sweating under a tight, starchy collar he hadn't worn for years, since someone's wedding or funeral in Jamestown. Tom was in loose cotton shorts, and a singlet with the Lindisfarne crest.

Sam started to reread the article, as he did every day. 'Local lad, Tom Lancaster, of "Yanda" via Merinee, showed the city kids what a farm boy is really made of ...'

As Sam headed inside, to the sound of the kettle whistling, he whispered the words he'd remembered. 'Tom has been boarding at

Lindisfarne for six years, as did his father and grandfather. But this lad is going places, athletically speaking ...'

Barb had a corned beef sandwich waiting. There was a clean table-cloth and the paper was set out, flat, just as Sam liked it. The teapot on its cork mat, covered with a cosy, steaming. There was butter in a saucer, stale bread and fig jam that was bitter beyond eating. Sam stood in the kitchen and looked down at the holes in his socks. Barb noticed and said, 'Leave them, I'll get to them tonight.'

He went into the dining room and sat down. Smoothed the *Argus* and read the headlines. 'The land they're giving those returned soldiers,' he said.

'What about it?' Barb said, coming in with a jug full of milk.

'Look at it, north of Port Augusta. They're setting them up for failure.'

She poured the tea. 'I suppose they gotta do something.'

Sam couldn't see it. 'Get 'em building dams, or fixing roads.'

'You can't do that. They've just been to war.'

No one bothers asking, he thought. Typical government. Some fella gets an idea and that's that. 'They should look at us,' he said.

'There's still money in sheep.'

'Some.'

Barb watched her husband read. Grey hair. Bleached-boot skin, calcified by a sun that ruled and ruined everything. Wheatsack eyes that drooped as they emptied across a face of spreading liver spots and varicose decay. Fat chin. Permanently rheumy eyes. A shoddily ploughed forehead, the tynes set too deep. And all this on a man barely forty. Working at beef made no less edible by gravy. 'Is it tough?' she asked.

He held the words back with a finger, finishing the small, smudged chunks of newsprint. Eventually he looked up, met her eyes and said, 'It was just a matter of time.'

'What's that?'

'Cutting back the train. Three times a week. So if I want to go down on Friday, I can't come home until Tuesday.'

'Doesn't affect us.'

'It's not the point. Too few votes up here.'

Off he goes again, she thought. But he didn't. Instead, clearing his throat, sipping black tea and reading.

Barb looked at a picture in the middle of an otherwise empty wall. Ten-year-old Tom done up in his blazer and tie, smiling, or at least trying to. She could remember their visit to the photographer in Port Pirie. The day before he'd caught the train to town, to his new life as a boarder at Lindisfarne College. He'd been anxious, undecided about leaving his family and friends at the local six-horse school. Crying and pleading with them to let him wait one more year.

But Sam had been adamant. He'd been ten. It was the right age. Not so young he'd miss them (too much); not so old his education would suffer.

It was a Sunday, and the photographer's shop was closed. Sam had knocked on the door for a minute, maybe more. Eventually a man in a singlet had put his head out of an upstairs window and said, 'We're closed.'

'We'd like to ask a favour,' Sam had explained. 'He's off to school tomorrow.'

'It's Sunday.'

'Just one shot. We got him ready especially.' Touching his son's shoulder, pointing out the new blazer and a shirt with an over-tight neck.

'Sorry,' the photographer had replied.

'Ten minutes, mate. You've got kids, haven't yer?'

'Yes, and I'd like to spend some time with them.'

'Please,' Barbara had said, flattening Tom's hair.

The photographer had taken a moment. 'You got cash?'

'Yes.'

'Hold on.'

And the window had slammed shut.

Back in their small dining room, Sam was straightening the *Argus*. 'Christ!'

Barb waited for the usual lecture. 'What is it?'

But he just kept following the text with his finger.

'*What?*'

He looked up at her, then checked the words again.

'Sam?'

'I didn't think they'd do it.' He stood and walked from the room, leaving his sandwich mostly uneaten. Through the kitchen, down the hallway and out the front door.

'*Sam?*' She moved around to her husband's seat, pulled the paper closer towards her and read.

Cowards' List to be Published.

The Department of Defence has advised the State Government that it will release the names of all soldiers considered to be derelict in their duties in the 1914-1918 conflict. This list will include all deserters, self-mutilators and Cowards. The Argus promises to publish all names provided as an act of Goodwill towards men lost in fighting, their families and the Empire.

Barb sat back in her husband's chair. Looked up at the photo of her son and whispered his name.

Meanwhile, Sam sat on his toolbox. He was anxious and sweaty and could feel his heart beating fast. He undid his top button. 'Tom,' he whispered. 'Where are you, boy? Where are you?' He looked at the trophies, but there were no answers. 'Tom.'

'Sam!' Barb called. 'Come in, will yer?'

He waited until there was silence. Stood, opened his toolbox and took out a long rope. Took a few minutes to tie a rough noose at one end. He knew how it was done; he'd thought about it a hundred times. Imagined it all: the knot pulling itself tight, the creaking timber beam (he'd chosen the one, and he threw the rope over it now), the post where he'd tie off, the rope's texture, the pattern it made as it snaked around the pole, the way he'd position the stepladder and the thud it would make as it hit the ground after he kicked it away.

He paced for a few moments, thinking, crushing almond shells. Then turned to the shelf of trophies and took the shot-put. Dropped it in the pocket of his overalls and shook it to make sure it wouldn't fall out.

'Sam!'

She was coming towards the shed. He panicked, forgetting what step he was up to, where he'd left the stepladder, how he'd position the knot, whether he'd keep his eyes open or closed, or if he had a choice. His head was full of disasters: the beam breaking (although he'd swung on it to test it), Barbara coming in and cutting him down, and him having to look her in the eyes over a thousand cups of tea, guessing she was disgusted at how all the Lancaster men were cowards.

He pulled the rope loose and threw it behind the stripper only seconds before she entered.

'What are you doing?' she asked.

'Thinking.'

She looked around. 'What's in your pocket?'

He produced the shot-put.

'What are you doing with that?'

'Thinking ... remembering.'

She noticed the end of the rope resting on the stripper. '*Christ.*' Took the shot-put and placed it on the shelf, but it rolled, upsetting trophies and falling to the ground.

'Come in,' she said, taking his arm.

He went to pick up the shot-put.

'Leave it.'

Three days passed, each progressively warmer. Clover and medic breathed nitrogen. The sun sank and swam in its paddle pool. Stubble crackled as Sam crossed his paddocks. He thought he could smell rain, but it was never more than a promise. He was consoled by a cool breeze smelling of sheep, and Barb's stew. Standing in front of a small garden, he studied his carrots. Struggling, their green tails limp. He watered them from a leaking bucket, but the soil resisted. Picked up his hoe and started chipping the weeds between the vegetables. Stopped, looked up at the sky, and remembered.

> Dear Mr and Mrs Lancaster
>
> It is with regret that I write to you regarding your son, Private Thomas Lancaster, 2419387. At evening roll call on Tuesday 21 July 1916 Private Lancaster was found to be missing. Inquiries with his officers and NCOs revealed nothing. Dozens of infantrymen from the 32nd Battalion were interviewed but none had seen him since the previous evening.

Sam had remembered these words too, every one of them – the way they were arranged into paragraphs, how the typewriter (with a fading ribbon) dropped its K, a finger smudge on the bottom right-hand corner of the letter. He still had it in his shed (although he'd told Barb he'd destroyed it). Still in its Department of Defence envelope. He even remembered the sender's details. 'Colonel Arthur R. Griffin, 32nd Battalion, Fromelles'.

He returned to his weeds. Made himself fetch more water, and refill the valleys.

The battalion was involved in heavy fighting on the 19th, but a survey was taken of the Fallen, and your son was not among them.

He could remember Barb crying as they sat on the front porch, three years earlier. He could still hear his own voice, and see his hand trembling as he read. Remembered looking at her and saying, 'At least he's not dead,' and Barb replying, 'Well, where is he then?'

'Lost.'

Mr and Mrs Lancaster, I must inform you that Tom has been recorded as a deserter. This means that he is presently wanted by the Military Police. I hope that some information comes to hand that disputes this view, but at this time we have no choice but to consider him a Coward.

The day after receiving this letter Sam and Barbara drafted a reply.

Our son is no deserter, they said. He is a school prefect and champion. He lives for his mates and would die for them. We consider your use of the term 'coward' an insult. Tom is no coward. Surely what you mean is 'missing'? Maybe he is dazed, confused, lost? Captured? We don't like to think of it, but perhaps he is dead, and not found. We read that many bodies are never recovered, properly, we mean.

For weeks after they read about the 32nd Battalion's defeat at Fromelles. The 718 casualties, and how ninety per cent of their boys, their young men, their heroic sons and fathers, butchers, tailors and schoolteachers, were killed on one day.

A sunny day, with low cloud. Gardening weather, Sam guessed, as he picked up a snail and threw it a few yards.

They read how the boys of the 32nd Battalion had been so full of energy and spirit as they'd trained with the 5th Division in Egypt only a few weeks earlier: tanning themselves beside the Nile; drinking beer that resembled sheep dip; buying big, hessian bags full of strong tobacco and fold-out postcards of women with big bums and legs, untreated moustaches and crooked smiles. They imagined Tom enjoying all of these things. Imagined him happy but anxious, ready for adventure. They knew the statistics (and Tom had read these things too) but there was an acceptance, a resignation.

On the dock at Port Adelaide, Barb had held her son for a minute before she'd let him join his mates.

'Careful,' she'd whispered, 'I've only got one son.'

'I'll keep my head down.' Smiling.

Sam sat on the dirt beside his carrots. Dropped his head between his knees. 'Coward,' he whispered, playing with the word.

The official version – the version in the letter, and government filing cabinets. The wrong version, he thought, but the official version. The unchangeable version. The version history would remember, as well as their community, friends and maybe even family. The version the stonemasons would consult when it came to making memorials to the Fallen.

And although no one said as much, this is what the official version suggested. That when the shelling started, Tom ran away and found a quiet spot. Sat in a hole, or hid behind a bush. Screamed, and cried, and eventually ran towards a nearby forest. Hid there for days, until the fighting stopped, before wandering off (at night, of course) towards some nearby farm. That he hid in someone's hayloft. Stole clothes and made his way to the coast. Found a boat heading to England, and posed as a discharged soldier, finding work on some farm: growing wheat and carrots.

They'd written a dozen, maybe fifteen, letters over the years. Asked why, if Tom was still alive, he'd made no attempt to contact them? How had he moved around France and Europe unnoticed, during a war? How would his sense of fair play have allowed him to stay silent for so long?

Instead of condemning our son, they said, you should be helping us find him. If you want to refer to him as a coward you have to prove that he was one.

This was the sense of confusion, of unofficial grief, they had to live with for years. Without rain, in every sense of the word. When asked about their son they would say, 'Yes, he is missing in action,' and someone would reply, 'I'm sure he'll turn up … directly.' Eventually the conversation would come around to, 'So, they never found his body?' and Barb would reply, 'They were in the way of heavy artillery.'

And that's where they'd left Tom: pulverised in some French paddock. That was *their* official version. But they knew that if he was alive there was a *reason* he'd fled: a new piece of psychological research, a footnote to a yet-to-be-published article, an idea still forming in some doctor's head. Barb spent hours thinking it through, remembering: Tom in her arms, crying for attention, or scared, in a corner, as Sam ranted and raved about tax, or his evil aunt from Glen Iris, or the weather. She could still see the look in her son's eyes – the turn-away-from-the-world fear that gripped him the night before returning to school, or when Sam tried to get him to kill his first sheep; his refusal to deal with bits of the world he disliked. Mulesing, maths and turnips. She could remember, still feel him trembling in her arms, as Sam paced the room mumbling, 'Don't baby him, Barb.'

Sam saw a cart travelling along his eastern fence line. He squinted and made out Mr Gall, their agent. He stood and started walking, then running, towards the front gate.

Mr Gall saw him coming and waited. 'Morning, Sam.'

'John.'

A box of groceries and a fresh copy of the *Northern Argus*. Sam looked up and studied the older man's face. He was convinced he was holding back. 'Anything in the paper?'

'Usual stuff. Hoggets down again.'

Sam nodded. 'Always down.'

'Yes.' He paused, then tried to smile. 'How's Barb?'

'Good … yes, good.'

'Tell her we can't get no more dressmaking stuff until next month.' He slowed. 'Apparently there's shortages of that too.'

Sam knew he'd seen the list. Knew in his face, his voice. 'Something up?'

John couldn't help himself. 'What the hell they put Tom on that list for?'

Sam kicked the dirt. 'It's there, is it?'

'What a thing to do after … you losing him.'

'It's a mistake,' Sam said. 'If they haven't found any trace, that's what they do.'

'Don't worry, Sam, me and Sue will tell anyone that asks.'

'Thanks.'

'He was a nice kid, Sam. What a thing to do. I tell you what, I'll be writing to that paper and tellin' them.'

'No,' Sam replied. 'Thanks anyway. Best to let it all blow over.'

'Well, I'd stop stocking it, if I could, Sam.'

'I know.'

Sam picked up the box of groceries. 'See you next week, eh?'

'Yeah, and throw that rag in the bin. Toilet paper – that's all it's good for.'

Sam was livid. He was walking, almost jogging along Ellen Street, Port Pirie, clutching a letter addressed to 'The Headmaster, Lindisfarne College, Adelaide'. He was dressed in his old suit, newly repaired and ironed. His shoes were polished, but he could feel the hole in his sock opening up again.

'Sam.'

Nicholas Irving, the Mid North stock agent for Elders, stood in front of him, smiling. He was carrying a bag of wool samples and lanolin was blotting the paper. Producing a tuft of wool, he presented it to Sam. 'There, feel that.'

Sam wasn't interested, but he felt it anyway.

'Stephen Cartwright's,' Nick said. 'I've got a buyer from Stafford's. They want it for suits. Suits!'

'Good.'

'How's your mob going?'

'Fine. I got to get along, Nick.'

He knows too, Sam guessed.

'I'll come see yer,' Nick said. 'Next week?'

'I'll have to let you know.' Before walking on.

Sam entered the post office, purchased a stamp and attached it to the letter. Held it in the mouth of the postbox, but stopped short. 'Why?' He approached the counter and asked for a line to Adelaide.

'Where to, Mr Lancaster?'

'Lindisfarne College.'

He waited, and a few minutes later the attendant directed him to a booth. He closed the door, picked up the handpiece and started speaking slowly and clearly. 'The Headmaster, please.'

'Brother Koltun is busy … can I help you?'

'Who are you?'

'Brother O'Sullivan. Can I help?'

Sam took his time. His mouth was dry. 'My name is Sam Lancaster. I'm calling from Port Pirie. My son, Tom …'

'Yes, I remember Tom.' A warm, but curt voice.

'I've heard through a friend that his name's been removed from the Honour Board.'

A long pause.

'Are you there?' Sam asked.

'Yes … from the Honour Board?'

'Yes.'

'Why?'

'That's what I'd like to know.'

O'Sullivan chose his words carefully. 'I wouldn't know, Mr

Lancaster. I can't think why. I'll have to get Brother Koltun to call you.'

'I don't have a telephone.'

'Can you wait?'

'He's not there?'

'He's taking a class.'

Sam tried again. 'What's your position, Brother?'

'Deputy Headmaster.'

'Well, then, if such a thing had happened – '

O'Sullivan had heard enough. 'Listen, call back at lunch, just after two. Otherwise, I can get him to write to you.'

Sam's voice echoed around the booth. 'Listen, that's enough bullshit. I want to – '

'Mr Lancaster – '

'Tom was an old scholar. If this is all about – '

'I don't know, Mr Lancaster.'

Sam hung up. Stormed from the booth and posted the letter.

A friend of Barb's appeared in front of him. He couldn't remember her name. 'Good morning,' he managed.

'Sam.' She stared at him, and down at his ill-fitting suit. 'How are you?'

'Fine.'

'Where's Barb?'

'Home. She doesn't like coming to town anymore.'

'Oh, why?'

You know, you old bitch, he wanted to say. 'I'm picking up some cotton and thread.'

'Bet she made your suit.' She felt his jacket. Met his eyes and smiled. 'No word on Tom?'

'No.'

'Just a matter of waiting.'

'For what?'

'News.'

He couldn't stand her tone. 'You don't read the *Argus*?'

'What?'

'You know … it's Mary, isn't it?'

'Yes.'

'You know, don't you, Mary?'

'I know?'

'The cowards' list?'

She wiped the tip of her dry nose. 'The cowards' list?' And shook her head. 'I'm not sure, Sam.'

He stepped towards her and she almost fell back.

'Give Barb my love,' she said, turning.

'Your love?'

She walked off. Sam stood alone, defeated, feeling ridiculous in his suit in the Port Pirie Post Office. He could feel eyes resting on his woollen jacket, and skin.

Heavy artillery, he wanted to say. Or maybe someone took him in.

He made his way back down Ellen Street, and people stopped and watched as he passed.

Go on, say it, he wanted to shout. At least have the courage to say it.

When he got home he gave Barb her material. 'We'll get John to fetch that from now on.'

Autumn 1920

The end of a hot day. Northerlies, still, the stone cottage seeking shadow, and the sweetness of dill pickles, brandy custard, kept cool in the safe. Sam and Barbara sat on their front porch, surveying fallow paddocks. There were only a few leaves left on the almond trees. In the corner of the yards a pepper tree flourished.

'Look, reds,' Sam said, as a group of kangaroos grazed the stubble.

'Pests,' Barbara replied.

'Better than rabbits.'

There was cloud on the northern horizon. Sam watched as it drifted past, avoiding them by a hundred miles. 'There's no rain.'

'It's not coming this way.' As she threaded darn onto a heavy gauge needle.

Sam squinted. 'Who's that?'

Barb looked up. There was a man standing at their front gate. They watched as he walked towards them.

'Recognise him?' Sam asked.

'No.'

When the stranger was close enough they could see that he was tall, unshaved, wearing corduroy pants and a brown shirt with half of its buttons missing. He had long, blonde, uncombed hair. Barb noticed his fine eyebrows and blue eyes.

'Hello,' he said, coming closer, climbing and stopping on the first step of the porch.

'G'day,' Sam replied, standing up.

'You Sam Lancaster?'

'Yes.'

The stranger looked at Barbara. 'Well, you must be Tom's mum?'

She took a moment to think. 'You know Tom?'

'Yes.'

The stranger dropped a hessian bag on the step. Barb stood and moved towards him. 'You know where he is?'

'No, no one knows where he is ... but I knew him.'

'You fought with him?' Sam asked.

'Yes.'

They took him inside and gave him barley water. Barb retrieved leftover lamb, cabbage and carrots from their bowl of scraps and served them with some of her own tomato sauce. The man shovelled food into his mouth with his fingers. Chewed it three or four times before swallowing. 'Tom was a top bloke,' he said, looking up long enough to meet their eyes.

'You were mates?' Sam asked.

'Yeah. He told me to come visit, once we got home.'

There was a long silence. 'That would've been nice,' Barb finally managed.

'I've always worked on farms. I need a job.'

Sam was massaging his chin. 'I'd like to help … I don't even know your name?'

'Neil. Neil Lindsay.'

'Neil … but you've seen this place. We're just gettin' by ourselves.'

'I don't want no pay. Just a roof, and a bit of food perhaps. Tom said you'd be good for it.'

Sam studied the man, and felt that something wasn't quite right. 'He did, did he?'

'Yes.'

Barb looked at her husband. 'Sam?'

The stranger licked his fingers and pushed his plate away. 'Thanks, Mrs Lancaster.'

'Barb,' she said. 'So, tell us a bit more about Tom.'

'What would you like to know?'

'How was he, the last time you saw him?'

Neil sat back, covered his mouth and burped. 'You want the truth, Barb?'

'Yes, yes, everything,' Sam said. 'We got a lot of questions need answers.'

Neil wiped his mouth again. 'Well, I suppose you could say … Tom didn't take to fighting.'

'How's that?' Sam asked.

'At first, we were back from the front, training. We could hear artillery, and even machine guns, and all day there'd be planes flying over.' He paused, studying their faces. 'Well, you know, he was a happy fella, wasn't he?'

'Yes,' Barb said.

'But the noise started getting to him. He didn't sleep, and you could see his hands shake.'

'He was scared,' Barbara whispered, looking at her husband. 'Sam?'

'They were all scared. Go on, Neil.'

'He went off his food.'

Barb dropped her head, stared at the ground and started rocking.

'He was nervous, jittery, all the time,' Neil continued. 'Should I go on, Mr Lancaster?'

'Yes.'

Neil took his time, watching Barb, choosing his words carefully. 'Then when we went to the front ...'

Barb looked up. 'What?'

'We knew it was heavy fighting. We'd heard the stories, and seen the casualties.'

'How was he?'

'Vague. You'd talk to him and he wouldn't answer. He'd be staring into the distance, and mumbling to himself.'

Barb looked at her husband again. 'See, I knew. He was sick.'

'Was anyone else like this?' Sam asked.

'A few, but they'd come around. But Tom ...'

'Didn't someone notice?'

'Yeah, the NCOs, but they just told him to grow up. They shouted at him. Extra drill. Then at night, you'd hear him crying.' He looked Sam directly in the eyes. 'I hate to tell you this, Mr Lancaster, but it's true. You'd hear him crying, and he'd curl up in a ball, like a baby. Me and a few other fellas, we'd have to drag him out of bed in the morning.'

Barb was still watching her husband. 'We need to tell someone.'

But Sam was busy with Neil. 'That's it?'

'We went into battle. It was late afternoon. He could barely hold his rifle. The whistle blew and he … fell down.'

'Shot?' Barbara asked.

'No, he just collapsed. He was screaming, louder than the shelling. I tried to help him up but I couldn't. I had to move forward.'

Barb was sobbing. She said her son's name over and over. Sam was thinking. After a few moments he said to Neil, 'That doesn't make him a coward.'

'I agree. He was ill, Mr Lancaster. They should've helped him. But it wasn't like that. You just had to get on.'

'And that was the last time you saw him?'

'Yes. Although there was a rumour … Some fella said he saw him running away. Over a fence and into a paddock.'

'That still doesn't make him a coward.'

'True. Shell shock, Mr Lancaster.'

'Someone should've helped him,' Barbara whispered.

'There were fellas put bullets in their feet cos they couldn't face it. Or stabbed themselves. But they'd just fix 'em up twice as quick.'

'You didn't see him run?' Sam asked.

'No.'

'So it mightn't a been him?'

'It could've been some other fella. I bet you it was, Barb.'

It was dark, and the stranger looked tired. So Sam said to his wife, 'Fix him a bed, in the shed.'

Half an hour later Neil was sitting on the edge of his camp stretcher. He had fresh sheets that smelt of lemon and camphor laurel. Barb had given him a pair of Tom's pyjamas, and the legs dragged in the dust. He stood, approached the trophy shelf and spent a few minutes reading. Then said, 'Sorry, old fella,' and went and lay on the stretcher.

Barb knocked and came in with more of Tom's clothes. 'I've just ironed these. I'll turn up the legs and sleeves if you like.'

'That's all right.' Taking the clothes. 'He'll want them back, won't he, Mrs Lancaster?'

'Barb.'

She noticed his top was undone. He had no hair on his chest and his skin was tanned. She looked up and he met her eyes. 'How are you?' he asked.

'It hasn't been easy, Neil. Terrible years.'

'For everyone.'

'Yes, you must have been through hell?'

'I was lucky.'

She was still holding the clothes, and he squeezed her hand. 'He was a good mate,' he said.

'Yes?'

'And funny.'

She smiled. 'He could have me in stitches.'

'So, you probably didn't want to hear what I had to say?'

'No, Neil … it's best.'

'His sister would probably want to know.'

Barb took a moment, unsure. 'His sister?'

'I thought he said he had a sister.'

'No … he said that?'

'I'm getting him mixed up with someone else.'

She noticed his arms: solid, brown, lined with veins. 'You've worked with sheep?'

'For years.'

'Good. Sam could do with a hand, even though he'd never admit it.'

Neil stayed and worked and was rewarded with lamb shanks, mutton, week-old pork and sherry that Sam had been storing under the house. Every night they'd settle around the table and he'd tell them something new about their son. About the way he could never stay in step, his taste for duck (stolen from a nearby farm), his impressions of their CO, his love of Dickens (yes, I knew he liked Dickens, Barb concurred, but I didn't know he'd taken a book), his dry sense of humour, his sarcasm and how he could throw a grenade further than anyone in the battalion.

'You've seen his trophies?' Sam asked.

'Yes.'

'So, it did come in handy.'

On the morning of his eighth day at Yanda, Neil emerged from his hot shed wearing a white shirt, suit jacket with its arms turned up, grey canvas pants and old boots. He saw Barb in the chicken pen and approached her. 'Need a hand?'

She held up a knife. 'Sam usually does it for me.'

He came into the yard, picked up the fattest animal he could find and said, 'What about this one?'

'She'll do.'

Barb turned away as Neil knelt, put the chicken across his knee and removed its head with three or four passes of the blade. Stood up, returned the knife and said, 'Finished.' Finally, held up the twitching hen and smiled proudly.

She took it by the legs. 'Thanks.'

Neil picked up the chicken's head and threw it out of the yard. Then he wiped his hands on his pants, picked up the bowl of scraps and started scattering them about.

'You just pretend it's a German?' Barb asked, but he wouldn't be drawn. Then she said, 'Can I ask a favour?'

The chicken stopped twitching. Dripped blood onto her shoe. She put it on a nearby bench and said, 'Could I ask you to talk to Sam?'

Neil looked surprised. 'About … Tom?'

'Yes.' She looked at the chicken, then back at his broad hands. 'I mean, we talk, But it's not the same coming from your wife, is it?'

'I don't know.'

'It's not. But maybe from someone he can talk to. He can talk to me, but the thing is, all of this business has hit him hard. Tom was his boy. He meant everything to him.'

'I could imagine.'

'He was gonna have the farm. You know, they were mates, best mates, and these last three years … Sam's been lost.'

Neil had seen it – the pictures on the wall, the way they'd left his room, full of old bears and zebras, tin soldiers and a golliwog she'd made. The way they talked about him like he was due home any time, and how Barb always cooked an extra portion. He'd heard it in the stories – how Sam and Tom had built a raft out of old timber and a couple of 44-gallon drums. How Sam had bought a pirate's flag from a shop in town, and how they'd flown it above the raft. Stripped down to their underpants. Sailing on the bit of water in their dam.

And how the turkey nest dried up every September.

Neil had seen their raft, rusted and broken up, overgrown with weeds, and time.

The stranger emptied the last of the scraps. 'I can talk to him, but what do you want me to say?'

She moved closer. 'I want you to tell him it's not worth it.'

Neil wasn't sure. 'You can tell me, Barb.'

'He was gonna kill himself.'

'Jesus.'

'I think. And when they published the cowards' list … Tom was no coward, Neil.'

'I know.'

'But Sam's taken it to heart.'

Neil took her arm and said, 'What was he gonna do?'

'He has a rope, in the shed. I'm scared, Neil.'

'What makes you think …?'

She explained: the knot she'd seen in the rope, the day after the list was published; Sam's changing moods, sentences becoming words, grunts, then nothing; his talk about selling the farm. 'A few years ago he had all these ideas – fertilisers, machinery, new types of wheat. He was determined to improve things. But now he's let go. You've seen the weeds? Last year there was no crop, and he said he doesn't care about this year. And look at those sheep, half of them are flyblown.'

'Maybe we should both talk to him?'

'No, you … please.'

They were startled by Sam's voice. 'Neil.' And he stood looking at them.

'G'day, Sam.'

'You got half an hour?'

The men went inside. Sam made Neil a cup of tea and sat him down at the table. Found some writing paper, and a pen, and placed them in front of him. 'From the heart, eh?'

'Sam?'

'We'll go right to the top: Monash. Leave the address, we'll find that out later. Start by saying how you're writing on behalf of me and Barb, and how you fought with Private Tom Lancaster. His number is 2419387. Write that down.'

Sam watched as Neil started scribbling.

'Then tell him what you saw; about Tom's mental condition. His shaking and crying and screaming. Go on.'

Neil wrote. 'Slow down.'

'And say, what we want is an inquiry. With doctors, psychologists, experts. Tell him how we want Tom's name cleared.'

Neil looked up. 'Sam, I'll write your letter, but I'll need time. To set it out properly. Make sense.'

Sam stared at him. 'If you do it tonight, I'll take it to town tomorrow.'

'Good. I'll try.'

'I appreciate this, Neil.'

The next morning Sam was up early. He washed his face and dressed in his best suit. Ate breakfast as Barbara slept. Just before sunrise he went out to the shed and knocked on the door. 'Neil?'

No reply.

'Neil?'

He went in, but Neil was gone. Clothes. Wheatbag. Gone. The bed hadn't been slept in. The paper and pen he'd given him were sitting on the toolbox. He picked up what he thought was his letter and read it.

> I'm sorry, but I've never been to no war. They said in town about Tom. I needed work. Seeing how your farm was so big. I been stupid, I know. I wish you all the best with Tom. Your good people. My name's not Neil, so I hope you can forgive me.

Sam sat on the bed for a few minutes. Noticed a box of old books the stranger had been looking through: a coverless Donne from Barb's school days, a mouse-eaten Bible, a manual for his stripper. There was a recipe book, magazines, stock journals and a copy of *Oliver Twist* with Barb's handwriting in the front: 'Happy 12th Birthday Our Artful Dodger'. And on top of all this, three and four year-old newspapers, with references to the 32nd Battalion underlined.

Sam let the note fall to the ground and it settled on the almond shells.

The first light of morning was coming through the cracked window. He could hear his sheep, and distant thunder. He could smell rain, but didn't care anymore. He stood and looked at his son's trophies. It was like he'd never grown up, shaved, left home, worn a uniform. Like he'd never left his side (as they sat, busy with the alligator). There was a bowl, where they'd soak the almonds, get them out of the skins. It'd dried, and rust from the roof had crumbled into it. He could ask him to rinse it, so they could get started.

Then he slipped the shot-put in his pocket.

The One-Eyed Merchant

1936

THE *IRON DUKE* stood proud and defiant in the ship breakers' yard.
At 9823 tons deadweight she was all muscle and bone, her salt-eaten
skin flaking in the last gasp of a north England summer. She'd ferried
tourists to the Continent before the army had claimed her for troop
transport in 1916. After the war she was sold to the Adelaide Cruise
Company and, on a cold December morning in 1919, steamed south
to warmer waters.

She was still an impressive vessel (propped up by a frame, wallowing
in a swamp). Two funnels, held up by cables, which were being cut.
Her cabins were all wood – floorboards, walls and ceilings. Men
brought up armfuls of spruce and oak and dropped them overboard.
Boys gathered the remains and threw them onto flat-top trucks.

The *Duke* had steamed the coastal run off South Australia –
Adelaide to Ports Lincoln, Pirie and Augusta, meandering on to
Whyalla and Port Hughes on its famous Gulf Trip. For £6 you could
get seven days of quoits and cardboard horse racing, fancy-dress
parties and visits to barley-smelling towns.

But now the *Iron Duke* had returned home. Settled in a dry dock,
dropped any pretence of dignity, exfoliated, cast off her husk and
shown the world her skeleton: rows of ribs from the world's best
welders. Bulkheads that would yield, to the river, the scrap merchants.
An autopsy carried out by teams of little navvies stripping wire from
the bridge and cabins; sinks and marble benches from the kitchens;

shower heads and taps from the bathrooms; and half-inch-thick iron plates from the hull.

The *Duke* had a double hull, so there were men inside the ship, removing more iron plates, forcing them through gaps to fall again, closer to workers who lifted them into small carriages, pulled by a tank engine that took these materials back to the main yard. A scaffold had been erected above the waterline and teams worked their way along – cutting, hammering, prying away the plates until they fell into the mud. There were two men, high up, laughing to themselves, working slowly as they complained about the weather, the price of meat and the fact that they were never given asbestos gloves anymore. The taller of these two men finished cutting a plate, peeled it back and loosened it with a kick from his steel-capped boot. It fell and landed sideways in the silt that was rinsed twice a day by a weary river.

His friend, a shorter, grey-haired, possum-like man, saw it first. He gazed into the shadows of the freshly opened hull and said, 'Christ!'

The taller man looked and agreed. 'Jesus …'

They stood staring. The foreman called up to them but they ignored him.

Then the taller man stepped forward, knelt down and removed a small piece of cloth from inside the hull. It was an old yellow handkerchief, gathered and tied in a knot to hold something. He undid the knot and removed two fresh pennies from the bundle. Studied them and noticed the dates: 1898, 1900. Then stood and looked back into the hull.

The bell sounded for lunch, but neither of them moved.

1901

George Barham lived above a dress shop in Chart Street, Draper. He was nine years old, but small for his age. He'd finished with school – or more correctly, it had finished with him. But even before he'd left, once he'd turned eight, he was still the smallest boy in his class. Once, his teacher had met his mother at the front gate and asked, 'Do you feed him meat?'

'When I can afford it.'

'Fruit? Vegetables?'

She'd just glared at him. 'His father was a small man.'

The teacher's eyes had narrowed. 'His father has passed?'

'Dead. Trying to stop a fight. He was a policeman.'

There was a big photo of him, young and happy, clutching a cricket bat, hanging in what passed as their lounge room. George had some of his things – a hairbrush, a button from his tunic, a letter he'd written him, yellow, cracked along the folds.

His mother shook his shoulders and he woke. 'Come on,' she said. 'You'll be late again.'

He rolled over, pulled the rug up under his chin, but then sat up. 'What day is it?'

'The day after yesterday.'

'Is it Friday yet?'

'Yes it is.' She pinched his cheek.

He dressed in a pair of old calico pants that came up past his ankles; pulled on his boots, without socks; a shirt; and a loose jacket that allowed him to crawl easily inside the big ship's double hull. Then he sat at an old table in what passed as their dining room, the same room as their lounge room, bedroom and kitchen; all contained in what passed as their flat, their building (with its chunks of old stone falling off, hitting the hopscotch girls on the head) and finally, what passed as a suburb, a community of uncollected rubbish and wild dogs running loose.

Although they only had a single room, if you tried, you could imagine it as some sort of palace. The bed he shared with his mother, and some nights, one of her friends – before he crawled out and slept in the hallway. A long bench that passed as a kitchen (he'd told her about the *Duke's* marble benches). A pot that she squatted over during the night.

'Eat up,' she said, placing a bowl of watery oats in front of him.

He decided not to complain. He ate half and said, 'You have the rest.'

'Eat!'

'What's for lunch?'

'Corned beef.' Wrapping his sandwich in wax paper and slipping it into his dad's old satchel.

'I've had beef all week.'

'Think yourself lucky.'

'The men have stew.'

'So?'

And again, he stopped, choosing old meat over what his dad called 'your mother's dramaticals'.

He studied his mother as she washed dishes. Her hands, still soft and white, her arms, thin and tapering, as if they could be snapped with a gentle twist. A small curl that hung down beside her left ear. Her neck, long, whiter still.

Returning to his bed, he sat down on his old sheets, took out a book from under his pillow and opened it to its mark. Read a line or two about Mr Jeremiah Cruncher before his mother said, 'What are you doing?'

He looked up. 'It's not time.'

'I want you to go early, and stop at Mr Gordon's. I need plain flour, quarter of a pound. Can you remember that?'

He continued reading.

'George!'

Looked up. 'Plain flour, quarter of a pound.'

'Well, get going.' She threw his satchel onto the bed.

'Can I finish this page?'

'It's twenty to seven.'

'So?'

'So, go.' She stood with her hands on her hips. 'Without your rudeness, young man.'

'I shouldn't have to,' he whispered.

She placed three coins in his hand and closed his fingers around them.

He stood, slowly, slipping the book into his satchel, glaring at her as he fastened it, before slinging it across his shoulder and leaving without a word.

The small boy, George Barham, trudged through Draper in the early light of day, past the railway station, through Swansea, Largs and Lulu Terrace. There was a foundry on Sugar Street. He could see flame from inside a giant shed, the still shadows of horses and men, machines thumping hard against themselves, and the earth, spitting out rivets, hinges and metal plates for the big ship. There was a row of shops along Musgrave Street. Some had their lights on, but only one had its door open. It was Skurray's, the boot-maker, dark apart from a smoky candle; quiet, apart from a tap that hissed somewhere in the back room. George stopped at the door, studying the boots lined up on the floor, the work table covered in scraps of leather and tools.

I could steal a pair, he thought, studying new-looking hobnail boots a few feet from his reach.

But then he heard his father's voice: There's only one thing I ask, son.

He turned and studied a wooden box perched on a stand. Read the big gold letters at the top: 'The One-Eyed Merchant'. There was a dial on the front, broken into twelve segments – six images of heaven and six of hell. He studied the harps and pitchforks and noticed the words: 'Your fortune for a Penny'.

Before he'd even thought about it he'd slipped a penny into the slot. Mr Gordon could always be convinced. The wheel turned six times and then stopped on the border of a fire-scorched hell and a blue-sky heaven. He read the painted words: 'You are proud, defiant and strong-willed. All of the world's riches will fall into your lap'.

He walked to Mr Gordon's shop. Waited outside. The light was on but the door was locked. He stepped up to the big, glass door and knocked. No one appeared. 'Mr Gordon,' he called. 'My ma wants flour.'

No one. He knocked again, fingering the two coins in his pocket.

Five minutes later he could smell the river. Cabbage and oil; coal-smoke and the dead fish they took away for fertiliser. He followed the road that led to Cable Wharf. The giant sheds of McFarlane and Sons, Shipbuilders, consumed most of his morning sky. More light seeped from the seams between roof and wall, the walls themselves, and he thought, If the shed itself was launched, it would sink in five seconds flat. '*When father papered the parlour, you couldn't see him for paste ...*' Singing, as he continued, imagining a shed growing legs and arms, a head full of a thousand teeth, reptilian skin – moving along the bank, knocking over the *Duke*, squishing the early shift as they brewed tea, and screamed for mercy. Mercy, mercy, mercy! No such luck. The way their brains would pop from their skulls. He smiled. 'Bad luck, boys!' Continuing: '*Slapping it here, slapping it there, paste and paper everywhere.*'

He followed a set of tramway tracks as they entered the sheds from the rear and reappeared several hundred feet later at the front. On one of the old doors someone had scribbled in chalk: '55.66905°N, *in honorem*.' The tracks ran between two long slipways that led down to the river's edge.

The *Iron Duke* sat on the downriver slip. So far it had a keel and a frame, and perhaps half of its double hull. There were teams of men, high on the scaffolds, preparing for their day – gathering tools, stretching, testing the ropes and block and tackle they used to raise the iron plates and rivets.

George looked up at the ship with admiration and disgust. He'd never been able to work out how so much iron could float. Someone had once explained: because the air it contained was lighter than water. But he couldn't reconcile this with the fact that iron was heavier than air, water, concrete, in fact almost anything. Iron, it seemed, was a marvellous material. Bridges that crossed wide valleys, supporting tons of human and horse flesh, carts and coal.

But iron was not a happy material. Not like wood, or stone. Eight men and three boys had already died on the construction of this monster (as he saw its eyes opening, winking at him). He'd even been there, four feet away, when Ian Truscott's son, another George, had fallen from a scaffold and impaled himself on an iron bar. George had watched George quiver and groan for a full minute before becoming still, relaxing and draping himself across the bar. George could still see the boy's eyes, open the whole time, seemingly fixed upon a puddle on the ground.

He went into the foreman's office and hung his satchel on a hook. Initialled a chart that had his name, and the date, and a thousand grease and oil smears from the hands of riveters and boilermakers. He was early, so he took out his book and started reading by the light of a flickering lamp. Other men came in, signed on, ruffled his hair or twisted his nose, and went out into the shed. But he still had four minutes.

Until one of the young foremen came in and said, 'Resting, before you've even started?'

He went out to the big ship and stood looking up. There was nothing new. More iron, more rivets, noise, heat, burns. The rest of his life mapped out in metal, although when he thought about this, he thought about the fact, the certainty, that he'd one day be a writer. Instead of iron there would be a wooden desk; instead of rivets, a pen; grease, ink.

He climbed a ladder that led to a long platform, that in turn fed into smaller scaffolds that terminated on the sections of hull that were being plated. As he climbed he looked up at the hundreds of steps above him, and then at the parts of the hull they'd finished. He never looked down. He'd always been told: never look down. He could still see George Truscott's eyes, studying the puddle full of muck, his wrists, his ankles, all bone.

He reached his platform and his riveter, Ted (an old man, he guessed, judging from the hairs in his ears and nose), was waiting. George thought it strange how Ted seemed to live his life (eating, shaving, washing) on the scaffold (after all, he was always there before he arrived, and after he knocked off). Ted said, 'Good day for it, George.'

'For what?'

'For working. You're changing lives, son.'

He couldn't see it. 'How's that?'

'All the people that'll benefit from the old girl.'

He thought, So what? I won't. Mum won't. Dad certainly won't. What's to be happy about?

'How's the French Revolution coming along?'

George seemed to light up. '"To the eyes of Mr Jeremiah Cruncher, sitting on his stool in Fleet Street with his grisly urchin beside him, a vast number and variety of objects" ... ah, I've forgotten the rest.'

'Keep at it.'

'I know the speech from the end ... "It's a far, far better place ..." do yer wanna hear it?'

'Later, George. We got work to do.' Ruffling his hair, wondering, again, if one day he might say something to the boy's mother.

It was perhaps half past one, George thought. His corned-beef sandwich had settled and he was hungry again. As he moved inside the two-foot gap of the double hull he could feel his knees and ankles starting to ache.

He supported himself by standing on a portion of the bulkhead. The interior skin of the ship had already been fixed, so he stood facing out. He could see the sun, the sky and seagulls. An iron plate would cover him and it would be dark. The hot rivets would slip into the holes in the plate and he would hold a second heavy plate behind them as Ted hammered them home. When all eight rivets were in Ted would say, 'Next,' and he'd move back into the sun. Another plate. Another eight rivets.

'Next.'

But then Ted said, 'I missed one.'

'Sorry?'

'Four plates back, three down.'

'Four back, three down?'

'Go on then.'

So he crawled across, and then down, counting the plates. The light seeped out of the hull and it was completely dark. He felt his way by counting the rivets. He held up his hand but couldn't see, smell or even sense fingers or flesh.

He stopped. Called to Ted. No reply. Looked for the hole, for any light it might provide, but couldn't find any un-riveted holes. He calculated: four across, three down. That's twelve rivets across, nine down. Nothing. 'Are you there, I can't find it?'

His heart was racing. He made himself stop, and breathe deeply.

Of course, he figured, I haven't gone far enough. He moved awkwardly, squeezing his body between the plates and the bulkhead, struggling to straighten, turn and twist his ankles as he moved. He counted down another three rivets, then another three; just in case, he counted across another three. No hole. No light.

'Can you hear me?' he shouted.

Silence. Just his own voice echoing in the double hull. Blackness.

Then he panicked. He thought, I have to get out. Moved up, three plates, four, five – nine, twelve, fifteen rivets. Down two plates, three plates – six rivets, nine rivets. Stopped. Shouted, 'I'm here, here, can anyone help me?'

He hammered as best he could in the small gap. Then he was tired, and stopped, and rested.

Two more down, three more across – six rivets, nine rivets.

He hammered.

He screamed.

He couldn't tell if he was high in the hull, or low. He needed a piss and he thought, If I can just wait a few more minutes …

Three down, four across – nine rivets, twelve rivets.

'Someone, please!'

Then he pissed himself, and it was warm on his cold, chicken-bone leg.

'Ma!'

And all he could think of was how angry she'd be about her flour.

A Descriptive List of the Birds Native to Shearwater, Australia

3.30: The Shearwater Choir

MARK AND SUSAN CROSBIE-MORRISON watched the choir file out of the old bank building, line up (tallest in the middle) in two rows, wait for the conductor, and begin. Peter Allen's 'Tenterfield Saddler'. Since it was a dwarf choir, there were no sopranos, or altos, or basses, just thirteen flattish, mostly out-of-tune tenors. They reminded Mark of sheep: the protests they made as they were moved by angry dogs. Nuts and broken pretzels in a stale mix. He grinned and whispered to his new wife, 'Fuck.'

She refused to acknowledge him.

'Check out the fat one in the front.'

He was an old dwarf, dressed for the forge. They'd just watched him (standing on a fruit box) hammering away at a horseshoe.

Susan said, 'So?'

But he didn't reply.

The singers were lusty, determined, but Mark was only getting what he came for. 'This is possibly the worst choir I've ever heard.'

Which wasn't saying much. Mr Loussier had made him sing in the Year Five Mixed, but since then, nothing. Still, this was entertaining enough. A selection of the little people, from the little town, giving their all. A Sovereign Hill Carnival, minus the history, scholarship, humbugs, mines, café. Everything, really. Although Shearwater 'Aussie' Dwarf Village had other joys. The History of Aussie Dwarfism interactive display, in which conventionally statured visitors (adult entry $15.50, including tea and coffee) could reach for groceries on nine-foot-high supermarket shelves, use more fruit boxes to reach public phones, ride on oversized bikes, run for simulated buses, risk getting hit by cardboard cars whose drivers refused to look down, and on it went.

Susan wasn't enjoying the day at all. It seemed like a silly idea. Finding an old town (Shearwater's mining days were well and truly over) and converting it into a tacky themed village for ... she wasn't even sure what they were called. In fact, she wasn't comfortable at all. Paying five dollars (extra) for a boy dwarf to tap dance in the foyer of the former town hall. An expensive two minute clunk for them, a family with a few bored teenagers, an old couple with mints and socks up past their knees. 'Can we go?' she asked.

'We just got here.'

'It's so ... tasteless.'

'Rubbish. We're supporting them. This is how they make a living.'

She couldn't see that this was so, and if it was, was right. Who'd heard of a dwarf village in the Australian wheatbelt? Was it even legal? Hadn't *Today Tonight* done a piece? Hadn't there been protests? What if there was one now, and they were filmed, and family and friends saw them on the telly coming out of Shearwater? This was the sort of thing she normally protested about, but here she was, and why? Because of Mark saying: 'This Shearwater place, let's have a look.'

'Are you kidding?'

'Interesting.'

'What?'

'Yeah. And we'd be supporting them.'

But she'd known better. Mark, with his search for the under-breath, nasally-dispelled laugh. 'I know why you want to go.'

'Why?'

'You arse.'

The choir finished, and wandered off, and each man, woman and child returned to their job.

4.00: Weaving display

There was a loom, set up in the old school, and three women worked it. They were dressed in old-fashioned bonnets, aprons, long dresses, leather shoes. Mark whispered, 'Look how small their feet are.'

Susan shook her head.

He smiled. 'Little dwarf feet. So cutesy-cute dwarf feet.'

His new wife was staring at him, wondering.

'What?'

One of the women approached them. 'Weaving has always been a way for us to make a living.'

Mark didn't understand. Why weaving? Was it because they'd always been locked away, denied proper employment, shunned by their respective communities? But he didn't think there was any point asking.

The woman said, 'Here at Shearwater we make cardigans, jumpers, and sell them.'

Susan tried her best. 'In Myer?'

'Selected outlets.'

She didn't know what this meant. 'And this loom, has it been modified?'

'Yes. See, the raised pedals. It all began in Manchester, a hundred years ago.'

Mark didn't think this sounded right. The mills had all closed by then.

'This machine is original. My great-great-grandmother wove on it.'

And he thought, How? Manchester? Disassembled? Sent to Shearwater? It didn't add up.

Susan asked, 'How many jumpers can you make in a day?'

'Three, four. Sometimes rugs, and sheets. Pillowcases. Whatever people want.'

Mark did the maths. Three. How could that keep them going? 'Must be hard competing with cheaper, imported stuff.'

'Not really. People support us.'

And he thought, Feel sorry for you. But that was false economy. And couldn't last. Like everything at Shearwater, it was founded on an incorrect assumption. Still, it was a bizzaro Sunday afternoon out, and only two hours from town. Close enough to work in a few wineries on the way.

They continued their tour. Down the main street, its old fish shop a new fish shop, the teenagers sitting at an empty table. They went in, ordered Chiko Rolls, sat down and waited. Watched as the girls loaded the fryer, dropped it into the oil, talked about Uncle Murray. 'After this, can we go?' Susan asked.

'No.'

She wasn't even sure what she'd married. What was this streak? She'd been noticing it more since their wedding. As they drove past Aborigines drinking in Conrad Square. He'd slow, and study them, and say, 'I don't get it.'

'What?'

'They just sleep all day, like sloths.'

'They don't sleep all day.'

'Well, what are they doing?'

'Sobering up.'

'They're not. Look, flagons, casks. I don't get it. And look, their kids are there, playing. Why aren't they in school? Look at that woman, she can't even stand up.'

'Why don't you go help?'

'What am I gonna do?'

She'd look in his eyes and see what it really was. He hated them.

Letting his disgust bake, before he removed it from the oven, and continued with his six-figure town-planner existence.

The Chiko Rolls were served, and bitten into, but weren't cooked, and he complained, and the girls said they could put them back in the fryer, but he said, 'Don't bother, I'm not hungry anymore.'

4.30: Feeding the animals

They watched as two men fed pigs and chooks from buckets of scraps. They scattered the food, and the animals came running. One man said, 'Shearwater is entirely self-sufficient. We butcher our own sheep, and cattle, and pigs. The meat is processed, packaged and frozen, and sold in town.'

Mark wondered why they'd come so far to see animals being fed. It wasn't like it was a distinctly dwarf activity. You didn't have to be short to look after animals. One of the pigs was as big as one of the men. This, he guessed, was worth the price of admission. He wanted to take a picture but when he took out his camera Susan poked him in the side. 'What?'

'I know what you're doing.'

'I wanna get a snap.'

'Of the pig?'

'Yeah.'

'Because?'

She was giving him the shits. Why couldn't she play along, have a laugh? Like the inhabitants of Shearwater, life was short, and had to be enjoyed. It wasn't like he was laughing *at* them. They'd started the place. Dressed as ballerinas (even the men). Organised weddings. Invited the controversy. He was just supporting them. *They* were the ones who looked like something out of Dickens. What did that have to do with being a dwarf? Really, they hadn't thought it through. They were, he guessed, their own worst enemies. But, he deferred. Switched off his camera and waited while the pigs ate.

Susan was getting an uneasy feeling. Not about the little people – they were just trying to get by. She was having flashes. As they walked down Hyland Street. The old man with his trolley full of sacks of cans and bottles. The way her husband looked at him, moved, turned and stared as he passed. Saying, 'I wonder where he sleeps.'

'Probably in an alleyway somewhere.'

'His clothes are black. He's probably never washed them, or himself. Do you think?' Looking at her. 'He's probably covered in sores. I can't believe, in this day and age, people still live like this.'

Again, she'd said, 'What are you gonna do about it?' And he'd just shrugged, and she'd taken this to mean he did care, sort of, but not really enough to act. That was a good sign. It meant he was compassionate, and maybe one day he'd want to help out: Vinnies, or teaching in Africa. But now, now she suspected she'd misread him completely. Compassion, or a forensic fascination? A desire to pin every man onto a foam backing board, watch him wriggle, die, and dry out, write a label that said, 'Can man', 'Aborigine', 'Dwarf'. To close the box and forget, knowing he'd made some attempt to understand, but really just to observe, to know, to control.

5.00: Dance troupe

Back in the main street, the same thirteen (perhaps, Mark couldn't tell) appeared dressed as Morris dancers. Frilly pants, boaters, bells, ribbons and vests with sequins. They formed a circle, raised their hands and waited. One of the fish-shop girls started a tape player and they were off. Up and down, jiggle-jiggle, around, linking arms, separating, executing their tightly choreographed moves. Susan was impressed, but Mark was grinning, again. 'They're actually quite good,' she said.

'Yes.' He studied their faces. There was no mucking around. This was serious stuff. 'Their little legs ...' He loved how stumpy they were; how the very short ones had to run to keep up; how their arms weren't long enough to make a daisy chain, and how the links kept breaking. One stumbled, rolled, and got up. Mark laughed, but Susan poked him again.

She could remember the look on his face. From when they'd slowed to twenty-five, driven past the road crew gardening in Parkville Acres, a dozen or so retards (yes, he'd used the word) mowing, line-trimming, weeding beside the highway. The look on his face: how his forehead compressed, his cheeks bulged, his eye-slits narrowed, his tongue wet his lips, his head jutted forward. 'Do you think they pay them?'

'What?'

'For gardening. Do you think?'

'Of course they pay them.'

'That's nice, isn't it?'

'What?'

'That they have a job. Something to do all day. What else would they do?'

She'd just looked at him, as he'd studied them, the way they held their power-tools, interacted, just got on with the job, despite the need to keep stopping and scratching their faces and arms and legs and arse and biting at the air and spitting, all of which made them less efficient, but at least they were doing something useful.

'It would've taken hours to learn this dance,' Susan said.

'Yes.'

'You gotta hand it to them, they've gone to a lot of trouble.' But despite saying this, she didn't feel any easier about the idea of the dwarf town, or coming to visit, which, by definition, was some sort of validation of something that seemed quite wrong.

Another dwarf tumbled, and Mark laughed again, and this time the little man looked at him angrily. He stopped. The man returned to his spot and turned little circles that made him dizzy and he nearly stumbled again. Mark managed to keep a straight face.

5.30: Aviary

It was a big aviary, with perhaps a hundred birds lined up on branches, arguing on the poppy-seed floor. A man stepped inside, closed the gate and said, 'Hi everyone, my name is Irwin.' Then he pointed out the hardhead, the brown songlark, the robust whistler.

Mark hated birds, but admired the way Irwin moved, spoke softly, allowed a bar-tailed godwit to land on his head. How he caught an eastern spinebill, stepped out of the cage and passed it around. Told them about its call, preferred habitat, life span. Shared his knowledge, and affection, which (Mark thought) seemed different from, more than, the Shearwater way.

Mark took the bird. Waited. Realised it wasn't about to fly into the unwired sky. Let it sit in his hands. Still warm and soft and heavier than its size might suggest. After a few moments he returned it, and watched how Irwin stroked its head. Like a baby he'd just adopted, and fetched from the hospital.

Mark moved into a world of small, satisfying things. Fingers on beaks, warm breath, little tubby heads that were no longer tubby. No dwarves or looms or Chiko Rolls. 'How far north does it live?' he asked.

Irwin told him. He explained how its habitat had shrunk, mainly because of deforestation, but how that applied to all the birds, and their struggle to survive, find food, a place to breed.

Mark turned to his new wife and said, 'It's getting late, we should go.'

'Give me five minutes. I need the toilet.'

He waited on a log. Remembered. Holding a slingshot, attacking seagulls, as the kids in his class egged him on. Whack! Straight to the leg, dangling as it took off, falling onto the oval, as everyone applauded, and he felt good, and bad, at the same time. Felt the need to take up his slingshot and try again, but the necessity of making sure he missed. After all, it was unlikely a seagull could survive long without a leg. It'd land, stand, and fall over. Like a dwarf. Just fall over. And that wasn't terribly helpful, or good to think about. Especially if you'd caused it.

Thwack! Again and again, but his marbles didn't hit the seagulls. So that the other boys lost interest, and ran off to kick the footy, and he sat, on some other log, and felt bad. And wondered how he could be these two people. One good; one rotten. One decent; the other unknown to him, but always there. He just didn't understand. Wanted to get in his car and drive home.

It wasn't like Susan needed impressing. Quite the opposite. Still, something had brought him here, and something was driving him away.

Standing, he walked back towards the aviary. Irwin was still inside, sprinkling seed. The birds were quieter now, as if they sensed it was safe, the performance over. He studied the bird-keeper. He wore shorts, and his legs were like sides of beef. Little sides of beef. He could see his mum holding him, and squeezing his leg, and pulling on pants, and socks, and getting him ready for school. Lowering a singlet over his body, which was compact and meaty but still childish. And he could see her holding him close and saying, *Just another day. If you can get through it ...* He knew for a fact she rubbed his chest with Vicks, and tied coins in a hanky so he wouldn't lose them before lunch. *Just another day ...*

He knew why she was saying this. It was what every mother had said to every child since the beginning of time. And Irwin was listening, but not happy to go to school, where other boys shot at birds, and said things, and laughed, and seemed to be glad that he was the one in the opportunity class.

Mark could remember Irwin. The boy who liked birds. Who'd scolded him about the slingshot. He'd pushed him and said, 'Fuck off you little oompa-loompa', and felt good and bad again, all the time sensing it was necessary.

Irwin had said, 'You better stop that.'

'Why?'

'It can't look out for itself.'

And he'd said, *'It can't look out for itself.'*

Laughter.

'You're only doing it to yourself.'

'What?'

'Not the bird. *Yourself.*'

This had so angered Mark that he'd picked Irwin up, approached a chain-link fence, and hung him up by a loose wire. Irwin had squirmed, kicked, called for help, before falling, tearing his jacket, and cutting his calf on a wire.

Everyone had scattered, including him. But he'd hidden beside the sport shed, and listened when Irwin said to a teacher, 'I might need a doctor.'

The teacher had said, 'Who did this?'

He'd replied, 'Me.'

She'd waited for the truth.

'I was climbing. I slipped.'

Back in his aviary, Irwin knelt, and the birds ate from his hand, and Mark knew why he'd come. He approached him, and stood looking. Noticed the long scar on his leg and said, 'That looks nasty.'

Irwin noticed. He looked at him strangely. 'It's old.'

'How did it happen?'

'A fence. I wasn't looking what I was doing.' He stood, exited, closed the door and walked away.

Then the birds settled, ignoring the last of the seed on the ground. Until it was almost silent. Just his mother, shielding him from his father, who was shouting, still, about the government, and his boss, Reynolds, who wanted him gone. His father, who leaned forward, and squeezed his chin, so much that it hurt. So that he could feel it now. His father, holding a shard of Easter egg in the air, high enough that he couldn't reach, and saying, 'Go on, jump'. Which he did, as the chocolate got higher, and higher, before it was given to the dog. Press-ups. Three bricks on his back. Which would do him good. Thrown into the water. The best way to learn how to swim. Until his mum came in after him ('Let him be, he'll learn!').

He noticed that Irwin had left a book behind. *A Descriptive List of the Birds Native to Shearwater, Australia*. He picked it up, flicked through, recognised a few from the aviary. Then turned and walked off.

They drove home in silence. Susan guessed he'd had his lot for the day. He was happy with what he'd seen. This couldn't make her happy, as the Shearwater Dwarf Village had left her feeling flat, deflated, depressed.

He'd bought a book (or so he'd told her). She looked through. It was old, and she recognised it, but couldn't see how he'd understand it.

The Keeping of Miss Mary

BROTHER PHILIP VELLACOTT lived in a small cottage across the road from Lindisfarne College. Most of the students had worked out where he lived, and on their way home of an afternoon would slow past his gate and look in the windows, hoping they might see him semi-clad before a mirror, lifting weights, or maybe even living up to the stories their lapsed Catholic uncles had told them about Brothers caught *in flagrante delicto*. Yes, there were scraps of mostly imagined folklore, but the most anyone had seen was Vellacott in a singlet out fertilising his roses. Generally he kept his blinds drawn, except, perhaps, on a Sunday afternoon when he'd let in some light as he prepared his homily for the boarders' mass.

Brother Vellacott was a frugal man. Some of the ladies from the local parish shopped for him, leaving his groceries at his back door. But if Brother Vellacott found himself hungry on, say, a Saturday afternoon, he'd walk across the road to the college, and the canteen, and use his master key to help himself to a pack of barbecue chips or a few frozen kranskies he'd take home and warm up for himself and Miss Mary.

Brother Vellacott had shared his cottage with Miss Mary for seventeen years. No one at Lindisfarne knew, of course. It wasn't so much deceit as an error of omission. He'd consulted God and He'd given him permission, and that was good enough for him. There was no point telling the big boss at Lindisfarne, or the little ones, wrapped up in their climate-controlled offices. No point telling the kids, or his brother, or the bishop or archbishop. Miss Mary was his little secret. She had her own life and her own room. They ate and watched MasterChef together, but they'd never kissed, or touched in a romantic way, or even squeezed hands at the end of a sad movie (the sort she was always making him watch).

Miss Mary was his trial, his test, and for this he thanked God and promised to work, to struggle, to overcome. She was bedridden. Had lost the use of both legs in a car accident, aged twelve. Her father had stopped at a T-junction. Indicated to turn right. Looked left, and right, and left again, then pulled out. But a gravel truck from the local quarry had collected them anyway.

Afterwards, after they'd buried her father and sister, her mother had sat at her bedside and said, 'We are lucky.'

'Why?' she'd asked.

'The truck only clipped us. A quarter of a second earlier we'd all be dead.'

'Or,' she replied, 'a second later and we'd all be alive.'

'There's no point thinking like that,' her mother had said, shaking her head. 'Just be thankful God saved us.'

She'd stared at her mother with disgust. 'If God saved us then he must have killed Dad and Joan.'

Which was the beginning of Miss Mary's God versus Doubt wrestling match, still going on fifty years later, with Brother Vellacott in one corner and a life of wasted opportunities in the other.

Brother Vellacott's day would start early. He'd wake at five, shower, dress in black slacks, a shirt and tie, and slip on one of a dozen light jumpers he'd bought at Kmart. Then, every second day, he'd shave. There wasn't enough to bother about every day, he thought, although one of the boys had called him Brother Michael. The class had laughed and he'd just asked, 'Who's that?'

'A singer, Brother.'

'Like Sinatra?'

'Yes, Brother, like Sinatra.' And they'd laughed again.

At six he'd make a cup of tea and two slices of toast. Watch the early news, trying, all the time, to see world events from a Catholic perspective. Planes didn't crash because God willed them to, he believed. God was too busy for all that. Planes crashed because nuts and bolts fell off, because the weather turned bad or the pilot had entered the wrong coordinates on the flight computer. The rest, the making the best of it, was what we had to do with God's help. That's what he'd told Miss Mary a thousand times. Life is for the living, and God will smooth our way when he can. That's the most we can hope for, Miss Mary: love, understanding and a helping hand.

After rinsing his dishes he'd go into Miss Mary's room, open the blinds (letting in dappled light from an old jacaranda) and say her name a few times. 'Miss Mary, it's time. Look, what a beautiful day.' He'd sit beside her, and smile, and their eyes would meet. 'Good morning, sleepyhead,' he'd say, and she'd smile, the same smile every morning, revealing the teeth he helped her clean every evening after the late news. Then he'd ask if she was decent, pull back her sheets, help her out of bed and into her wheelchair. He'd find her cardigan, wrap it around her shoulders and ask, 'Ready for another day?'

Some days she'd just lift her eyebrows, and frown, and he'd say, 'Come on, there's a movie with Farrah Fawcett later.' Other days she'd smile, look out of the window and say, 'I think Dad's already out on his tractor.'

'Your dad's dead,' he'd reply, refusing to indulge her.

She'd look at him, shocked. 'Dead?'

'Yes, you remember, in that car accident?'

And she'd stop to think. 'Dead?'

'Yes.'

'But I can hear him, on his tractor.'

He'd try to smile, remembering his promise to God. 'No, that's Mr White mowing his lawn.'

'Dead?'

He'd wheel Miss Mary to the lounge room. Park her in front of the television and make her breakfast. If he spied bare skin through her unbuttoned nightie he'd look away and think of that morning's lesson: Year Eight Pythagoras, the sum of the square of two sides is equal to ... Eventually, returning with her tea and toast, he'd lean over and button her nightie. Then there was no need for Pythagoras, or other forms of self-correction.

He'd wheel her to the bathroom. Turn on the water, adjust the temperature, close his eyes and lift the nightie from her shoulders as she held her arms in the air and wiggled her body. Then, with his eyes still closed, he'd push her over the lip of the shower and under the water. 'You're okay for a moment?'

But there'd seldom be a reply. Such was her state of mind.

He'd return to the early news, checking his lesson plans, rolls, correspondence from the Catholic Education Office. Every minute or so he'd call out, 'Miss Mary, how goes it?' When he was satisfied he'd continue reading about requests for canned food for Nigerians, clothes for the poor and his availability to perform an extra mass at St Kevin's.

Brother Vellacott hardly ever said no. If there was someone, anyone, who wanted to hear about God and the amazing adventures of Jesus of Nazareth (which is how he sold the biopic to his Grade Sevens), then he was more than ready, willing and Abel (although no one got the joke) to tell them.

He'd started off teaching at a small outback school. Badjaling was a hundred kilometres west of Whyalla. Three pubs, a post office and a row of shops that clung desperately to the highway. There was a small church attached to an even smaller hall. He had anywhere between four and six students, depending on the harvest. After September he was often by himself in his vestry-storeroom-cum-school, passing his days writing reports to his Catholic overlords about how the children were prospering and learning, growing in the Lord as they fumbled their rosary beads between bouts of Lawson and little lunch. On Sundays he said mass. Four-and-a-half years; one worshipper. Worship, in the broadest sense, for like Miss Mary, the old dear only sat and stared at him, unblinkingly, for the thirty or so minutes it took him to get through an express Eucharist. He'd look at her, and then at the back wall, at the host, the back of his hand, the worn carpet (that he vacuumed every Saturday morning), the broken clock, the crack in the wall, her (again!). Then he'd see the old girl to the door, ask about her gout, almost push her down the front steps and lock the door, secretly praying she might die before the following Sunday.

Lindisfarne College, in comparison, was Paradise regained. There was hot soup and salami-and-alfalfa baguettes in the Gold Room at five past one every day. He had a glass-walled office in the new administration wing and there was a swimming pool and spa he had to himself on Saturday afternoons. Classrooms with smartboards and projectors and a gym where he dared to reveal his legs to the Year Nines.

As Assistant Principal (Religious Education) Brother Vellacott was one of the small big fish at Lindisfarne College. As he sat on his lounge, every weekday morning, calling to Miss Mary, he was aware of the weight on his shoulders: eleven hundred boys, one hundred staff, a sprawling school that cost seven million dollars a year to run, and Miss Mary.

'Miss Mary, are you finished?' he'd call.

No reply.

'Miss Mary?'

'Yes, Philip.'

He'd return to the bathroom, enter, close his eyes and wheel Miss Mary out of the shower. Hand her a towel and wait. 'Done,' she'd say, and he'd return her to her bedroom, open a drawer, take out a clean set of clothes and lay them on the bed. Then he'd wait outside as she got dressed. When called he'd return her to the lounge room, place the remote control on her lap and say, 'Must be off.' She'd smile at him, and sometimes he'd touch her arm or shoulder.

Then he'd leave for school. Out the back door, through the side gate, so none of the boys would see him. He'd wait at the crossing until one of the Grade Six monitors stopped the traffic. Cross, greeting parents, students and teachers on duty. 'Peace be with you,' and they'd reply, 'And also with you.' He'd teach his Pythagoras, phone a few parents, make a coffee and return to his office. Then, sitting comfortably in a leather chair, he'd stop to think about Miss Mary. He'd pick up the phone and call her. 'Miss Mary?'

'Yes, Philip?'

'Is everything okay?'

'Yes, yes,' she'd manage. 'Are you stopping by the shops on your way home?'

'I can.'

'I have a craving for FruChocs.'

'Of course, dear. Of course.'

There'd be a long pause. 'They had Bryce Courtenay on the telly,' she'd say.

'Really?'

'He has a new book, and I think I'd like to read it.'

He'd smile. 'What's it called?'

Another pause. 'I can't recall, although there was a convict involved.'

The next Saturday, or on his next visit to Kmart, he'd buy her the book. It'd sit on her bedside table, unread, on top of a dozen others. Eventually, after a few months, he'd move them into a bookcase full of unread books.

The dilemma of neglected books wasn't something he was happy about, but they were the only things she ever asked for. He couldn't deny her this simple joy. Maybe the physical object gave her some pleasure. Maybe it took her back to some other time. Perhaps when her father would read to her.

Back in his office, he'd open his desk drawer, take out a framed photo of Miss Mary and place it beside a pot of plastic foxgloves. He'd stare at his girl's face – her small brown eyes, her button nose, the lips he'd help decorate every Sunday morning before they sat down to watch *Songs of Praise*.

One day, called from his office on an emergency, he'd left his photo of Miss Mary on his desk. When he'd returned his superior, Brother Tobias, had asked, 'Is that a picture of your sister?'

'My sister? Yes, yes.'

'Where does she live?'

'Now? Melbourne.'

'I never knew. It's funny, I tried, but I can't see any family resemblance.'

Yes, the keeping of Miss Mary did have its moments. Why, he often thought, should he be ashamed of doing good deeds, of showing charity, compassion, love? Sometimes he felt like a German hiding a Jew. But Miss Mary was no Anne Frank. She was a living, breathing, crying-at-the-end-of-*It's a Wonderful Life*, angry, loving, forgetful human being. She was flesh and blood, an aching, longing bag of bones who just needed someone to care for her, talk to her, understand her.

Years before, when she'd first arrived, someone would knock at the door and he'd wheel her to her room and spray the area with deodorant to remove any feminine scents. He'd open the door to discover it was a charity collector. These days he just left her in front of the telly, kept the chain on the door, opened it and asked who it was.

One day it was Brother Tobias, dropped in for a coffee, and he said, 'I seem to have some bug. Can we make it for another time?'

Brother Vellacott would go home for lunch. Fill a plate with finger food from the spread in the Gold Room, leave the low-pitched hum of his office and walk out into the sun. Cross the road and let himself into his cottage. Present the food to Miss Mary, go to the kitchen and return with two cups of tea. 'So, Miss Mary, how was your morning?' he'd ask.

But she wouldn't reply, too caught up in Farrah Fawcett's golden locks.

Then he'd hear the postie, go outside to fetch the letters and return to his tea and sandwich.

'Bills,' he'd say. 'Bad news and bills. Oh, and here ...' Opening a hand-written letter. 'It's from Brother Cope, remember him?'

As he read, and Miss Mary worked on a cold samosa.

'He says he's taken the show to Broome, and they're loving it.'

The 'show' being what Cope called his 'Sidewalk Sunday School', a truck that pulled up in front of skate parks, schools and shopping centres in disadvantaged neighbourhoods, opening a curtain to reveal a stage. Cope would be there, lit up, music playing, dancing about on the floor of his old Dodge as his offsider distributed ice creams and plastic flags to attract the local kids.

Vellacott had first seen the show in the early eighties. He'd been working at a parish school in the outer northern suburbs when, one day, unannounced, Cope had pulled up on the oval, parked his truck and started his show. He remembered watching him use a dummy to entertain the kids. His hand in the back of the little boy's head, moving his mouth.

'Good morning, Willy,' Cope had said.

'Good morning, Brother.'

'There's no need to call me Brother.'

'Well, you sure ain't my sister.'

Laughs. As he marvelled at how Cope kept the most unruly kids under his spell.

Brother Vellacott would return to school, mark a few tests, write an inspiring piece for the college newsletter and finally, just after the bell, retire to the toilet to change into his shorts and Lindisfarne coach's top. He'd take to the oval with a series of infamous strides. Stand with his hands on his hips, his whistle in his mouth, and call for the Cricket First XI to line up. Then he'd show them how to get their shoulders back, their stomach in and their head high. 'Let's acknowledge our one weakness: fielding. We're letting too many through.' A dramatic pause, eyes narrowed, searching for any weakness on the peach-fuzzed, pockmarked faces of his 'Magnificent Eleven'. 'Today we'll work on the art of the perfect catch: full lob. Here, cupped hands, close to the body.' As he demonstrated. 'Right, two lines, off we go.'

Once, he'd brought Miss Mary to watch. Helped her into the front seat of his little black Golf, driven her across the road and parked her behind the nets. He'd covered her legs with a rug and left her with a thermos of tea. 'Will you be alright?'

'Go on, get to your boys.'

For the next hour he'd kept looking over, waving, making sure she hadn't fallen asleep. One of the boys had asked, 'Who's that, Brother?' But he'd just smiled.

At five o'clock on a Thursday there'd be an executive meeting: the big fish, the little ones, the business manager, heads of departments and sometimes Monsignor Pascal, in his black splendour, a gold crucifix around his neck and a solid, silver ring. They'd discuss curriculum and resources – whether to drain and retile the pool, revarnish the floorboards in the gym, replace the twenty-year-old maths textbooks. One day, as he sat listening to the big fish talk about Edmund on his donkey, his pager went off. He unclipped it from his belt and read the message. The big fish looked at him. 'Is there a problem?'

'Yes.'

He'd told Miss Mary only to page him in an emergency. This was only the second time his pager had gone off. The first was a hot February afternoon when she'd tried to bath herself. He'd found her arse up, legs over the side, almost drowned. So this time, as he excused himself from the meeting, he was worried.

He fumbled his key in the lock, tried again, burst into his cottage and called, 'Miss Mary?'

No reply. He didn't have to look far. Miss Mary had fallen from her wheelchair and her left leg was twisted, caught under her body.

She lifted her head and looked at him. 'Philip?'

'Stay still.'

He assessed the situation, and then took her under the shoulders, lifting her into her wheelchair. 'What happened?'

'I was reaching for the telly guide.'

'But I left it ...' He looked at the coffee table. It wasn't there. 'Where?'

She pointed to the bookcase.

'Miss Mary, I'm sorry.' Kneeling beside her, holding her hand and kissing it. 'I was in a rush.'

She smiled. 'Get up. It doesn't matter, there's nothing broken.'

Which was something. The prospect of having to take Miss Mary to hospital had often worried him. 'What's your relation to Miss Mary?' they'd ask, and the cat would be out of the bag. And what about when she died? How would he explain the ambulance and the flashing lights? The frail old lady, her face covered, wheeled from his cottage? What would he say to his shocked neighbours, the coroner, the police? Who exactly *was* this Miss Mary, they'd ask. And what exactly was your relationship to her, Brother Vellacott?

That night, to punish himself for leaving the television guide in the wrong spot, he turned his shower up hot and made himself stand under it for five minutes. The next day, and the next, he called in sick. When the principal stopped by to ask how he was he didn't answer the door, although the big fish could hear Miss Mary singing along to the 1957 cast recording of *Oklahoma!*

Brother Vellacott often took Miss Mary through the McDonald's drive-through. He'd turn to her and ask, 'Was that with or without pickles?' Once he'd said to the girl at the window, 'My wife likes to get out for a drive.'

She'd looked at him strangely.

'She's bedridden, you know, but she has a thing for Quarter Pounders, don't you, dear?'

One night he'd taken her to see the Christmas display along the River Torrens at Hindmarsh. 'Look, there's Thor,' he'd said, indicating the papier-mâché god and his sparking anvil.

'I used to play down there, as a child,' she'd said.

'You did?' Shocked she'd offered something of her past.

'Yes, with my brother.' Sighing, looking into her lap.

'I didn't know you had a brother.' Watching the traffic, eventually finding a spot and pulling over.

'Yes, his name was Jack. I can't remember much about him.' Bowing her head, lower.

'Was he killed in the accident?'

'What accident?'

'The accident that killed your father and sister.'

'Who was killed?'

'Jack.'

'Who's Jack?'

'Your brother.'

She'd frowned, looked annoyed and shook her head. 'I never had no brother.'

He'd driven around Hindmarsh for another hour, hoping it might trigger more memories, but in the end Miss Mary had just asked, 'Will we be home in time for Ernie?'

'Ernie who?'

'Sigley.'

Weekends were often a conundrum. He knew they couldn't just sit and watch television, or talk, or deadhead roses in the backyard. Once the papers were read, the dishes washed, the clothes hung out to dry, there was a deep, cold pool of nothingness. Boredom led to trouble. It was always the way.

One Saturday afternoon, as he sat reading a story about Pierre Menard, he looked over and noticed Miss Mary was asleep. Noticed her dress was undone down past her nipple, and that she hadn't bothered putting on a bra.

He felt the call of the Devil. Satan made him stand, walk over, kneel in front of her and slide two fingers inside her dress. It was the Fallen Angel who guided his hand over her wrinkly tit, cupping the weight of her breast, feeling (and lingering) on the cold, sallow nipples.

Then he removed his fingers from her dress, and studied them. He looked at Miss Mary's sleeping face and all at once felt like the worst person who'd ever lived. He stood, went to the bathroom and washed his hands four, five, maybe six times. Looked out of the window and studied the sky. 'Forgive me?'

He went to his room, sat on the bed and started to feel physically ill. He doubled over in pain from a stomach cramp. Slid to the ground and curled up into a ball, shrinking, smaller and smaller, so as to avoid God's gaze. 'Forgive me?' Before starting on a round of Our Fathers.

Nothing helped.

He sat up, opened his bedside drawer and inserted the tips of the guilty fingers. Then slammed the drawer on them, again and again, until they numbed with pain and started to turn red and black. Then returned to his foetal ball and began a round of Hail Marys.

He was brought around by Miss Mary calling for him. He returned to her and she was rested, happy, smiling, as though in a sign from God.

No, he guessed. Better to keep busy.

So they'd go on a Saturday afternoon outing. Generally these were as far away from Lindisfarne as possible: the Calvos flower markets (returning home with a dozen roses), a stroll along the Semaphore foreshore (coal smoke settling on Miss Mary's hands), the fish market (a pair of tommy ruffs), a book sale (Cavafy and Spender), the Himeji Gardens, cemeteries, low tea at poky nurseries or maybe just sitting in the sun beside a playground, listening to children sing and shout.

But no matter where they went, Miss Mary's legs were always covered with a rug, her body wrapped up in coats and shawls, her face hidden by fine netting from an old black hat. People would stare at her, straining to make out her strong features, before looking at Philip and smiling. There was something about her, they thought. Something stern and stiff. A stillness that was a refusal to move with gravity, the wind, the rhythm of her chair.

Once, he wheeled her across to Lindisfarne. Gave her a tour of his school: the classrooms and ovals, the administration wing and gymnasium. Took her into his office and wheeled her close to the glass wall that overlooked the Valley, the ancient creek-made garden that ran through the middle of the college. Then he wheeled her up to the farm, showed her the bantams and Rhode Island Reds, the merino flock and the goat that had almost hanged itself while climbing a tree in search of fruit.

And then Sam Wheeler, the Ag Master, was standing in front of them in bloodied overalls. 'Brother Philip.'

'Sam.'

'I've come in to slaughter the meat birds,' the farmer-turned-teacher said. 'There's no use trying when there's kids around. You want one?'

'No thanks.' Thinking on his feet. 'I can't see myself cleaning it.'

'I can do it for you.'

'Thanks, anyway.'

Then the teacher looked at Miss Mary.

'This is my sister.'

Wheeler was still staring at her, a single furrow deepening across his forehead. 'Hello, Mrs …?'

'Miss Mary.'

'Hello.' Extending his hand, but then retracting it. 'No, not with all that blood. Glad to meet you, Miss Mary.' He waited, but there was no reply.

At night they'd follow a set routine. He'd go to the supermarket on his way home, purchase meat, a simmering sauce and rice. Come home, present the jar to his girl and say, 'How about we try something new?' Put on his apron and start cooking as he watched the five pm news on a small television on top of his fridge. He'd set the table, and generally there were a few flowers from the garden. Light a candle, turn off the radio and television and manoeuvre Miss Mary into position.

After tea, perhaps, there'd be a DVD. Something light, a story where a couple rekindles their relationship. After that he'd read to her, and return her to her room. If she was wearing makeup he'd wet a flannel and help her remove it. Cut her fingernails, brush her hair and put it in its net, take out her teeth, go to the bathroom and clean them, and then deposit them in a glass of murky water.

He'd help her into her nightie. Take her under her shoulders and lift her into bed, adjusting her legs, and feet, and eventually tucking her in. Then he'd sit beside her and say, 'Another beautiful day, Miss Mary.' Sometimes she'd reply. He'd pull the sheets up under her chin and think of kissing her, although he never did. If her arm was crooked, askew, he'd move it so it rested comfortably on the quilt. If it creaked, or crunched, or tried to spring back into position, he'd say, 'We must get you fixed, Miss Mary.'

Then he'd switch off her light, and retire to the telly, knowing he'd done his penance.

Guarding the Pageant

I SAW MY FUTURE in the budgie's beak. It was the Earth Fair, and you could have your fortune told by a small yellow bird – one revelation for three dollars, two for five. Of course I just laughed it off, but my daughter, a clever, anti-*Saddle Club* sort of kid, urged me to have a go. So I paid my money and sat on a stool in front of the cage, and a short, wiry-haired woman said, 'Go on, talk to him.'

'Talk to him?'

'He has to know something about you.'

'What's he want to know?'

'What do you want to tell him?'

Christ, I thought. What was she going to say next?

'He can see into your mind. He knows your inner thoughts, feelings and desires.'

Was she trying to be funny or was she (more alarmingly) serious? At least you could excuse the bird – he was only after some seed.

So I told the bird my name (Sam 'Mad Dog' Morgan), address (17 Brookfield Heights, Wynn Vale) and place of employment (Lindisfarne College). I told him about my eight-year-old daughter (Sarah), ten-year-old son (Liam) and wife of sixteen years (Avril). The bird's eyes seemed to glaze over. Not much of an expression. Although it did have some nice-looking throat spots I wanted to tickle.

Then the old girl said, 'Now, tell him something about *you*.'

'Me?'

'Yes.' She smiled.

'Well,' I began, hesitantly, 'some people think I'm a bit of a comedian.'

'Go on.'

'I've written a few comedy skits, and sent them to Channel Nine.' I wondered why I was sitting in the middle of a school oval sharing my thoughts with a budgie.

'Tell the budgie about the narcolepsy meeting,' my tall, buck-toothed, brown-eyed son grinned.

'Yes,' I said. 'You see, it's the Narcolepsy Association's AGM, and one by one they fall asleep, until the camera shows the whole table, with everyone snoring.' I waited for a response but the budgie wasn't impressed. 'Then there's this skit about a priest blessing pets at a school, sprinkling holy water on them, like this.' I showed the budgie. 'But then he gets to this stick insect. So, you know what he does?' I looked expectantly at the bird. 'He takes out a pipette and fills it with holy water.'

By now there was a queue of people waiting for the budgie to tell them how much weight they were going to lose, if a terminal aunt would leave them any money or if they'd be promoted. The woman said, 'That should be enough.' She produced a seed tray, half-filled with budgie food and half with folded notes. She opened a door on the cage and placed the tray inside. The hungry bird started picking at the seed, swallowing a few grains, before picking up a piece of paper. After he'd dropped it she slid a hand into the cage and retrieved it. Opening it, looking at me, smiling and saying, 'Lucas knows.'

'Lucas?'

'He says, "Follow the way of truth, it leads to happiness".'

'What does he mean – God?'

'Not necessarily. Truth.'

My son Liam was pulling on my sleeve. 'Come on, Dad, you said we could do the three-legged race.'

A lot's changed since then. If I were having my fortune told today I'd have to tell the budgie: name, Sam (not-so-'Mad Dog') Morgan; address, living alone in a one-bedroom flat in Salisbury Downs;

employment, Four Squares Security; relationships, nine-year-old daughter and eleven-year-old son, eighteen months separated from wife of sixteen years. From Friday prawns and Corona to a constant diet of Don-the-Greek's steak sandwiches with the lot (minus pineapple). From freshly ironed button-downs to synthetic polos doused in deodorant to make them wearable for the third day running. From teaching physics to guarding pageant floats on South Terrace. And all because of that budgie. Okay, it was slightly more complex than that, but I'm sure the budgie wouldn't mind me laying a bit of guilt at his little Christ-like claws.

The story I'd like to tell took place last night, on the eve of the city's annual Christmas pageant, six weeks out from the big day. As five other guards and I made sure no one tampered with the floats. Since there are so many floats, and since there's not enough time on Saturday morning to drive them all over from the warehouse, they're ferried over by a small army of drivers the night before. Parked in a line that concertinas two times before moving to the next stretch of road and doubling up again. This way about two hundred floats can be parked along a three-hundred-metre stretch of road.

And there they sit, through the night, waiting for their big moment. When thousands of Credit Union employees arrive on Saturday morning, pull on their fluorescent clown wigs and oversized novelty boots, and practise riding their knee-high bikes. For the marching bands to find their place between the floats, the fairies to start sprinkling glitter, the fiddlers to fiddle, the tellers-dressed-as-farmers to harness their motorised sheep, and for Father Christmas to gather his sack of toys (as all the kids think, Has he got enough for everyone?) and settle into his sleigh.

As jobs go, this is a good one. At least there's something to look at. I'd just spent the last month standing outside the Klemzig branch of the National Bank. We're told we can't use our phones, listen to music or make conversation with customers. No, we're there to work; to stand and look menacing. Yes, we can walk around (within a two-metre radius of the entrance), have a drink and even eat our lunch, but if we read anything (even a gas bill) we can face instant dismissal. We're meant to have our eyes open and watch for trouble. This is the sort of job I warned my students they'd end up with if they didn't study. Last week one of my old Year Twelves walked past, but I pretended I was looking for something, and turned away.

Guarding the pageant is a very important job. What if, for instance, some little hooligan came along with a screwdriver and punched holes in the floats' tyres? There'd be no pageant. Hundreds of thousands of people would have to be told to stay home, but many would already be in the city, picnic rugs down, and imagine their anger, and how congested the trams and buses would be, and all of the crying children.

Our group of guards met at six o'clock outside the Green Dragon Hotel. Apparently, life hadn't been any kinder to them than me. One guy had ironed his clothes and shaved (the ambitious type, he'd already told me he was applying to join the police force for the fifth time in seven years); one wore a too-small uniform, I think, to show-case his enormous muscle bulk (like he was some sort of stripper, and might rip the whole lot off at any time); the others had alcoholic eyes, a week's growth, food on their shirts. Not really enough of a threat to stop anyone doing anything, except living, eating, talking, even being with them. I didn't feel like I belonged. Had I fucked up my life *that* completely? Regardless, we were given our pistols and some curt instructions. 'No one can come within three metres of the floats. They can look, they can take photos, but hands off, folks.'

I started my night beside the pirate float: a twelve-foot-high Bluebeard, his broom bristle mo fluttering in the breeze as birds sat and shat on his cap. Helped by a scrawny pirate using an old bottle as a telescope and a two-ton pig-man-cutthroat guarding a treasure chest full of coins. Finally, a navy officer in a boat attached to the float, rowing as fast as he could to get away from the pirates.

Cute. I knocked on Bluebeard's boot. Hollow. The pageant could transform flesh into fantasy. I remembered sitting behind the blue line with Sarah and Liam two, maybe three, years before, watching this same float drive past. Remembered the smoke coming from Bluebeard's ears and the pre-recorded growls and pirate-speak over an old PA. The clerks-as-pirates threatening onlookers with cardboard swords and hook-hands. And Liam, looking up and saying, 'This is the best one yet.' As he smiled so hard I thought his cheeks would pop. And then, perhaps, my eyes frosting over, and me wiping them, feigning hay fever.

As I wished the pageant would last forever.

But it didn't, and doesn't. I can also remember Avril staring at a mother (in a cotton twill asymmetric jacket) and father (with a half-ton Tiffany CT60 watch) who'd sat their kids in front of Sarah and Liam. She'd spoken up, as usual. 'I believe our children had the front spot,' as I said, 'Don't worry, they can share.' But she wasn't having any of that. 'Typical eastern suburbs attitude.'

As the other mother said, 'Pardon?'

'You heard me. Today's meant to be about the *kids*,' (who by now had all moved to accommodate each other).

I paraded my stretch of South Terrace, passing Nellie the foam elephant, who would be accompanied by a group of teller-types bathed in fake tans to make themselves look Malaysian, or Thai, or something faintly North China Takeaway. Glaring blue, yellow and red velvet jackets, three-quarter pants and sandals. Bamboo canes to tap the diesel-driven beast on the rump.

Darkness settled across the grammar school on one side and the paddocks on the other. Yellow lights on Stobie poles blinked to life and it was officially night. A few families with excited kids strolled along the terrace, dads looking at me as if to say, What if you turned your back for a few minutes? Just after nine a group on a buck's night emerged from the Green Dragon and one, a short, stocky kid with shaving cuts and a high voice, jumped the cordon and grabbed Nellie's horsehair tail. 'She won't shit on me?' he asked, as the others laughed.

I just shrugged, remembering my buck's night, what seemed like a lifetime ago. I was so excited to be marrying Avril, to be leaving home and starting a new life. I wondered what the budgie would've told me back then. *Don't do it. Just don't do it.*

I strolled past floats that reminded me of other times, other places: the Seven Dwarfs, the Timber Cutters, the *Anything Goes* cruise ship and the red and green School Daze. Wood, fibreglass and paint provided flashes of fantasy, worlds beyond acceleration coefficients and broken line-trimmers, wildly fictional orthodontist bills and staff meetings that ran past six. Beyond Mike and Carol marriages and *Neighbours* communities. Ali Baba instead of algorithms. Tom Sawyer instead of tax returns.

Frank, a twenty-year Four Squares veteran, brought me a coffee and we sat on the Toyland float to rest. 'Nice job?' he asked, with his Godfather voice.

'Different,' I replied.

'Someone said you're a teacher.'

'I was.'

'So what are you doing here?'

'I quit.'

'Why?'

'To annoy my wife.'

'Serious?'

'Sort of. There was more to it … she didn't appreciate the sacrifices I was making.' I stopped, realising I hardly knew him. He slapped me on the shoulder, slurped his coffee and wiped his mouth on his forearm. 'Women are bitches,' he said. 'They get their claws in, you know what I mean?'

'I know.'

'You did the right thing.' Then he stopped to think, looking into the sky and tilting his head. 'Bet you miss the money?'

'What's to miss?'

'Got another girl yet?'

'I don't want another girl.'

'I got a cousin.'

'I could imagine.'

'If you just want sex.'

'Thanks anyway.'

A few minutes later he set off to check the other guards, and I continued my stroll. It must have been after ten when a mother and father with a six- or seven-year-old daughter wandered past the Toyland float. The girl couldn't believe her eyes: hundreds of presents, some of them as big as washing machines, piled up at the base of a five-metre high Christmas tree. She slipped under the cordon and climbed onto the float.

'Get off,' her mother called.

The girl ignored her. Crawled towards the pile of presents, grabbed one and discovered it was stuck on. Pulled at it, but it wouldn't budge. Looked at her parents and scowled. Her father started laughing, but her mother kept repeating, 'Get down, this instant.'

The girl looked like Sarah: mousy blonde hair, a button nose bisecting a pair of demonic eyes, strong piano hands and a will that couldn't be tempered by reason. Sarah. Christmas morning. Ripping through presents like an angry tornado, examining plastic-wrapped dolls and games and exploding with joy, throwing herself at me with open arms and saying, 'Thank you, Daddy.' Between kisses, although it was generally Avril who'd bought the presents. If she found one of Liam's presents she'd throw it across the carpet or just brush it aside or say, 'Liam, that's the basketball you asked for.'

Eventually the girl crawled back to the edge of the float and the father helped her down. She crossed her arms, stamped her feet and said, 'They're not real.'

'What did you expect?' the mother replied, turning and walking on.

I watched as the girl smiled knowingly at her father, taking him by the hand and lifting the yellow rope for him to walk under. She noticed me but just raised her eyebrows as if to say, So, what are you gonna do about it? I smiled and the father winked at me, and I wondered if Sarah was home asleep or reading or watching television. I felt, as I did thirty times a day, that I'd made the wrong decision by putting myself first, especially when it seemed like every other parent on the planet was doing the right thing.

But then I remembered a warm March afternoon, last year, walking in the front door, Avril on the phone. I put down my bag, smiled, waited until she was finished. Then, 'Guess what?'

'What?'

'I quit.'

She smiled as she stirred something on the stove. 'Quit what?'

'Work.'

'One day.' She kept smiling.

'No, today. I quit.'

Then it dawned on her. She turned off the stove, stepped towards me and said, 'You didn't?'

'I did.'

Then the fireworks. 'Why?'

'Because I don't enjoy it anymore.'

She asked about the mortgage, school fees and bills and I reminded her we had enough savings for a year or so.

'While you do what?' she asked.

'Write this novel I've been planning for the last eight years.'

'Are you stupid?'

'And after that I'll get another job. There's plenty of work for physics teachers.'

'But you didn't even ask me.'

'I did, for the last five years, and you always said, "One day, when the kids have finished school".' And I whispered, 'I could be dead by then.'

'We all could.'

'That's the thing, isn't it? You couldn't give a rat's arse. As long as I'm earning ...'

'I supported you for years.'

'So what?' I waited. 'We'll make it work. I'll get my book written and you – '

'Ring the principal. Talk to him. It's not too late.'

But I just smiled.

The beginning of the end. She kept pleading for another few days, and I kept ignoring her, locking myself in my study and reading about Daisy Bates for the Great Australian Novel. She tried a different approach – ignoring me back, talking to me through the kids and refusing to acknowledge my presence in the house. After two days of this I said, 'Come on, grow up, it's not such a big deal. Twelve months.'

'You didn't even ask me.'

'I did.'

'You only think of one person.'

'Bullshit. I've spent years thinking of everyone else.'

'You could've asked for leave.'

Everything I'd been thinking for the past few years crystallised – small compromises leading to bigger ones. The words of the budgie were sounding in my ear.

'What do you think of me?' I asked.

She didn't reply, and I knew. I couldn't remember when I'd ever loved her, or how, or for how long. She'd become a sort of assembly-line foreman, telling me how to put my life together, inspecting the finished product and putting a defective sticker on it. In a fit of rage and revelation I went to our bedroom, took a case from the robe and started packing. She followed me and stood staring, her arms crossed. 'Nice performance.'

To be honest, I think I was mainly bluffing. 'You think I won't?'

'Gonna tell your kids where you're going?'

I decided. Twelve months. Daisy Bates would get written. I'd get to rediscover the 'Mad Dog' in Sam Morgan and she'd be brought back down to earth.

At least that's how I remember it happening. Then there were the three nights in a motel, the flat, the lawyers and money taken out of my account. Four Squares. The National Bank. The Christmas pageant.

As Daisy Bates went unwritten.

I moved to the Barn Dance float. Red, blue and green planks of wood. The loft full of fresh hay, paddocks mined with nibbling sheep, hungry pigs, grunting. An area had been left for cowgirls to dance with milk pails. Lanterns. Wagon-wheels and a Hills Hoist with a thousand corks blowing in the doughnut-scented breeze. I could just hear the music and see the dresses flying in the air.

It was still, and mostly quiet, except for the hum of a distant air compressor. I piddled in a bed of red and white petunias and returned to sit on the Barn Dance float. Someone had painted a line of horses, nose-to-tail: simple two-tone ponies minus mouths and ears, their eyes a single dot of watery paint that had run, leaving them crying milk-white tears.

Liam was the artist in our household. I'd given him money to buy canvases and a set of oil paints and he'd painted aliens landing in our backyard, Jackson Pollock-inspired psychoscapes, portraits of Avril and Sarah and one of me filling a blackboard with nonsensical physics formulae.

I touched one of the horses' white eyes and the paint flaked off.

'What do you think of this one?' Liam asked me, as he sat in the corner of the living room of my flat the previous Sunday.

'What is it?'

'The budgie, remember, at the fair?'

'I remember.' It was a Picasso budgie – fat, misshapen, its yellow body striped with pink and purple paint. The note in its beak had grown to the size of a large encyclopedia and I wondered if it was the budgie (or Liam) telling me that life is far more complex than a fortune cookie. I sat on the floor and asked, 'What's written on the note?'

'I can't remember.'

But I could – 'Follow the way of truth, it leads to happiness'. Or this, sitting in a hot flat that smelt of cooking oil and petrol, its shag-pile carpet full of dust mites and dirt, the sun beating on the cracked window as the air conditioner made enough noise to drown out the telly without actually cooling the room.

The Truth? Happiness?

'That's a damn fine budgie,' I said. 'But I think he was wrong.'

He looked confused. 'How?'

I just put my arm around his shoulder. 'I'm sorry,' I whispered, without thinking.

'Why?'

'Because of ... all this.'

He shrugged. 'Mum says you'll get over it, when you're finished with Daisy.'

I touched the tip of his nose, and almost laughed. 'She does, eh?'

'Who's Daisy?'

'She ran away too.'

'From what?'

And then I pointed to the painting. 'I didn't know budgies had teeth.'

It was almost five-thirty when the horizon started to lighten from black to purple, to a blue that promised day between the rooftops. I sat yawning, rubbing my eyes, beside the Jolly Swagman, an over-sized sheep rustler who'd slept the night (and his whole existence) beside a cellophane river, waiting for a giant cod to take the bait. He wore patched jeans that were held up by a length of twine; his toes dangled in the river and his nails, smelling of fresh paint, were clogged with real dirt.

I took an envelope from my top pocket, opened it and produced a pile of colour photos. Sarah and Liam playing under our nectarine tree. I looked at them – tall, lanky, brown-skinned – and decided I'd make a phone call when I knocked off. If I drove straight to Wynn Vale, picked them up and returned to the city, I'd be back in time for the pageant. I could find a nice spot on the southern end of King William Street and settle in with them. That way I could reclaim the pageant. Our pageant – fantasy made flesh. I could tell them, 'I almost fell asleep on that float,' and they could think, So what?

The next photo showed the kids eating spaghetti, their faces covered in pasta sauce. Avril stood beside them, trying to wipe their faces with a flannel, as I (I suppose) just stood laughing, reaching for my camera and telling Avril to let them go.

Avril – growling at the world at the front of her own Bluebeard float, forming fibreglass skin, donning an eye-patch and shaking her hook at every potential enemy. Which made me the Jolly Swagman, my felt hat down over my eyes as I snored, waiting for a fish that would never bite.

But that's life, I guess. You make your own happiness, or misery.

Christ, I thought. *That's* what the budgie meant.

I looked at Avril's eyes and decided I didn't need her anymore. I took the spaghetti photo and threw it in the bin beside the float.

She picked up the phone when I rang. 'Are the kids doing anything this morning?'

'Sarah's got netball.'

'Ah.' A long pause, as I took a deep breath. 'I was gonna take them to the pageant.' I could almost hear her thinking.

'Hold on, I'll ask them.' But she stopped to think. 'How's Daisy going?'

'Still in the desert with the black fellas.'

'Like you?'

'Me? I am a black fella, eh?'

'Hold on.'

So I reached into the bin, retrieved the photo and put it on the bottom of the pile. I couldn't edit her out of my life, or back in, yet, perhaps. But photos are good like that: they compress time, showing you what's happened, what's happening and perhaps what's to come. Flesh and fantasy in a snapshot.

I turned and saw the big beast. Hippo's Hot consisted of a giant purple hippopotamus sitting in a cooking pot. I assumed that soon the natives would arrive to paint their bodies, don their grass skirts and gather their spears. Then they could tend the fire under the pot as Hippo, thinking they were giving him a bath, continued cleaning himself with a scrubbing brush, sponging his red-hot face, popping the bubbles and laughing as though this was the best day of his life.

Akdal Ghost

DH LORINS WAS BEST KNOWN for his music videos. Ken had seen one: three bearded men strumming their guitars as they sank into a swamp, as seagulls with streamers on their legs landed on their heads, as fireworks went off, lip-synch, baby-baby, no life without you, and Greek grandmas ate yoghurt in the background. Silly stuff, but that's what the kids watched, apparently. DH was bell-and-whistle: mutton-chop whiskers and a nose ring, but … no, stop, Ken Fletcher told himself. What did it matter? As long as the kids learned about the End. The seconds, minutes and hours when He'd walk from His own swamp, extend His hands and say, Come with me, Ken, we have work to do. And smile. Cos that's what He'd do. Telling him: Let's gather the followers, Pastor Fletcher.

That's all that mattered. Lorins' badged-up beret. So what? His eye shadow, even (although what did it mean – was he bum happy?).

Lórins had tried a few takes, but wasn't happy. He approached the young man, Charlie Clarke, and showed him (again) how to hold the Akdal Ghost. Tight, but not trembling. Raise it like this, and look down the sight, into the camera. Cock it. The viewer has to think you're gonna pull the trigger. You wanna kill them. Or, if not, you're so angry you could be persuaded. Like this. Camera. Raise. Cock. Find you mark. Let's see your finger tightening on the trigger, then, don't worry about then – *then* we'll cut to black, and the words …

'Which words?' Charlie asked.

Lorins turned to Ken. 'What did you want?'

'"If he's given up on God, who's next?"'

Charlie thought about it; he still didn't understand. *'Who's next?'*

Ken wouldn't be drawn. 'Just do what Mr Lorins says, Charlie.'

But Lorins was curious, too. 'So, what you're saying is, if he's given up on God, then this is the result?'

'Not at all,' Ken explained, slowly. 'If this boy doesn't find God … we're all lost.'

Lorins didn't really care. It was a quick job, in and out, one day, thirty seconds. None of the major networks we're likely to run it, no matter how much they were offered. But, he supposed, Fletcher would put it on the net and millions of apologists would see it, and agree with him, and feel satisfied that they were the ones chosen (for that's what they'd get out of it, somehow – a sixteen-year-old in a singlet, walking along a country road, raising his gun, angry face, cold eyes, the sound of gravel under his bare feet; that's what the old prick wanted; why he was willing to pay fifty thousand).

Ken stepped forward, lifted Charlie's arm and said, 'Hold it like that, strong, like you've already decided.'

'What?' Charlie asked. He had no idea what he was doing, but the old man had offered him two grand for a day's work. The old man who'd approached him in the supermarket as he'd stacked sauce. Who'd said, 'You have a serious face.'

'Sorry?'

'Square. Solid. No-nonsense.'

'Are you after something?'

'I'm making a short film, for my church, to promote our views.'

Two thousand? 'How long?' (as he'd thought, weeks, a month …)

'Should be done in a day.'

'For your church?'

Lorins waited for Ken to finish. Then: 'Mr Fletcher, if you want *me* to make the film …'

Ken studied the holes the seven or eight earrings had made. 'I was just suggesting …'

'You need to leave it to me. That's why you're paying me, isn't it?'

Ken stepped back, watching the young *man*. He put his hand in his coat pocket and felt the nine millimetre lumps of lead and copper. From where he'd removed them from his Akdal Ghost. Handed the pistol to Lorins, who'd given it to Charlie Clarke. Charlie had smiled and said, 'It's heavy, isn't it?'

Ken had thought, It's got a lot of killing to do. Not actual killing, but killing of sin. Removing it from the world. Via these few images. Not that he agreed with guns. In fact, hated them. But he'd wanted his film to look authentic, and he wasn't about to risk someone recognising a prop gun. So he'd gone into Wembley's Shop, and persuaded a friend to lend him a pistol, and the father and son had produced the Ghost and showed him and said, 'This was a good idea of yours, Ken. Get the young ones thinking, eh?'

'Absolutely, John.'

'Scare the shit out of them. Get them back to church, eh?'

'Correct.'

'So, you just want it for the day?'

'I'll give it back after we finish filming.'

And then he'd given him the Ghost, but he'd forgotten to remove the Parabellum bullets, so Ken had done this himself, and he was feeling them now, cold, in his pocket.

Charlie tried again. Walked up the road. Stopped, raised his hand.

Lorins shook his head. 'No, nothing threatening on your face. Remember? Angry, but cold, calm, like you've decided.'

'What?'

'To wipe away the sin,' Ken said.

Lorins turned to him. 'Ken, you gotta let me do it.'

'But that's the point. People have got to know, they won't find the answers in Coke, and teeny-bopper music. They'll find them in Genesis, and Revelation.'

'Leave it to me.'

'They've got to *feel* it, DH.'

'They will.'

Ken just looked at this boy-man, full of an ungodly arrogance, the three necklaces, the shirt open to his bellybutton to show his chest hair. He might've been Satan himself, with horns somewhere in his mop, nails growing from his fingertips, goat horn equipment, ready to pop up and spread his swampy seed to the kids, over them, fertilising evil with his repeated bass riffs and hi-hat tingles. He wondered if he should've got Alf, after all. Alf from the church band (*Ascensiones in Corde*). With his hand-held and computer software for editing. The whole thing (he'd promised) for five grand. Easy. On the web by Monday. He wondered. This fella had some other agenda.

Lorins called for a break. Ken watched as his cameraman, and soundman, and the girl who'd done the makeup and costumes (not that there was anything to do, the boy had brought his own singlet) sat on canvas chairs and talked. Looked at him, smiled, and laughed. Wasted the time he was paying for. The time he'd borrowed (in the form of money) from the Bank (in the form of Evil as bricks and mortar). From the church account (truth be known). Although the online ads would soon take care of that.

Lorins approached him and said, 'Apologists?'

'Sorry?'

'Is that what they call you guys? Apologists?'

'No.'

'But you think people like me are done for?'

Ken noticed how the cuff on Lorins' jeans was worn, how he was wearing sandals, like Jesus, gathering the Faithful, which is what he was doing, maybe, but not really. Just working some technical magic. A means to an end. To an End. 'You're not done for, if you believe.'

Lorins smiled. 'In what?'

'The same stuff they taught you in Sunday school.'

Lorins almost laughed. 'You don't really believe ...' But stopped. After all, it was good money. Jesus or not, it'd pay a few bills. Although, he worried, he might get a reputation. And it wasn't like you could put a disclaimer on it: The director wishes it known that Sinners will not be shot in the head by a sixteen-year-old in a singlet walking along a country road. Yes, that was a worry. But it was so much money. 'I still don't get it,' he said to Ken. '"If he's given up on God, who's next?" I mean, the meaning's not clear. You go to all this effort, and people still don't understand.'

'They will.'

'I don't think so.'

'I do.'

'I've been doing this a few years. One thing I've found, you gotta keep it simple, the message clear. You got thirty seconds to get in and out, why fuck around?'

Ken didn't like his potty mouth either. But all of these things would have to be ignored, for now. He noticed Charlie sitting on a log beside the road, playing with the gun. 'Careful of that,' he called.

Charlie looked up, but then continued.

'The point is, DH, people will be left to think about it.'

'What?

'Not mattering, which comes from not believing, and how this makes love, and grace, impossible.'

Lorins had no idea what this meant, but he suspected Ken didn't either. What a load of shit, he thought. Ken could see that this is what he was thinking. He said, 'You think I'm simple?'

'Believe what you want. You're paying me to get a professional film. You'll get it. I've got a few ideas for a neat edit. You still set on the no music idea?'

'All the focus on the sound of gravel, feet moving, the gun cocking, the boy's breath.'

'Some violins, perhaps, soft at first – '

'No.'

'Or synth? Not enough that anyone would even notice.'

'No.'

Lorins examined Fletcher's whiskers, and the few nasal hairs that whistled as he breathed. Nothing passed between them. No sound. Not even the rub of a rag on the lens cap, as the director planned his next move. He looked at Charlie again. He was drinking Coke, wiping his mouth, playing with the torn knees on his jeans. Then he asked Ken, 'Why him?'

'That's the future, Mr Lorins.'

'DH.'

'Look at his eyes. Vacant. Nothing going on. How can there be, without God?' He looked into the young man's eyes, almost pleadingly.

'That's such bullshit. There's plenty going on. He was telling me about his girlfriend ...'

Ken walked away, uninterested.

'And his results for _'

Turned, and said, 'Shall we get on with it?'

Again, stationary camera, Charlie walking towards it, looking into the lens, raising his arm, waiting.

'No!' Ken called.

Everyone looked at him.

'He's walking like he's taking a stroll down Commercial Road. Listen, Charlie.' He came forward, and held his arms. 'You gotta walk with determination. You know who you're pointing that gun at, don't you?'

'No.'

'Does God matter?'

'I dunno. Does he?'

Ken knew the boy was lost; but not the cause.

'You gotta – '

'Mr Fletcher!' Lorins half-shouted. 'You either want me to direct this, or you don't.'

'But you've got to make him walk like he means it.'

'Means what? You won't tell me.'

'Like he wants to shoot someone in the head.'

'Who?'

'His mother, his father – they didn't tell him about Christ. But now he's found out, and he's angry.'

Lorins took a deep breath, and indicated for Ken to stand back.

Ken moved. He felt in his pocket. Parabellum. And was pleased with the feel of them. Their density. Their refusal to compromise their view of the world. All soft things, that could easily be penetrated, destroyed, made to not exist. Like Evil. Washed away with a hose of gun smoke, like dog turds on a driveway. How beautiful was that? Gone. If only people could see this. How easily it was done. They might sit up and take notice. Yes – the graphic example. Like Jesus on his cross. Inspiring thousands of followers for thousands of years. Cos of a simple, single image. All visual. For the visual age.

They tried again, and again, and Lorins still wasn't happy: with the walk, the way Charlie's shoulders moved, with how fast he cocked the gun, the way he licked his lips. With a million things.

Ken was silent; deep in thought. He'd been put in his place. But it didn't matter. He knew DH was a good director, and the kids loved him, and the film would end brilliantly, and have millions of hits, and viewers, and media beyond anything he could've hoped for as he stood at the front of the Westridge Church preaching Proverbs and Daniel and the End of Days and give generously for our new Creation Museum. It would end beautifully. Fifty thousand well spent. As the world looked on, as Charlie in his singlet became famous, a star, more films, several wives, children who drifted on and off of drugs.

All because of the power of the image. A girl running along a napalmed road. King. Hitler. Little John Kennedy saluting his dead dad. Man on the moon. Lennon in bed with Yoko. OJ live on the highway. The events that defined.

'My feet are getting sore,' Charlie said.

It wasn't fine gravel. Big lumps. And they were cutting into him.

'Last time,' Lorins said.

Ken watched his director as he finished rolling a cigarette. Why couldn't he just use a bought one? The way he lit it, spat out a bit of tobacco, and started smoking. All the fires of hell. There was probably a girlfriend. Loose. Telling him he was a genius. Clawing at his pants. Working him up. Drugs. Injected. Although he wore long sleeves, so you couldn't tell. But all this, when it came out, would make it even more poetic, and meaningful. He could see his film. How, like a little Bible of his own times, it would change the world. How, like Jesus, someone would have to star, become a symbol, feature on T-shirts and animations, be remembered for generations to come. Charlie? With his tight lips and flaring nostrils.

Fifty thousand well spent.

'Charlie?'

'Yes, Mr Fletcher?'

He motioned for him to approach. 'Quick word.'

Lorins said, 'I wanna finish, Ken. We've got plenty of takes to choose from.'

'One more.'

'His feet are bleeding.'

'Like Christ.'

'Screw Christ. *His feet are bleeding!*'

But even this didn't worry Ken.

The boy stood in front of Ken and said, 'I can barely walk, Mr Fletcher.'

'I know, son. One more, please?'

Charlie took a deep breath, and released it slowly. Ken felt in his pocket. Nine millimetres. Took one. Took the gun from the boy's hand. Said, 'I've had this idea. Instead of pointing the gun at the camera, cocking, firing, you point it at Mr Lorins' head.'

'His head?'

'Off camera, you see? I think it'll be a lot more effective.'

'How?'

'Just do.'

Charlie was confused, but not concerned. He just thought of the money, again, and how he was here to do as he was told. 'So, same thing, but …?'

'Yes.'

Charlie called out. 'DH?'

'No,' Ken said. 'You can't tell him. It's gotta be a surprise. He reacts, you react, we see your face, see … whole different feel. I think it'll work.'

Charlie shrugged. 'If you reckon.'

Ken handed him the Akdal Ghost. 'I know your feet are hurting, but this one last time. Then it'll be perfect. We can go home. Everyone can watch you on the net.'

Charlie smiled. 'And you reckon the television will screen it?'

'I'm sure.'

'And it might lead to something?'

'Yes.'

'I reckon I could act. For a living. If I got lucky.'

'Lucky. Exactly. Now, one last time.'

Charlie returned to his spot, further up the road. Lorins called action and the boy-man-Christ started walking towards the camera, with its little red light.

The Barmera Drive-in

TREVOR ROPER UNLOCKED THE GATE. It swung on a single hinge, so he lifted it. He pushed it against the waist-high grass growing around the entrance to the old Barmera Drive-in. He got back in his car and drove down the side road that led to the parking bays, the old projection room (covered in graffiti, its windows smashed in, its walls kicked out) and, at the back, the cafeteria. It hadn't sold anything for years. Since its closure in 1987, when the owner looked out of his office, across the drive-in (at the two cars that had come) and decided enough was enough. The following week there was a 'FOR SALE' sign on the fence, but although he'd built the drive-in, no one had come. Not one single offer. He'd dropped the price, again and again, but it had done no good. No one wanted a Riverland drive-in.

Trevor drove back to the cafeteria. It still promised Choc-tops and Pluto Pups, cold Coke and hot chips, but like everything else, it was a ruin. He got out and looked around *his* cafeteria (since he'd signed the contract to buy the old Barmera Drive-in). Since he'd walked into Oranges and Lemons Real Estate the previous week and asked, 'The old drive-in?' Since the old fella had looked at him. 'The drive-in?'

'What are they asking?'

'What are you offering?'

'I'm willing to pay a fair price.'

'But it's been for sale for twenty-five years.'

Trevor had smiled. 'I know. How much are they asking?'

As he stood looking across the asphalt, he felt proud. That something more than a house or car was his. That he finally owned this

Super Duper Saturday-sized field of dreams. That he'd reclaimed his, and every kid's, history: every movie he'd ever seen on every Saturday night he'd come as a child: from *Willy Wonka* to *Kelly's Heroes*, *E.T.* to *Freaky Friday*. Each film a chapter of his own life, summarising the chronology (and sad and happy bits) of his own Barmera childhood.

It'd been a *Citizen Kane*, San Simeon kind of thing. Decades of passing the drive-in on his way to school or work, always remembering, always saving, always hoping the 'SOLD' sign wouldn't appear. Planning for this day. The first of many. When he'd start the process of reclaiming his childhood by reclaiming the drive-in.

He walked into the cafeteria. Again, the walls had been kicked out and there was wood and asbestos everywhere. Old signage, parts of the ice cream machine, chip racks and the deep-fryer that had deep-fried his childhood. Everything. Hot dogs and bananas, Chiko Rolls and Mars bars.

'What are you seeing tonight?' he asked a boy, standing, waiting.

'*Rocky*,' he replied.

'You like Stallone?'

'Not really. I wanted to see *The Omen* tomorrow night but Mum said I was too young.'

'For *The Omen*? Rubbish.' He stopped to think. 'Although ... there are other ways.'

The boy just looked at him.

'You know the willows, over there,' he indicated. 'You can sit and not be seen, and you can hear the sound from the cafeteria speakers.'

The boy smiled. 'But they won't let me out.'

'Well, tell 'em you're going to a mate's place.'

'They'll find out, they always do.'

'Not if you arrange it with Keith.'

The boy seemed shocked. 'You know Keith?'

'Of course. He's everyone's best mate.'

Trevor walked out to his car and drove across to the projection room.

He studied the slab where the projector had once been bolted down. Even now there were shards of film on the ground. He picked one up and studied it: a horse, and some hills, still searching for lamplight decades after they'd been trimmed from the reel. There was an old canvas seat the projectionist (an old man, his grandfather's friend) sat on working on his crosswords as the film hummed and spoke and sang beside him. Trevor used to watch him, sitting outside, leaning against the door licking his pencil. He'd wonder why he was more interested in his book than the film. How could it be? A film was the best of the world: the history, the drama, the songs, the costumes. Perhaps, he'd guessed, the old man had seen it too many times to care. Or perhaps he was only interested in solid, real, dependable things: two across and one down.

'What's showing tonight?' he asked.

'*Jaws*. Again. Two months straight.'

'Scary, eh?'

'Not particularly. It's all shit. Next week it's *Convoy*, then *Revenge of the Pink Panther*. We were offered *The Deer Hunter*, but they turned it down.'

'Why?'

'Said no one would come. Like we're all idiots. Thing is, you keep it up, people will stay away. You've got to challenge your audience.'

'You reckon?'

'Absolutely. This is like throwin' Christians to the lions. People'll get sick of it eventually.'

Trevor went out to his car. He opened the boot, took out a card table and projector and a dozen extension cords that had been joined together. He unwound the cords as he walked across the drive-in towards the gate, along a hundred metres of highway and into the carpark of the deserted Cobby Fruit Mart. He inserted the plug into a wall socket he'd noticed fifteen years ago, when the plan was only half-formed in his head. Then he returned to the projection room and set up his equipment.

He walked back into the night and stood looking at the screen. Despite being grey and faded, and bird-shat-on, it was intact. He wasted no time. He untied a ladder from the roof of his car, found a brush and tin of white paint in his boot and began. Soon he was six metres up, hovering above the playground for the young kids who'd got sick of the film. There were still monkey bars, and a slide that burned the back of their legs on hot summer nights, but the weed-mat had yielded to the fat-hen and caltrop.

He painted the part of the screen he figured he'd need. As he worked he was aware of Gregory Peck beneath his bristles. He felt like Michelangelo on his scaffold, tackling the Sistine ceiling, honouring his own gods in paint. But these were fleeting gods, flickering for a few hours before vanishing into the night. Like the bell for the end of recess; little worlds surrendered to active verbs and Oliver Cromwell.

As a child he felt the world was imperfect; still did. There was little colour in it (except citrus-orange and red- and white-grape), little music, little poetry. But these were things he liked: Oliver Twist on his balcony watching soldiers march down Mayfair; Peter Sellers at the sort of party he never went to (just fat uncles telling him about botrytis). He felt the drive-in was the only way to escape his own world of ever-darkening freckles and never-resolving long division. In a way, these were the only hours he was alive. Maybe, by watching movies, you could escape the real world. Maybe not. Maybe school and mashed potatoes *were* the only things to look forward to. But why would people choose this life when there were Manhattan galleries and African safaris? Why? Even now he didn't know.

The fear struck him again. What if by doing this, nothing was better? Would that mean he was wrong? Would it mean that life was just a succession of mortgage payments and toasted sandwiches?

He saw lights at the gate. A patrol car drove in and stopped. He waved. 'Over here.'

The car continued. He climbed down and walked over to greet the sergeant. The car stopped and a middle-aged man with a pot belly got out. 'G'day.'

'How are yer?'

'I haven't seen anyone in here for years.'

Trevor was half-worried, half-proud. 'Well, I've bought it.'

'What?'

'The drive-in.'

'The whole thing?'

'Yep.'

The sergeant looked around. 'Why?'

'Why not?'

'You gonna reopen it?'

Trevor wasn't sure himself. 'Perhaps. But for now, I wanna do it up, get it working again.'

The copper didn't get it. 'So you can reopen it?'

Trevor shrugged.

'You'll fix the whole thing, so ...?'

'So I can sit and watch movies.'

The sergeant noticed the extension cords, the projector, and smelt the paint. 'Couldn't you just hire a DVD?'

'I could, but this is the real McCoy. Didn't you come here when you were a kid?'

'No.'

'Don't you love the drive-in?'

'No. It's either raining or too hot. That's why people stopped coming. You either froze yer tits off or sat sweatin' in yer car. I think yer better off at home.'

Trevor guessed that drive-ins were something you either got, or didn't. Like rock climbing, or growing orchids, they didn't bear analysis.

'Come on, Sergeant, there must be something a bit *wild* you like to do.'

'Wild?'

'Yeah.'

The sergeant was a practical man. 'This place would cost hundreds of thousands to get goin'. You're tellin' me ...'

'I've been saving for twenty years.'

'For this dump?'

'It's not a dump. It's where I grew up.'

The policeman shook his head. 'Well, good luck to yer.' He got back in his car and drove off, avoiding a minefield of smashed speakers.

Trevor returned to the screen. He reached as high as he could and soon had a three-square-metre patch painted. He climbed down, resealed his paint and returned to his car.

Then there was the folding chair, the esky (with its Choc-top and cold Coke) and the chips. He ordered a pizza and the delivery man didn't understand his directions. 'But that place has been closed for years.'

'I've reopened it.'

'No shit?'

As he waited for his Meatlovers he loaded the DVD into the projector, aimed it onto his white patch and focussed it. The pizza arrived. He paid, and tipped, and at last, settled in to watch.

It was after eleven, and he was eight years old again.

The Eiger Sanction.

Clint Eastwood. George Kennedy.

'Dad, he's in the middle!' his sister called out.

'Trevor, move your bloody head,' his father said.

His mum opened her door. 'Righto, who wants some hot chips?'

And they all agreed, hot chips would hit the spot.

Trevor watched her walk back to the cafeteria but when he looked, ten minutes later, she was standing under the porch sharing a fag with one of her girlfriends.

'Where's your mother?' his father asked, looking back.

His sister pushed him aside, but he was small, and could only see Clint when he edged round the headrests (his dad had tried to remove them, but they wouldn't come out).

Eventually the chips arrived, and there was Coke (brought from home, by now warm and flat). The film was so-so. He became bored. He watched the old man work on his crossword, and all the little kids fall from the slippery dip and bang their heads on the concrete. He felt happy. He tried to stop and dissect this happiness, but couldn't. It just was. For all the shitty bits, and his parents arguing over poor reception, and his sister kicking him – he was happy. The screen was big, the faces broad. It was them, up there: his Uncle Brian, who refused to talk to him because he'd once hit him with a broom; his Gran, who'd been asked to come, but wouldn't go out after dark; Mr Meus, his teacher, who was always telling them about the Bee Gees and other tins of paint.

Trevor settled into his chair. He started thinking about how much paint he'd need, and how much scaffold he'd have to hire, and how much glass he'd have to replace in the cafeteria. Then there was the fencing, and the box where the ticket men stood. That would have to be rebuilt completely. All of these things could be done, of course. He was forty-five, and might live another forty years, and by then it would be a grand place – somewhere for mums and dads to bring their kids again.

The ticket man came along. 'One ticket, one film. Tickets please.'

He reminded Trevor that he only had a single, and would have to leave before the late feature. Trevor wanted to remind him, about what had happened, and how he was in charge now – but he didn't, couldn't. He'd have to play by the rules: one ticket, one film.

His sister punched him in the arm. He complained and his dad managed a grunt, but as far as he was concerned, it was every man for himself in the back seat. The windscreen was fogging up. His dad opened a window and turned on the demister. His mum started wiping the glass with her hanky. It cleared, but five minutes later it happened again. Then it rained, and they had to put on the wipers, and his dad had to turn on the engine because he was afraid of flattening the battery. And when he did this his lights flashed the screen and everyone tooted. Then his sister kicked him again, and his mum said, 'This is as boring as shit,' and got out to go for another fag. And it went on like this, summer, winter, autumn and spring. Nearly every Saturday night (except for when someone died, or there was a wedding to go to).

They were all gone now, which meant, in a way, there was no rebuilding the drive-in. No point even trying, perhaps. But the alternative was letting it all go, and that was a shame beyond description.

So he priced the hardware, the wood, the steel, in his head.

He looked out of his side window. It was so hot, and there was nothing they could do but sit and sweat. He took off his shirt and his sister gave him a nipple-cripple.

'What's on next week?' he called to his dad. He didn't reply. Perhaps he didn't hear, or perhaps it didn't matter. They'd come anyway.

The Confirmation

January 1976

THE MINIBUS HELD EIGHT, but the short man with the missing tooth had been off sick. So, Patrick Bowen had two seats to himself. He stretched out, his arms across the headrests, and watched familiar country: a dry-stone wall that ran most of the length of this stretch between Gilford and Banbridge; low-grazed pastures; a wind-chimed cottage containing a dreadlocked, naked arse tribe of wild Scots who they'd often see washing in a dam; fat cows; rain.

The seven men were returning from a building site. They'd spent the morning raising frames for a row of flats on the outskirts of Gilford. They'd be the usual, dreary, can't-swing-a-cat, hear-every-thing-your-neighbours say sort of homes. They'd put up most of the walls, and braced them, but then the rain had started, and stayed, and now they were heading home early. Coughing; someone laughing; someone reciting in their best Richard Burton: ' "*Twice every day the waves efface of staves and sandalled feet the trace.*" '

This suited Patrick Bowen. Tonight was his son's confirmation. It was to be a big night with family and friends, Father Gilman and even a few neighbours gathering at their home beforehand for fish and chips, beer and Coke (for his tall, shaggy-haired son, Michael, the reluctant Catholic). It would be chaos, he imagined, as he sat in the bus watching the sky clear. There would be running, shouting, the Bay City Rollers rattling windows, wet wood smoking in the fireplace, his brother arguing with his dad, dogs barking, drink spilt on the carpet and maybe even a prayer or two muttered in the relative quiet of their lean-to laundry.

Confirmations were always a big deal in his family. 'Send forth upon the sevenfold Spirit the Holy Paraclete,' he could remember Father Gilman half-singing at his own ceremony. He could still see himself standing in short shorts on the altar of their local church, his bow legs shivering; the sleeves of his suit (freshly pressed) hanging down past his fingertips and his tie pinching his neck. His bright, red and yellow silk sash (as he watched Jesus melting on the wall). His mum and dad in the fourth row, grinning, his sister sticking out her tongue. He could recall every smell, every clunk of the organ keys, every genuflect and forehead wet with chrism.

And this, he hoped, is how it would be for Michael.

Father Gilman's voice hadn't changed in the intervening years. 'I mark thee with the sign of the cross and confirm thee.' He could still feel the priest's hand brushing his cheek, and smell the beer on his breath as he mumbled, 'Peace be with you.'

Back in the bus, he turned to Aidan Hay (Saint Aidan, as they all called him), their foreman, boss and motivator (and sometimes, when the company was working them too hard, or paying them too little, their spokesman and peacemaker) and asked, 'What about your weekend then?'

Aidan pinched the tip of his nose and said, 'Still helping my uncle – painting.'

'Glen?'

'He could afford to pay someone, but why would he do that when he's got me?'

'And what's he do in return?'

The bus came to a sudden stop. Aidan half-stood and saw a car parked across the road in front of them. 'What's this?' Then, in a moment flooded in light reflected off the wet road, four men in black balaclavas emerged from the car, spoke among themselves and turned to face the builders.

'Fuck,' the bus driver, an old man, moaned.

All seven men were standing, their heads bowed under the low roof. 'Okay, boys, just keep calm,' Aidan said. 'They just want to show us how brave they are.'

Each of the men on the bus had a vacant expression – as though they'd just cut a piece of expensive timber to the wrong length. One, an apprentice, dropped back into his seat, put his head in his hands and said, 'Jesus ...'

Of the four men in balaclavas, two had semi-automatic rifles and two had pistols. One of them, the tallest, came towards the bus and hammered on the door.

The driver looked at his passengers. 'What should I do?'

There was silence, then Aidan said, 'What's the point, you're going to have to open it.'

The driver opened the door and the tall man in jeans and boots stuck his head in and said, 'Okay, boys, everyone out.'

They looked at each other, and then Patrick said to the man, 'We're just builders, heading home to Banbridge.'

'Out!'

They stumbled out – tripping over each other, knocking their heads – and were told to line up beside the bus. 'Bremer Coaches', in blocky letters, splattered with mud. To a casual observer it might have looked like a holiday snap. The four men stood in front of them, silently, almost nervously, squeezing, releasing and playing with their weapons. The tall man said, 'Any of you fellas belong to the Holy Roman Catholic Church, would you be so good as to take one step forward.'

'What do you want from us?' Aidan asked.

'All in good time.'

Patrick froze. All he could think about was the confirmation. Would it go ahead without him? Tonight, next week, next year, never? He saw Michael's face, smiling, and could see how he played with the sash that had been his. He could see his own brother's face, two or three weeks previously, and remembered asking, 'So, do you want to sponsor your little nephew then?'

'I don't have to say no fuckin' prayers, do I?'

'You just gotta nod.'

'Sure?'

'It's meant to be an honour.'

'I didn't say no, did I?'

There was silence along the line of eight men. The driver said, 'I got nothin' to do with this. I work for Mr Bremer.'

'Shut up,' one of the other four men said. 'Or you'll be first.'

There was a deeper silence. Dread. Shallow breath. The apprentice was looking into the cold, blue sky, searching for a Sunday school Jesus, his legs almost giving way beneath his weight. 'I am Protestant,' he said, slowly.

None of the four men responded. One of the other builders said, 'You're acting like cowards. This won't solve anything.'

Then the tall man repeated, 'If you're Catholic, please step forward. Let's get this sorted, gentlemen.'

Patrick knew he was the only Catholic on the bus. He knew each of the other men, their families, the Protestant churches they worshipped in. He didn't know the driver, but he guessed he was Protestant too.

'I'm only going to ask one more time,' the tall man said.

No one moved.

No way to know who the four men were. No clues that might help: a voice overheard at St Mark's church, a limp, turn of phrase, familiar pair of boots. There was only one choice: to step forward or stand still. That's what their lives had come down to – a flip of a coin. There was no point trying to reason, plead, explain or offer photos of children and wives.

Patrick knew he'd have to step forward, or they might all end up dead. He imagined how he might do it – one foot forward, then the other. Wondered if it'd be a quick shot to the head, or if they'd take him aside, into the irrigation ditch that ran beside the road. Which of the four would do it, and what they'd say. You Catholic dog. You and your IRA mates.

'Where does our church say anything about this?' one of the other builders said.

'Shut up.'

'We're not political people. We build homes.'

'I just drive them,' the driver repeated.

Patrick thought of his wife. Juggled words of gratitude and thanksgiving. Nothing he'd ever say to her face. They'd been married too long for that. He wanted to turn to one of the other men and give him a message to give to her but that, he sensed, would be the last irony. Still, she'd know. Turn their lounge room into a sort of shrine. Take down photos of dead cousins and uncles and hang him beside their cross.

There was silence in the small patch of country. He heard a flock of birds in a tree somewhere but dared not turn to look. There was still a chance he'd survive, somehow.

He knew what he was about to pay for. A group of Protestant paramilitaries, perhaps this lot, had shot and killed an IRA leader in some town (as he tried to think of its name) to the west. The next day a bomb had exploded in the vestry of a Protestant church, killing seven, including three boys who were preparing to sing in the choir. Perhaps, he thought, these were some of their fathers. That might explain their awkwardness with their weapons. The images of the blast had appeared on the front page of every newspaper in the United Kingdom, and beyond, accompanied by headlines such as 'IRA Atrocity' and 'Pity The Innocents'. Photos of prayer books, a woman's shoes and a pram in the rubble.

So, there was nothing for it, he thought. He could see his son's face, and the chrism rolling down his skin, and chin. 'I mark thee with the signs of the cross,' he whispered, and one of the four men looked at him and said, 'What was that?'

He shrugged. Took a deep breath and decided, in a moment of clarity and grace, that it was time to step forward. Just then he felt a hand touching his. It was Aidan, and he knew he was saying, Keep still, keep quiet, we won't turn you in.

For a moment he felt safe, and hesitated. Imagined the four giving up, getting in their car and driving off. But then thought, What if? What if they kill us all, not so much as to be sure, as to finish what they'd started.

So he stepped forward.

'Thank you,' the tall man said, moving towards him.

He wondered if he should try and fight him, but he allowed himself to be dragged back, by the collar, to the bit of grass behind the four.

Silence. He knelt, and dropped his head. 'Send forth upon the sevenfold Spirit,' he whispered, before the loud fugue of firearms filled the green Irish afternoon with death and smoke. He leaned forward and tightened himself into a ball. Heard the bus driver say 'Christ' as he fell against his bus. Heard a groan, and the apprentice managing the words, 'It's all wrong,' before he slid to the ground.

The firing stopped. He dared not look up. The four gunmen didn't speak. He heard a tractor on the hill behind them and airbrakes from a truck on a distant road.

Then the tall man said, 'Next time, when you're asked … And I reckon you might pick some better friends.'

He heard them walk off, disturbing spent cartridges on the road. Listened as they talked as they got in the car, slammed the doors and drove off.

He looked up. Saw Aidan sitting against the bus, blood on his shirt and a black hole in his throat. Bullet holes in the side of the bus, and legs and arms.

He stood and watched the car disappear into the distance. Turned away from his friends and saw a farmer in a distant paddock, sitting on the idling tractor, watching him.

The Adult World Opera

ALTHOUGH ONLY SIX, Jay Foster had built his own fort, stocked it with food and drink, books, a blanket and other necessities, and even made plans for its defence. Its walls were an iron fence, a diosma, a pile of bricks and a piece of plywood. It was dark in Jay's fort, from an overhanging cherry plum that dropped small, bitter fruit on his head most of the summer. To him, the best thing about it was that his mum and her boyfriend didn't know it existed. They'd appear at the front door of the house and call out, 'Jay, y' little fuck, where are yer?' and he'd retreat into the darkest corner of his terra-rosa world.

Then Chris, his mum's boyfriend, would come down the front steps and look under the old Datsun some relative had left on their front lawn years before. He'd flatten the grass that grew up around the car and say, 'Wait till I get my hands on you.' He'd look in the car through the non-existent windscreen, and perhaps shoo the cats that had lived and raised families on the vinyl seats. He'd look behind the piles of tyres that Sean Foster, Jay's real dad, had stacked there before Jay was even born.

Then he'd come back up the front steps. He'd look behind the old fridge – full of mouse shit, and shells Jay had collected when Sean had taken him to the beach. He'd look under the cane lounge he'd taken from someone's hard refuse. Then kick a cardboard box, half-full of empty bottles, and go inside.

Jay stood on the dolomite driveway, listening. He could hear three types of birds, but when he looked up into the big wattle that grew beside their gas box he could only see a single honeyeater. He stood watching it, and then smiled. Tried to replicate its call but had trouble whistling because of the scar from a split lip. 'Hey,' he called, as he clapped his hands.

Jay Foster had his dad's wild hair, starting flat at the top and falling in long, loose curls. He had big brown eyes that reflected most of the light that came near them and a nose that only lifted from his face as it reached its tip. His mouth was such that by doing nothing he seemed to smile, his teeth receding towards dimples that Sean used to poke and promise (one day, when he was asleep) to fill with Polyfilla. Jay's arms and legs hadn't begun to stretch into boyhood proper and sometimes Melanie, his mum, would pinch his baby fat with its light and deep purple bruises and say, 'Look how much you been eatin'.'

He could hear noises from inside the house – from his mum's bedroom. Chris telling Mel to mind her business; a lamp falling onto the floorboards; silence. He'd been led to the back door by Chris, pushed outside and shooed like the fat tabby who was Lord of the Datsun.

He shifted the broken plywood and entered his fort. Sat with his face resting on his knees, and closed his eyes. 'Godly,' he started whispering to himself. 'Godly.' He picked a dictionary from a pile of books, opened to a bookmark and continued. '"Godmother: parent; Godown: storehouse; Godsend: good fortune."' Then he closed the dictionary, and his eyes, and repeated: '"Godmother: parent; Godown: storehouse; Godsend: good fortune."'

He was the only one in his class who read the dictionary. His teacher, Mrs Partridge, had told Mel he was a clever boy. She'd smiled with pride, but when the teacher had said, 'We must start him reading harder books,' she'd just replied, 'What, you mean we should buy them?'

'No, I have some I can give him.'

These now made up most of Jay's pile: *Journal of an African Safari; A Descriptive List of the Birds Native to Shearwater, Australia*; explorers; spaceships; middle-primary readers and even a 1950s *Boys' Guide to Working Timber* that Mr Partridge had been encouraged to surrender.

But Jay had read them all. He'd moved on to the dictionary – letter by letter, word by word, marvelling at the sound and shape of *oxalic acid* and *lincrusta, ballerina* and anachronisms like *heretofore* (which he'd try out on Mrs Partridge, as she grinned and turned to sort the lunch orders).

Jay retrieved a butter knife he kept hidden under some branches. He used it to dig the soil. A few minutes later he retrieved a small wooden box from the hole, sat it in the valley of his crossed legs and opened it. Inside were the things his dad had given him: a pocket knife (he opened it, ran his finger along the blade and pressed the sharp edge into his leg without cutting it), a leather key ring, more shells and a packet of chewing gum. He took three pellets, put them in his mouth and started chewing. Then he heard Chris calling, 'Jay, come on, your mother wants you inside.'

He stopped chewing.

'Don't make me come look for you.'

He took the gum from his mouth and put it in the box. Reburied it, hid the knife and opened the door to his fort, letting the sun stream in.

It was hot inside. There was a small fan blowing warm air into every corner of the room, through Mel Foster's hair and across Chris Collins's shaved head. This was Mel's job: to set Chris up in a chair in the backyard with a tea towel wrapped around his neck; to run an extension cord from the kitchen and connect it to the clippers; to shave his head. Then Chris (stretched back with a cigarette dangling from his hand) would say, 'Go a bit easy,' and she'd reply, 'You do it then.'

Mother and boyfriend were sitting on a couch in the lounge room. They were watching a man demonstrate a duster that rotated for more efficient cleaning. Chris said, 'Forty bucks, for that piece of shit?' He kept watching, regardless.

Jay came in and said, 'Can I have breakfast?' Neither of them replied.

Chris was sitting in his singlet and footy shorts. He had a flat chest he worked on every morning and afternoon. This was the focus of their backyard – an outdoor gym consisting of bench press, weights, an old exercise bike and a rubber mat where he did his sit-ups.

This was another reason Mel loved Chris. As she sat on the couch reading her magazines, all she had to do was reach over and run her hand across his chest, or feel the solid muscles on his arms. He'd never protest, no matter how often she did it. In fact, most of the time it ended with Jay being led to the back door and locked outside.

Jay stared at Chris, sitting slouched, drinking from a bottle of iced coffee. Chris looked at him and said, 'What?'

'Can I have breakfast?'

'You know where the kitchen is.'

Jay walked past the dirty clothes that had spilled out across the hallway. He attempted to push them into a pile. Even at his age he sensed there must be some sort of order, some alphabetical sorting of things that made up the world. There was dirt, body odour and blood on the clothes and he wished they were clean, folded, sitting neatly in one of his drawers.

He passed into the kitchen to find more of the same: a pile of dirty dishes in the sink, empty beer bottles, butter left open and melted on the table. He found some two-minute noodles in the cupboard, removed the plastic wrapper, pulled back the lid, emptied the flavour sachet, then used a chair to get up to the bench, and put the kettle on to boil. As he waited he looked out of the kitchen window. His mother had hung some clothes on the back line but she hadn't bothered pegging them. A towel and T-shirt had fallen to the ground and mixed in the dust of their dead lawn. He made a mental note to pick them up and bring them back in.

The kettle boiled and clicked off. He lifted it, but it was over-full and he had to use both hands. As he started pouring the water into the foam cup his foot slipped off the chair and he fell. A few moments later he was on the ground and the kettle was on top of him, emptying water onto his left hand and forearm.

He screamed.

'Fuck,' came the reply from the lounge room.

He could feel the pain on his skin and see how it was turning red. He sat up, still screaming, and as he did Chris entered the room. Without saying a word, he grabbed him under the arms, rushed him into the bathroom and turned on the shower. He took the boy's arm and thrust it under the cold water.

Jay's voice modulated between groans, whispers and more screaming. He tried to reclaim his arm but Chris held it under the water.

'What the fuck were you thinking?'

'I slipped off the chair.'

'On a chair, with boiling water? Are you stupid?'

'I wanted breakfast.'

'*I wanted breakfast.*'

Mel was standing behind them with her arms crossed.

'You okay, pup?' she asked.

'If you'd just got his breakfast,' Chris growled at her.

'He's okay.'

'Obviously fucking not.' Indicating the welts that were rising on Jay's arm.

'Don't blame me,' she said. 'You coulda got off your arse.'

Chris filled with rage. He stood, lifted his fist and drew his arm back before stopping. 'It's your fucking kid,' he said. 'You can fix this mess yourself. And while you're at it, clean the fuckin' place. It's a disgrace.' He stormed from the room, down the hallway and out the front door.

She looked at her son, who was grimacing. 'Look what you've done now.'

It was just after seven that evening and Jay was standing at the window in his room, staring out at his neighbour's Christmas lights. There was a cardboard Santa in his sleigh on the front lawn, and four reindeer with broken legs repaired with gaffer tape. Every year there were less reindeer. It had become a local pastime to steal them, tear them up and frisbee the parts over the fence into the Big W Garden Centre or the high school with its razorwire-topped six-foot fence.

Jay had been locked in his hot room for almost three hours while his mum and Chris were out. He was red-faced, covered in sweat. His curls had flattened in clumps against his scalp. He'd stripped, and stood at his window wearing nothing but underpants with broken elastic, and a bandage wrapped around the burn on his arm.

The burn was aching, pulsing with pain. He tried his door again, shook the handle, pushed and pulled it a few times. Then he returned to his window and looked out again.

The tap – the hose.

He worked at the two latches that held his fly screen in place. After a while it moved, loosened and dropped out. He squeezed under the window, through the opening and jumped down into what was left of a vegetable garden he'd planted with his dad. His feet crushed the husks of old peas and he could feel small carrots between his toes. He moved but tripped on an old tomato stake and fell hands down in grass full of cat shit.

Standing, he walked over to the tap, turned it on and started running cold water from the hose over his bandaged arm. He stood for ten, maybe fifteen minutes as the worst of the pain subsided.

Feeling the sun on his shoulders and back, he covered the tip of his hose with his finger and sprayed his face and body with a fine mist that made a rainbow from one side of the yard to the other.

He turned off the tap, retreated to the shade of a plum tree and sat down. He leaned against the tree and the bark bit into his back. The little bit of pain was a distraction from his arm. Looking down the road, he wondered where his mum and Chris might have gone. If he could find them, and ask them, he thought, they might take him to a doctor, and the doctor might put him in hospital, and then he'd have clean sheets and cold custard.

Maybe they've gone shopping, he thought.

He could see them walking down the biscuit aisle, arguing over cream versus plain, Chris slipping off to the bottle shop as his mum piled cups of noodles, fish fingers and party pies into the trolley.

Maybe it's the tavern, he thought.

He was waiting in the car watching people come and go. They were all dressed up, their hair slicked back, the men's faces shaved clean.

Yes, the tavern. He'd heard Chris say it, they were going to win money, and Chris was going to buy himself some boots.

He stood, ran to the fence and jumped over. Headed down the street – towards the shops, the tavern. The footpath was hot on his feet so he walked on the nature strip, the gutter, the road. Stopping at an intersection, he looked both ways. Then he chose left. He could remember turning left more often than right. It led to the tavern. It must lead to the tavern. It should. Perhaps.

He stepped onto the road. A tall boy in baggy white clothes, with his baseball cap on the wrong way, smiled at him strangely and said, 'Hey, little man, you got some clothes?'

Jay looked at him.

'Some shoes?' the teenager asked.

Jay kept walking across the hot intersection. A car slowed and sounded its horn. It stopped and an old man opened his door, stepped out and said to the boy in white clothes, 'Your brother just about killed himself.'

'He's not my brother.'

'Where are you from?' the man called to Jay.

Jay looked confused. 'Mum and Chris are at the tavern.'

It was after eight when the old man returned Jay to his house. As he pulled into the driveway, Mel and Chris were sitting on the cane lounge on the front porch, eating chips and drinking Coke. The old man stopped the car, looked at Jay and asked, 'Is that them?'

Jay smiled and nodded.

The old man had taken him home to his semi-detached, with meticulously clipped lawns and old black and white photos of his dead wife. Jay had listened as he'd rummaged in a back room, eventually appearing, smiling, holding a school uniform hanging from a fabric-covered hanger. 'Here it is,' he'd said. 'I reckon it'll just about fit you.'

Jay climbed from the old man's car proudly wearing the pants and Lindisfarne College blazer, and a pair of black leather shoes. Mel and Chris stood and came towards them.

'You his dad?' the old man asked Chris.

'No,' Chris replied.

Then to Mel, 'You his mum?'

'Yeah.' She looked at Jay. 'Where the hell did you go?'

He shrugged.

'We told you to stay in your room.'

The old man, who had a neatly trimmed moustache, said, 'He was in his underwear, on a busy road. He was nearly knocked over.' He stared at Mel and Chris.

Mel approached her son, knelt down and grabbed him by the lapel. 'You know how worried we been? What the fuck were you thinking? You know better than that.'

The old man looked at her – at the tattoo on her shoulder, her black fingernails, a cigarette glowing between her fingers. 'I should've taken him straight to the police.'

'He would've come home,' Chris said.

'He wouldn't have made it home, son. You're just lucky it was me.'

'Thank you,' Mel said. 'But we don't need no lecture.'

'I think that's just what you need.'

Chris stepped forward. 'Watch yerself, old man. You oughta be careful, pickin' up kids off the street.'

The old man clenched his fist. 'In you go, son,' he said to Jay, messing the curls he'd tried to comb flat with his wife's old ivory-backed brush.

Jay went inside, through the mess, to his room. They'd bought him a Happy Meal, and left it on his bed. He unwrapped the cheeseburger but it was cold, and with a belly full of the old man's vegetable soup he didn't feel like eating it. He just examined how someone had sewn a picture of a book onto the pocket of the blazer. Then he looked out of the window and could see the three of them arguing. Chris pushed the old man and he fell back, steadying himself.

He tried the French fries, but they were cold too.

22 December

The next morning he watched a movie about a girl who'd lost her dog. During a commercial he checked to see if Chris and his mum were still on the porch. He quickly darted into their room, closed the door, placed a chair against the built-in robe and slid the door open. There, on a high shelf, were the presents. He reached up and rummaged, turning the parcels into the light to read the tags.

To Chris, Merry Xmas

To my One and Only Muscle Man

To Jay (and he shook it, and felt it, but had no idea)

To my old Hen, Mel – You know what it is!

Mel

He kept searching. There were probably more towards the back, he thought. One of the presents dropped and he jumped to the ground to retrieve it.

To my darling Chris

He threw it back up but another fell out. He retrieved this one and slipped it back on the shelf. Then he heard a car in the driveway, a door slamming, voices. He slid the robe shut, replaced the chair and ran back into the lounge room.

'G'day, killer,' his dad said.

Jay ran to his father and wrapped his arms around him. 'You've come?'

'Course I have. Here, an early Christmas present.' Sean Foster handed his boy a small stocking packed with an assortment of chocolate bars, balloons, plastic toys and a whistle.

'Thanks, Dad,' Jay said, examining the stocking but returning to embrace him.

Sean Foster was short, olive-skinned and brown-eyed like his son. He had hair that fell in curls, too, but he'd cut it back to stubble. He had broad, muscled shoulders that came from his job lifting crates at a fruit market.

Mel was standing behind him with her arms crossed. 'Want a coffee?'

'That'd be good.'

'I'm goin' the pub,' Chris called from the porch.

'He's not feeling sociable?' Sean asked his ex-wife.

'Don't start,' she replied, walking into the kitchen with her arms still crossed.

Sean led his son to the couch and they sat down. The television showed a choir singing 'Silent Night' beside the makeup counter in a department store.

'So, what is it?' Jay said to his dad.

'The big present?'

'How big?'

Sean smiled. 'Let's just say, it barely fits in the boot.'

'Is it heavy?'

'Very.'

'Do you need to plug it in?'

Sean knew the game. 'No, that'd be giving too much away.'

'Come on,' Jay pleaded.

'No.'

'Does it make any noise?'

Sean noticed his son's arm. 'What happened?'

'I burned it.'

'How?'

'I was making noodles, and I fell, and the kettle fell on me.'

He held his son's arm. 'Does it hurt?'

'No.'

'What was he doing with boiling water?' he called to Mel.

No reply.

'Mel?'

'What?'

'What was he doing with boiling water?'

Mel appeared in the doorway. 'He didn't ask us,' she said. 'We had no idea.'

'You should be watching him.'

Her brow creased. 'Fuck off.' She returned to the kitchen.

'Is it bad?' Sean asked his son, but the boy's face was blank.

He noticed a series of small bruises on his son's neck, as though someone had held him. There were more bruises on his legs and thigh. He took the boy's hand, led him to the kitchen and showed Mel. 'What the fuck's this?'

'He's always falling over,' she said, busy sugaring the coffees.

'That's bullshit. How do these come from a fall?' Indicating the fingertip bruising.

'He plays with other kids.'

Sean led his son back to the lounge room and they sat down. 'Tell me,' he whispered. 'How did you get these bruises?'

Jay was biting his lip; his head was shaking.

'Was it Chris?'

Jay could see into the kitchen. His mum was listening. 'I just fell over.'

Sean stood, walked into the kitchen and said, 'He looks a mess.'

She shrugged.

'What kids is he playing with?'

She turned on him. 'What's your fucking point?'

'If your mate touches him, I'll rip his throat out.'

'Fuck off.'

'Try me.'

She tipped his coffee down the sink. 'Visit's over.'

Jay laid awake in bed. He looked at the blazer hanging on the back of his door. He remembered the old man's smell, the top of his singlet showing towards his neck, his ironed pants (with a crease down the middle) and the way he sanded his feet with a sort of shrunken cheese grater. Remembered him telling him about his own son, as he flicked through an album showing him in the same blazer, overalls (three months into his apprenticeship), the suit he hired for his wedding, his bathers and a Santa costume for his work picnic. And he remembered the old man saying, 'You got problems, you come and see me.'

As he smiled.

'What I mean is, if they're not looking after you.'

Jay watched the shadows the trees cast on his curtains. They were twisting, shortening, lengthening as they moved with the wind. One branch was a mop; another a giraffe's head; another a book opening in the wind; and yet another, Chris, with his ball-and-socket shoulders, standing in the dead peas and pumpkins under his window.

He moved back against the bed head and pulled the cotton sheet up under his chin. He saw Chris's shaved head and big ears, his square jaw and beefy neck.

Jay, the shape whispered. Come over here, you little fucker.

He closed his eyes. 'Fistful, fisticuff, fistula … Dad?'

He heard his mum switching on the telly: 'Hark the Herald Angels sing, Glory to the Newborn King,' he sang, drifting back to his dictionary: '… kingdom, kingpin, kink …' He heard Chris's car in the driveway; the door; footsteps.

'Where you been?' he heard his mum say.

'Where do you think?'

'Thought you were coming home for tea?'

'I thought hubby might stay.'

'I pissed him off.'

'Why?'

Their voices dropped, whispering. Jay listened intently. He slipped out of bed, crawled across his floor and opened his door to hear more.

'Sean … what do you think I said?'

And then Chris shouting. 'If that little cunt's said anything.'

Jay jumped back into bed and pulled the sheet up under his chin.

'Quiet!' he heard his mum say. 'He didn't say anything. Christ, what's the issue, we didn't burn him.'

'Then y' got FACS on your door in the morning.'

Silence.

'Little fucker.'

Jay was shaking all over. He slipped from his bed to the floor, then crawled to the wardrobe and got in, shutting the door as the voice grew louder and louder. He held his legs, trying to still them.

'Idol, idyll, ignite ...'

There were footsteps in the hallway and his light came on.

'Where are y'?' Chris shouted.

The wardrobe door opened and a hand reached in for him. Grabbed his neck, launched him across the room, leaving him sprawled on the floorboards. He tightened his body into a ball and covered his face with his hands.

'What did you tell him?' Chris shouted.

'Nothing.'

'Nothing,' Mel repeated, standing at the door. 'Leave him be, Chris.'

Chris knelt down and pointed his finger at the boy. 'If there's any fucking trouble ...'

'Chris!'

Jay could smell alcohol on Chris's breath.

'What did you tell him?'

'He wanted to know about my arm.'

'And you told him it was us, didn't you?' Chris raised his open hand and slapped the boy across the face.

'No,' Jay pleaded, shaking violently, finally wetting himself.

'Get off,' Mel said, stepping towards her boyfriend.

'Shut up,' he shouted, without looking at her. Then he took the boy by the shoulders and started shaking him.

Jay felt faint. He closed his eyes. Mel reached over to stop him but he pushed her back. She landed against the wardrobe and old toys fell on her head, and on the floor. Then she stood still. She folded her arms and started sobbing.

'So?' Chris said to the boy.

She ran from the room.

Jay was mostly unaware of what was happening. His eyes closed, then opened, and he saw the shadows on the curtain.

Then he felt a boot kicking him hard in the side. He rolled over, clutching the spot, searching for the pain that was like a hundred kettles burning him at once. Thinking, Galoot, galore, galosh, as the twelve days of Christmas drifted in from the lounge room.

He couldn't sing, speak, think or feel. There was just pain, and piss cold on his legs.

Jay woke in bed in the darkest, quietest part of the night. Someone had placed his stocking on the sheet that had been tucked in across his chest. He opened his eyes and noticed an empty coat hanger casting a shadow on the back of his door.

'Mum,' he called.

He sat up, removed the sheet and managed to walk across to the window. Opened the curtain and in the half-light of a clouded moon studied the red mark on his side. He touched it and it was sensitive. Dropping to the floor, he rested on folded legs, leaning forward so that his head almost touched the ground. 'Mum.' He stood and, leaning forward, shuffled from his room. Walked slowly, so the floorboards wouldn't creak, so *he* wouldn't wake. He stood at the door to the front bedroom and saw Chris, naked, lying diagonally across the bed. Then he moved to the lounge room and saw his mother, fully dressed, asleep on the couch.

'Mum.' He pressed her arm with his finger but decided not to wake her. Finally, he went to the toilet. It was painful taking a pee, and when he'd finished he noticed there was red in the water. He returned to bed and curled up in a small ball. Small. Smaller than anything he could imagine.

23 December

He woke tired. It was after ten and Mel had opened his curtains, letting in bright light that settled to the sound of sirens, a chainsaw and an old fan clunking. He closed his eyes and turned towards the wall.

'In three weeks you'll have your own six-pack,' a voice promised.

He felt his side, the area below his stomach, his skin and whatever plumbing was inside (that's how he imagined it, like the pipes under the kitchen sink) and it was raw and sensitive. 'Mum?'

Mel was in the front yard watering an apricot tree. She loved apricots – loved the juice on her wrist as she bit into them, loved them on her cereal, and best of all, in a fruit salad she ate doused with whipped cream.

Then, with a flash of flesh and limb, there was a small moon face standing at the gate. 'Can Jay come out to play?'

'Hi, Harrison.'

The boy was shorter than Jay, browner, wearing an old Hawaiian shirt. There was snot under his nose, spread across his top lip, and what looked like the start of school sores.

'You should wipe your nose,' she said to him.

'So, can Jay come out?'

She watched the water soaking into the ground around her apricot tree. 'No, he's not feeling well.'

'What about later?'

'No.'

'Okay.' He walked up another three houses and went in someone else's front gate.

Mel turned off the tap, went inside and crept into her son's room. 'You awake?'

He tried to look at her. 'Yes.'

'What's wrong?'

'My tummy.' Grimacing.

She lifted the sheet and looked at the red mark and swelling on his lower abdomen. 'You'll be alright.'

'It stings.'

'It doesn't sting. Bees sting. You've just got a bit of a gut ache.'

She looked around the room, remembering the previous evening. The toys were still on the floor, the lamp beside his bed had fallen, and the globe had broken.

'Come on, up for breakfast,' she said. 'The day's half gone.'

He twisted his body to lift from the bed but then dropped back. He was biting his lip, and taking short, shallow breaths. 'Can I stay here?'

'Get up.'

He tried rolling from his bed. His legs dropped to the ground and he attempted to straighten his body. 'I can't.'

'Christ, drama queen … Get back to bed, I'll get you something.'

She watched as he climbed back into bed. She wanted to call Chris and get him to sort it out. Get him to fetch food and drink all day, read stories, bath him, dress him and generally fix whatever problems he'd created.

When she returned with toast and cordial a few minutes later he was asleep again. She put the plate and glass on the ground and sat beside him. Moved hair from his eyes and studied his fine features: the little bags under his eyes; the red in his cheeks and the crease between the tip of his mouth and his nostrils; his red lips, dry now, and Sean's button nose. And then, for a moment, she felt bad. She didn't know why. None of this was her fault. Stuff just happened. They'd all move on, and Chris and Jay would be the best of mates.

Chris was at the door. 'I'm out of fags.'

'So?'

'So – go get us some.'

She refused to speak, hoping he'd leave the room. But he just stood there, at one point picking something from his teeth. 'What's your problem?'

She turned on him. 'What do you think? Look at him.'

'So?'

'*Look.*'

'He's always sick. I've never seen a kid like him.'

There was another long pause.

'So?' he repeated.

'What?'

'Are you gonna get my fags?'

Jay turned down a jam sandwich for lunch, despite Chris saying he should be made to eat it. Mel settled him on the couch in the lounge room with a pillow and Coke, and a *Jungle Book* DVD that Sean had given him the previous Christmas.

Jay was awake long enough to watch his hero swing through the trees, ending up in a sort of high-rise homette in a giant fig; he watched him talk to monkeys and reason with elephants; drink from coconuts and battle a fast-flowing river to rescue a potential jungle girl. He could imagine retreating to the privacy of his own tree fort with the girl – they could share books and salt and vinegar chips, juicy apricots, picked from their own forest, and they could swing from the engine hoist that Sean had set up years before in their shed.

Jay drifted in and out of sleep. Chris's brother dropped by and Chris showed him the boy on the couch. 'So, this is Sean's kid?' he heard the brother ask.

Jay was awake, but he kept his eyes closed.

'She looks after him, as you can tell.'

Jungle Boy was followed by *Bananas in Pyjamas*. When Mel came in she saw her son smiling and felt better. 'How is it?'

'They're funny.'

'I gotta go out for a while.'

'Where?'

'The doctor.'

'I don't need anything.'

She stared at him. 'It's for this mole on my shoulder. You never know with moles.'

'Why?'

'They can be cancerous.'

Jay looked back at the television. 'Who's looking after me?'

'Chris.'

He retreated into the images, silently.

'Anything you want?'

'No.'

After she'd gone he went to the toilet and managed to sit down in a way that caused least pain. When he pushed it hurt more, and more, until he was doubled over with his head between his legs.

'Chris,' he called. 'Chris …'

He walked back to the couch, his body bent in half. Sat down, and his eyes engaged the screen, although he didn't really know what he was hearing or seeing.

It would get better, he guessed. It always did. The pain would go and the bruises would fade.

'Mum' – the pain intensified and he curled into a ball. 'Mum.'

Chris came in with the books from his fort. He dropped them onto the ground and said, 'If it rains, they'll get wet, and we won't buy you new ones.'

Jay was groaning, fighting for breath. His body was shaking, again, and he was hot.

'What now?' Chris asked.

'When will Mum be back?'

'*When will Mum be back?* You put on yer little fuckin' act, mate. It might work on her.' He took out his phone, pressed a few buttons and started filming the boy. 'Go,' he said, smiling, 'we'll show her when she gets home, eh?'

'Mum ...'

'You weak little fucker.'

And then the boy was quiet, still. Chris turned off his phone and put it in his pocket.

Then he went out for a smoke.

The lounge room was hot, and the light warmed dust in the air. The television showed a couple of flowers with human faces, singing about water and sunshine and the taste of fresh fertiliser and how one day they might end up in someone's vase.

The Syphilis Museum

Reeves. Four blocks, Civic Park, monkey bars and a self-flushing toilet. Immaculately conceived. In need of Resurrection. A sign on the way into town says Population 1245, but no one believes that. The Davids had a saw-mill, but that closed. A thousand, perhaps, although god knows where they work. There's a chicken shop, and a pub, and Boston's Motor Repairs, although they put off Rose Shaw's boy. Eight hundred at a stretch. Sign looks good. Makes you think someone'd want to live here. Maybe five hundred. But judging from all the 'FOR SALE' signs …

Which leads me to Bill Redman. Bill did a lot for Reeves. As people moved on he bought their shops, put them to good use. It started in 1983 when the Dukes closed their record parlour. Before that it had been a haberdasher, but when Bill bought it he cleaned it out and set up his own little museum. Guessed it might attract a few tourists. Museum of Pestilence. No one really understood. It was the year after a bad locust plague, and Bill had worked it out. The First Horseman was on his way. Insects as a sign of God. He'd studied his Bible, Revelations, Daniel, and worked it out. There was no point worrying about people leaving, or grain prices. After 21 March 2012 it'd all be over.

Bill lined the walls with photos of locust plagues. Display cabinets with larvae, pupae, adults, a giant papier-mâché mock up, bones, real bones, of people who'd died in locust-induced famines. Can't remember which Horseman. Wasn't the pale one – maybe he was blue. He'd spend his days in his museum. Taking the one dollar entry. Showing people around. Starting with *Chortoicetes terminifera* in copulation, explaining the differences between the American and Rocky Mountain varieties, Desert, Red, Jesus, God, an eternity of damnation. That was all up on the wall, too. Pictures of Messianic A-bomb detonations, cleaning out the sinners.

People'd stick their head in the door. 'How are yer, Bill?'

'Good. Comin' in for a look-see?'

'Maybe later. Got a boot full of pullets.'

The word got around. The old boy's lost it. Too much Bible. You could only feel sorry for him. He put up a sign on the way into town: a March 21 Jesus standing in a field of locusts. The mayor at the time, Sid Lehman, told him to take it down, but he refused. Said it was the only tourist attraction Reeves had left. Which was sort of right.

Bill was what you'd call catholic, and Catholic. His little house, tacked on to his only remaining museum, was full of holy cards and framed verses and Matthew and Luke. Pictures of a Charlton Hesty Jesus. A big Bible, with everything underlined. Little bottles of holy water to boil his eggs. Ryvitas, which he cut into hosts using a scone-cutter. Altar wine; two bob a gallon. Lived alone, although he had the visiting priest, Ken MacLeod, over once a fortnight after their session at Saint Jabber-Jaw. Just them, and a few shakers they wheeled across the road from the at-capacity nursing home (oh, I forgot, there's a few more jobs).

Back to the museums. 1989. Middle of a particularly bad drought. Mrs Maxwell died, so the Public Trustee sold her wool shop, and Bill bought that too. Museum of Famine. Horseman number two. Don't ask, I couldn't tell you. Maybe red. Bill was up and running again. Photos of the Okies, and Dustbowls, and barren paddocks around Reeves, and more Jesus, God, A-bombs with Jehovah saying, 'For thou art my child, and walk with me, blah, blah'. Pestilence was open Monday to Wednesday, Famine Thursday and Friday (Saturday to wash his Kingswood and put on a few bets, Sunday for a couple of hymns, a strong cuppa and *Midsomer Murders*).

People grew concerned. Bill wandered town at night, writing in chalk on the footpath: '21.iii.2012'. With a copperplate flourish, like that Stace fella. He'd go into the front bar of the Commercial and hand out Famine and Pestilence leaflets and say, 'Oi, Sid, haven't had a visit yet'. And Sid (or whoever he was pestering) would say, 'Come on, Bill, give it up, mate. Bowls Club is looking for new members'. Worse, he'd set up a chair and bang a tambourine whenever someone stopped on the way through to somewhere else (we get a lot of that). Excuse me, missus, thought you might be interested in visiting my museums.

Then Bush went into Iraq, and Bill had it all figured. War. Number three. Purple, perhaps. About then the Black and White café closed, and Bill was in like Flynn. Pulled out the cookers, all the furniture, painted the place white and put up another sign. Museum of War.

Monday-Tuesday Pestilence. Wednesday Famine, Thursday-Friday War. And so it was, for another twelve years. As Bill aged, and shrank, and scampered from one shop to another. All well and good, until ABC 736 Country heard about it and sent a fella with a digital recorder, and it was all over the place. City radio. Breakfast television. And a decent spike in numbers, according to Kurt Westermann at the Hacienda. Of course, me and a lot of other people reckoned it was for the wrong reasons. The nation's not laughing *with* us ... Within a year it all died down, and people forgot. Bill was happy. He'd done what JC had asked. 'Spread the message, Willy Redman, and I will prepare a seat by my side.'

Speaking of which. About this time Bill had some hip problems. Had an operation, but it didn't take. Could barely hobble down the street, and we were thinking, Hi-ho, here we go, he can't keep it up. But then he appears in a wheelchair. Says, 'Just as well, I guess, the gout was makin' it hard to stand all day in Pestilence-Famine-War. Look at this. Press the button. Forward. Press it again. Backwards. Fellas, I reckon I can go another twenty years. Maybe, maybe ...' (and you could see the glimmer in his eyes) '... *maybe I'll make it to 2012.* What do you reckon? We can all go together.' Although he gave us this look like he didn't think we'd be going anywhere.

Which leads me to why you're reading this story, I suppose. 2003. Conrad's Shoe Shoppe closes and Bill's there again. Goes into the estate agent and says, 'Listen, you got ten empty shops in the main street. No one's buying nothing. I'll give you two thousand dollars.' Of course, Haddy Gabman argued a bit, but that was two grand he hadn't been expecting. So, a few weeks later we had the Museum of Syphilis, or the Syphilis Museum, as it became known.

Now, Famine-Pestilence-Plague is one thing, but clap's another. We got together and went to the front door, and I said to Bill, 'Why can't you just call it plague?'

He said, 'This is the modern plague.' Then some stuff about fornicators, and whores, then, 'This is my greatest achievement. People can bring their kids and show them the price of *transgression*. What better way to prepare Reeves for the End of Days?'

There wasn't much we could do except insist (and he was accommodating) he black out the front windows so the kids couldn't see anything. Still, they'd look in the door, and see the posters on the wall: bacteria blown up ten thousand times, scurrying in and out of tracts, a model donger the size of a Sherrin football. Completely infected. Secondary syphilis.

Of course, no one went. Not the sort of place you'd take your girlfriend. Bill would just sit there for hours at a time. No one knew what he was doing. Vacuuming the rugs? Cleaning the cabinets? Keeping the tea urn topped up (losses entirely due to evaporation).

Then, one day, the strangest thing. These fellas came in a truck and emptied Famine-Pestilence-Plague. Took it all away. Till there were three empty shells, and three signs: '21.iii.2012'. Bill told me he was getting too old for the Four Horsemen, so the One would have to do. And what did it matter? He could still preach his gospel in Syphilis. Yep, he'd miss his locusts, and American Army hand grenades, and the smell that droughty soil gave off, but his spiral pallidums would have to suffice.

And so, to the events of last November. Bill had been cutting back. Opening later, closing earlier. You'd go in (I did) and he'd smell uriney, his clothes never washed or ironed. Permanent five o'clock shadow. His chair was seizing up, so a few of us greased it and welded a few spokes. But more than this, he rambled, never quite made sense. It'd be, 'Well, the Commandments were quite clear, thou shalt not ... Oh, my sister used to leave the gates open, and the ewes'd get out ... And the third one said yer shouldn't covet yer neighbour's wife ...'

So we organised Meals on Wheels, and someone checked him every day. Mrs Horowitz did his hoovering once a week, and a few of the old girls washed his clothes and hung them out across Redman's Farm. That's what he called it. Redman's Farm. Wasn't much of a yard, but enough for a few rows of veggies (which, despite his condition, he kept perfect), Rhode Islands, a goat and six pigs. Landraces. Fat bastards. Stunk like hell, and Trevor Lehman, Sid's son, who'd inherited the mayorship, told him he couldn't have pigs in town, but Bill pretended not to hear him. Man needed a few pigs. Cut up a pig, you could feed a family for three weeks, and maybe, if the End was drawn out (say some sort of heatwave that went on for months), you'd need some meat. So, that was it. Pigs.

He'd be up at the crack of dawn, feeding his animals, watering his cabbages. Then in for a shower in his wheelchair-friendly bathroom (courtesy of Rotary). Put on his jacket and tie and polish his shoes and open the front door of Syphilis. Look, wondering who was there. Which was no one. Ever.

That was his life. Infected lymph nodes and lesions in jars of preservative. And a texta sign: 'Bacteria grow in their billions, and this is the result. *"For thus said the Lord, Thy bruise is incurable and thy wound is grievous*".' Mrs Horowitz covered his cabinets with towels so she didn't have to look. Plaster-cast torsos with warts and maggoty old noses dripping mucous. And she'd say, 'What you got all this for, Bill?' And he'd tell her about the Naaman, and their seed, and the clinging clap, and she'd just turn up his Tom Edmonds and the old cross.

Then, the strangeness began. It was a warm night. We'd asked Bill if he wanted an air conditioner, but of course he'd said no. If God wanted to test us, to make us toss and turn and sweat all night, then you couldn't challenge His will with a two-horsepower Kelvinator. He'd just locked Syphilis, turned off the light, wheeled himself into his room, hoisted himself onto his bed, changed into his pyjamas, read a few pages of Paul and switched off his light.

Midnight, one am, two. Poor Bill and his insomnia. Comes from a man thinking too much. Analysing a world full of things that happen just because they happen.

Anyway, Bill's drifting off. Maybe three, maybe bit after. Then he hears his pigs. Squealing. The lot of them. On and on it goes. And he thinks it's the cats from next door, because this happens a bit. But the noise keeps on, then, suddenly, silence. That isn't right, he thinks. So up he gets, into his chair, down the hall, through Syphilis, out the back door, pops on his torch. 'Who's there?'

Quiet. Just a bit of grunting, and the goat coming over to see if there's any food. Down the ramp, the path, to the pig shed. Two. Dead. Lying together like Hitler and Eva. Shines his torch. 'Who's there?' Nothing. Just the sound of the generator from the IGA. So he gets closer and manages to stand and have a look but there's no sign of any interference. No puncture marks, indentations, cuts, nothing. Sits down, goes in, calls this new copper by the name of Bullock but he says, 'Mr Redman, it's very late, I'm not coming for no pigs.'

'They don't die in pairs, son.'

'I'll pop round in the morning.'

'If there's a prowler, he might come back for the others.'

'Who'd wanna hurt your pigs?'

'Couldn't say.'

So he went back to bed, but just rested, thinking. Who? He hadn't made any enemies. Unless … unless Satan had murdered his pigs? That was a possibility, although, he believed, angels rarely manifested themselves in such obvious ways. Droughts, perhaps, and meningovascular syphilis, but not a couple of pigs. Bita hot weather, perhaps, car crash, someone's aunt with the cancer, but swine?

Despite all this, he managed to get some sleep.

The next morning the constable came, and they had a good look-see at the pigs, but they seemed perfectly okay (apart from being dead). The copper suggested changing their feed, but Bill told him it wasn't that.

So, he went in, got changed, and opened Syphilis an hour late. Just in case it was the Devil. He'd show him. The light forever shineth. Sixty watts. Crusted with dead moths.

That day Bill had a couple of visitors. It'd been quiet. He'd been inflating wine bladders, so he could hang them over his nectarines, stop the parrots. He was blowing when he heard a knock. Wheeled himself over to the door and welcomed a blind lady, with a stick, sixty, not much older, tapping and smiling and saying, 'Mr Redman, is it? I've heard all about you.'

'All good?' he asked.

'Yes. And your museum. You're famous.'

'Well, it ain't all about me. Not even this bug, scientifically called *Treponema pallidum* subspecies *pallidum*. No. It's about something else. Someone else.'

But she didn't seem interested. Just moved into the middle of the room and stood waiting for her tour. 'You'll have to help me, Mr Redman. Perhaps a bita description?'

'I understand Mrs …?'

She took a moment. 'Bly. Flora Bly.' And offered her hand.

He shook it.

'And this, Mr Redman, is my granddaughter, Annie.'

Bill looked around. No one. Some sort of phantom memory? Gone, like her ability to focus on objects, consider sunsets, admire Russell Drysdale's drought pictures.

'Annie?' she said.

He wondered. Annie? Felt grateful. Yes, the bladder was leaking (he'd torn up a towel, and used the strips in his jockeys), the mind wandering, but he could still tell real from imagined.

Then the girl appeared at the door.

'Nan?'

'I told you to come in.'

She came in, looked around, screwed up her face and turned to Bill. 'They reckon you're a disgrace.'

'Annie!' Flora Bly thundered. 'Don't be so rude.'

Bill just smiled. 'Don't matter, Mrs Bly, I'm used to it. Whole places thinks I'm nuts, but they reckon it's better to humour me. They figure I can't keep going more than another five, six years.'

The girl and her nanna waited.

'But they might be surprised.'

'How's that?' Flora asked.

'I'm on a mission, Mrs Bly. And I'm not alone.'

'No?'

'Twenty-first of March, 2012.'

'Flora. Call me Flora. And this is Annie. Annie?'

Annie stepped forward, offered her hand, and Bill wheeled himself closer, and managed a wet, weak shake.

They started with a cup of tea and two stale biscuits. Bill had made a sort of lounge area, cluttered with literature, a pile of old *Watchtowers*, some Gideons the Gideons had left, giveaway holy cards and a bowl full of crosses he'd carved from a fence post, each with the date of the big day burnt onto the beam. Bill was curious. Always. Why someone had come to Syphilis.

'What brings you to Reeves, Flora?'

'You, Mr Redman.'

'No?'

'I read about your museum.' She looked around, although she didn't. 'I always say, Mr Redman, best way to learn ...'

He waited.

'Is to see the outcome? Don't you agree?'

'Yes, yes.'

'Quick tour and Annie'll be set for life. Won't you?'

Annie didn't answer. She was too busy studying a model. She looked at Bill. 'What's wrong with that?'

'Spirochetes.'

'Sorry?'

'That's what the bacteria are called. They grow and grow, and that's what you've got.'

Annie shrugged, and ate her biscuit. She asked her nan, 'What's for lunch?'

'We'll worry about that later, when we're done.'

Bill was wondering if it was suitable for a child, but then thought, So what, God's coming to gather everyone.

'You mentioned a date?' Flora said.

'Yes, March twenty-one. Still a few years off, but I believe we have to be ready, Flora.' At which point he explained the Four Horsemen, his three defunct museums, syphilis as plague, but it might just as well be AIDS, HIV and such abominations.

'AIDS?' Flora said.

'That's God trying to tell us something.'

'What's that?'

'We're not listening. He's trying to get our attention.' He turned to Annie. 'Do you understand?'

'What?'

'*Pardon?*' Flora said.

'*Pardon?*'

'The End Days are here.'

Annie took another biscuit. You could do that with a blind nan. 'I dunno about that,' she said.

Bill indicated the displays. 'The proof's all around, isn't it?'

Annie noticed the specimen jars. 'Sorta like that movie?' she asked. 'You know, where there's a meteor headed for earth.'

'Exactly,' Bill said. 'But in this case, it's survivable.'

Annie just looked at him. Silly old prick.

Flora was biting her tongue. AIDS. Didn't some kid get it from a dodgy transfusion? How was he or she responsible for the sins of mankind? Still, if a quick visit could save Annie from a life of hepatitis.

'Ready?' Bill asked.

The tour began. A bust of a patient with tertiary syphilis. 'Gummatous syphilis,' Bill explained, as Annie soured. 'Now, Flora, we're looking at a cast of an elephant man. Horribly deformed, which is a characteristic of this stage. Maybe you'd like to feel?'

She nodded, so he guided her hand onto the bust and she explored the face.

'Nasty business,' she said.

'Yes.'

She turned to Annie. 'See, that's what comes from philandering.'

'What's that?'

'Pokin' around where you're not welcome, or where are you are, which is probably worse.'

Annie got it, but wasn't about to admit it. You got jiggy, and stuff happened, and you ended up looking like the Elephant Man. She couldn't see how this affected her. She didn't even like boys. Will Carey, perhaps, but he was smart and wore glasses. But most boys were dopey, and watched *Transformers*, and only cared about hamstrings.

Bill showed them another model he'd bought from a scientific supplies company. A brain, shrunk, cut in half to show the grey matter. 'Now, Flora, Annie, one of the worst things you can get is neurosyphilis. This is when the spirochetes – you remember those, Annie? – enter the central nervous system, the brain, and so forth.' He indicated a poster, then remembered. 'Flora, I'm showing Annie a model brain, diseased, and an illustration of what comes after that.'

She seemed satisfied with this.

'Now, Annie, you gotta understand, a man needs to stay in charge of his mind, doesn't he or she, Flora?'

'Yairs.'

'Neurosyphilis can lead to blindness, and madness. Two hundred years ago thousands were locked away in asylums, just cos of our friend *Treponema*. Shouting out all day, banging their heads against walls.'

'But haven't they got pills for it now?' Annie asked.

'Indeed they do, but I guess it's easier not to catch it.'

'But if you do, you're not gonna go mad?'

'Well ...'

'So why have you made a museum?'

Bill wanted to take her by the collar, lead her out back, throw her to the pigs, but realised Flora would hear. 'That's okay if you live in a rich country, Annie, but millions the world over don't have access to antibiotics.'

'So why don't you make a museum there, or help them?'

Bill took a deep breath. 'I'm too old for that. Just do what I can, Annie. Show people.'

'You could raise money for medicine and send it there?'

'How do you know I haven't?'

'Have you?'

Bill could feel his nostrils flaring. 'Shall we move on?'

Flora was led by her granddaughter.

'Initial diagnosis is difficult,' Bill said. 'Blood tests are the best way for the newly infected. Here we see a variety of posters from all around the world, urging young people to get tested. Here, Spain, 1936, and if I translate it, "False Shame and Fear may Destroy your Future". And I suppose, if you think about it, that applies to the pride of man.' He smiled at Annie again. 'How we have fallen in the eyes of the Lord, but refuse to be tested, to submit, to *fix* the problem.'

Why are you looking at me? Annie thought.

'Now, Flora, this poster shows a young man and woman looking down at the ground ...'

Annie didn't get it. 'Mr Redman?'

'Yes, Annie?'

'What's this place really about?'

'How's that?'

'The end of the world, or syphilis?'

'Both.'

'And that's why there's pictures of Jesus everywhere?'

'Yes.'

She read: '... "the Lord smote Nabal, then he died".'

Bill waited.

'Cos he had syphilis?'

'Possibly.'

'He didn't?'

'He might've. That's the point. This is a museum of plague, as described in Revelations. I thought that syphilis was the most relevant to our times.'

'Although, you're saying it's about the end of the world, but no one dies from it anymore?'

'It's a sign.'

'So why don't you have a cancer museum?'

'I've only got one shop, Annie. And like I said, I'm an old man in a wheelchair. There's only so much I can do. Which is why it'll come to people like you, to carry on.'

'What?'

'The message.'

'March 2012?'

'Yes.'

Bill wondered what Flora was thinking. Why wasn't she supporting him? At least in a syphilitic, non-Apocalypse sense. Maybe that's how it was with blind people. Maybe all of their senses were stunted.

He was feeling tired. Guessed that might be enough. 'I like to finish over here,' he said. 'Prevention and treatment.'

Flora shuffled over, as though she knew the way. There was a model of a naked man sitting in a barrel of water, and Bill told them it was mercury infusion, and how they used to think it'd help. But it didn't. A booklet on a table. Billings. An example of wrong-time and right-time, a thermometer and a chart where you wrote down your temperature every day. Annie studied the objects. 'What are these for?'

'Knowing,' Bill said.

She didn't get it; didn't care.

Bill said, 'Here, Mrs Bly. Just showing Annie the Billings method.'

'Does it really work?' Flora asked.

'Ninety-five per cent accurate.'

'Righto.' Though she knew it wasn't true. Could see her dad coming in from feeding the pigs, taking off his shirt, kissing the back of her mother's neck.

'Mind you, there's only one effective way to stop syphilis.' He explained what the Catholic Church had to say about sexually transmitted diseases. 'If only people could be strong.' He could see Flora's hand shaking, but she didn't say a word.

'You okay, Mrs Bly?'

'Yes.'

'Strong?' Annie asked.

'Resist the urge.'

'What urge?'

Bill couldn't see how this was his job. Nanna had brought her, and Nanna could tell her. But Flora didn't say a word. Her hand was tensing and relaxing on her cane, and the scratched name: Bert Bryars.

'Don't you agree, Mrs Bly?'

'Sorry, Mr Redman?'

'Abstinence. It's very simple. But some people just don't get it, do they?'

And then, he fancied, she clenched her teeth.

'Mrs Bly? You okay?'

'No,' she said. 'Some people just don't get it ... but given time, Mr Redman – '

'Bill.'

'Bill. Given time they come to see.'

'Yes,' he said, sure he was making progress. 'They see, don't they? The light, the flash at the very End. And hopefully, they're ready, eh, Annie?'

Flora Bly tapped her way along Dalrymple Street. Annie said, 'We're going the wrong way.' Tap, trip, stumble, walk, faster and faster, away from town, back, down an alley, as Annie pulled on her sleeve and pleaded. 'Nan!'

Flora was determined. 'If it comes to it, and I murder him ...' She passed through a gate, into a paddock on the edge of town. Right across, through the stubble. Could smell smoke, but didn't stop. Annie tried to turn her around. 'Nan, there's a fire!'

A farmer on his tractor called: 'Get out of it!' He'd lit a stubble fire, and it was burning towards them. Flora kept going, and then they were up to the flame front, and her dress was on fire. The farmer ran over with an extinguisher and put her out and called her a madwoman and led her back to the road. And all the time, Annie was wondering, What had really happened at the syphilis museum?

They headed into town. Passed beneath the Brandenburg gate. Six columns towering above Commercial Street, plinths, and four Diggers in a chariot. Should never have been built, most agreed. But Vermes was mayor at the time, and he'd lost two sons. Finally, Annie stood in front of her. 'Nan, you gotta slow down.'

Flora stopped. 'See, that's what comes from sleeping around.'

'What?'

'*Disease*. That's why I took you, Annie, so you could see what might happen.'

A couple of shop-girls walked past, and seemed surprised, but Annie didn't care. 'Look, here's a café. They got buns, Nan.'

They went in and sat at a plastic table with empty pepper and salt shakers and a couple of flies licking juice. Flora caught her breath. Annie waited. 'Funny sort of place,' she said.

'Were you paying attention?'

'Yes.' But she knew it wasn't about spirochetes, Snowy Mountain versus Desert, Jesus as Lord, March 21, or any of that stuff. 'Why was he so strange?'

Annie noticed her nan's tight fists. Studied, again, the grey skin, the deep wells that were her absent eyes. Wondered whether she could really see her.

Flora had calmed. 'Catholics are the worst.'

'How's that?'

'There were nine of us.'

'Who?'

'Us kids. But only five survived.'

Just over fifty percent. A pass, a C, but her parents wouldn't be happy with that.

One of the shop-girls came, and they ordered, and Flora rallied. 'You listen to what he said, Annie?'

'Yes.'

'Remember it. All of it.'

Annie thought she might as well try. 'Did you have syphilis, Nan?'
She didn't get angry. 'No.'

They waited silently. The milkshakes came, and the flies
moved on.

The following day Flora returned to Syphilis. Knocked, waited,
then Bill let her in. She entered cane-less, just like a sighted woman,
no stumbling or feeling her way. Carrying a box.

Bill was surprised to see her. 'Come in, Mrs Bly, please.'

They returned to the lounge, and he switched the urn to high,
and they sat and ate more stale biscuits. Flora could hear the pigs
grunting, and said it reminded her of the farm, her mum and dad and
brother Bertie and sisters and horses and sheep and fox-dead lambs
on cold winter mornings. Bill said he'd just given them a bucket of old
cabbage leaves cos by God, pigs loved cabbages. Then he said, 'I'm
surprised to see you back, Mrs Bly.'

'Flora.'

'Maybe I gave you some food for thought?'

'Maybe.'

'And Annie. Clever thing, eh? I think we mighta made an impact.
This is just the thing, Flora. If parents, church, science, everyone,
come together, the moral standards ...' He stopped, realising he was
getting preachy.

Flora wasn't really listening. She was watching her dad lead her
mum into their not-so-private bedroom. She could see the look of
horror on her mum's face. Like she knew what this meant, and what
would come of it.

Then she opened her box, and said, 'I've brought a few things for
your museum, Bill.'

Bill. Good sign, he thought. 'Well, that's fantastic.'

She produced a diaphragm. 'I thought you could put this out, to
show people.'

He just looked at her.

Then she reached in and found a banana, and a condom she'd stretched over it.

'And this?'

'No, that's not my mission, Flora.'

'Your mission?'

'"Responsible men can become more deeply convinced ..."'

'Ssh!' She leaned forward, silencing him. Indicated her broken eyes. 'Can't see: blind. Can't hear: deaf.'

He didn't know what she meant.

'I wanted to ask you, Bill, if you'd consider ...' She produced foil-wrapped pills. Hormones to fool the unwary.

'This is why you returned?' he asked.

'Yes.'

'But I assumed ... the girl?'

'This one is called an IUD, and it's very simple to use.'

Bill just shook his head. 'My museum has a very clear purpose. On March – '

'I know, Bill, but I'm not asking a terrible lot.'

Yes, Bill was disappointed, but it wasn't the first troublemaker he'd had.

Flora waited. Thought. Decided. 'I'm a reasonable woman, Bill. Do you have a copy of the *Humanae Vitae*?'

'Yes.'

'I'd like to discuss a few passages.'

Reasonable, he thought. He wheeled himself out to the kitchen and searched the drawers. Nothing. Then into his bedroom, and a sort of improvised library of religious documents, *Pollyanna* and Kafka. Not there. He stopped to think. 'It's here somewhere,' he called. He opened his wardrobe, leaned forward and retrieved a box of books. Searched through. No. He knew he had it, and perhaps she could be convinced.

Then he heard pigs. Pigs. From ... inside? Louder, squealing, grunting. Louder. 'Flora, you there?'

He managed to turn around, wheel himself back out to his museum, and saw pigs. His remaining landraces, rooting around in the biscuit jar, the kitchen, the toilet, all over the place. 'Get out!' He could smell solvent. Looked around. Saw his curtains billowing out of the window. They combusted. Immaculately. Burned. Consumed the ceiling, walls, the wood of the old shop.

'Shit! Flora!'

No time. He manoeuvred his chair around the pigs, tried to round them up, but it was a big job, even for a sure-footed man. They ran away, squealed, and the fire consumed more of the room. Specimen jars exploded and pustules trailed across the floor. He coughed, tried to cover his face, but the syphilitic smoke was growing. He tried the pigs one more time. 'Go on, get out of it!' But even with the smoke and fire, they wouldn't leave the museum. Posters caught, flared, and the elephant man started melting. He took a breath, but there was nothing to take. Formaldehyde fumes and the urn exploding tea and coffee water on the rug.

Squeals, as pig became bacon. Flora stood beside her granddaughter on the footpath on the opposite side of the road. She could hear sirens, but knew it was too late.

A few neighbours were using garden hoses, but there was point. The place had gone. No surprise really. A small crowd was gathering. Flora heard someone say, 'I hope he's not inside,' and the response, 'Probably best if he was.'

Bill had painted '21 March' on the front window, and that was burning too. The last squeal of the last pig. And then the roof fell in.

As the fire engine arrived, and unwound its hoses, Flora took Annie around the shoulder. She'd sent her for ice cream, and when she'd returned, the girl had found her nan standing on the footpath, looking across the road. She'd said, 'Isn't that smoke coming from the museum?'

Flora said, 'There's one type he didn't tell you about.'

Annie looked up. She still suspected she could see her. 'One type?'

'Congenital.'

'What's that?'

'That's when yer dad's a philanderer, and he comes home, and he ...' She stopped, realising Annie knew enough.

'Go on.'

They watched the water working on the flames, but the old shop had gone.

'Anyway, it's when a mum's got syphilis, and as the baby comes out, it gets on her eyes, and all them billions of spirochetes, Annie.'

She waited.

'And it gets so bad so quick the baby goes blind.'

Annie knew she could see her. Could see everything, despite her blindness. The way down the hall, the few steps, the gate to the hutch, back inside, the box, the bottle of thinners, the matches – all of this was simple if you knew how. She just ate her ice cream. She liked watching fire. Flames were best, but they couldn't last forever. Like an A-bomb flash, soon gone, and forgotten. And when it was all over, the smouldering begun, she smiled with recognition as the wheel of the upturned chair turned because the men had kept it oiled.

Eventually her nan looked at her. 'Pity,' she said. 'He was a decent fella. All the Redmans were. Even Bill's father, a doctor – he used to come to our place. Always telling Mum what she should and shouldn't do, what was right, and wrong. And she believed him. Like his word was gospel.'

The Shack

Iᴛ's ᴀ sᴍᴀʟʟ ʜᴏᴜsᴇ ᴡɪᴛʜ ʙɪɢ ᴡɪɴᴅᴏᴡs: possum eyes staring out across the Murray. An old engine on a tree stump. A box of kitchen utensils, a vacuum with a split hose and a frypan the retarded boy (now a man) burned his arm on in 1969. Inside, Frank Harris, a man who, at seventy-five, has already shrunk to the size he was at fourteen, lies awake on a camp-stretcher. He wears a singlet and shorts covered in fish scales, and blood. Looks at his watch and mutters, 'Christ!' Wipes sweat from his forehead and starts to cry. Then, just as suddenly, stops. 'Christopher,' he says, noticing a hole in the wall where his son once hit it with a hammer.

After four or five hours of sleeplessness (he doesn't count any more) he sits up and tries to breathe. He steadies himself on the stretcher and takes a deep breath. Reaches over and picks a mask off the floor. Checks the tightness of the tube that joins it to an oxygen bottle sitting in a cradle beside his stretcher. Turns a valve and the oxygen flows. Places the mask over his face, tightens the elastic around the back of his head and breathes again.

He can feel the gas in his lungs. Sucks it, again and again. After a few minutes he feels clear-headed; his hands and feet tensing and relaxing; his legs and arms ready to move. He sits up, but then slouches.

He wonders if there's any point.

Switching off the oxygen, he removes the mask. Coughs and spits onto the old lime carpet. He can almost feel the fibres in his lungs. The clumps, the masses that clog his alveoli; each growing, swelling, bursting and releasing more cancer into his bloodstream; cells gliding through his arteries, capillaries and veins, coming to rest in his brain, liver, spine – any of the eight places they found before they stopped looking.

Frank clears his throat and spits again. This time it hits a wall, and he can see blood mixed with old mucus.

Despite the fact that he no longer cares about dying, he reaches for the mask again, holds it over his face and breathes deeply. Looks across the room, and his eyes settle on the couch where his son slept for twenty-nine years.

Until he built the shack on the river at Morphett's Flat.

It's a leather couch that has split open from a series of creases that now sprout white cotton tendrils. There's a chain bolted to the floor and, attached to this, a leather shackle that he purchased at a XXX shop in the city. It's covered with bite marks where Chris, in the middle of one of his turns, would work at it until his gums bled. Over the years he managed to lose three or four teeth.

If he wants to be toothless, let him be toothless, he'd say to himself. If he wants to sit in his own piss, let him.

Once, years before, the government sent someone. Frank covered the chain and shackle with a rug. Although it was hot he made Chris wear a jumper that covered his wrist. When the man asked what had happened to Chris's teeth, Frank replied they had no money for a dentist. So the man made a note of this and arranged for one.

Franks surveys the cough drops, pills and broken clock on his bedside table. He notices his old *New Testament* sitting open to Matthew 25. Picks it up, holds it in one hand and smells the pages. He can hear a soft voice reading, and see the same words underlined in blunt pencil: 'Then shall the kingdom of heaven be likened unto ten virgins ...'

He starts to cry again. This turns to a cough and he clears his throat and spits, this time on his own foot. He does nothing about it. He throws the mask onto his bed, but makes no attempt to switch off the oxygen. Frank Harris, former builder and plasterer, places his hands on his knees and stands up. He feels faint, and steadies himself against the wall. 'Righto,' he says.

As the first suggestion of light warms the horizon beyond his window, he almost smiles.

Righto, he keeps saying to himself as he hobbles across the room, picks up his .22 calibre rifle and slings it over his shoulder. He picks up a box of cartridges and empties them into his pocket. Turns, steps forward and puts on a pair of slippers.

Again, he takes a few deep breaths and feels he's up to it. He intends visiting his son in the asbestos shack he built him on the riverfront. He lifts his head and his chin juts out. Rubs his four or five days' worth of whiskers and runs his tongue around his mouth.

'Come on then, Frank, get on with it,' he mumbles to himself. As he stands at the front door he looks back into the living room of his house. There are no memories, he guesses – no thoughts, no feelings. That's all unnecessary. Always has been. He steps out of his house. Pulls the door closed and turns to look at the river.

'Righto,' he whispers, as he sets off down the dolomite path.

He sees rabbits darting about in the scrub. Chris is a crack-shot with a .22. He can see him now: his still hands, his head dropping over the sight, his breathing slowing … Crack. As the bunny drops. As Chris looks at him, seeking approval, as Frank takes his son's head in his arm and kisses it. 'You're a clever boy, Christopher.' As Chris's hands start to shake, his body fits, his wordless drone returns as saliva dribbles down his chin.

There's still little light. Frank checks his watch and wonders whether he should leave it until later – but what's the point? There's a gibbous moon but it's smothered by cloud. The milky light settling on his house creates long shadows on the pigeon grass.

He walks past his 1978 Commodore, its panels rusted around

the edges. The engine still ticks over, nervously; its shattered windscreen (Chris with his hammer again) has been replaced with plastic. Frank's been driving it unregistered to Morgan for years, all the time watching for coppers, pumping the brakes to bring it to a stop every few kilometres so he can top up the radiator.

Along the side of the car, from the petrol lid to the front panel, someone has scratched the words: 'mosquita fish, gold fish ...'

He can still remember the night. He's sitting at the front bar of the Commercial watching the Belmont races. Chris is waiting in the car.

'Who owns the little prick?' a voice calls from the door.

Frank turns to see a hard-faced farmer holding Chris by the ear. 'Christ,' he mutters, jumping from his barstool. 'What's he done?'

The old man glares at him. 'Come and have a look.'

A small group heads outside to the carpark. The light is dim but the words on the side of seven or eight cars, vans and utes, are easy to read: 'carp, perch, catfish, smelt, cod ...'

Frank steps towards his son. 'Is this you?' he asks, indicating.

'Yes.'

'Well?'

Chris holds up a single page of newspaper. 'You told me to copy,' he says. 'Everything – you said everything.'

He walks on. Follows a path of sun-baked dirt. Fifteen, maybe twenty minutes later he sees the shack. It's a plain, square box sitting in the shade of an old willow that drags its arthritic fingers through the mud. Made from asbestos, cut on-site by hand, nailed onto a wooden frame of salvaged pine. The joins are covered with strips of wood so the whole place has a European appearance.

Asbestos: tough, hard-wearing, solid, dependable. Over the course of his career as a builder in Adelaide he's built hundreds of homes from asbestos. Lovely stuff. Whack it up, nail it on. A coat of paint and everyone's happy.

Frank stands thirty metres from the shack. The tip of the sun has split the horizon. The light is bleaching the bush and small things are becoming clear: the nylon line on the rods, the words 'Chris's Place' burned into a piece of wood hung above the door.

After years and years of saying he would, Frank gave his son independence. Also, reclaimed the balance of his own life. The building materials were delivered by punt and carried up through the scrub. This was the southern-most limit of his land, or so he believed at the time.

He would build a shack for his son (he did). Hand-mix the concrete for the slab (they did). Build a frame and have it up in a day (it was). They would do all this together – father and son. They would allow the skin on his wrist to heal, once and for all. Share a beer around a campfire at night (they did) and sleep on the rough slab under the stars. Then they would finish the walls, and roof, and make solid furniture that would outlast them both.

Frank fights to breathe. He forces his ribs to expand, his lungs to open and air to enter. At the end he's exhausted. Walking the final few steps to the door of the shack, he enters, and steps inside to find Chris asleep on the ground. Sheets, rugs and pillows twisted around his body where he's fallen from his own camp stretcher.

He makes his way through a carpet of mess – a tin can bleeding beetroot juice onto the rug, a pile of lures, plates and bowls and a pile of Lego the forty-seven-year-old man returns to every few days. He sits in a chair beside the camp stretcher. His foot is only a few inches from his son's cropped hair. He rests his rifle on the floor, clutching the barrel with both hands. 'You awake?'

He notices lasagne sitting open but uneaten on the bench beside the sink. A few flies sit on the cheese that's healed like a scab. He goes to stand, to cover it, but sinks back into his chair. Quietly, he clears his throat again, spits the phlegm into his hand and wipes it on his trousers. Struggles for another breath, and another. Then looks at his son's face.

He is a boy still. His face is soft, thin, rounded. He shaves every day (has done for thirty-three years) and there's no hint of the interruption to boyhood that whiskers create. His nose has a scoop that follows the rise and fall of his cheeks; he has a Roddy McDowall forehead that consumes two-fifths of his face, a small mouth (the top lip forward from the bottom) and a chin that's neither prominent nor receding.

To look at him now, Frank thinks, everything is normal. He half expects him to spring up, greet him, cook a three-course breakfast, go for a morning jog, dress in a suit and tie and head off for work. But he knows Chris will always be alone in his shack. No roads to wander onto; no cardigan-warmed CWA grandmothers to offend; no chocolate to steal; no cars to drive; no voices to overhear him praying to 'Dear God, Jesus, Lord Darth Vader' in the back of two-dollar shops.

This had been a hard but important lesson. He'd gone to town with Cheryl, his wife, and Chris, his nine-year-old son. They'd visited the Children's Hospital. Walked into a specialist's office and there, through the window, Chris saw an enormous adventure playground. After the specialist had examined him, Chris pointed to the playground, started biting his finger and jumping up and down in his seat.

The specialist nodded and Chris was told by Frank (a clear-lunged, white-eyed Frank) to go left along the hall, straight down the stairs, through the double doors and out into the playground.

So, the specialist kept talking and ten minutes later Frank noticed that Chris still hadn't emerged through the double doors. He stood, studied the playground and said, 'Where's he got to?'

Cheryl and the specialist stood and moved to the window. 'I wouldn't think he's lost,' the specialist said.

'Can you see him?' Cheryl asked.

Frank ran down to the playground. Searched the foam-ball pit, the safety swings, even crawled through the Aladdin's Cave maze. Then stood, looked up at his wife and the specialist, still looking concerned behind a double-glazed window, raised his hands in the air and shrugged.

At eleven pm that evening he was searching the back streets of Moreau with a pair of police cadets; at midnight he was walking across the ovals, and around the classrooms and playgrounds of Lindisfarne College; at four-thirty he was walking along the river, saying to Cheryl, 'I didn't want to let him go.'

'Hospitals are meant to be safe.'

'I didn't want to let him go.'

'We'll find him.'

Later, a police car took them back to the hospital, to their son, wrapped in a blanket, sipping cocoa in the locked-up cafeteria with its blinking fluoros and cauterised floors. Frank sat beside him, stroked his cheek and said, 'You okay?'

'Can I sleep now?'

Back in the shack, Frank is still staring at the boy. He's glad to be here, in the warm, with him. He's always glad to be with him. Although he can't imagine living with him, he's unable to imagine life without him. And he knows the boy is really only a function of himself – a fifth limb, a toe, an incomplete breath of air. They are a pair of well-mannered parasites, taking and giving as the mood, the times and the weather dictates. Where one sings the other smiles; food is cooked, removed from the can and shared in separate places.

Frank coughs. He reaches into his pocket for his handkerchief. Opens it, spits and replaces it. Feels a letter in his pocket. He retrieves it, and unfolds it.

Dear Mr Harris

Staff at the Titles Office have repeated the search on the titles Folio 9/379 (1946) and 9/74A (1952). There is no doubt that the land in question is Crown Land. There were some adjacent transfers of land in the late 1940s but

none of these coincide with the land on which you presently reside.

As stated previously we have agreed to let you remain
on the land for now. There can be no guarantee of this
beyond the next 12-18 months. We accept the present
circumstances of your illness and your son's disability ...

Frank studies the map that has been stapled to the letter. Notices
the lines that run around, across and through their land. He can see
how someone has highlighted them.

The letter is many years old. The folds have nearly broken, leaving
him with six odd-shaped squares that have ruined his life. He rereads
it to make sense of it, although he never has. This is why the letter has
been the subject of endless phone calls, return letters, front bar rants,
but mostly just dejection, disappointment and despair.

For thirty years he believed it was his land. Was told so. By an old
friend called Reg. As young men they'd pooled their savings, all three
hundred pounds, and Reg went to see his mate the real estate wizard:
'No office, no lawyers, no nothin', mate, just dirt cheap property.'
They'd looked at several country blocks before settling on Morphett's
Flat, south of Morgan.

This will be my half, and this yours, Reg had declared, and Cheryl
and Frank had agreed.

But what he meant was (Frank now realised) this bit here, this bit
we bought, will be mine, and this, the Crown Land, will be yours.

Frank felt stupid. For not checking the title, the map, the description. He felt like this has been the course of his life – one fuck up after
another. But he felt glad, sort of, that Reg had ended up dead with
liver cancer (not before selling the land).

Still, Frank had saved some money and decided to find someone to
take care of Chris when he was gone.

He found a place in Renmark called Waratah Village. Worked out that with what the government puts in there'd be enough money to keep Chris comfortable, fed, and perhaps even happy. The manager of the home did the sums and reassured him everything would be okay. But then this same man, who was tall and always had a smile on his face, took him on a tour of the home.

Frank saw rows of old people lined up in a sunroom; he saw nice enough young men and women feeding them, wiping food from their chin, and talking to them (despite the fact that they never replied); he smelt the piss and shit and porridge; he was told by the smiling man that they'd had plenty of people like Chris over the years, and that they'd all fit in, found friends, gone on day trips.

Frank fumbles in his pocket for a single bullet. He loosens the bolt, loads the bullet and rests the butt of the rifle on the ground.

The room is almost light, but Chris is still fast asleep. Frank looks at his son's face again – he notices a red flush in his cheeks, and shadows where his oval-shaped face catches the little bit of sunlight.

Now they are landing their boat at Morphett's Flat. Retrieving an esky full of food, and bait, and carrying it, one handle each, towards the shack. Chris is quiet. There is something on his mind, Frank can tell. He looks at his son and asks, 'You okay?' and the boy replies, 'I have redfin, in case we don't catch any.'

Frank just smiles. 'Of course we will. We always do.'

Chris grins. 'Always?'

'Always.'

The Photographer's Son

On from Barmera, towards Cobdogla. All the way round Wachtels Lagoon to Moorook, then half-way to Loxton. Country that had been over-grazed, stripped of vegetation, the soil left to wash and blow away, exposing limestone in honeycomb sheets that could be cut (and had been) to make blocks for building. Then south along the Murray, the small ghost-filled inlets with their marshes and shouldn't-have-been-planted willow trees. Along Alcott Road (*keep going, keep going, all the way to the water*) to the farm that no one knew about, or visited.

Hugh Heyward had started it. He'd taken his wife, Sarah, and set off from Adelaide. Boarded a riverboat at Tailem Bend and journeyed all the way to his block on the Murray. Jumped off the boat, onto the shore, and held his arms out for his wife. The second mate had lifted her, deposited her, but Hugh had underestimated her weight and dropped her in the water. They'd surveyed their sixty acres. Hugh had said, 'Nice country' (although he wasn't really sure of this). They'd walked up the bank, across sandy flats into thick scrub. Hugh had said, 'How about we build the house here?' Sarah had replied, 'No, higher. I don't want to be flooded out.'

Sixty years had passed and the house was still there. Sarah had named it 'Querelle', despite not knowing what it meant. She'd made Hugh carve a sign on a piece of redwood. He'd hauled every stone from Cobby on the back of a cart, dumped it on the clearing, fitted it, laid it, pointed it.

Now, Hugh and Sarah were dead. But their son, Des, was still running things. He had fruit trees, mainly, and some vines. Cattle.

A flock of sheep and a few goats. In fact, he hadn't really worked out where the good money was, so he'd hedged his bets. He was still searching for the pot of gold at the end of the rainbow. Des was a practical man, but not overly ambitious. He had no desire to make millions, to tame the land (that always seemed to be taming him) or move beyond the smell of burnt bread and beeswax candles at Querelle.

Des was out chopping wood. His wife, Lucy, was in town, organising men for the harvest. His only son, Adrian, was standing on the porch of the house, looking out across the bloated river that crawled towards the sea. The boy was eight, but told people he was nine, ten, even, depending on who he needed to impress. He was short for his age, and his head always drooped like the golliwog his aunt had bought him – as though it was too heavy, or perhaps just because he couldn't be bothered holding it up.

Adrian had finished spreading the hay for the sheep. He'd finished burying the latest lamb. Preparing the fire. There were other jobs but he wasn't in the mood. He could do them, and Des would probably praise him, but he wasn't interested – didn't feel the need for his father's hand through his hair.

He went into the house, and his parents' bedroom. Climbed onto their bed and reached on top of their wardrobe. The photo box was heavy and he overbalanced and fell back onto the mattress. Some of the photos spilled onto the quilt. He gathered them and went into his room. After closing his door, he sat on his bed and started removing photos from the box. There were a few of him: a portrait taken in Renmark, his hair cut and combed back over his ears; his mother's sisters and brothers; postcards from his parents' honeymoon in the Blue Mountains; even some old newspaper clippings for agricultural implements his father had planned on buying.

Then, his favourite: a formal photo of Hugh and Sarah, kneeling on the lounge room floor of Querelle. They were both dressed formally, Sarah in a black dress that reached below her ankles, Hugh in a rough suit he kept for Sunday service, funerals and trips to town to discuss the mortgage. There was a girl lying between them. Adrian wasn't sure, but he guessed she was nineteen or twenty, perhaps a bit older, judging from her sun-baked face. She was also wearing a good dress. Pearls. Her hair was done up in a bun. Like Hugh and Sarah, she was looking at the camera, but he couldn't see much in her eyes.

'Adrian!'

He heard his dad in the kitchen. Froze. He wasn't doing anything wrong, much. There was no rule against looking at the photos, but sometimes, when his mum got them out at night, and got a bit teary, his dad would gather them and storm out of the room and say to her, 'Just leave them. Doesn't do no one no good.'

'Adrian!'

He heard footsteps in the hallway. Realised there was no point trying to hide the photos; the little bits of life he'd known, or heard about, forgotten, imagined. The dead people. The places other people had gone.

'What you up to?' Des asked, opening the door and coming into his room.

He didn't reply.

'The family jewels, eh?' He sat down on his son's bed. Picked up a photo, smiled, and threw it back down.

'I finished everything,' Adrian said.

'Good boy.'

Adrian studied the bristles on his father's face, the scars on his neck, the hairs poking from his nose. Smelled the eucalyptus and cow shit, the black mud on the bottom of his shoes.

Des took the photo from his son's fingers. He looked at his father, and mum, and the girl.

'Who was she?' Adrian asked.

'I've told you, haven't I?'

Adrian didn't reply. It seemed that would be disrespectful – like saying his father was forgetful, or hiding something.

'No? Well ...'

Maybe she was a family secret, Adrian thought. A retard. Like the ones in the special school in Berri. The boys and girls who sat on the porch watching him walk by in his Sunday suit. Maybe she was a relative who'd fallen pregnant and been sent to Querelle.

'My sister,' Des said.

He looked at him, confused. 'But you don't have a sister.'

'I don't, but I did.'

He reclaimed the photo. 'Your sister?' There was no way this could be his aunt. He'd never seen, heard or been told stories about her. And stories, he already knew, were the way people proved something was true. If you hadn't done something funny or dumb or stupid, it was like you'd never existed.

'Look closely,' Des said to him.

He studied the girl.

'See, she's dead,' his father said.

'No ...'

'Yep. That's a *memento mori.*'

He looked up.

'A photo people used to have taken so they could remember someone.'

Adrian thought about this. It made sense. You could remember a face for a month, a year perhaps, but eventually you always forgot what people looked like. The boy who'd drowned at Pyap, for instance. Who'd been in his class. Blond, and a round face, but he couldn't see him to think of him.

'Elizabeth died when she was nineteen. No one never knew what of, cos she was just buried.' His father was remembering. 'See, the tallboy, the table, that's our dining room.'

173

Adrian could even see their mirror, covered, and the old organ he'd never heard played.

'So, this is what happened. Of course, I wasn't around at the time. I was only told later. She got some infection, and took to bed, and sweated and tossed and turned for days. And then one morning your grandma went in and she was dead.'

Adrian kept studying the photo. 'Was she upset?'

'You would be, wouldn't yer? But as I said, I wasn't there. Anyway, after they dealt with the shock, Hugh said, We ain't got no picture, have we? Sarah thought, and said, No.'

He noticed how Elizabeth's hands had been arranged, each finger woven like his mother's crochet. It was like she was praying.

'Hugh said, I'll drive to town and fetch the photographer. He got dressed and went out to the stable, but had forgotten the horse had slipped a shoe. So he just turned and started walking – out the front gate, towards Barmera.'

'He walked all that way?'

'It was a stinker. He walked and walked. No one went past to offer a lift. He slept under a tree on the first night, then walked the next day, then slept in a hay shed the next night – then he got to town.'

Adrian had never heard this story. He wondered whether his dad was just making it up, but knew (from his face) that this wasn't so. Maybe it was something he thought he was ready to hear; maybe he'd never got around to telling him. Still, this was unlikely. This was a house full of stories: deaths, lost babies, drownings, people with their arms caught in mangles.

'Meanwhile, Sarah was left with Elizabeth,' Des said. 'She wasn't sure how long Hugh would take, so she stripped her off and put her in the bath and covered her with water. Then she just sat beside her … holding her hand perhaps.'

He knew his father was starting to improvise. There was no way he could know that sort of detail. But he didn't care. A story was more real than the thing, after all. The thing just happened, but the story you could control. 'For two days?' he asked.

'Two days. So it wasn't like she was really going to … turn.'

'Turn over?'

'You know, start stinkin'.'

Adrian almost smiled. Almost asked, How long would that take then? But wasn't sure how close his father had been to his sister. 'Where were you all this time?'

'I was busy elsewhere.'

'Where?'

'Listen. Hugh walks into town and makes straight for the photographer's rooms. He walks in, and this man, Bernie Padfield his name was, looks at him and says, "How can I help?"'

'Is this true?'

'Believe me, it's true. I wouldn't be here if it wasn't. And you wouldn't either.'

Now Adrian was confused.

'Hugh's pretty messy, he stinks, covered in dust, so Padfield's a bit curious. Hugh explains about Lizzy, and how they want a photo to remember her, but you know what Padfield says?'

He played along. Knew that questioning was one of his father's story-telling techniques. 'No.'

'He says, "Sorry, no time to be drivin' all round the country. You can bring her here." "How am I gonna do that?" Hugh asks. "Sorry," Padfield says.'

He could tell his father was hitting his straps. By the way he sat forward; raised, and modulated, his voice; spat as he spoke.

'Hugh exploded. He shouted. "Padfield: You will come with me, sir!" Padfield shouted back: "I will not, sir!"'

Dramatic pause. Adrian knew what was expected. His eyes lit up, he sat forward himself.

'Then, Hugh picked up a knife from Padfield's table and held it to his throat. He'd had enough. His daughter was dead! He was tired, thirsty, sore all over. He said: "Sir, you will come with me, and you will take my daughter's picture."'

He waited.

'Know what happened next?'

'No.'

'Padfield said no.'

'No?'

'Yep. Knife or no knife, he wasn't going anywhere. So ...'

'What?'

'Just then, the photographer's son walked into the room. Hugh felt he had no choice. He sprang forward, took the boy by the arm and held the knife to *his* throat.'

He was lost in the story.

'"You will come with me," Hugh said to the photographer, as the boy just shook and ...'

'Yes?'

'Wet himself.'

Adrian sat back. 'How do you know?'

'Don't worry. I know. So, Hugh waited with the knife to the boy's throat as Padfield went out and harnessed his cart, gathered his equipment, and loaded it. Then, Hugh led the boy out and they all got in the cart and set off.'

Adrian knew the drama had to surge and recede, like the river, wetting and drying the roots of big gum trees. But Des also knew that if the horse slows too much it stops.

'They headed to Querelle. All lined up on the front seat: Padfield, the boy (his throat nicked, and bleeding) and Hugh Heyward. For the first few hours there was silence. But then Hugh started telling them about Lizzy. Her smile, her sense of ... lightness, her ear for music, and the way she could make the organ sing like a choir of angels. How she was the light of her parents' life.'

Adrian realised it was getting dark, and cold, but to stand and light a candle, or start a fire, would ruin everything.

'The photographer listened to Hugh and, despite the knife, started feeling sorry for him. As the sun started setting, he guessed the farmer was harmless.'

His father had left the room, and another man was telling the story. This man was someone like Dickens, or Twain, or even Kipling. He *was* the story.

'Hugh told them everything about Lizzy. How she could tackle the hardest sums, and always get them right, and cook ... how she could make old mutton taste ...'

Adrian was in the cart, too, sitting, listening.

'Then, all of a sudden, Hugh stood and threw the knife into the bush. Padfield pulled up. Hugh looked at him and said, I'm sorry. About all this, and your boy ... for scaring him. "I'm sorry. I wouldn't never have hurt no one." Then he sat down. And Padfield put his hand on his arm and said, "I understood all that. Right from the start. How about I come with you and take your daughter's picture?"'

Adrian could tell his father had descended, on the verge of tears that were story tears, but real tears. He was slowing, savouring every word, every action, every smile, every second of pathos.

'Hugh said, No. But Padfield didn't care. He looked at his son and smiled, and the son agreed – they should take Lizzy's picture.'

'He was a good fella, this photographer,' Adrian said.

'Yes,' Des agreed. 'A decent man. Ones you don't see so much these days.' He knew the story had to continue. More than anything, once started, it had to be finished. 'They stopped for a rest and the photographer fetched his equipment, and set up, and took a photo of Hugh and the boy.'

Des took out his wallet. Produced an old, torn photo Adrian had never seen. He handed it to his son, who studied it. It made sense. It all made sense. Hugh and the photographer's son stood together against the bush, and the distant river that ran through their lives. There was blood on the boy's neck and shirt. He looked at his father. Lifted his hand and touched the scars on his neck. 'You ...'

Des smiled. 'I was gonna tell you ...'

'But ... how?'

'We went home, and Sarah was waiting. They got Lizzy ready with her dress, and her pearls, and Dad, *my dad*, took the photo.' Des reclaimed the *memento mori* and studied it.

Adrian sensed the story had stopped, and something else had begun. *My dad ...* Hugh, or Bernie Padfield? It wasn't clear to him anymore. 'I still don't understand.'

Des was lost. 'I can still remember, standing watching as they got her ready, adjusting her hands in her lap.'

'I don't understand ...'

'Later, we all went out onto the porch for a cup of tea. I went off to play and Dad, Bernie, talked to Hugh. This bit I'll have to make up.' He smiled. 'Bernie said, "Listen, Mr Heyward, I can see you're a decent man. The thing is, I've done you a favour, and you could do one for me."'

Adrian felt cold. It was almost dark outside. The room was full of shadows. He could barely see his father's face.

'"Hugh," Bernie said, "my wife, she went to Sydney, and she never came back." Then, I imagine, there would've been silence. Then, Bernie would've said, "I was wondering if you could watch my son. For a few weeks at most."'

From a knife at the throat to a favour; threats to something that already resembled friendship, perhaps even love. This is what Bernie Padfield had come to think of Hugh, and Hugh of the photographer.

'So?'

'Hugh said yes. What else could he do? The poor man's wife had run off, with some other man as it turned out.'

'And he never came back for you?'

'No.'

Des took the photo of him and his father, Hugh Heyward, standing before the bush, and put it back in his wallet. 'He never came back. Couple of years later, Dad told me, he heard he'd been stabbed. Maybe by the fella that my mum had run off with, maybe someone else.'

'And?'

'I was angry, cos he'd dumped me. But later, I realised he'd gone to get my mum because he loved her. Didn't mean ...'

'And Pop?'

'Once he'd heard about the stabbing. Once a year had passed with no word. Then he knew. He was always a practical man, so he said, "No use waitin', son." He went to town and signed some papers and that was that.'

Adrian still wasn't sure if the whole thing wasn't the most ambitious, grandest story his father had ever invented. But, he concluded, it must be true. And if one bit was true, then it was all true. He guessed that it had taken his father eight years to tell him this, simply because it had taken eight years to tell him. 'How did you feel?'

Des sighed. 'Not good ... not good. I came back to the porch and ... Dad, Bernie, told me what they'd decided. And he left me there. He messed my hair, kissed me, and told me he'd be back soon, and that Mr Heyward was a good man and would look after me. And then he got in his cart and drove off. And that was it.'

Now it was pitch black. They sat in silence.

'That's me, the photographer's son,' Des said, packing the photos into the box.

Adrian felt happy, and sad, that he was here because of this story, and these people, and their weaknesses, and goodness, and charity. He felt love. A dad was a valuable thing, no matter where you found him, and if his stories went all night, into the dark and cold, you listened. You never moved. Not an inch.

Des was still watching his father drive through the gates at Querelle.

He was still waving. His father didn't look back. He supposed this was because he was busy planning his trip east. He turned and looked at Hugh, the farmer in the torn and dusty suit. 'Will you need a hand digging?' he said.

'Tomorrow, son.'

Datsunland

William Dutton was still walking towards school. Two decades after he'd finished, still. Carrying his guitar, head down, mumbling to himself, resenting that he had to go, waste another day, fill in shitty little forms that he always got wrong, screwed up, started again, or forgot to attach, eliciting a reminder email. He didn't even like schools, but where else could a guitar teacher get work? He didn't like how the bell was the same bell as in the seventies, loud, metallic, unable to compromise, still cutting days into geography-sized pieces, unwilling to allow sunshine, Ginsberg's hipster funk or fun. Fun. Fancy that. Fuck he hated schools. The way teachers stood in hallways discussing assessment criteria and performance standards, like the boys were goats to be fattened to fetch the best price at the abattoir. He hated his pigeonhole, because it never contained anything he was interested in, just more work, more shit to fill in, more complaints from parents. And he hated them too. Why couldn't they just teach their own kids, or feed them, take them to sport, imbue manners? Yes, manners. They had to be *imbued*. He couldn't understand what people talked about in staff meetings. What did it matter if socks were worn below the knee? Or if no one had completed their sixty hours of professional development. What was professional development? How to make an effective rubric? Rubrics. Fuck. More shit, less interest than *Mein Kampf*, although at least that started a war.

He entered through the big iron gates, crossed the Brother Blah-Blah Memorial Lawns and stopped to admire a life-sized statue of Mary. She was wearing a smock filled with needles from nearby pine trees, and there was mud on her feet from where the principal's car drove past every morning. And the principal, Mosby, he was a barrel of laughs too. Anyway, Mary's arms were missing. A sign explained how this was the work of vandals.

> Good Friday. 1954. The Virgin was desecrated, and partly restored. Due to a lack of marble, and suitable craftsmen, the Holy Mother was left in her present state to reflect the suffering of Jesus on His cross.

Nearby, a brass plaque beside a carpark told the story of Irish monks who'd inspired the founding of Lindisfarne College – a lifetime spent copying Bibles, developing cataracts and freezing in a cave. That was devotion, the boys were told by the college's surviving Brother (as he squeezed their shoulders). Eadrifth and Ethilwald, the love of God and porridge.

Tons and tons of it, still served in vats in the boarding house.

William Dutton was suffering on his own cross: the prospect of seven hours of guitar lessons. His small room in the music suite. Eight teenage boys murdering Deep Purple, each of them fresh from PE lessons, smelling like old plums gone bad on someone's back lawn. He'd taken to keeping a can of deodorant in his room but only used it after they'd gone, unable to tell them they stank. Again, their parents' job. Why the hell couldn't they say something?

He walked past a sandstone mansion that had once been the centre of this forty-acre property. Now it was the administration building. The tiles on the entry porch had sunk, and cracked. The white paint was peeling. There were proud flags, but these too were threadbare around the edges. Still, there were iceberg roses, figs in giant pots and BMWs and Audis left running on the gravel drive as mums ran inside to pay their fees.

Lindisfarne House, as it was called, was the college's showpiece. For years its floorboards had creaked under the weight of black-robed

Christian Brothers, the boys who carried their books, red-necked boarders and Van de Graaff generators. Now it was home to HR managers, finance officers and assistant principals with massage chairs. He'd seen them, at four in the afternoon, gathered around the mini-bar in the boardroom (as another fee increase was discussed).

Lindisfarne College was the poor cousin of a family of elite schools. It had managed to borrow and beg enough to build an Olympic-sized swimming pool, a new science centre and library, but it still had plenty of hot-in-summer, cold-in-winter classrooms from the forties and fifties. Cracked mortar rooms, their old wiring covered with asbestos, cornices coming away and walls crumbling where nails had been hammered in. Threadbare carpet and the smell of boys – eighty years of them, caught in an eternity of Pythagoras and cold showers, waiting for Godot as the smell of paint and more perspiration filled their rooms, and dreams.

Boys – foursquare and basketball in the twenty minutes between Latin and Bach. Pasties with burnt edges dropped over the Thoreau Wing balcony. Cricket bats in cracked leather cases. Leftover spag bog in Tupperware eaten cold under dying jacarandas. Boys – grunting, spitting, picking fights over whose brother had the hottest Monaro.

William entered the music suite and climbed the stairs to his teaching room. His first student was already waiting. 'G'day, Charlie.'

'Sir,' the boy replied, catching his teacher's eye then looking away. 'Been waiting long?'

'A few minutes.'

William entered the room and switched on the light. The fluoro flickered and then came to life. That was the Lindisfarne way – things working despite age, ability or lack of maintenance. Like most of the teachers – grey-bearded, nasal-haired men with their own body odour issues. Yes, they all knew their stuff – got their boys through with near-perfect scores – but whenever you turned them on they always flickered. Lindisfarne teachers always had at least one button missing from their shirt. Some had descended to picking their nose in class.

'Sit down, Charlie,' William said, pulling up a chair for the boy. 'I'm late. Am I late?'

'No, I'm early.'

'Good. Should we start with some scales?'

Charlie took his acoustic guitar from its case as William spread the sheet music on a stand. 'How did you go?' he asked.

Charlie bit his lip. 'Okay, I guess.'

'You guess?'

'It's just remembering.'

'Well, let's see. Sit up straight.'

Charlie straightened his back, looked at the music then slouched again.

'Straight,' William repeated. He stood, came around behind the boy and pulled his shoulders back. 'Like that. Can you stay like that?'

'I guess.'

'How tall are you?'

'Taller than my dad.'

'That's not a height. You must be five eight. You're gonna have to put your shoulders back.' He continued applying pressure. 'Can you keep them there?'

'Yes.'

'If I let go?'

'Yes.'

William let go and Charlie held himself straight. 'I can't do this and play.'

'Try.'

William sat down and the boy began. He started on a low E and made his way up the fretboard. William watched his fingers: long digits covered in sun-bleached skin. Knuckle-bound fingers – clumsy, craving precision – stretching and twisting up a path of semitones.

William was consumed by the small, simple movements. He slipped in and out of this hypnosis, trying to make a remark, but failing. He wasn't really listening or watching. His eyes moved onto the boy's long and slender arms. Awkward, bent up at improbable angles – marionette limbs, bouncing about in defiance of music. 'Good,' he said, coming out of his trance. 'But you've slouched again.'

'You never see Chris Shiflett standing like that.'

'He doesn't need to. He's got millions.'

'I don't want to be classical.'

'That's not the point.'

'I'm not interested in Mozart.'

'Listen, Charlie Price, I'm getting paid to teach you good habits. All of the Kurt Cobain stuff, and the wanky solos, that comes later.'

Charlie had a broad smile across his face. 'I didn't say I wanted to be Kurt Cobain.'

'It was just a wild guess.'

'I just want to be a good guitarist.'

'Well, sit up then.'

Charlie straightened, and then slouched. 'What?'

'Christ.' William knew there was no point pursuing posture. It wasn't that Charlie didn't agree, he just didn't care enough. His mind couldn't make the connection between a straight back and a blues riff. William understood. He'd once been fourteen years old. He could remember not seeing the point of folding and putting away clothes he'd be wearing the next day. Of hanging up towels that dried just as well on the floor. Of having to tell his parents about the book he was reading when they didn't read (or seem to care about) books.

'I tell you one thing,' he said. 'You wanna be a star, you learn how to write a good song.'

'I can.' Charlie took out his iPhone. He offered William an earpiece and took one for himself. He pressed play and they listened. It was solid, grunting, granny-flat rock – Charlie and two mates – guitar, drums, bass and vocals. The song described how love made you feel when it's hot, when it's cold, when you're down, when you're happy, when you've had enough. There was barely a riff that hadn't been stolen, a chord progression borrowed or lyric reworked. Charlie was still blue without you, suffering without his lover (like no other) and searching for a way to fix this thing that's torn us apart. Despite this, the song worked. It was fresh, catchy, in-your-face, smelling of Rite Price teen spirit.

He stretched back in his seat, tapped his feet, stare at the wall and smiled.

William could see how tall he really was. It was as though his legs had been stretched by some device. They were more scaffold than limb, clamped at the knees, narrowing into wishbone ankles that somehow supported his whole body. He studied his face. His pine-blond hair, twisted into small dreadlocks (yes, there'd been a letter home, but it was still in his school bag); a refined nose, ending in a chiselled tip, flat, broad cheeks and blue eyes that were hidden, curious, peeping out through slits like gun emplacements.

Charlie looked at him. William closed his mouth, removed the earpiece and said, 'Not bad.'

'Not bad?'

'It's fine … it's got quite a catchy chorus.'

'You think?'

'Yes, keep at it. You fellas played anywhere yet?'

'Just my living room, when Dad's at work. Mr Ordon lets us have a room at lunch sometimes. If the Glee Club's not singing.'

William was caught up in the boy's eyes. 'That'd be your thing, wouldn't it?'

'Doris Day.'

'You wouldn't know who she was.'

'On Moonlight Bay.' Screwing up his nose.

A week later William was back outside the Lindisfarne College music suite. He looked at the whitewashed walls, the tinted windows and brass plaques to honour former music masters. He didn't know why this annoyed the hell out of him, but it annoyed the hell out of him. Wasn't music meant to be risky? Wasn't it meant to say something? Didn't it have the job, like books and poems and paintings, to question? So why the obsession with Beatles medleys, 'My, my, My, Delilah' and ABBA tributes? Was it that music, and what he was meant to pass on, had become so much wallpaper? Admired, and made, by the ordinary? And if so, where did that leave him? A perfectly respectable Sid Vicious.

'Dutton!'

Pete Ordon, Lindisfarne's head of music, approached him from behind and held his shoulder. 'How are you, Jimi?'

'Good,' William replied, pointing to a pair of school-blazered, saxophone-playing teddy bears in the window. 'Your idea?'

'One of the mums – she hand-sewed the blazers.'

'Desperate housewife.'

'You should go clean her pool.'

'I'd rather fuck a donkey.' He visualised a Volvo mum waiting outside a classroom, trying to catch a glimpse of something else to complain about. 'We should make them do something useful.'

Pete knew when William was getting started. He didn't have the time or inclination to listen, so he asked, 'How are your students going?'

'Fine. Usual bunch of little rock stars.'

The stocky teacher smoothed the greying hair on the sides of his head and grinned. 'Well, you're just the one. What's your group called?'

'Nimrod's Cat.'

'Very eighties.'

'That's how long we've been playing.'

Pete loosened his tie and said, 'Don't give up … any day now.'

'Fuck off, no one's paying you to compose symphonies.'

'No one listens to symphonies any more.'

William smiled. 'That's okay then. Sit back and teach. Whatever happened to that string quartet you had performed?'

'It was recorded, and copies distributed.'

'What, ten, twelve?'

'Three hundred. What about Nixon's Cat?'

'Nimrod's. You'd be surprised.'

Pete started to go but then stopped. 'I meant to ask if we have any decent guitarists this year?'

William visualised the faces – the sweaty brows and big ears, the pimples, the peach fuzz and clumsy fingers. 'Little wog called Alessio … Scuzzi, Scuzzioso, something. Very classical. Straight back. Bought himself a foot stand.'

'Good.'

'And Charlie Price, you know him?'

'Yes.'

'Great kid. Very serious. Works his arse off.'

William could hear himself saying it, but didn't quite believe it. Charlie was an average student, not the type who could sight-read a new piece. William could see himself in Charlie – all of the desire, the rock'n'roll fantasies, the smashed guitars (he couldn't really afford to smash) and witty replies at the press conferences he held in his head – but whether he had the determination, stamina or talent to achieve anything of this remained to be seen.

'Do you get much out of him?' Pete asked.

'Well, he's a nice enough kid.'

'I had him last year. Shy as all hell. Reckon I got three words out of him all year.'

'Really? He talks to me.'

'Good, he must like your lessons. Not that he's unpopular. All the other boys flock around him – you know, being athletic. But he never seems that interested in them. Often see him in the library sitting by himself, reading.'

William thought this was strange. 'Some of them mature earlier.'

'I suppose. His mother died of cancer a few years back. I remember them having a service in the chapel. The whole junior school was there. Charles was in the front row with his mates, and his dad, and I thought it was strange how he just stared at the ground the whole time.'

'That explains it, eh?'

'What?' As he remembered conducting the choir at the service, looking around and noticing Charlie. He could still see his feet, turned in at an angle, and his hands in his pockets. Could remember talking to him afterwards, and not knowing what to say. 'Charlie, we're all here for you,' he'd managed, holding his shoulder and smiling at his father, Damien.

William waited. 'Well, that's handy to know, eh?'

The music department secretary stuck her head outside the door. 'Pete, parent on the phone.'

'Tell 'em to fuck off.'

She wasn't happy.

'Coming.'

And he was gone – past the school crest on the wall, the coat-of-arms acid-etched into the glass doors and a young boy waiting with his saxophone. 'Mr Ordon swore.'

William took a step towards him and said, 'Keep it to yourself, he's under a lot of stress.'

He started his day with Alessio, who explained how he'd been studying a video of Segovia and wanted to learn to play in the same manner – the runs, the fingerpicking, the dancing fingers and light touch.

'As I say to everyone,' William explained, 'it all comes back to scales.'

'I know as far as F sharp.'

'How much practice do you do?'

'Three hours a night.'

William knew it couldn't be true. Three hours would produce a half-decent 'Cavatina'. But here was a small, stove-shaped Italian who could barely produce an in-tune 'Three Blind Mice'. 'Three hours?'

'Yes.'

There was no point arguing. He'd only tell his mum and then she'd be on the phone blaming him for her son's lack of Segovia-like attributes.

After Alessio there were another three beginners, and an hour and a half of clock watching and wandering thoughts. At one point he saw himself standing up, walking from the room and strolling across the Lindisfarne lawns. He could see himself sitting under a pine tree, lighting a cigarette and stretching out on the soft grass, covering his face with a cap and cursing the armless Virgin. The city skyline tasted of Turkish coffee, garlic sauce and cold beer. But then he opened his eyes and saw ten stumpy fingers murdering 'Yesterday'.

A simple melody, he thought. How can you get it wrong?

'No,' he said to the boy, moving his fingers. 'Up close, *behind* the fret.'

But then, his last lesson before lunch, he looked up to see Charlie standing in the doorway. He stood to greet him. 'Come in, Charlie, sit down.'

William pulled out a chair and they both sat. As Charlie unpacked his guitar he flicked through the boy's music folder with refreshed eyes. 'So, how did you go?'

'Okay, I guess.'

'You're still guessing?'

'The more you do it the worse it sounds.'

William held up a finger. 'That's a good sign – repetition. That's how you learnt your times tables, wasn't it?'

'And Hail Mary, and Our Father. They're more interested in that crap here. Sorry, you're not Catholic?'

'It might come in useful one day.'

'When?'

'When you're on your deathbed.'

Charlie laughed. 'Tables'd do me more good.'

'Okay, let's hear you then.'

Charlie looked at the music, squinted, adjusted his guitar and positioned his fingers.

'Watch the music, not your fingers,' William said.

'Then I won't be able to play.'

'Try.'

He started with a G major scale. As he played he bit his bottom lip, pushed his tongue against the inside of his mouth, fumbled, stopped and looked at William apologetically, then kept on slowly and carefully as he moved up the fretboard.

William was studying his face.

Cancer, he wanted to say. That must have been hard.

I guess, he could hear, as a reply.

Do you miss her, he imagined saying, but this time there would be no reply, as the boy looked down at the ground, and shrugged.

Instead he said, 'Excellent. You seem to have the pattern. Keep it up. Use it as a warm-up. I know you'd rather be playing "Smoke on the Water", but any idiot can do that stuff. Now, your pieces.'

Charlie continued. William looked at his tightly twisted dreadlocks. 'I like your hair,' he heard himself saying.

Charlie stopped, surprised. 'My sister does it. She's a hairdresser. I can ask her to do yours if you like.'

'No, I can't see it. I had a mullet at one stage, a permed mullet, but that was before you were born.'

Charlie was smiling, and William felt he had to keep going. 'My mate's girlfriend was training to be a stylist, so.'

Charlie screwed up his nose. 'You, with a perm?'

'They were strange times.'

'You'd look good with dreads. She wouldn't charge.'

William could feel himself approaching the line, and watching and listening to what was on the other side. He could smell youth, and fear, and the excitement of everything for the first time. He could hear a buzzing guitar, and flat notes, and felt the vibrations through his fingers and toes. Staring into Charlie's eyes, he wondered what to say. At last he managed, 'You should come and play a few numbers with my band.'

'That'd be great. I'd love that. What sort of things do you play?'

'Mostly original. A bit of distortion, a bit of attitude. You know, Iggy Pop?'

'Of course.'

'We're a little bit punk.'

'Fuck, that's what I want to play.'

William just smiled.

'I better not say that, eh?'

'Just make sure no one's listening.' And then, continuing to forget he was a teacher, he showed Charlie a few blues patterns he could play for solos.

Charlie had also forgotten it was a lesson. This was black and sticky, and rock'n'roll; it was a recording studio at three in the morning, a hotel room, a front bar – anywhere but school. He was no longer sitting beside his teacher. It was someone else all together. As he practised the box pattern, bending notes, hearing real attitude coming from his fingers for the first time – he forgot everything.

He was no longer wearing a uniform, a tie. He'd moved beyond linear equations and yard cards into a world of his own devising. There were no rules, no paths to stay on, no tenses to stick to – just a string of unremarkable sounds that followed each other into melody. He had no control over them. They seemed to have their own life.

They sang – ranging high and low, groaning, fading. This was a lesson that couldn't be taught. 'It's so simple, but it sounds so good.'

'Exactly. It's the blues – poor man's music.'

And he was back on the strings, obsessing.

William looked at the clock and noticed they'd gone fifteen minutes into lunch. Still, he didn't say a word. He played some chords and Charlie improvised over them. Half an hour later the lunch bell sounded and he said, 'Okay, that's it. I think we lost track of time.'

'Who cares?' Sliding his guitar into its case.

'Your mum might.' Realising his mistake. 'Or your dad.'

'He wouldn't care.'

'Yes, he would.'

But Charlie just looked at him and shook his head. 'Next Thursday?'

William extended his hand and Charlie shook it. 'Rock'n' roll.'

'Fuckin' eh,' the boy replied, grinning.

'It's just unlike you,' Damien Price said to his son, as they sat opposite each other in their living room.

'I didn't realise the time.'

'Well, he should've.'

Charlie had no reply. He just sat back with his feet on an old coffee table, staring at another dumb game show. At fourteen he'd already worked out that most people were stupid. Magazines provided ample proof: baby bumps, Malibu mansions and a thousand Barbie dolls lip-syncing their way through life. That wasn't the worst of it. At least they'd found a way of making money. It was the morons who paid to read about it. And here, more peanuts jumping around on the telly.

He watched the audience encourage the contestant. Yes, this is why there's rock'n'roll, he guessed. In the absence of revolution, anarchy or sensible people running things, a guitar, bass and drums would have to do.

'Tell him to sort it,' Damien Price said, picking a crumb from the corner of his mouth.

'It was my fault.'

'This goes on your record.'

'No, it doesn't.'

'It does. I'm not paying eight thousand a year …' He trailed off, and sat looking at the card in his hand:

LATE SLIP: Charlie Price

LESSON: Biology

YOU ARE TO REPORT TO STUDENT SERVICES, TUESDAY, 12.55, COLLECT GLOVES, BAG AND TONGS, FIND A YARD DUTY TEACHER AND COLLECT RUBBISH UNDER SUPERVISION FOR TWENTY MINUTES. FAILURE TO COMPLY WILL RESULT IN AN AFTER-SCHOOL DETENTION.

'What were you doing?' Damien asked.

'Practising.'

'Can you at least look at me when you talk?'

Charlie looked up. 'We were practising.'

'You must have heard the bell.'

'It's a soundproof room.'

'Bullshit.'

'Okay, bullshit, but it is.'

Damien sat forward. 'Watch your tone.'

Charlie watched an ad for an exercise machine. He looked at the male model and said, 'He shaves himself.'

Damien sank into his seat. The springs were gone, but there was no money for repairs. That's what Charlie didn't understand: there were a lot of other uses for eight thousand dollars – a stove with a working hot plate, rising damp in the bathroom. He knew there was no point nagging him. He didn't listen, and he certainly didn't hear. He called it Charlie's World. Charlie lived in Charlie's World. Unless there was something he wanted to hear.

Damien had his son's long face, but it had been pushed out by time. He had his blue eyes and arching brows, but his nose was flatter, finished with a few fine capillaries. He had the Price shoulders – flat, strong and mechanical where they attached to arms. His body was narrow, too, although he had a pot belly that doubled as a personal dining table. 'So, now you're stuck picking up papers.' Undoing his belt, loosening his tie and refolding the yellow card.

'You've gotta sign it.'

'And what if I don't?'

'I'll get an after-school detention.'

Charlie watched as his dad took a pen from the pocket of his Datsunland shirt. He looked at the cursive letters trailing across his chest: 'It's a World of Datsuns out there'.

And wankers, he thought.

Damien signed the card and flicked it across to him. 'So what else happened today?' Opening a can of beer.

'We're learning about mitosis.'

'What's that?'

'Cell division.'

Damien drank then wiped his mouth with the back of his hand. Disgusting, Charlie thought. Still, it wasn't as bad as the way he always hitched his pants, blew his nose into a handkerchief he refolded and pocketed, walked around the house in his undies, cut his toenails on the lounge, cleared his throat and spat in the garden. It wasn't as bad as the dumb game shows he watched, the way he called women *love* and *darls*, the way he unpicked his undies from his bum and said, 'Yes, too true', as he listened to shock jocks.

'Cells … like bacteria?' Damien asked.

'Yes.'

'And that's it?'

No reply.

'So that killed an hour. What about the rest of the day?'

'I dunno. Stuff.'

'Stuff?'

'Vectors, statistics … boring.'

Damien had no idea how to connect, to create some sort of spark. All that was required of him, it seemed, was silence, cash and food.

I could put you in a state school, he felt like saying, but didn't. His son was at Lindisfarne because his wife, Carol, had wanted him there. It was one of the last things she'd said to him. 'He's so handsome in a blazer, isn't he?'

Damien dropped his stare, following his son's leg down to the old rug. 'I got you pasta for lunch tomorrow.'

'Thanks.'

'You wanna do the crossword with me?'

'Not now, Dad. I do that stuff all day.' He stood and looked at the television.

'We gotta fix your hair, or there'll be another letter home.'

'They can't make me.'

'They can.'

'It's my hair.'

'It's their school.'

Charlie looked at the monkeys jumping around, clutching their oversized cheque.

'Perhaps Nicole will come over,' Damien said.

'You'd think they'd worry about other things.' He went into his bedroom and sat with his guitar on his lap. Then he tried to remember the box patterns William had showed him.

After tea he was back at it, and at eleven o'clock his father called out from his room, 'Put that damn thing away, and get to bed.'

So he switched off the light, and continued practising without plucking the strings.

Still, Damien could hear him. He said nothing. He spread a newspaper out across his bed and started searching the classifieds. He checked that all of his Datsunland ads had been put in correctly – a 2001 Toyota Camry, new tyres and low kilometres; a 1993 VP Commodore with reconditioned engine; a chirpy Volkswagen Golf, a couple of Corollas and a Nissan Skyline that was equal parts attitude and horsepower (he knew he'd have it sold before the end of the week – some nineteen-year-old with a pocketful of McDonald's money and two capped teeth).

He turned the page and started reading the death notices.

De Fazio, Simon. 1971-2010. Now you're in God's arms …

He remembered sitting on his bed with Carol as she read the notices aloud. He recalled saying, 'What do you read those for?' and her replying, 'They're sad.'

'You're morbid.'

He remembered thinking, All very nice, but what's it got to do with us?

Now he knew. Everyone ended up in the classifieds, one way or another – birth, marriage, food processors, death. It was just a matter of time. The classifieds brought people together. They were most people's most public moment – all that was left of a life that had seemed bigger and more promising.

He remembered how long it had taken him and Charlie to compose Carol's notice. How they'd agonised over every word. *Loved mother.* Although this couldn't begin to describe how they felt. Nonetheless, it would have to do. He still had the notice in a photo album somewhere. And the invoice from the paper, the same one he got every week in the mail at work: subtotals, units, rates, GST and the amount payable within fourteen days. So that even in, and despite, death, the economy kept moving.

He let his hand drop back onto his pillow. Pushed the paper off the bed, thought about switching on the radio but was asleep before he could decide.

William was waiting for Charlie when he arrived for his next lesson. He took him into the music suite's performance room – a space big enough to seat two hundred people, decorated with photos of everyone from Handel to Santana, smelling of a new carpet with the school's crest. He took him onto the stage and showed him the set-up – two stools, music stands and a pair of electric guitars plugged in to Marshall amps. 'Have a seat,' he said, indicating.

Charlie put down his bag and acoustic guitar and sat on one of the stools. Then he picked up a black Stratocaster copy.

'Go on,' William said. 'It's mine.'

Charlie laid the guitar across his knee. He turned up the volume and played a chord. The sound came out of the amp in shards, and William reached over to turn it down and switch pickups. Charlie tried again. 'Smooth.'

'Try the pedals.'

He looked at the pedals at his feet: distortion, reverberation and a little green box flashing with frequency shift. As he tested the sounds he grinned at William, who sat back contentedly, occasionally leaning over to adjust the effects. 'The distortion was the first one I bought. When I was sixteen.'

'Nice,' Charlie said, feeling the music through his feet. 'I've saved a hundred-and-fifty dollars – but I want to spend it on a decent guitar.'

'Good idea.' William picked up the other guitar and sat down. He took a moment to think, adjusted the volume and said, 'I tell you what – you save two hundred, I'll sell you that one.'

Charlie's face lit up. He moved the guitar around, felt the varnish on the neck and the roughness of the strings. 'It feels great.'

'It's a nice instrument. I mean, it's a copy, but not like the Korean shit … stuff, you get today.'

Charlie looked at the guitar, and then his teacher. 'Okay, deal.'

'It's got a case, cord and strap.'

He was already thinking of ways to save the money faster. He'd just thrown in a paper round, refusing to work in forty-degree heat for three cents a paper when Murdoch had billions. He could always ask his dad for a loan, but probably wouldn't get it for a guitar. Then there was his sister, Nicole, and her boyfriend, David, who'd already offered him a few loose joints.

Even bribery crossed his mind. *Dad, you'll never guess what Dave offered me.*

Charlie said, 'Please don't sell it to anyone else.'

'I've had it twenty years. I'm not in any rush.'

'Give me a few weeks.'

'Take your time.'

Soon William was fingerpicking some jazz chords and Charlie was playing his box patterns over the top. William watched how the boy had learnt to bend notes, flick his fingers off the strings, repeat phrases with minor variations and improvise melodies and riffs that were complete, sweet and singable. 'Very good,' he said, as they played. 'Maybe you won't be a Segovia.'

But Charlie was consumed, his eyes lost on the fretboard, his thoughts dissipating in a haze of blue notes, fade-outs and amplified fifths. He remembered the pedals. Went from one to the other, testing their effect on a lead break, lapping up the growl of fat chords. After a while he said, 'I suppose I better show you my scales.'

William shrugged. 'No, that's okay. As long as you're still practising them.'

'I am.'

'I can tell.'

Charlie hit the distortion pedal and played 'Smoke on the Water'. Then he said, 'I got a detention the other day.'

'Why?'

'Our last lesson … I was late for science.'

'We weren't that late.'

He leaned forward. 'It's this prick I've got. He locks the door at five past two and makes you wait outside. Then he lets you in, with his hand out.' He lifted his head and pouted his lips. '"Your diary, please, Mr Price. Perhaps next time you'll clean out your ears. I'd have thought a musician could hear a bell." Wanker.'

'And what about your dad?'

'Yeah, the usual speech.'

William tried to make light of it. 'Well, that's his job I suppose.'

'Apparently. Still, he doesn't go on about it.'

'He's a good dad?'

'He's okay … I guess.'

'You guess?'

'Yes, I guess, Mr English teacher.'

William adjusted his guitar on his knee. 'Well, you're lucky. My dad made me practise outside. Forty degrees, out you go – under the bloody peach tree. Half an hour a day, then he'd make me put it away. "This is why you're failing maths", he'd say. Which was probably true.'

'Dad doesn't mind. As long as I'm still getting A's.'

'All A's?'

'The stuff they give us isn't that hard. I know more geometry than my teacher. So, Dad expects it from me now.'

'He's a lucky dad.'

'Well, you know, I can't afford to lose another parent.'

William wondered if the boy was inviting him to ask, or whether it had just slipped out. 'And your mum died?'

'Shit happens.'

'Not when you're fourteen.'

'I was twelve.'

William knew he wasn't good at death. 'Do you miss her?'

Charlie licked his bottom lip. 'I was twelve.' He tried to remember her. He could still see the outline of her face – her long hair, brown eyes – but he was concerned about the detail. He knew she had freckles, but couldn't see them. And what were her eyebrows like – black, brown, did they finish short, or curl up on the ends? Was her neck long, and wasn't there a small mole towards the back? Were her lips smooth, or marked with light creases? He looked up. 'But you know, she bought me my first guitar.'

'When?'

'When I was little. One of the half-size numbers from Kmart. And I'd just strum it and sing. I have a video of it. It's awful.'

There was Damien, sitting on the lounge on Christmas morning, looking at his wife and shaking his head. 'What were you thinking?'

'Cheer up,' she was saying. 'He'll lose interest.'

'Bullshit.'

Charlie was a blond seven-year-old in summer pyjamas, swimming in a sea of wrapping paper, sticking his tongue out at the camera his sister was holding.

Back in the rehearsal room, Charlie reached down and turned off a pedal with his foot. 'She'd be happy, if I got good.'

They returned to their jam and before long slipped into a twelve-bar blues that soon transformed into a poorly croaked 'Hound Dog'. Charlie laughed at his teacher's voice, before taking a chorus himself. Then he stood, shaking his hips, sticking out his tongue, hammering at the strings and unsuccessfully attempting a fingertip solo on the fretboard. They became louder and faster until he ended up on his back turning circles on the carpet. William just watched, laughed. A marvel, he thought, seeing so much potential in front of him. What could be – smart, inventive, original. Before all the planning, scheming, wanting, thinking critically about how much a bridge could support or what drove Lady Macbeth, before girls, and women, before facial hair and man boobs and comments muttered when someone else got the promotion *he* deserved. Failing to see that there were other solutions. The correct path. The path of no regrets or suffering. The path that no fourteen-year-old in history had ever found among the undergrowth of the adult world.

Pete Ordon came in and they both stopped. A dozen or so new parents stood behind him and he said, 'This is Mr Dutton, our guitar teacher.'

William's lips zipped and his eyes bulged. He looked at Charlie. The boy broke up laughing and played one last chord.

Charlie, Nick and Aaron, a sort of Three Stooges combination, sat with their backs against a wall watching the Year Sevens and Eights play basketball. It was cloudy but warm, and the bit of drizzle that fell was dry before it wet anything. Charlie had just finished the sandwich he'd made that morning: tough fritz and spongy bread, allowed to sweat in Gladwrap and cook in his bag, crushed by textbooks.

'How can you eat that shit?' Nick asked.

'I've gotta make my own lunch. What have you got?'

'A Chickadee.' Displaying a deep-fried chicken portion that oozed fat from every crumbed pore.

'Why don't you buy something?' Aaron asked, struggling with a pie that was coming undone around the edges.

Charlie watched a pair of younger boys mucking around, pushing each other, until one of them said the wrong thing, or shoved or pulled too hard, and then they were exchanging blows. A few friends pulled them apart and there was a standoff. Aaron spat gristle from his mouth and called, 'Go on, get into it.'

Then it was over, and the boys continued their game as if nothing had happened. Soon they were passing the ball to each other and laughing.

'Pity,' Aaron mumbled.

Silence. Flies. Someone spitting. The sound of balls hitting hoops. A voice calling, 'Penis head!' Chip packets shoved into the cracks between the bricks of the wall.

'What's after lunch?' Aaron asked.

'Edwards,' Nick said.

'Fuck.'

'He's okay,' Charlie said.

'Yeah, blah blah, twenty minutes later he's told you what a carnivore is. *It eats meat!*'

Silence. Nick looked at Charlie. 'Let's see the letter.'

Charlie took the note from his pocket, unfolded it and handed it to him. The small, snotty boy started reading.

> Dear Mr Price,
> In reference to our recent discussion, I must say it is disappointing to see Charlie arrive at school today with an even more inappropriate haircut.

Nick and Aaron examined Charlie's hair more closely. Yes, the dreadlocks were gone, combed out into the usual peroxide frizz, hair sticking out in every direction but down, but in their place was an even more creative style, courtesy of his sister. She'd come over the previous evening, especially. Set him up in the backyard with a towel around his neck.

'You got in trouble for the dreads?' she'd said, connecting the trimmer to three short extension cords.

'So?' He'd rubbed his toes through the dead grass on their lawn. 'It's my hair.'

'Dad wants me to get rid of them.'

'You don't have to.'

'They'll suspend you.'

'They never suspend anyone.'

So there she was, as day turned to night, spraying and combing his hair, pulling at the knots as he ground his teeth, squinted and told her to be more fucking careful.

'Fighting words,' Dave had said, sitting on the porch rolling a cigarette.

'It fuckin' hurts.'

'Watch yer language, y' little prick,' his sister had said, slapping his shoulder.

'Go easy.'

'This letter, just said no dreads? Didn't say …?'

'What?'

'Something nice and short?'

'Not too short.'

She'd grinned, bit her tongue-ring and set to it. A few minutes later Charlie had looked at Dave and asked, 'What's she doing?' But he'd just smiled.

Ten minutes later she'd said, 'There, that'll do.' She'd handed him a mirror. He'd looked at himself and said, 'Fuck.'

She'd shaved the sides of his head almost clean. Then etched a lightning bolt into each of his temples, shaving down to bare skin to get sharp lines.

'What's wrong?' she'd asked.

'Now I will get suspended.'

'Bullshit.'

'Dad will freak.'

'No, it's fine. Short, clean and Catholic.'

'Fix it, come on.'

But she'd just folded her arms. So he'd taken the clippers, switched them on and had a go himself. 'Cow. You can tell Dad.'

'Fine.'

Luckily, Damien had stayed back at Datsunland for a sales meeting. When he'd got home he'd called out, 'Charlie, you in bed?'

'Yeah, I'm tired.'

'No more guitar then?'

The next morning he'd tried to wait until his dad left but couldn't draw it out. When he'd emerged from his hole, Damien had said, 'What the hell happened to you?'

'It was Nicole.'

And then there was the usual lecture about rules, respect and responsibility. 'This will go on your school record. One day you'll ask for a reference, and what are they gonna write?'

'She went stupid, I told her not to.'

Damien had stopped to think. 'It's the bloody boyfriend. Just you watch who you end up with.'

Nick and Aaron were laughing too. 'It looks shit,' Aaron said. 'You should've just left it.'

'My sister's a bitch.'

Aaron ran his fingers through the stubble. 'At least if you'd left it you coulda got some street cred – told people your dad was a Fink.'

Is this the best I can do for friends? Charlie thought. He looked at Aaron, licking meat from his fingers, swatting a fly and wiping his nose along his forearm. 'What did you get for the geometry test?'

'D, I think.'

No, there wasn't much to be said, or learned beside the basketball court, he guessed. Just more of the same – balls through hoops, sweat, comments about Mrs O'Brien's cleavage (visions of her leaning over to check their spelling), banana skins softening on hot concrete, untucked shirts and red cheeks. He stood and gathered his books.

'Where y' goin'?' Nick asked.

'The library.'

'Why?'

But he didn't answer, sauntering across the patched bitumen, dragging his feet, his shoulders drooped, his back bent. He made his way to his locker and dumped his books inside. There were five German soldiers climbing the walls: the beginning and end product of a father-son model-making phase.

Twenty minutes later he was sitting alone in the library, staring into a monitor, studying the lyrics of Xavier Rudd. William had played him a few of his songs, and he was hooked – the rhythm, the untamed hair; words that were angry in the nicest possible way; a man at peace with the patch of earth he'd been plonked down on, with whatever god had put him there, and the prospects of a musical life.

Xavier Rudd. Yes, he'd buy the album. Or, alternatively, put the money towards his new guitar.

He was surrounded by half a dozen groups of chess-playing geeks. He studied their pimples, and steady hands, and wondered where he really belonged in the Lindisfarne scheme-of-things.

William and Charlie ran down Ferngrove Street in the rain. Covered their heads with their guitars, skipping to avoid puddles, hitching their backpacks and laughing. 'Shit,' William said. 'All of my music will be wet.'

'Run!' Charlie shouted, charging across a driveway, narrowly avoiding a reversing car.

They finally arrived on the porch of number fifty – a rental warhorse with dirt for lawn and weeds for a garden. The landlord had supplied the guts of an old washer and a cut-down 44-gallon drum as a plant pot. The iron fence had come away from its posts, although someone had tried to repair it with wire. There were remnants of a concrete path and a hole filled with cracked plastic where someone had once put a pond.

Charlie shook what hair he had and the spray caught William in the face. They entered a hallway cluttered with unpacked boxes, an ironing board (still in its plastic), soccer balls and tennis racquets. There were piles of books that rose like crankshafts from the carpet, folders full of yellowing lecture notes, a box full of chipped Buddhas and even a wetsuit and skis. William opened a linen-press, took out a towel and handed it to Charlie, who knelt down to dry his guitar case.

'Should you dry yourself first?'

He wiped his face.

'Do you want dry clothes?'

'I suppose.'

'Well, it's better than I guess, I suppose.'

William creaked across the floorboards, into his room. He closed the door, stripped off and changed into an old business shirt and shorts. Then he opened a drawer and found a clean T-shirt and shorts for Charlie. When he returned the boy had dried both guitars, standing them up against the hallway wall.

'There you go,' he said, handing him the clothes. 'Bathroom's there.' He indicated.

He went into the lounge room, collapsing onto a vinyl sofa. Sorted through a pile of CDs on the floor, looking for his latest Nimrod's Cat demo. When he looked up – out of the room and across the hallway, through a gap in the bathroom door – he saw Charlie standing in his shorts, drying his long, brown legs. He stopped to ask himself what he was doing. Wasn't this breaking some rule? Something in the fine print of his registration documents? Something about familiarity, decency, duty-of-care?

Charlie had been his last student for the day. He would've had to dismiss him at 3.25 anyway. There were only so many times you could play scales, and studies, and poxy little folk songs about maidens in meadows fair. Music became stale, and that's when kids lost interest.

So, he'd thought, why not take him home and show him my guitars? What's the harm? I'm the teacher. In *loco parentis*. And I could hardly bring my whole collection to school.

Still, he was sure he was doing something wrong. He'd gone through life with this feeling. That he'd forgotten an exam, missed his mum's birthday, shrugged once too often or looked uninterested.

Charlie came into the room and stood barefoot in front of him. William looked at his flat feet and asked, 'Drink?'

'No, thanks.'

'Here it is.'

He produced a CD with a plain cover. Someone had listed the names of the tracks in a small, blue scrawl.

1. The Spider Revolution (Dutton and Fraser)
2. Me (Dutton and Fraser)
3. The Day before Yesterday (Dutton and Fraser)

He loaded the CD into a disc player. Charlie took the cover and read it. 'Who's Fraser?'

'An old friend. Bass. Not that he can play beyond the first three frets. And not that he actually writes the songs – but it keeps him happy.'

The music started. Loud. Distorted. Thrashed out in major and seventh chords. Driven by a simple bass line and frenetic drums.

Charlie sat on the lounge and listened to his teacher's singing.

> Here, coming out of the sky
> There are moons and stars and plastic forks
> Brides with their hair on fire
> And postmen on zimmer frames.

More guitar, more smashing cymbals and a buzz-saw riff. Charlie started playing it in the air, biting his lip. 'What's a zimmer frame?'

William held out his hands and attempted to look frail. 'You know, the thing old people have.'

'What's the song mean?'

'What's it matter? It's rock'n'roll.'

Charlie laid back and looked at the ceiling. Rock'n'roll, he thought, trying to imagine a postman with a zimmer frame.

Here, coming out of the ground
There's holes and steel and plastic pipe
Boys with their arse on fire
And firemen with cobblestones.

It's a Spider Revolution
Coming out of the sky
Spider Revolution.

Charlie's first reaction was dumb, dumb, dumb, but then he looked at William and said, 'Rock'n'roll?'

'Well, it's bound to annoy someone.'

'Which is good?'

'Isn't it?'

'I think.'

William sat forward. 'Charlie Price, where's the rage?'

'The rage?'

'School detentions ... this is how you get back.'

'"Firemen with cobblestones"?'

'Okay, bad example. But what about the cruise ship that just docked? A quarter of a million dollars for a ticket. Meanwhile, half the planet starves. See, rage.'

'But you didn't write about a cruise ship.'

'I should've.'

'You didn't.'

'I might.'

'You didn't.' Charlie didn't even grin. 'Anyway, cruise ships don't piss me off.'

'What does?'

'Biology teachers.'

'There's your first song.'

'What, "Fuck off, Biology teacher"?'

'Why not? Only, don't tell anyone I suggested it.'

Charlie smiled. 'Yeah, Mr Attitude, *don't tell anyone I suggested it.*'

William moved across and took him around the neck. He tapped him on the head a few times and said, 'Hello, anyone home?'

Charlie was laughing. 'Get off.'

'"Fuck off, Biology teacher" ... the headmaster would love to hear me play that one.'

'You're gutless.'

'I'm forty. You're fourteen. You write it. You sing it.'

Charlie pulled himself free. 'I will then.'

William looked at him, and believed him. 'Well, just be careful.'

'Why? Scared?'

'Be careful.'

'"Firemen with cobblestones" ...'

William was torn. There was no denying it, twenty years did make a difference – between what you thought, and what you said; between poems scribbled in the Ab-Flexor hours and words left unwritten; between lifted eyebrows, head shakes and mumbled comments, and diplomacy. It seemed that growing up was about packing things away in your head. Reaching compromises with yourself. Watering yourself down. And no amount of pretending, of cryptic lyrics or catchy riffs, could change that.

The second song started slow, decorated with fingerpicked guitar.

> Me
> All of the bits that you see
> The broken glass and torn shirts
> The remains of the years, blown away
> The tears
> Sitting forgotten beside gas bills, and old shoes, and love.

'They're your words too?' Charlie asked.

'My attempt at poetry.'

'No … it's good.'

Me
Nothing left to see
With the best bits taken away
Brushed from the skin like a sting
The years
Emptied of someone I love, her smile, her hair in my eyes.

Charlie listened as the guitar improvised. William looked across at him. 'It's hard to get the words right.'

'Is it about someone?'

'No.'

'I bet it is.'

And the final chorus.

The years
Emptied of someone I love, her smile, her hair in my eyes.

More quiet arpeggios. Then Charlie said, 'That's it. I leave school, write songs, change the world.'

'That's the tricky bit. I tried.'

'Just gotta be honest, say what you think.'

'Which is?'

'That I'm surrounded by fuckwits.'

'For now. Later, you don't have to put up with them. And you meet other people … people you recognise.'

'And I get to leave Datsunland?'

William said, 'Shit, I forgot why I brought you here.' He led Charlie into a back room, switched on a light and said, 'Welcome to Axe World.' A dozen or so guitars on stands, amplifiers of different shapes and sizes, posters of Frank Zappa, Santana and Segovia. 'Well, what do you think?'

Charlie ran his hand over an old Telecaster. 'How did you afford all these?'

'They just sort of … appeared. Supplied by the guitar fairies. If you have enough they breed.'

William explained his collection: a pair of resonator guitars – one wooden and one aluminium-bodied; acoustics – nylon and steel-stringed; two basses; Stratocaster copies; a Telecaster; a mandolin; a ukulele; and the pride of his collection – a black Les Paul from the 1960s. 'The real thing,' he promised. 'This would set you back fifteen thousand now, but I got it from a pawnbroker for two hundred. See, you gotta keep your eyes open.'

Charlie felt the Les Paul's varnished wood.

'Go on.'

He sat on the floor with the guitar in his lap, plugged it in and switched on the amp. Played a single chord. 'What a sound.'

'Try the pickups.'

He switched from one to two to three pickups and tried again. 'Sure you won't sell me this one?'

An hour later they were still there – Charlie sampling the guitars, improvising and starting spontaneous jams with his teacher. Eventually he looked at his watch and said, 'Shit, not again.' He stood.

'Wait,' William said, picking up the black Strat copy he'd promised. He put it in its case and said, 'You may as well take it now. It's just sitting here. You could be playing it.'

'What about the money?'

'When you're ready.'

He threw a cord in with the guitar and presented it along with a small practice amp. 'There, can you carry it all?'

'I'll try.'

Later that evening, Charlie was dry. Still wearing his teacher's T-shirt, and now, a pair of Fred Flintstone boxer shorts and woollen socks with holes for the toes. He had his feet on a coffee table covered with junk mail. His acoustic guitar nestled in his lap – its veneer scratched where he'd tried to fit screws for a strap. As he sat cocooned in his chair, his shoulders slouched, his head drooped, the guitar seemed to become part of his body – an extra, clumsy limb that moved in time with his torso.

'Go on then,' Nicole said, pulling stringy cheese from her toast.

'What do you want to hear?'

'What do you know?' Dave said.

Charlie started fingerpicking a sequence of broken chords he'd learnt from William. Some of the bass notes were wrong and he acknowledged this with a shake of his head. Then he stopped.

'Keep going, it's good,' Dave said.

'I just worked it out.'

'You're really getting into it, eh?'

'It's hard to put it down.' He worked on a difficult chord. 'And it's good when you come up with something.'

'But getting good's only half of it,' Dave said. 'Then you gotta be able to sell yourself. So, start with friends.'

'We're not gonna laugh,' his sister added, kicking his leg.

'Doesn't bother me.'

'Go on then.'

This time he started with full chords, played to a strong rhythm. He sat up, his back straightened and the music became louder, cleaner, driven. Then he was singing Xavier Rudd's 'Messages', his eyes drifting across the carpet, his licked lips and bitten tongue gone, his flat feet tapping as a toe emerged from its hole with a long, crooked nail.

His body started to rock and, although he was tall and lanky, there was a measure, a sense of proportion, a pulse – movements that went beyond the awkwardness of his fingering and timing. There was an inner music, and he was following it – not in any thought out way, but a learning-to-crawl, walk and run way.

Charlie was a boy who listened and learned, observed and imitated, mastered and excelled at nearly everything he set his mind to. That's why Damien knew he was the luckiest father alive – why he never really worried about Charlie's future. He was a set-and-forget sort of kid, a teenage crockpot, an aspidistra that kept growing in a dark corner. He'd watched his son's temperament develop. As he became serious and smart, funny and ironic, and with this, slightly superior (without saying as much). He'd watched his will harden, so that when he decided to win, he would win. If he decided to give he would empty his pockets, and heart, of everything. If he decided to daydream he would invent other worlds and if he decided to love, he would walk across hot coals to share whispered thoughts.

He stopped playing.

'Fantastic,' Dave said, wiping crumbs from his attempt at a beard. 'Does your little group play that one?'

'No, they just want to hammer the same three chords.'

Nicole was smiling her look-at-little-brother smile. 'Has anyone else heard you?'

'No.'

'Dad?'

'What do you think?'

'Well, if he heard that he might be more interested.'

He couldn't see it. 'I don't think so.'

'Bullshit,' Dave said. 'You got it all, buddy, except one thing.'

'What?'

'In yer face. You gotta learn to say, Here it is, like it or lump it.'

'Na, people make up their minds.'

'People are fucked in the head. They're told to like Adele and they do. They're told to watch *MasterChef*. You gotta be there, right in their face.'

'That's not me.'

'It's not anyone. You gotta make yourself.'

Charlie stopped to think. Dave was probably right.

Breasts on a billboard, that's what William said. That's what it took to get ahead in music – breasts on a billboard. And for the rest there were a hundred half-empty pubs, ringing ears and work on Monday. You could always find a gimmick – eighteen earrings and pasted-on attitude – or else there was an eternity of Motown revivals. But, Charlie guessed, the only real choice was to be honest and say, This is me, these are the chords I pluck and the words I sing. 'Xavier Rudd, he's good,' he said.

'Yeah, but he's out there,' Dave said.

'So am I.'

'No, you're in here.'

'It's early days.'

'You have to play that for Dad,' Nicole said.

'It's not his thing.'

'What is then?'

'Trade-ins.'

'Bullshit. Have you played that for anyone else?'

'Once.'

'When?'

He stopped to remember the afternoon on the tennis courts. A few friends were playing and he was sitting in the shade, serenading them. Then a small group of girls in their early teens approached. By the time he saw them it was too late to stop – so he cut his losses and fingerpicked a few simple chords he couldn't stuff up. He diverted attention by watching the tennis, calling out comments.

But there they were, gathered around him, sitting down on the concrete. 'Do you know any Coldplay?'

'I don't play pop.'

'What *do* you play?'

'Hard rock … grunge.'

'Go on then.'

He reluctantly played a few bars of 'In Bloom', but then stopped and said, 'I can't play that stuff on an acoustic.'

'What about Taylor Swift?' a girl asked.

'Fuck.'

Back in his lounge room, Charlie looked at Dave and said, 'I couldn't get rid of them.'

'So what did you do?'

'I packed up and came home.'

'Why?' his sister said. 'All those girls?'

'So?'

Nicole shook her head. 'You should've asked one of them to meet you at the Plaza on Saturday.'

He played a series of harmonics across the bridge of his guitar. 'Twelve year olds?'

'So, you gotta start somewhere.'

'No, thanks.'

She grinned. 'Charlie Price?'

'What?'

'There's no special lady in your life?'

He turned red and threw a cushion at her. 'What about you?'

She grabbed Dave's arm. 'I've got my man.' They kissed.

'Do you mind?'

'I bet there's someone.'

'I go to a boys' school.'

'All the more reason. What about that friend of Dad's … his daughter?'

'Fuck off. Just cos you started early.'

'What?'

'That kid from Magill.'

She moved towards him. 'Yeah, so what do you reckon – '

'You're the expert.'

'What?'

'That day Mum came home, and you two were in your room, and she couldn't get you out.'

Nicole sat back and remembered, eventually sniffing and wiping her nose on the back of her hand. 'I reckon you saw that in some movie.'

'I remember.'

'And so what if we did?'

Charlie knew there was no point arguing with his sister, so he started playing again. He picked and strummed the chords he'd already worked out for William's 'Me'. There was a descending bass – long notes underscoring a melody all loss and indecision.

The first thing he'd done when he arrived home was put William's demo into his disc player, tune his guitar and start playing along. He soon had the melody in his head, and then the words, and the feelings behind them.

Neat, he'd thought, that even a teacher could come up with something so effective. Which proved that music was within his grasp – and maybe that William, this unshaved, foul-mouthed excuse for a teacher, was someone far more than just report cards and scales, impatient eyes and the tedium of a thousand 'Streets of London'.

Me
All of the bits that you see
The broken glass and torn shirts
The remains of the years, blown away.

Nicole could hear the longing in his voice. He's calling for Mum, she guessed.

As he had for the weeks and months after she died, as he lay awake in bed, eventually turning over and burying his head in his pillow.

Some nights it was tears, others loneliness, a catalogue of practical matters he'd now have to deal with himself. Who would be there, talking to the mums at school pick-up, or organising the notes on the fridge so he got to football on time? There were buttons that would never get sewn on and problems that would never get explained (such as why his aunt and uncle had separate beds). Who would cook his favourite chow mein and polish his shoes?

Nicole was still living at home at the time and she'd come into his room and crawl into bed next to him. 'You okay?'

'Fine.' Turning towards the wall.

'You better get to sleep,' she'd say, choosing to avoid the mud they'd already waded through a hundred times.

Months later, the longing was still there, as was his father, standing in the hallway at one am, his hands on his hips. 'Charlie, just close your eyes and get to sleep.'

The tears
Sitting forgotten beside gas bills, and old shoes, and love.

Which was the image Nicole had of Damien, towards the end of their mother's illness, as he sat at night at the dining table surrounded by accounts, unfinished homework, X-rays. She would try to talk to him, but he'd only ever mumble, and return to his pink and yellow forms.

'Come on', Charlie, she'd say, and they'd go out into the backyard.

Carol was there, sitting in a plastic chair in a ring of camellias, staring at the grass. She'd look up, smile and reach into the pocket of her dressing gown.

'There,' she'd say, handing them a ten-dollar note.

Moments later, Nicole would have the pool ladder over the back fence and they'd escape down the laneway and around the corner to Nick's fish shop.

Once, coming back over the fence, Charlie slipped and cut his leg on the galvanised iron. And although she was sick, Carol came running.

It wasn't so bad, and soon all three of them were sitting on the grass eating vinegar-soaked chips.

The sort of shit you remember, Nicole guessed.

But this memory wasn't so much in the words as the music, in the chords as the falter in her brother's voice. There was nothing either of them could say that hadn't been said.

Damien came in and stood looking at them. 'Go on,' he said, as Charlie slid the guitar between his knees.

'Go on,' Nicole insisted.

Damien dropped his keys in the ashtray on the coffee table and sat down. 'Know any Neil Sedaka?'

'No. It's one of Mr Dutton's songs.'

'Mr Dutton? The musical guru?'

'He plays in a band.'

And then Charlie realised he was wearing his teacher's T-shirt.

'Something soothing,' Damien said. 'I haven't sold a car in three days.'

Charlie continued, avoiding his father's eyes.

> Me
> Nothing left to see
> With the best bits taken away
> Brushed from the skin like a sting
> The years
> Emptied of someone I love.

He slowed, realising, lapsing into a round of fingerpicking and hummed melody.

Damien looked at Nicole. He's good, he said with his eyes.

Someone I love, that's what he said, Damien thought. Which, he guessed, was a Neil Sedaka sort of thing. He waited for his son to clarify this but there were no more words. Just someone. Mr Dutton's someone. 'That's very sad,' he said, when his son had finished.

'No, not sad, it's beautiful,' Nicole said, wiping the last of the crumbs from her top.

'Nice,' Dave said.

Damien was studying his son's face. 'Who's it about?'

'I dunno, these sort of things are generic.'

'Generic?'

'Anyone, everyone.'

Dave sat forward. 'Play the Rudd, Charlie.'

'No.'

'Go on.'

So he sat up and tried again. The rhythm started slow, but then took care of itself. Nicole and Dave sang along and Damien tapped the beat on his polyester slacks. No denying it, he thought, as he sat back in the lounge – this boy's a marvel, a proper little jukebox. Maybe there's a few quid to be made somewhere: a couple of weeks on *The Voice*, Carols by Candlelight, Hi-5 or the classical set.

Charlie looked at his father and saw the hint of a smile, and found the will to keep going, to struggle with the last verse.

Half an hour later, Charlie was sitting in his room, sprawled across a bed that hadn't been made for weeks, scribbling chords on manuscript paper. Occasionally he'd look up at the few posters tacked to the walls – stripped-down Chili Peppers, a Bavarian landscape his mother had put up, Hare Krishnas in a shopping mall, Ian Thorpe with a sharpened arrow drawn through his head, and a photo of Heinrich Himmler to remind him of school.

He could hear his father, sister and the boyfriend in the lounge room. Long pauses. Someone rustling paper, then Nicole reading.

On September three, two years ago to the day since you went away. And yet there's never more than an hour or two goes by that we don't think about you. Around the table, you're still here, and every time we have scones, we think of how yours were the best.

And his dad, in his gruffest, no-nonsense tone. 'What have scones got to do with it?'

'I was trying to personalise it. I hate all that *forever remembered* bullshit.'

There was a long pause, maybe as Damien read. Then, 'How much will this cost?'

'We want to pay.'

'It's about eight dollars a line.'

'Not that much.'

'For a Saturday ad – '

'Dad! We don't care about the money.'

'It's money you can use for other things.'

'It's for Mum.'

'She'd agree with me.'

'It's not the point.'

Charlie looked up at a crack in the mortar, and studied it. He could guess why his dad had fallen silent. The usual response. According to his father, you just had to get on with life. Otherwise it would turn into a soap opera. There was a photo on the telly, and of course you could talk about the way she laughed, or used gallons of spray to kill flies, or never changed a toilet roll. Real things. Solid things.

But there was no point going on all night, or too often.

He heard his dad say, 'You're determined?'

'Yes.'

'Well, let me pay half.'

'No, we want to pay, Dad.'

Charlie couldn't hate his dad for this. After all, he was no more demonstrative himself. He looked at his new song, the piece he'd promised William – an ode to every foul-breathed science teacher on the planet. It was a string of words stuck together with attitude – half-thought-out feelings that described some mostly imagined angst. But that was okay. It was rock'n'roll, and allowances could be made. He picked up his new guitar, plugged it into the amp and switched it on. There was a hum, and he adjusted the volume. Then he started playing the sequence of chords he'd come up with.

He followed his chart carefully. Yes, he was interested in his words, but this performance was more about introducing his new axe to his dad.

Instead, there was Damien, standing in the doorway. 'Where'd you get that?'

'I'm buying it.'

'Buying, or bought?'

Charlie knew it wasn't sounding good. 'Mr Dutton was selling it, and he gave me a good price.' He played a riff, high up on the fret-board, as if this might help his cause.

'So you still owe him for it?'

'A bit.'

'What's a bit?'

'Thirty bucks.'

'D'you think you should've asked me first?'

'I got it cheap. If I'd bought this in a shop ...'

'You've already got a guitar.'

'An acoustic.'

Charlie watched his dad waiting, thinking, biting his bottom lip, each of his thoughts advancing and retreating.

'Mr Dutton asked you if you wanted it?'

'Yes, when I went to his ...' He stopped, teetering on the edge, trying to think of other ways to justify a guitar. 'It's not gonna affect my grades.'

'I didn't say it would.'

'It's a hobby.'

'How much was it?'

And they were off, on a discussion of money – learning to save, part-time jobs, setting goals: a car, uni fees (yes, if you set your mind to it, you could be a doctor), a flat, an investment property (fella at work, his son's nineteen, he rents out three places), a holiday (you and me, we could go to the Gold Coast). 'My point is,' he said, 'just cos you got it doesn't mean you have to spend it.'

'What do I buy?'

'Look at me, I haven't sold a car for two weeks.'

'You just said three days.'

'Closer to two weeks. And don't be smart. If there are no sales, there are no school fees.'

'What's that got to do with a guitar?'

Damien pointed at his son. 'Listen …'

Nicole was in the hallway. 'Dad.'

'What?'

'Come here a minute.'

As he stared at his son. 'You can give it back.'

Charlie sat up. 'Why?'

'If you want a guitar, ask me. We'll get you one for Christmas.'

'That's another three months.'

'So?'

'He's letting me have this one.'

'It'll still be there.'

'Dad!' Nicole called.

'What?'

She took him by the arm, and led him back to the lounge room. Then she sat him down and said, 'Calm down.'

'Him telling me …'

'Calm down.' She sat beside him. 'It's what he needs.'

'It's not the point.'

'He likes it, and he's good.'

'He can't just go spend hundreds of dollars. He needs a new blazer.'

'Kids don't care about blazers,' Dave said.

'Well, they bloody well should. If he wants he can always go to a state school.'

I don't care, Charlie wanted to call out, as he sat listening in his room. I never asked to be sent there. Jesus and first fucking XI cricket. So, pull me out, if that's all that matters.

He turned to see himself in the mirror, and looked away. Breathed deeply, and then cracked the knuckles of his left hand. Wait, he told himself. Wait. He knew that when his father settled things would be okay. And Nicole, she could steer him around, in the same way Carol could.

Charlie heard his sister say, 'How about, instead of putting this in the paper, we help him with his guitar?'

'No, you wanna do that, you do it.'

There was a long pause.

'Well?' she asked.

'He can keep his guitar. It's just, he's got no bloody concept of the value of money.'

'He's fourteen.'

'That's old enough.'

'It's self-expression,' Dave said. 'These are the angst years, Mr P. Remember?'

'I was already running bets when I was fourteen.'

Nicole held her father's knee. 'Dad, you shouldn't expect too much too soon.'

Later that night, Damien went into his son's room. 'Sometimes, Chucky-boy,' he said, sitting on his bed, 'you have a way of ...'

'Pissing you off?'

224

'Yes.'

'It's just that it was cheap.'

Damien looked at the scar on his son's leg. 'I know. If you like, you stick with it. But get good.'

'I want to.'

'Treat it like a violin. You wanna be in an orchestra, you gotta take it seriously.' Then he thought, If nothing else, it beats selling cars. 'Still, I'd rather you be an engineer. I heard those fellas in the mines make a hundred and fifty, a hundred and eighty a year. And you've got the brains for that. You *know* you've got the brains.'

'That might be okay too.'

'More than okay. You don't want to end up selling cars.'

'Why not?'

'Why not? Christ.' He let his head drop.

'I'd be an engineer, if it interested me.'

'And have your band on the side?'

Charlie waited, looking at, but avoiding, his father. 'But you still like your job, don't you?'

'It's just what you get used to.'

No, not good enough, Charlie thought. Not when every day you get up and shower, pull on your pants, your shirt, your tie, your socks – forty years of pulling on your socks.

'The thing is, they just keep sending those bills,' Damien said. 'And engineers, that doesn't bother them at all, but the guy that works at Datsunland ...'

Charlie looked at his new guitar, leaning against the wall. 'So I can keep it?'

Damien finished the last of a chalky finger bun and sipped sweet tea as he thought about a weekend already spoken for – lawns and a blocked gutter, shopping, a tyre to be changed on Nicole's car (since the boyfriend had no idea how to do it). There would be a constant battle with Charlie – to get him out of bed, motivated, working on something apart from songs. He walked down the hallway, opened the door to his son's room and went inside. 'What a bloody disaster.'

Charlie turned to face the wall.

'You can deal with this today. Okay?'

He produced a sound that wasn't quite a word.

'Okay?'

'Okay.'

Damien turned on the light and started gathering clothes from the floor – a tie, shorts and seventy-five-dollar school shirt. 'The laundry's two doors away.'

No reply.

Socks – grey turned brown, embedded in the carpet – and at the bottom of the pile, his blazer. 'You could at least hang this up.'

'Sorry.'

Damien picked it up, brushed it off and sniffed the air. 'What's that?'

It only took a moment for Charlie to remember. He'd gone onto the main oval to play soccer, but lost interest. Seen a few friends sitting under the scoreboard, staring at him, grinning. He'd wandered over and asked, 'What's up?'

'Sit down, Chucky,' one of them had said.

He had. The boy had looked around, and then at him, before producing a half-smoked cigarette. 'Go on.'

Charlie had scanned the oval and stopped to think. 'You'll get suspended.'

'No one's ever been suspended. Go on.'

He'd looked at the cigarette – red-tipped, glowing and whispering his name. Come on, it said. One puff, no obligations. If I'm not as good as you think – stand up, walk away. But if I am … You'll be joining our little group, Charlie. Don't you want to?

He'd taken the cigarette. Wanted to try it more than anything in the world. But like Mr Keane had said, for every action there was an equal and opposite reaction. It was a law of physics – you couldn't get away with anything. Someone was always watching, writing in the detention book, asking for your planner and saying, Your parents will need to sign this.

'Go on,' the boys had urged. 'It's burning down.'

Back in the bedroom, Damien was sniffing the blazer. 'You haven't been smoking?'

Charlie could feel the morning cold on his chest and fastened a single button on his pyjama top. 'I sat with these kids at lunch and one of them got out a pack.'

Damien just waited. More bad news. Shit he'd have to deal with, behaviour he'd have to explain, plead, all the time wondering what the hell was happening in his son's head.

'Dad, that's the last thing I'd do. You get suspended. I'm not that stupid.'

'Well, you must be, you were sitting with them.'

'It's not so easy, just to get up and leave.'

Damien smelled the blazer again. 'It's bloody easy. That's what you've got legs for. If they suspend one, they'll suspend you all. What else would you be there for?'

'Just sitting.'

'Is that what a teacher would think?'

'I dunno … yes … no.'

Damien was looking for eye contact, but Charlie was studying stickers peeling from his wardrobe door. 'What?'

'That's the truth?'

'Of course.'

'I know some experiment. But others …'

'What, now I'm taking drugs?'

'I didn't say that. Even fags, that'll go on your record.'

'I'm not stupid, Dad.'

Damien guessed his son was telling the truth. He threw the blazer in his lap. 'You better hang it out to air. Smells like you've been in a pub.'

'I'll pick up my clothes.'

'I'll be on a pension if I wait for you.' He picked up the T-shirt William had provided on the day of the rainstorm visit. 'This isn't yours?'

'Let's see.'

'It's an adult's.'

Charlie searched for a story, but nothing came to mind. 'It's Mr Dutton's.'

'Why have you got it?'

'He lent it to me … when my shirt got wet.'

'When was that?'

He explained, and when he'd finished Damien asked, 'What, he asked you there?'

'Yeah, so I could see his guitars.'

'And this was when you were meant to be having a lesson?'

'Yes.'

'An eighteen-dollar lesson?'

'It's all part of it, Dad.'

'I wouldn't have thought.' He looked down at his faded moccasins. 'That man's not a bit … strange?'

'How do you mean?'

'You just looked at his guitars?'

'Yes.'

Damien waited. 'Well, I tell you, he's not meant to do that.'

'Why?'

'There are reasons.'

'What?'

'Don't you mind. He asks again, you say no.'

'Why?'

'Cos I said so, that's why. And the law says so.'

Charlie couldn't see the problem. 'He's okay.'

'Was someone else there?'

'No.'

'That's the problem. Supposing something had happened?'

Charlie wasn't stupid. Years of evening meals had been eaten and homework completed to a soundtrack of current affairs programs. Dodgy developers, loan sharks and thirty-day diets had competed for time with slightly bent trigonometry teachers and Little Athletics coaches. Much had been hinted, but little described in detail, in the six-thirty timeslot. Nonetheless, it didn't take much imagination.

Charlie didn't always reveal the full scope of his understanding to his father. He'd learnt to pace himself, release information sparingly, and even to act. Nothing melodramatic, just a shrug here and there, a look of surprise, a sudden lapse of memory

'You tell him, Dad's paying for lessons, at school.'

'Okay.'

'A teacher should realise these things.'

'He does, but it was just ...' There was no point arguing. 'Okay, I'll tell him.'

'You just played his guitars?'

'Yes.'

As he loaded the powder and clothes in the washing machine, Damien wondered whether he should speak to someone. Guru Dutton seemed to be becoming a strange presence in his son's life.

Charlie's smart, he told himself. He saw him reading the *Australian* for hours, watching documentaries about deep space and studying stray textbooks he'd found in labs. He'd ask questions about vectors and what Mormons believed, the cause of King George's madness and how many shillings and pence made a pound. But Damien wasn't sure if smart meant savvy.

Charlie slipped down into the yellow seat cover.

This, he thought, is the worst moment of my life.

He studied the three-foot fibreglass chicken head on their bonnet. 'Drop me around the corner,' he said to his dad.

'Don't you want to show your mates?'

'Not particularly.'

The chicken car had arrived at Datsunland as a trade-in. A yellow Volkswagen with wings painted on the side, blood red hackles dangling from the doors and a plastic beak wired to the grille. 'Charlie's Chicken Feast' (in the shape of bones) on the side of a pair of drumsticks bolted onto the roof. 'Just here,' Charlie said.

'It's too far to walk.'

'No, it's not.'

It wasn't the first bizarre trade-in Damien had brought home. There'd been a rib delivery Cowasaki (a motorbike with a cow's head and tail) and a Disco Festiva with shag carpet, mirror ball, strobe lighting and a turntable connected to a boom-box in the boot.

Damien pulled over and Charlie got out with his guitar. He looked around, but luckily the street was deserted. 'Are you bringing it home again?'

'Of course. I might even keep it.'

'You're kidding?'

'Why not?'

Charlie knew his dad was joking. He was rubbish at hiding things: his smile, the tongue in the side of his mouth.

'Thanks for the lift.' He closed the door and stepped away from the chicken car before anyone noticed. Walked the extra block to school and arrived late. Then went straight to the music suite for his lesson.

William was waiting. 'Late night?'

'No, I had to walk,' he explained. 'Dad has this chicken car.' He told the story of how Damien had arrived home the previous evening, sounding his Dixie horn; how he'd taken him for a drive, waving to neighbours and friends and saying, 'It smells like KFC.'

Charlie sat in a sweaty chair, opened his bag and produced William's shorts and T-shirt – freshly ironed, folded, smelling like lemons. 'Dad did them,' he said, placing them on the table.

William's face drained of blood. He took a moment to study the razor-sharp folds and asked, 'Your dad?'

'Yeah.'

'So, you mentioned your visit?'

'Of course.'

'I suppose I better teach you something.' He opened his book of scales and flattened the pages on the music stand. 'Should we make a start?'

'I guess.'

'You're still guessing?'

Charlie took out his guitar and threw the vinyl bag aside. 'Thanks for showing me your guitars.'

'No problem. Now, D major, two sharps – all the way up to the tenth fret. Off you go.'

Charlie looked at the music and started playing. He could feel William's eyes on his hands and fingers. He made a mistake and stopped, looked up and smiled.

'Don't stop every time you make a mistake.'

There was something missing from his teacher's voice, and he felt flat, disappointed. 'Usually I don't.'

'Most of the time people won't notice. It's called bluffing.'

'Are you good at that?'

'Apparently.'

He started again. Finished D major and moved on to A and E – pages and pages of scales. Finally, he asked, 'Is that enough?'

'Believe it or not, this is about the most important thing I can teach you.'

'No, it's not.'

'It is.'

That's not what you said before, he wanted to say. What happened to rock'n'roll, in your face?

'Right, "The Ash Grove",' William said, opening another book.

'Is there something wrong?'

'We've been wasting too much time.'

'It's not a waste. I've been practising these pieces – '

'"The Ash Grove".'

'You've got the shits.'

'And you're gonna have to watch your language. I got into trouble for that too.'

Charlie stood his guitar between his legs. 'When?'

'Let's take it from the bridge.'

'Tell me.'

William stopped to think. 'Who else knows you came to my place?'

'Dad.'

'Who else?'

'I've probably told a few people. So what?'

William leaned forward, took a deep breath, let it out slowly. 'I thought you would've guessed, Charlie. It's not something a teacher usually does.'

Charlie tried to remember exactly what he'd said to his friends as they waited outside the canteen. It had started off as a brag, but then someone had said, 'You went with him?'

'Yeah.'

'Fuck.'

'What?'

A few more people had overheard, and there was a mixture of silence, muttered comments and a wolf whistle.

'Fuck off,' Charlie had said, leaving the line and heading for the library.

Back in the bunker, Charlie waited for William. 'I just told a few people you had this whole room full of guitars.'

William was silent.

'I can't see the problem.'

'You remember Brother Powell?'

'But he was a perve.'

Everyone remembered Brother Powell. He was legend. His life had become a flummery of facts, lies and scenes stolen from books and smutty movies. The truth didn't matter any more – time only remembered the juicy bits: Brother Powell in a black robe, pacing change rooms, making no attempt to hide his wandering eyes.

'Okay, I get you,' Charlie said. 'I was just so impressed with all your guitars.'

'What did your dad say?'

'Said it's eighteen dollars a lesson, stick to the music.'

William clapped his hands. 'And so we do. "The Ash Grove".'

Charlie took a square of paper from his pocket and put it on the music stand. 'You remember, we were discussing attitude?'

'Yes?'

'And you challenged me?'

'I did?'

'"Fuck off, Biology Teacher". Remember?'

'Charlie ...'

'Listen.'

He started playing with a loud, syncopated rhythm. Tapped his feet and moved his body to the beat. Then started singing.

> String of Words
> Goin' round in my head
> Bullshit things that needn't be said.
> Words words
> Geometrical planes
> Signs and symbols, dates and names.

He crashed down on the strings for the chorus.

Take me away from this zoo
Let me do what I wanna do
Now it's time to be free
Let me be what I wanna be.

And returned to the syncopated introduction.

William smiled. 'Very good.' Picking up his own guitar, studying the chords and searching for the rhythm. Meanwhile, Charlie was off again.

String of Words
Filling my days
Spilling from lips in predictable ways.
Words words
Written in rhyme
Filling my head, wasting my time.

William was hooked. The song was fast, furious and angry, and better than anything he'd ever written. The lyrics were in turn poetic and threatening, heartfelt, dark and real. He studied the characters that formed these words: a capital R that should have been lower case; phrases crossed out three or four times before one was chosen; a stray sum; a drawing of Mr Shahriar, the student teacher; small, constipated cursive that crawled up, down and across the edges of the page.

They finished, and William congratulated him.

'It's just something I've been fiddling with,' Charlie said.

William thought it strange that his best student couldn't look at him as he said this. 'Charlie … you've got real talent.'

'Well, I suppose it's better than "The Ash Grove".'

'It is.'

'So I don't have to play from your book?'

William sucked in some air. 'For homework. And make sure your dad hears it.'

Charlie grinned and William stopped himself from taking his shoulder, or messing his hair. Is it too late to adopt Charlie Price? he wondered; Charlie, testing and rejecting; Charlie, stopping to think and stick yellow Post-it notes around his brain as a reminder of how the world worked, its cogs and gears, its pretensions and pains; Chucky, letting his thoughts and feelings settle across the Lindisfarne lawns like a mist of cheap deodorant.

'Again?' William asked, forgetting the rest of the speech he'd planned. Lessons about distance, and professionalism – hard work and friendship through respect.

'If you'd like.'

They were off again, Charlie singing his ballad of discontent about teachers other than William. They hammered through the chorus and found a harmony that filled out the melody, and sentiment.

This is what caught Pete Ordon's ear, as he walked past. He stopped at the door and listened.

> String of Words
> Goin' round in my head
> Bullshit things that needn't be said.

He peered inside and saw them playing, singing, their eyes moving between the music and each other.

Bodies, amorphic, interchangeable, flowing with the rhythm. Laughter, when the soundtrack slipped or they missed a beat. When they finished, just a few words, a nod and smile. Although no one seemed to be learning, or teaching, anything. It was a coffee clutch – unstructured, lacking books and pencil marks on manuscript paper. There was no sense of awkwardness or frustration. Just a can of Coke that they shared without wiping the lip.

The bell rang and they dared to keep playing for a few minutes, before they thought better of it.

'Would you mind if I took a copy?' William asked, picking up the food-stained page with its scribbled palimpsest of reworked words.

'If you think it's okay.'

'Listen, we're playing at The Gov tonight. I might show this to the fellas.'

'Fine.'

'You wouldn't mind if we had a go at it?'

'*At that?*'

William was glowing. 'Listen, Mr Price, this is good. Don't under-estimate yourself.'

Charlie started packing his guitar. 'That's what Davo says.'

'Who's Davo?'

'My sister's boyfriend. Dad doesn't know he sells pipes at the Brickworks on Sundays.'

'And you, you're little Mr Innocence.' Messing the boy's hair, grabbing his shoulder and squeezing it.

'I wish I could come tonight.'

'That'd be good, but difficult.'

'What time do you start?'

'Ten.'

'Past my bedtime.'

And William scowled. '*I guess.*'

Charles braced himself. He did up a button on his sports shirt, as if this might help – an inch less flesh, manners his mother had taught him. Then he stood in the doorway clutching his diary, looking out at his dad, watering the garden. 'Oh, I forgot,' he said to himself. 'You've gotta sign this … would you mind signing this … Dad, I think we better talk.' Although he was willing his hand to open the flyscreen door, it just wouldn't budge.

Damien was hosing gravel into the gaps in the driveway. Charles thought it strange how such small details always formed the background to the disasters of his life – staring at a crack in the wall as he cried himself to sleep whispering his mother's name; the mud splashed on the side of the ambulance parked in their driveway; Mr Chang's crooked fringe, as he led the memorial service. Debris that made enormous things small.

There was no point thinking about it. He opened the door and jumped down the front steps, hoping his father would start a conversation about roses or rusted fence posts. Instead, he just kept watering, head down, shoulders slumped.

'Dad?'

Damien looked up. 'I didn't know you were home.' Noticed the diary, and his face hardened. 'Tell me it's an excursion.'

'It wasn't my fault.'

'No?'

'It was Mr Neil again.'

'I come out here to relax, to sprinkle the lawn.'

'Remember, he gave me lines.'

'Pull a few dead leaves from the aggies, say hello to the neighbours.'

Charlie stepped forward. 'Listen to this: Neil says, "It's obvious that heavier objects fall faster than lighter ones." And I put my hand up and ask, quite respectfully, "Don't all objects fall at the same speed?"'

Charlie could remember the moment, and he wanted his dad to experience it too. He could see Mr Neil leaning across his desk, so their eyes were only a few inches apart. He could smell his Old Spice and see the hairs flaring from his nostrils; see the liverspots on his cheeks and the wrinkles around his eyes. He could hear him say, 'No, Charles, that doesn't make sense, does it?'

And he could hear himself reply, 'I remember this bloke dropping this match and this stone, and they both hit the ground at the same time.'

Mr Neil straightened. 'Who was this … *bloke?*'

'On the telly.'

'Ah, *The Simpsons* perhaps?'

His face screwed up. 'No, it was some science thing. And that's what they said – everything falls at the same speed. It's because gravity is a constant 9.8 metres per second, per second.'

Mr Neil returned to the front of the room. 'Now you're talking about acceleration.'

'No, gravity.'

'Not at all.' Pausing to double-check the facts in his own mind.

'It is,' Charlie said.

'Watch your tone.'

'It's the *same* thing.' He started flicking through his textbook. Neil came over and closed it. Charlie grabbed it back and continued.

'Give it here,' the teacher ordered.

'Why should I?'

'I won't ask again.'

Five minutes later, Charlie was walking across the tennis courts on his way to the Focus Room. He was already thinking about the consequences – the detention, the re-entry contract and his father's reaction – but he was so furious he just didn't care.

This wasn't the first time he'd crossed swords with Neil. There'd also been a discussion about reproduction, when his teacher had insisted identical twins came from separate eggs. He'd said, 'How could that be? Isn't it a case of one egg and one sperm, and the egg splits?' 'No,' Neil had growled. 'Eggs don't split.' He'd known he was wrong, but let it go. Soon Neil was showing them an overhead of a before and after penis. See if you can get that wrong, he'd thought. Neil was saying things like, 'It's there for one reason and one reason alone, gentlemen' – and he was almost grinning. Then there was a transparency of the girl's bits, and he'd mumbled something like, 'I imagine you all have a lot of questions, eh?'

He'd gone home and told his dad about Neil's lack of knowledge and Damien had said, 'Is that the best they can do for eight grand a year?'

So, he assumed his dad would understand when he invoked the name.

'Remember him?' he was saying, standing on the cracked path.

Damien was still trying to find solace in his watering. 'What did it matter if he was wrong? He knows most things, doesn't he?'

'But twins, that's so obvious. Fraternal, two eggs, two sperm.'

'It doesn't matter,' Damien said. 'He didn't chuck you out because of that.'

'He was wrong.'

'So what? I'm no bloody Einstein, but that doesn't mean ...' He trailed off, his eyes fixed on a lavender that needed pruning. 'This is all the bloody time now.'

'What?'

'You and your attitude.'

'*What?*'

'Listen to you. You know better than anyone, don't you?'

'Of course not.'

'Just cos you're a teenager doesn't mean you can be a pain in the arse. What would your mother think?'

Charlie couldn't fathom a reply. What did she have to do with it? With him, Neil, school, anything? She was her own truth, and life, framed on the wall, in fact, all over the house (although Damien had warned too much was no good).

'I'm wondering whether this guitar fella's got anything to do with it?'

'Cos I went to his place?'

'And other things.'

'What?'

'Watch your tone!'

The sound of water on dry dirt, the splash, the slap, like it could never be made wet.

'I reckon you should give that guitar back.'

'No.'

Damien turned off the tap and started reeling in the hose. 'Until you can learn.'

'I've already paid some of it.'

'So?'

'I won't.'

'You'll do what you're told.'

'Cos of a fuckin' detention?'

Damien stood up to him, glaring. 'You watch your mouth. When did you start talking to me like that?'

'Dad, listen ...'

'You can take it back tomorrow.'

'No.'

'You will.'

Charlie threw the diary into the garden and stormed inside. Damien listened as doors slammed and curses filled the hallway. He'd never seen his son like this before. Angry, yes, argumentative, but his passion was always curtailed by reason. Here was a different creature all together – loud and furious. Here was someone with a face and voice he could barely recognise. Something was pulling at him, and he was responding.

Maybe he was falling in with a bad mob. Cigarettes, attitude and fuck you stuffed into the bottom of blazer pockets. But why would he? He'd always laughed at the look-at-me mob, the rebels with nothing to rebel against, the Goths looking lost in shopping malls.

And then he emerged from the house in an unironed polo shirt, shorts, anklets and sandshoes. He walked down the path and out the front gate.

'This your big performance?' Damien said.

But he just kept walking.

'Where you off to then?' He was unsure of what his son was capable of. 'Okay then ... keep your bloody guitar.'

Still, no reply, and then he was gone.

Charles stood at a bus stop, watching as the 104 slowed towards him. The doors opened and he got on, took out his wallet and said to the driver, 'I need to go to the Governor Hindmarsh. Do you know where it is?'

'Other side of town.'

'Really?'

'I'll drop you in Grenfell Street, you'll have to get the 151.'

Charlie opened his wallet. 'Can you break a fifty?'

The driver felt in his pocket and produced a plastic bag full of coins and notes. Sorted through them and said, 'No.'

'Shit.'

'Go on, get on.'

The door closed and the driver pulled out. Charlie sat at the back of the empty bus. As they coasted down the hill he studied familiar streets, homes, driveways, stumped cars, the way gravel never stayed in the middle of the drive. People in pyjamas, work pants, business shirts and slacks. The details and necessities of living a life in one place doing one thing for years and years. The surrender to everything your life might have been. He knew this was an arrogant view, and probably wrong – but he wanted to trust his instincts. It was his right, he thought, perhaps even an obligation, to reimagine Lindisfarne (and his future) in a different way. He felt happy leaving his suburb behind – and could imagine doing it in a more permanent way.

He left the bus in the city, found the stop for the Port Road buses and waited fifty minutes for a 151. Then another slow drift westwards, past car yards and pawnbrokers, an old servo converted into a statue farm, and the brewery bleeding light and yeast into what was left of the River Torrens.

The bus dropped him across from the hotel. It was a stone building, trembling on a busy corner between factories and warehouses, workshops promising CV joints. The stonework had been painted black and there were neon signs advertising everything from dark lager to Drive-U-Home Safely cabs. Posters advertising bands, lingerie and even a vegetarian, multi-faith picnic in Bonython Park. The whole pub was protected from the sun by split awnings flecked with something that looked like vomit.

He entered through a hallway that smelt of beer and smoke. The music on the PA was heavy on the bass and he could feel it through his feet. He quickly forgot about his dad, and buses, and old men with their tomato plants. Here at last was some sign of life.

He noticed a barman kissing a girl, groups of men in expensive suits and a table surrounded by twenty-somethings smoking hand-rolled cigarettes, laughing on each other's shoulders, imitating people – politicians, perhaps, although he didn't know, and started feeling little-boy-lost, threatened, even. He wandered through a maze of smaller rooms and ended up in a large beer garden enclosed on two sides by shade cloth. There was a stage at the front and a drum kit with the name 'Nimrod's Cat' in black letters. A few of William's guitars on stands.

'Charlie!'

William stood in front of him, smiling. He grasped his arms and squeezed them. 'This is a surprise.'

'I guess.'

'Are you here with your dad?'

'No, just me.'

William took a moment. 'So?'

'He said it was okay. Said perhaps you could drop me home.'

'I could, but it'll be late.'

'That's okay.'

William wasn't convinced. 'Haven't you got school tomorrow?'

'Yeah, but I'm not ten any more.'

He paused, studying the boy's face for clues. 'Well, if you're sure.'

'I was surprised too. I said I'd like to come and he dropped me out front.'

With every word, Charlie could feel the walls closing in around him. Then he thought, So what? This is it. The Father, Son and Holy fucking Ghost. The hum of Marshall amps and the smell of Jim Beam. Noise to split your ear drums. Shredded vocal cords.

'Do you want a hand setting up?' he asked.

Meanwhile, Damien was driving around the back streets of Lindisfarne. He'd see someone and stop and ask about his son, but they'd just shrug or look at him like he was some old perve.

He'd waited an hour after Charlie left. He was ready for him to come in the front door, and he was going to say, Sit with your old man, and let me say sorry. He was going to be watching the television, as if nothing had happened. But then it got dark, and he started to worry. He searched his son's room, found his phone and looked up his mates' numbers. Phoned them, or their parents, but no one had seen him. Told them he was late back from swimming training, but not to worry, as he often ended up at someone's house and never thought to ring and tell him.

He pulled over and stopped to think. Took a piece of paper from his pocket and unfolded it. Then he read the scribbled words:

> String of Words
> Goin' round in my head
> Bullshit things that needn't be said.

Then, beside the title of the song: 'For WD, as promised'.

He wondered what the promise was. And wasn't that the sort of secret shared between father and son?

Christ, he thought, I haven't even seen this Dutton fella.

But again he figured WD must be okay. He was a teacher – educated, experienced with kids. And there were so many letters after his name on the reports that came home.

William was disappointed with the crowd. The usual group of friends, and their friends, a few regulars, one or two drop-ins, but no cult following, no word of mouth.

Charlie sat and watched as the band worked through a mix of covers and originals. He recognised songs from their demo and listened as they murdered 'Me' with raw guitar and thumping drums.

He sat at the band's table. Earlier, he'd listened to them discussing life, love and music. Marvelled at sentences containing four or five fucks, at the way insults, philosophy and song mixed in a salad of voices, at the way sex ebbed and flowed into the conversation until they remembered his presence. He listened as they agreed that marijuana was a domestic necessity (along with bread and milk), as they mocked Classic Hits radio and rap and laughed about people who wore the collar up on their polo shirts. He absorbed their body language and odour, their cheap cologne and stale clothes, their greasy, uncombed hair and two-week growth. He longed to be ten years older, and one of them.

They'd left plenty to drink on the table: half empty beers, vodka and William's untouched brandy and Coke; free grog: another benefit of the rock'n'roll lifestyle. He watched as cold beads formed and ran down glasses.

Fuck it, he thought. Just a taste, a half-glass. Why not? What's stopping me? I'm not the one threatening to take away people's property. Since when does doing the right thing ever get you anywhere? He could see his folder full of certificates, a wall covered with ribbons and medallions, trophies and the memory of aunties saying, What a clever boy!

Waiting until no one was looking, he picked up one of the beers and drained it in one long gulp. A few minutes later he tried the brandy, and then the vodka.

William was soaked with sweat. He was shouting into the microphone, growling each lyric so that it might resonate, scare, offend more than the actual meaning of any given word or phrase. And as he sang, he looked at Charlie.

The beginning of everything, he thought. Every word, urge and action. He met his eyes, and they both grinned. He studied his face and the lowset curve of his nose. Then, as he turned away, he noticed him picking up a drink and draining it. He looked at the table, the empty glasses, and met his eyes again.

The song continued, verse after chorus. William was tired, and mostly drunk. He kept moving on the spot to stay upright. He could feel his head spinning. Fell forward, back. Returned to the microphone and screamed the start of a chorus, but then ran out of voice and left the rest unsung.

Between songs he told the crowd, 'One of my students is here.'

Charlie held up his hand and looked around, but the room was spinning.

'We're gonna do a song.' Motioning for him to come up.

Charlie shook his head, but William unplugged his guitar and fetched him. The boy stood, walked around the table and tripped on a rug. Steadied himself, and climbed the three steps onto the stage. William handed him one of his guitars and as he strapped it on he said, 'This is my debut.' But no one seemed to care.

Then he started grinding away at the chords. William joined in and they managed a two-guitar version of 'String of Words'. After a loud ending, Charlie stumbled back to his seat. The other members of the band looked at William and smiled. He shrugged, approached the microphone and said, 'Charlie, no more grog.' This time a few people laughed.

They played a slow version of 'Blow up the Pokies' and Charlie watched as William raised his head and sang in a crying whisper as he reached for the high notes. For a moment he was with, and was, his teacher. In the middle of his warm, forget-the-world glow, he'd forgotten all about Damien, Lindisfarne College and Datsunland.

During a break in the performance, he headed to the toilet. Walked in and found William against a wall, hungrily kissing the girl from the front bar, as she ran her hand over his chest and the top of his legs. 'Charlie, this is ... Sarah, wasn't it?'

The girl said, 'Hi, Charlie,' and asked William, 'How old?'

'Too young for you.'

But she wasn't about to be put off. Stepped towards Charlie, and again, closer, before saying, 'You've got the bluest eyes.'

William seemed content to watch. As she kissed the boy, then used a single hand to guide him into a vacant cubicle.

Charlie was unsure. Maybe this was part of it, the fun, the game. But then she kissed him again, ran her hand over his chest, down across his crotch.

'Let him go,' William said, sliding down the wall to the ground.

But she just closed the door, pushed him into a corner, and started wrestling with his fly.

Charlie was terrified. He tried to protect himself, push her away, but she just became more determined. 'D'yer wanna show me?'

As William laughed. 'Leave him be ...'

She was in, investigating, and he froze. But responded, realising there was nothing he could do about it. The terror left him empty, vacant, unable to act. She just kept going, kissing his lips, face, neck, lower, as William said or did nothing, as she put her tongue in his mouth, as he waited for William to stop her, but realised he wasn't about to, and he'd have to save himself.

He pushed her away, fixed his pants and opened the door. Looked at William and said, 'What are you doing?'

William wasn't sure. 'She's just ...'

Charlie ran from the toilet, through the maze of rooms and out the front door of the pub. William took a few moments and then followed him. When he caught up he asked, 'Where are you going?'

He didn't reply.

'Listen, she was just ... you know ...'

Charlie stopped and stared at his teacher. 'You were gonna let her?'

'No, of course not.'

He started running. Turned into an alleyway and sprinted.

William tried to follow but couldn't keep up. Stopping, he looked in all directions – through mostly dead trees, parked cars, fences topped with razor wire – but Charlie was gone. He turned into a road protected by a boom gate and as he did a security guard appeared from a doorway. 'Private property.'

'Did you see a boy?'

'No.'

He returned to the road. Ran towards an intersection, looked around but couldn't see anyone. 'Charlie!' The name rolled down the empty street, echoing off factory walls. 'Charlie! Come on! I've gotta take you home.' He stood and listened. Heard a forklift reversing and the sound of metal dropping onto concrete. Then someone calling, 'Two inches, more like three.'

He turned and walked back to the pub. His heart was racing, and he felt almost sober. There were waves – the bitumen smell of the street, and the thought of what had happened. After a block or so this realisation flooded over him. He sat down on a planter box and dropped his head between his knees.

The music had gone. Now it was completely different. Now he was watching from his window, waiting, planning what he'd say.

Charlie sprinted the length of West Avenue – a kilometre of old workers' cottages, scrap yards and deserted factories waiting to become car parks. He tripped over gutters and cracked pavements, swerving to avoid low tree branches, post boxes and a couple walking home from a local pub. 'Slow down,' one of them said. 'What's the rush?'

But he just kept running. The endless hours of training, the PE lessons, the ribbons and trophies were coming in useful. Somewhere in front of him was safety – his father who, it turned out, was right.

He stopped and leaned against a brick wall. Saw the girl's fingers, and face, but tried to block them out. William's body, collapsed on the tiles, his heavy head, and red eyes. He continued, and found a main road. Looked both ways, unsure where the city lay, his suburb, home. Turning right, he kept walking up a gradual incline that stretched three or four kilometres before dipping behind a railway crossing. His legs were heavy, tired from running. Every time he heard a car he looked over his shoulder, ready to hide. He spat, but couldn't get rid of the taste. So he stopped and drank from a tap attached to the side of a MG dealership with an empty showroom.

An old sports car drove past, slowed and sounded its horn. A group of teenage girls waved and called out to him and someone asked, 'What's your name?'

Without thinking, he shrugged, and they laughed. 'Is the city this way?' he asked, and they replied by offering a lift.

'No. I'm okay walking.'

The car sped up and disappeared around a corner. The road was empty. His mind was racing. In a flash of light and noise he heard the band and saw the lights, and remembered. The evening had promised (and delivered, he guessed) a world of sound and smell, images in primary colours, raucous voices, massages and sanitised-for-your-comfort sex as seen in prime-time movies (as his dad told him to look away). It felt like he had lived three days in one.

The bus, when did I catch the bus? he wondered. Yesterday afternoon? The day before? And when did I argue with Dad?

His father? Still waiting for him, he supposed. Back home on the other side of the city. So far, and with the buses finished for the day.

Fuck!

A moment later he was kneeling in a garden of pine chips, vomiting, spitting brandy-flavoured chunks from his mouth. He looked up at a 'Mr Exterminator' sign, a pair of angry Rottweilers in a car yard, and cursed his teacher. He saw a taxi, crossed to the middle of the road and hailed it. It stopped and a small Indian man wound down the window. 'Where to?'

'Lindisfarne.'

'You were going the wrong way.'

He got in, and the driver planted his foot and completed a U-turn. 'You have money?'

'Yes.'

'Can I see, please?'

He took out his wallet, opened it and displayed a fifty-dollar note.

'Thank you. You have been drinking?'

'Sort of.'

'If need be, tell me before your sickness.' The driver indicated and turned right down a road Charlie remembered. 'Otherwise there is a sixty-dollar fee.'

'Okay.'

The driver looked at him in the rearview mirror. 'How old are you?'

'Seventeen.'

'Seventeen? You look too young to be out by yourself.'

'Well, I'm not. I've got a girlfriend.'

'Is she nice?'

His eyes were on the meter. 'That goes fast.'

'Don't worry, fifty will cover it.'

Greg Fraser, the band's bass player, stood waiting for William at the door of the pub. 'Come on, everyone's waiting.'

William walked past him, through the maze that led into the beer garden. 'I've gotta go.'

'But we've got another set.'

'The kid's pissed off ... that fuckin' bitch.' He climbed onto the stage, packed his three guitars into their cases, wound up his cords and approached the microphone. 'That's it.'

No one seemed concerned. The crowd had dwindled to a dozen or so. Someone called out, 'What about a refund?' But most people hadn't paid anyway.

'It's your bedtime,' William replied, and the voice mumbled something about them being shit anyway.

'What are you fucking good at then?'

A bald, beefy man stood up.

Greg pulled William aside. 'In the middle of a gig? Do you know how hard it was to organise this?'

'Do you think this lot will notice?'

'It's not the fucking point.'

He drove around the dozen or so blocks that made up Brompton and Bowden, accelerating, braking, looking down alleys and side streets, narrowly avoiding parked cars and knocking over a wheelie bin. He suspected he might have hit a cat, but didn't care. Just after midnight he emerged onto the main road and tried to decide what to do next. Only a few cars, mainly taxis. He drove towards the city, crossing the Parklands. A small fire, a few homeless people. Uni students headed for the next pub, a prostitute, perhaps, more taxis. He turned towards home, shutting off the radio so he could think.

The stillest part of the night. A rescue helicopter appeared from over the hills, flying low towards the city. Damien followed its path. Some cocky's son, smashed up in a ute, he guessed. He was pacing the brick path that wound through his front garden. This is where it had all started, and where it would finish, he hoped. He tripped on a paver and stamped it down with his foot. A branch had grown across the path, and he snapped it off.

He'd spent hours driving around Lindisfarne. Nothing. He'd walked through the school, checked the pool, the hay shed – anywhere Charlie might be hiding. He'd been stopped by a security guard and explained the situation, but was asked to leave anyway.

Nicole and Dave pulled up in an old Laser. Nicole got out, slammed the door and said, 'Nothing?'

'He won't be far.'

'It's not the point.' She came around to him. 'He'd know this would upset you.'

'He's a kid, they don't think.'

Dave jumped the fence and stumbled onto the front lawn. 'We walked all the way along Fourth Creek.'

'We gotta call the police,' Nicole said.

'No, then we've got Social Services coming in to interview us.'

They sat on a bench on the front porch. Mostly quiet, but after a while Dave said, 'I did this.'

Nicole turned to him. 'What?'

'Ran away. The whole day. Most of the time I was up a tree in the backyard.'

Damien leaned forward with his elbows on his knees. 'Why?'

'I can't remember. But I was always planning to run off. Had it all worked out. You know – No one gives a shit if I'm dead or alive.' He sat back and studied the stars. 'Don't worry, he's too smart to go far.'

'It's my fault,' Damien said.

'It is not,' Nicole replied.

'A bloody detention. Cos he argued with this teacher who was trying to tell them some bullshit. Charlie was setting him straight. Can you imagine it?'

Dave grinned, watching how the stars turned from white to red to blue. 'I can just hear him. Excuse me, sir, but is that right?'

'What was he saying? Identical twins come from different eggs. Any idiot knows that's wrong.'

Nicole nudged Dave.

'What? I knew that.' He noticed a meteorite burning up. 'Even the teachers at my crap school woulda known that.'

'So he argued with him,' Damien said.

'But he shouldn't have argued with you,' Nicole said.

'It was me.'

'He's smart, but he can also be a little prick.'

'I told him he'd have to give the guitar back.'

Dave sat forward. 'I bet that got his hackles up.'

Nicole looked at him. 'You don't even know what a hackle is.'

'I do.'

'What?'

'It's the red thing on a chook.'

'Bullshit.'

Silence. Crunching gravel. They all looked up. Charlie stood at the gate. No slouch, no expression, no torn clothing or cough or undone button.

'Welcome home,' Nicole said. 'Come in, I'll fetch your slippers.'

Charlie took a few steps forward. 'Dad ...'

'You alright, son?'

'Yeah.'

Damien walked through the garden, opened his arms and reclaimed his son. 'Jesus ... you had me worried.'

'I'm sorry.'

He held him close. Smelled the smoke and alcohol on his clothes, but didn't care. He took a few moments to feel his son's breathing, his warmth. Felt thankful that time had reset, again, the way it had begun. That Charlie was six again, and upset because of what someone had said; nine, left out; eleven, twelve, wanting to be with him, ask him questions, come to the car yard and sit in the Datsun that was left there for old time's sake, and the cats. That no matter how much his son grew, or learned, or was tempted, he always returned.

'I've been an idiot,' Charlie said.

'No, I have,' Damien said. He stood back and looked at him. 'You're not hurt?'

'No.'

'Where you been?'

He didn't answer, and in the gap, Nicole came forward. 'Well, where?'

'Walking.'

'Bullshit. You smell like beer.'

'I've been walking.'

She was studying his face, searching his clothes for clues. 'We've been looking all night.'

'Sorry.'

'That was bloody nasty, Charlie. Didn't you think about Dad?'

'I know.'

'You're lucky we didn't call the cops. Fuck, Charles, you're so selfish.'

'I'm sorry!' Glaring at her. 'I didn't think. I was angry.'

'We used a tank of fucking petrol looking for you.'

'Stop!'

Silence. Damien held his son's shoulder and said, 'It's all over now, eh, son?'

Charlie looked at him, desperately.

Damien turned to Nicole. 'That's enough.'

But she was still staring at her brother, her face set hard.

'Go on, hop to bed,' Damien said, and Charlie went inside. To his room, where he sat in the dark and watched his dad farewell his sister and Dave. He followed his progress back into the yard – as he stopped to pick a spent flower from a rosebush. He could hear him coming inside, carefully closing the flyscreen door. Could hear his keys rattling on a ring on his belt. The sound reminded him of the collection he kept on a chain at work. There were hundreds, labelled with little stickers with licence numbers. And every evening at five he'd go out into the lot and hand-lock each car. Watching his father drag himself from car to car always made him feel sad. He would watch him search the chain and then try two or three keys before he found the right one, working them in difficult locks, using his knee to force doors shut.

Sun-bleached, fender-dented cars; waiting for some kid or single mother to buy them out of desperation. Each car full of a hundred stories that hadn't quite vacuumed out – conception and trips to the emergency department, drive-throughs and drive-ins, baby vomit on the carpet and cigarette-burnt vinyl.

He could hear his father coming down the hall, his weight settling on the floorboards. Then he was in the doorway, whispering, 'How about we both have a day off tomorrow?'

'Okay.'

'Something we never do. Go see a picture, eh?'

'You and me?'

Then his dad said, 'It doesn't matter, son. Nothing matters.'

'I know.'

And he was gone.

Charlie pushed the clutter from his bed and lay down. His eyes adjusted to the dark and he could see the shadows the moon made across his wall. He noticed his new guitar on its stand, gleaming.

He lay awake counting the half-hours. Listened to his dad snoring and the old clock in the hallway that lost three minutes a day. Sometime in the coldest part of the night he opened his window and sat staring out at the shapes of trees and cars, porches and an old fridge in the neighbour's drive. He could smell orange blossom and it took him back.

He was sitting in the garden with his mum and he said, 'What's that smell?' She pointed to the mandarin tree.

That's all he could remember – a fragment. He didn't know what she'd said or what they'd done next. If it was a Saturday or Sunday, or even if it had really happened.

He took a book from his desk drawer. DH Lawrence. Not that he'd ever read it, but Carol had written her name inside the front cover. He studied the scrawl – the loops, the clumsily joined letters, the heavily dotted i – and felt even more alone. A tabby walked onto the lawn and looked up at him. He opened the book and found a small newspaper clipping.

> Price, Carol. Passed away peacefully on May 21. Dearly loved and devoted wife of Damien, loved mother of Nicole and Charlie. We are so grateful we were able to tell you how much you meant to us …

He closed the book and said a prayer to his mum. He told her he'd had a bad night, but that things would be okay. He said, in thoughts more than words, that there was no one, really, he could trust, and learn to love, and she told him (he sensed, somehow) that he was wrong.

He put the book away and returned to bed.

For the next hour he thought about the mess (he guessed) he'd created. He decided there was only one way to sort things out. He got up and walked from his room. Moving slowly into the hallway, he placed his feet where he'd learnt the floorboards wouldn't creak. Then he stood in his dad's doorway. There were no sounds, but his presence woke him.

'That you, Chuck?'

'Yes.'

'You sick?'

'No.'

Silence.

'What's wrong?'

Charlie tried to say it, but couldn't. Instead he whispered, 'Just getting some water.'

William had also made it home to bed. He was lying with his hands behind his head, thinking. It wasn't my fault as such … I guess … *although* … He thought about the boy and how, in a way, he was just playing with the idea of being grown up. Putting aside one thing to try another. Although some things weren't as plastic, flexible, forgiving. Choking hazards. That was made clear on the bag. Or skateboards – a fast-track to a greenstick fracture. But there were other things; that came too soon, too suddenly.

He put on his thongs, went out the back door, up the driveway and along the street. Walked for a full hour – along the banks of the river, up paths winding into the hills of Morialta, along old quarry truck roads – finally emerging on the edge of a high cliff overlooking the city. He walked towards the edge, but stopped well short. Looked down at the quarry below, the adjacent suburbs, nearby roads and shops. Estimated his height – fifty, sixty metres. Picked up a rock and threw it over the edge.

It fell quietly, slowly.

He looked out towards the distant sea. It was dark, and you could only tell it was there by the presence of distant freighters.

Then, back down the hill to Lindisfarne. A few minutes later he was standing outside Charlie's house. As he watched the boy's window, he wondered whether he shouldn't knock, go in.

Inside, Charlie was almost asleep. He opened his eyes when he heard the start and stop slap of thongs. Sitting up, he looked out and saw the dark figure, but it passed quickly.

It was a spot they'd returned to a thousand times: a stretch of asphalt behind Kmart. Cracked and full of potholes. No one bothered parking there. The Trimboli fruit truck always sat under a nearby fig tree, but that didn't bother them.

Charlie and Simon, his oldest friend, had set up their own BMX track, consisting of a series of jumps. Firstly, a shopping trolley laid on its side, with a piece of old particle board propped up as a ramp. This allowed them to fly a metre or more in the air before coming down on a couple of flattened cardboard boxes. Secondly, a garden bed they'd turned into a jump. This feature dated back to when they still fit on their bikes. Now they were far too big to ride them safely, but that didn't matter. In fact, it was just the point – knees sticking out over handlebars, feet too big for pedals, bums too big for seats.

Finally, there was a collection of fruit crates supporting more flattened boxes. These formed a series of cardboard valleys and hills that often collapsed under their weight.

Vince Trimboli didn't seem to mind their mess. They'd move it aside, and he'd come in and out with his truck. Sometimes, when other kids mucked it up he'd tell them to piss off. He'd give Charlie green bananas to give to his dad, but he'd always chuck them in the cardboard crusher behind Coles.

Charlie went around the course three times. Simon timed him. 'Fifty-four seconds,' he said, when Charlie skidded back beside him.

'Fifty-four? I counted forty-five.'

'How fast?'

'One-grandmother, two-grandmother ...'

Simon didn't care. 'Fifty-four, not a winning time, Chuck. You're losing your edge.' He handed over his watch, sat on his bike and said, 'When you're ready.'

'Go!'

Simon was off, over the trolley, through the garden and up and down the cardboard valleys. He went back a second time, and a third, pulling up a few inches from Charlie's thonged feet.

'Fifty-eight,' Charlie said.

'Bullshit.'

'Bullshit nothing.'

Simon shook his head. 'Okay, you still haven't beaten forty-eight.'

'Forty-eight my arse.'

'You sayin' I'm cheatin', Chucky?'

'You're full of shit.'

'G'day, Charlie,' a voice called.

Pete Ordon stood watching them. He was dressed in long shorts and black socks. He smiled at Simon, although he didn't know him. 'Nice little set-up you've got here.'

Charlie didn't know what to say. 'We can get around three times in under a minute,' he managed, thinking he was looking and sounding too childish.

'Very impressive. Haven't broken any bones yet?'

'No ... although I did chip a tooth when I was twelve.' He opened his mouth to show him but realised he was too far away to see.

Pete noticed a glow in his face. The real Charlie Price – in tattered shorts and a T-shirt, with a grease or oil stain. For a moment, he felt like he was seeing him through William's eyes. 'I'm after a hose reel,' he said, thinking several thoughts at once, and then realising.

Neither of the boys replied.

'Anyway, I'll let you get back to it.'

He walked on, almost tripping in a pothole. Simon looked at Charlie. '*Cleo*'s Most Eligible Bachelor.'

Charlie punched him on the arm. 'Ssh.' Then called, 'Mr Ordon?'

Pete stopped and turned back. Charlie rode his bike over and pulled up in front of him. 'I was wondering, there's another guitar teacher, isn't there?'

'Yes, but he mainly teaches seniors. Why?'

'It doesn't matter.'

'What's up?'

'Do you think he'd take on a Year Nine?'

Pete shook his head. 'We only change teachers if there's a very good reason.'

Charlie turned to go. 'It doesn't matter.'

'Do you have a reason?'

'No.'

Pete studied the boy's face. 'You don't like the way Mr Dutton teaches?'

'No, it's not that.'

'You don't get along?'

'No.'

'You look like you get along, when I see you working together.'

Charlie struggled with the words. He knew he shouldn't have mentioned it. Now there'd be questions, suspicions – more stuff he couldn't put back in the bottle. 'We do get along. I've learnt a lot.'

'So?'

'I just thought it'd be good to try someone different.'

Pete wasn't convinced. 'It doesn't work like that. You can't pick and choose.'

'Sorry. See you later.' He returned to Simon.

'What's up?' Simon asked.

'I was timing, it was forty-seven seconds.'

'That doesn't count.'

Charlie had had enough of jumps. 'Wanna ride into town?'

'It's miles,' Simon replied.

'Pussy.'

William's heart was racing. This was a moment he'd been dreading. He'd rehearsed it a hundred times. Tried to think of the right greeting. A solemn, Hi, Charles, or a pretend-nothing-had-happened, Hey, Charlie. He'd planned where they'd sit, and how he'd broach the topic. But as he watched the boy approach the music suite it all seemed to mean nothing. He sat down, placed his acoustic guitar across his legs and leaned forward, pretending to study music. Looked up at the door; down; up again.

'Hi,' Charlie said, in a monotone.

'Hi. Come in.'

Charlie sat down and took out his guitar. There was no conversation, and William guessed he was right to have been worried. No instant forgiveness; no best chums again.

Charlie looked at him without speaking. William let his eyes slip onto the boy's long neck, the gentle pulse of an artery. 'How are you?'

'Okay ... thanks.'

William knew he'd got it all wrong. Confused one thing for another. Fucked up a perfectly good kid, perhaps. Kid. Under the Christmas tree. He remembered it. How you sat, with your knees bent, as you unwrapped presents. But then shot forward when you saw one with your name on it. Kid. As you pretended it was quite matter-of-fact, but felt the world glowing.

Charlie played scales. Every note, perfect. He stopped and waited, and William said, 'I'm surprised you came.'

'Why?'

'I heard you were asking about another teacher?'

Charlie looked down, confused, but then said, 'That girl, she would've kept going.'

'Probably.'

'She would've.'

There was a long pause; just the hum of the air conditioning.

'And you just sat there, letting her.'

'I know ...'

'And you were laughing.'

William had nothing to say, because there was no excuse. She would've kept going, and she might've made him stay, in his corner, in the cubicle.

'I decided to stop learning,' Charlie said. 'But Dad wouldn't let me.' He explained how, when he'd brought this up, Damien had got out of his seat, searched through the receipt box and returned to him, waving a piece of paper in his face. 'Look,' he'd said. 'Ten lessons, one hundred and eighty dollars. Non-refundable. See that bit there?'

'Fine,' he'd replied. 'I'll keep going.'

'Too bloody right you'll keep going. I thought you liked the guitar?'

'I do.'

'What about Guru Dutton?'

'What?'

'You sick of him?'

'No.' Studying his face. 'I just thought I could try a different instrument.'

'You gotta stick to one thing.'

'I was thinking about clarinet.'

'Forget it.'

Back in the bunker, Charlie had moved on to his set pieces, some of which he hadn't tackled for weeks. He played slow, measured phrases. There was no attack, no anger, no straying from the small, black dots on the page. No *bullshit things that needn't be said*. William watched and listened, and felt he'd lost him. A wall of politeness, bars in their correct measure, which had grown between them. Although he was only a few inches from the boy, he knew he'd drifted too far. As the realisation fully dawned, he felt worse than ever. 'I'm sorry.'

Charlie stopped.

'You're a really good kid. Really grown up. So ...' But words eluded him. 'We're friends?'

Charlie dared to look up, but only for a moment.

William taught another four lessons. Luckily, he had drills to fall back on. The words were mechanical, the music lifeless, as usual. By mid-afternoon he'd made his decision. At four o'clock he packed his gear, left his bunker and walked into Pete Ordon's office. 'That's me done.'

Pete was busy transposing charts. 'See you next week.'

'No, that's me done.'

He looked up. 'What?'

'Finished.'

'For good?'

'There's one more week for the term. Tell the kids I'm sick, and I'll refund them.'

'What *are* you crapping on about, Dutton?'

'You'll fix my pay?'

Pete stood, came around his desk and closed his office door. 'Sit down.'

William stepped back and reopened it. 'Thanks.' Leaving the office.

Pete stepped out after him. 'For fuck's sake,' he said, as a couple of boys walked past. 'What's up?'

Charlie didn't touch either guitar for days. Then, on the weekend, he flicked on his amp and tried to remember a riff William had shown him. Damien popped his head in and said, 'I remember that one.'

'It's The Beatles.'

'Yeah … "Baby's good to me you know" … Is this the guru?'

'No, I heard it somewhere.'

Charlie had gone over William's words a hundred times. As always, bullshit things that needn't be said, excuses, little grovelling whispers that didn't attempt to understand or make good the situation. But, then again, everyone he knew was flawed. His father, of course, lost in a haze of retreads and cracked dashboards. His sister, with her allergy to work, dwelling in a *Young and Restless* world of celebrity-slimmer magazines. Wearing out couches as early visions of foreign correspondent-cum-author faded to a soundtrack of discount rugs – as hair went unwashed and armpits unshaved. Davo, floating through some dreamworld in a patched inner-tube, complaining about distant dictatorships as he failed to establish any sort of order in his own life. But all of them people. Real. Fully formed. Functional. Aware of their own limitations.

A week later he was back in the bunker. He was surprised to see a tall man with almost no hair, wearing a tie and business shirt, sorting through piles of music.

'Now, you are Price?' he asked, without looking up.

'Charlie.'

'Come in. Sit down.'

He did as he was told. The man turned and studied him, put on a pair of glasses, squinted, and crossed his legs. Then he sniffed, wiped the tip of his nose with a long, bony finger, and tried to smile.

'Where's Mr Dutton?'

'Gone.'

'Gone?'

'My name's Mr Lewis. I'm taking his spot.'

He didn't understand. 'What, he's on holiday?'

'No, he's left. So, you've got me.' He smiled a strange, crooked smile.

Charlie stared at a print of Weber hanging on the wall. He noticed his enormous sideburns and high collar. There were mountains, Bavarian hunting lodges and deer in the background, and he sensed that the scene was not quite right. He looked back at Lewis and asked, 'Why did he leave?'

'I don't know.'

'He didn't even say goodbye.'

'Maybe he owed someone money.'

Charlie glared at him. Fuckwit, he thought. He knew why his teacher had gone – given up his job, his income, maybe even his future.

'Okay, let's hear "The Ash Grove",' Lewis said, indicating the music on the stand. 'Mr Dutton said you were working on it.'

'So you've talked to him?'

'Yes.'

'And what did he say?'

'Good luck.'

He felt defeated, cheated. He remembered the afternoon in William's guitar room; smelt their wet clothes, and heard the chainsaw from next door. The air was heavy with wet grass, and soil, and damp. As though it had happened years ago. Although there was no forgetting the hum of the amps, the double-coil growl, the white feet folded in front of him – William, Bill, Dutton, dude, Mr, Sir, fuckwit, arse, *dirty* – uncut toenails, a hole in his T-shirt, a half-smoked cigar in a saucer. He could remember every word he'd uttered – descriptions of fuzz-boxes, caring for pickups, the joy of taking a Les Paul out of its case.

He played his piece and Lewis asked, 'How long have you been working on this one?'

'Six weeks.'

'*Six?*'

'As well as other stuff.'

'I see.' He tapped a pencil on his teeth. 'You're going into Year Ten, you need to know more.'

'Like what?'

'Sightreading, fingerpicking, sitting properly.' He stood behind him and pulled his shoulders back.

'Ask,' Charlie said, pulling free.

'Your technique, it's sloppy.' He sat down. 'Mr Dutton, I heard he liked his rock'n'roll?'

'We did.'

'Well, that's good, but you need a proper grounding.'

'We did all that. He was always making me play scales.'

Lewis had him playing exercises for the rest of the lesson. At the end he smiled with approval, saying, 'Excellent, you have made some progress then.'

Charlie leaned over his guitar and asked, 'Is that all we're gonna do?'

'No, we'll have some fun too.'

'Fun?'

'Rhythm and blues.'

'Is that what you like?'

'Muddy Waters.'

'Who's that?'

'*Who's that?* You wait!'

Charlie was examining the hair in his new teacher's ear. 'What about modern stuff?'

'Like?'

'Red Hot Chili Peppers?'

'That's easy ... if you're half-decent.'

Charlie sat back. 'Some of the riffs are hard.' But he drifted off, realising there was no point.

Two weeks of holidays passed and Charles returned to his world of unwashed T-shirts, cardboard jumps and walks through Morialta Park with Simon. They went to the city on the 104, drank gallons of frozen Coke and sat through martial arts films that Charlie couldn't stand. 'This is such bullshit,' he'd whisper, breathing in flakes of popcorn and coughing.

'Beats Hugh Grant.'

'As if I'd see Hugh Grant.'

He returned to school – fresh blazers and pants that couldn't be let down any further. A battery of pie warmers in the canteen, handball, leaves blowing across the tennis courts, mixing with paper, plastic and feathers from the farm. There was expectation, and holiday stories, someone's sister pregnant again and someone's dad trading up to an SS Commodore.

Mr Lewis gathered his four best students (the only ones who

could hold a melody, Charlie told Damien) into a guitar quartet he called 'The Bright Lights'. He made them practise every Tuesday and Thursday lunchtime, endlessly flogging the same three pieces until at last he announced, 'We're ready.'

'For what?' Charlie asked.

'Your first performance. Why else do we learn music, boys?'

None of them could provide a reason. Charlie had his own suspicions of what 'The Bright Lights' was all about: Mr Lewis trying to look good in front of his Catholic overlords. If he could prove his worth they might keep him on beyond his contract. Davo had told him how the whole world turned on three pivots – money, power and sex. He'd often stop and cross-reference his friends, teachers, relatives and daily events against these criteria, and to Dave's credit (surprisingly) he seemed to be right.

So, there they were, on stage in front of a full school assembly. They each sat in a plastic seat, one foot on a stand, their guitars placed neatly across their knees. Lewis stood in front of them with a baton. 'Sit up straight,' he whispered, and they all responded.

Fuck, Charles thought, looking out across the grinning faces. How did it come to this?

Lewis had polished his shoes and shaved an extra half-inch off his sideburns. He was wearing a pinstriped suit that threatened to cut circulation to his legs. He'd attempted a bow tie that sent entirely the wrong message to eleven hundred boys. He'd drowned himself in cologne that did little to counter four generations of stale BO in the Brother Dalrymple Memorial Hall. He smiled at the boys, cleared his throat and turned to the audience. After adjusting the microphone, he said, 'I'm pleased to introduce you to four very talented young men. This first piece is called "The Ash Grove". I hope you enjoy it.'

He counted them in and they played their parts from memory. Charlie was in charge of the melody; another, a counterpoint in bass notes; a third, arpeggios; and finally a short Italian named

Di Censo who played broken chords to disguise any bum notes. But there were none. Lewis had made sure of that. What the music lacked in soul it made up for in precision. They had become a steam engine. Their arms were pistons, their hands cylinders. They'd practised so much they couldn't have made a mistake if they'd wanted to. The 'Professor' (as they called him) wasn't about to let four smelly, awkward teenagers blow his big moment.

They finished and there was light applause. Made their way downstairs into a change room and packed away their guitars. 'That was a complete success,' Mr Lewis said.

Charlie wasn't so sure. 'They were laughing at us.'

'Nonsense.'

'Didn't you hear them?'

'*Calm* down, Charlie.'

'I felt like a complete …' He looked at the other boys. 'Well?'

No response. He returned to Lewis. 'Mr Dutton wouldn't have made us do that.'

'What did Mr Dutton teach you about performing?'

Charlie knew he was headed for the Focus Room, but he just didn't care. 'We played a real gig, at a real hotel.'

'If that's how you feel, maybe you should seek him out.'

'I will.'

Charlie realised that Lewis was being too reasonable. You couldn't argue with common sense. So he said, 'It's just, I like other things.'

'If you want Mr Dutton's number, I can get it.'

He paused, and continued packing.

'I'm not saying you can't like that stuff, Charlie, but I get paid to teach you something else.'

'As was Mr Dutton.' His eyes narrowed and he could feel his heart racing. 'You don't know what he taught me.'

And what he wanted to say – Music's the least of it, you silly little prick.

A few days later there was sun; a fern with four fronds burnt brown, an oleander dropping dead flowers, and a camellia in just the right spot, flourishing. A pergola, its wood rotten, its shade-cloth flapping in a light breeze, and an old barbecue built from leftover house bricks. Charlie sat in half-shade, on a cracked plastic chair, at a plastic table. He stared at a blank piece of paper, bit his lip, and finally started writing.

> Howdy Mr Guitar Teacher,
> It's me again. How are you? I'm shit at writing things. Hey,
> I've just taught myself Revolution. You probably know it, but
> I heard a slow version, and apparently Lennon was stoned.

The letter continued for a page and a half, outlining what he'd been up to. Most of it was a critique of his new teacher, the 'Incredible Shrinking Chrome-Dome', the chinless wonder who was forever scratching his balls.

He sealed the letter in an envelope, addressed it and thought, Why not? Walked the two blocks to William's place and slipped the letter into his box. When he got home he went to his room and picked up his guitar. He could hear the chooks, still, and the rooster you weren't supposed to keep in the suburbs.

William was content. Like a possum sitting in a tree, waiting for food to come to him. His plasticine face was finished with the hint of a smile. He held his body still, barely moving, breathing long, shallow breaths.

Greg counted them in and they started to play. It was Nimrod's Cat's weekly rehearsal, although they hadn't met for nearly a month. There'd been weddings, birthdays, work, an ingrown toenail and a dog to be put down. So they were rusty. The drums and bass didn't quite gel. The rhythm guitar was behind the beat and William couldn't reach notes he'd sung a few weeks before. There was a lethargy in the back room of his Shangri-La.

Still, they'd promised him a no-covers rehearsal. No Beatles, no Stones, no Pistols. Not even a 'Long Tall Sally' whipped off as a warm-up. Today it was all about engineering – the oxywelding of guitar, drums and bass. Improvising. Testing and rejecting dumb lyrics and over-complicated riffs.

Homestead Seven Hundred
I love your halogen plates
The cactus in your gravel
The sound your toilet makes.

William's new song was slow but loud, underscored with power chords and beefy bass notes. He raised his voice, shouting high notes until they were all gravel, nodding at the others when he needed a harmony. They were unsure, but followed their scribbled charts carefully, powering along when they finally reached the chorus.

Homestead Seven Hundred
Your quarter-inch snot-green turf
I'm coming through your French doors
You're Heaven here on Earth.

They stopped for coffee, to slouch on the lounge and watch *Viva Las Vegas*. As they took in the corny lines and lip-synced songs, William could see Charlie sitting on the rug beside him. He could see him scanning their CD, looking up at him and asking questions. Could remember the words he'd read that morning.

As he sits listening he picks snot from the corner of his nose.
Then I see him rolling it into a ball, and flicking it.

He could remember Charlie's description of his argument with Lewis in the changeroom, the quartet's performance, his new teacher's smell ('hair oil and cheap deodorant, burrito breath, and when he takes off his shoes ... disgusting'), his walk ('like he's got something up his bum') and the way he rolled his r's when he pronounced words like 'arpeggios'. He could remember the tone of the letter, hear Charlie's voice, see his smile, his hands moving in perpetual motion, his shoulders drooping. He could see the glow of his skin, the fine line of his eyebrows. And he could hear his half-child, half-adolescent voice breaking, conserving words like they had a dollar value.

Charlie was fuming. Storming down Edwards Avenue, away from Lindisfarne College – from D-average students who ruled the basketball courts, telling him he needed to 'shrink a little'; away from endless overhead transparencies – pages of facts no one was ever going to remember, thousands of words they were made to copy into their books for no good reason; away from the smell of the canteen – chicken-nugget rolls and hard-bottomed pies – as they were made to queue in the sun clutching a fistful of sweaty money; but worst of all – away from Mr Neil.

He tripped, turned and kicked the tree root. 'Fuck.' Hitching his school bag over his shoulder and continuing. He could remember Neil leaning over him, his face an inch away from his nose, smelling the science teacher's breath and seeing the yellow margins where his teeth met his gums. Hearing his voice: 'So, are we going to go through all of this again, Mr Price?'

'No.'

'Which reminds me, I never received an apology for last time.'

'For what?'

'You've got a short memory. If you look on your Focus Room card it says, quote,' and he took a yellow card from his top pocket, ' "Before re-entering class it is the student's responsibility to negotiate terms with the teacher." ' He looked up. '*Before* entering class.'

'I didn't realise.'

'How many years have you been here?'

Back on Edwards Avenue, Charlie was livid. He moved to avoid a pile of dog shit in the middle of the footpath. What sort of person just leaves it there, he thought, going on to consider the merits of its colour and shape, and how it was left in exactly the same spot every few days. He read fresh graffiti on a Stobie pole – 'The Vagina Cooling Machine' – with a picture of a man with his glasses bolted onto the side of his head. He crossed the road to avoid a mum with a pram and two kids in tow; she called something to him but he just kept walking. Then he realised she was an old neighbour. When he looked back she was gone. He kept walking, turning into William's driveway. He climbed the few crumbling steps to his front door and knocked.

Then he waited, feeling his heart racing. He wiped sweat from his face.

William opened the door. 'Charlie.'

'G'day, Mr Dutton.'

William was wearing a T-shirt, boxer shorts and thick socks. 'You okay?' he asked, sensing the boy's distress.

'It's Mr Neil.'

'*Ah.*'

'He sent me out of class again.'

William was trying to hide the relief in his voice, the simple, quietly spoken, thank-God-it's-all-over happiness that was washing over him. He could feel his fingers shaking, and his eyes were swimming in Charlie's. There was a drop of sweat about to run down the boy's cheek and he wanted to wipe it, but dared not.

'I could get suspended,' Charlie said.

'No one's gonna suspend you.'

'Neil said they might. He's such a complete fuckwit.'

William looked up and down the street. 'Come in.'

They sat in the lounge room. Charlie dropped his bag and took a moment to remember. The shaggy carpet. The springs erupting through the leather lounge. The piles of CDs and books. Then he looked at William. 'He hates me.'

'I can't imagine you taking on Neil.'

'He always starts it.'

William noticed Charlie's scuffed leather shoes, his long socks fallen down around his ankles, his legs, covered with new scars and bruises and a graze just below his left knee. 'You hurt yourself?'

'I came off my bike.'

He noticed his shorts, too tight, faded, fraying around the edges, and his shirt, stained with what looked like paint. 'So, what's Neil upset about this time?'

'We were doing this prac, mixing chemicals, and Simon, who was working with me, dropped a pestle and it cracked in half. Along comes old knob-nuts and starts in on me. I told him it wasn't me but he says, "This is typical of you, Price".'

'He wouldn't listen?'

'He wouldn't give me a chance. Eventually I just ... exploded, and called him something.'

'What?'

'I don't know ... wanker ... something. Then he says, "Teachers don't have to be abused by students". And I said, "It wasn't me". And Simon says, "It was me" – but he wouldn't listen. "Verbal abuse," he says, and he takes out his little yellow card.'

William was enjoying it. 'Once he said to me, "So, old man, you up for a bit of golf?" Like that ... old man. And I said, "No, I can't stand golf."'

'That sounds like him.'

'Well, at least you stood up for yourself.'

'But when he said verbal abuse, I just thought of what Dad would say. I tried to back off, I said, "Sorry, that just slipped out," but then the whole class laughed and he was even more pissed off.'

William couldn't help but smile.

'It's not funny.'

'I know.'

'I'm in deep shit.'

'If I could do something to help I would.'

Charlie's face mellowed. 'I guess I'll just have to tell Dad, eh?'

'Guess you will.'

'He'll freak out.'

'Maybe not.'

There was a pause, full of possibilities, and risks. William was the first to jump in. 'How you been?'

'Lewis made us get up and play "The Ash Grove".'

'So you said.'

Charlie saw his letter on the coffee table. 'You got it?'

'Thanks. It was funny. You're a very funny writer.'

'Cos I always fuck things up, eh?'

'Uh uh, language, Mr Price.'

'I fuck things up.'

'You don't. You just like to get to the bottom of things. You're honest, and you have a low tolerance of ...'

'Fuckwits.'

William stood. 'Fancy a drink?'

'Alcoholic?'

William's eyes narrowed. 'What about Coke?'

As William fetched a couple of Cokes, Charlie picked up his guitar and said, 'I told you I learned "Revolution"?'

'Yes.'

And he played – the blues chords, the elastic riff – and started singing. William returned and put the drinks on the table. He sat beside Charlie, busy playing around with the song – growling then whispering, throwing back his hair like a rock star, racing, shouting and then finishing with a flourish of chords that nearly broke a string.

William applauded. 'Very good. But what about your scales?'

'Screw my scales.'

He took the guitar from his student and said, 'Here's one I've written.'

Homestead Seven Hundred
I love your halogen plates
The cactus in your gravel
The sound your toilet makes.

He sang the song right through, occasionally meeting Charlie's eyes, looking away and back again. When he was finished, Charlie asked, 'Are you doing that with Nimrod's Cat?'

William nodded. 'The chorus sounds good with the big chords.'

'It was great playing with you guys.'

'We should do it again.'

'Well ...'

William censored his thoughts, but it didn't seem to matter. 'Look at this.' He showed the boy a small, hand-torn leaflet promoting a party they were playing in two days' time. Charlie studied the photo-copied image of the band. 'It's amazing, when you play a chord and the amps just roar.'

'There's nothing better, eh?'

'And your voice just cuts through everything.'

William picked up his drink. 'Well, ask your dad. See if he wants to come along.'

'You've got to be kidding.'

'I bet he'd love to hear you.'

'I bet he wouldn't.'

'Ask.'

Charlie folded the leaflet and put it in his top pocket. Perhaps, he thought, it was William's way of repairing things: Bring your dad, your sister, your uncles, everyone. From now on it's all about rock'n'roll. 'That guitar quartet,' he said. 'You should've been there.'

'And he conducted?'

'Like this.' Charlie imitated a conductor, flinging his arms about and almost knocking over a lamp. '"Come on, boys, nice strong beat." I'd just love to get up there with one of your amps.'

'Not much chance of that now.'

Charlie waited, screwed up his nose, like he'd just been embarrassed by one of his dad's farts. 'You know, you didn't have to quit.'

There was a long pause, the sound of roof iron expanding and a rubbish truck revving up a few blocks away. William said, 'I just …' But realised there was no way of explaining.

'You got more work?'

'Soon, I hope. At this school full of religious zealots.'

'There's no chance you could come back?'

Their eyes met. 'I was a real bloody idiot,' William said.

Charlie's didn't realise what William was saying; why he needed to say it, why there was, or ever had been, a problem. 'You'd need to work on your parenting skills.'

'How's that?'

'If you ever had kids … although, for that to happen, you'd have to attract an actual female.'

William smiled, and felt happy. He messed the boy's hair and pushed his head away. 'And you, with your tantrum. Oh, run away!'

And they were laughing, William pretending to strangle him, Charlie pushing him back. They fell to the floor, and William's head narrowly avoided the coffee table. He looked up. 'Focus Room!' Grabbed Charlie's leg and twisted it.

Eventually they sat opposite each other with their legs crossed. Charlie's top button had come off and William found it on the rug. 'Ask your dad,' he said, returning it.

'I don't think so.'

'At least ask him.'

Charlie stared at him. 'It's okay. I'm a big boy now.'

No words.

'So, what's he like, your old man?' William asked.

And Charlie started to explain.

The next day William looked it up in the book: Datsunland (PJV Nominees). He found the address, scribbled it on the back of an envelope, grabbed his keys and wallet and set out.

Datsunland was one in a string of car yards lining the northern arterial. Each looked the same – cracked bitumen littered with mid-priced Toyotas and low-kilometre Korean numbers for the kids. There were strings of coloured flags fluttering in the KFC-breeze, sandwich boards with 'Must Sell 2-Day' and scaffolded backdrops with images of everyone's favourite uncle in polyester pants.

Datsunland was down in the feeding chain of second-hand car yards. Its fences and gates were rusted, the ground cracked and full of weeds where deep puddles formed around the cars on rainy days. The office was a transportable purchased as Education Department surplus. Inside, there were still holes where the blackboard had been mounted, and above this, a faded alphabet that someone had tried to scrape off.

William pulled up in front of the yard. He turned off his engine and studied the cars. A few old Mazdas at the back decorated with fluorescent '$999' windshield posters. Towards the front, early model Magnas, Lancers and Corollas and an out-of-place Saab Cabriolet with a 'Low Price Today Only' sign sitting on its roof.

He got out and walked into the yard. Wandered between the cars, pretending to read information hanging in the windows. Strangely, he could only see one Datsun: an early-eighties 280ZX. Judging from the faded sign at the back of the yard, he guessed it was just a name that had stuck. Maybe someone thought it too good a brand to give up. *Datsunland*. Oz with hubcaps – some sort of fantasy world minus the fantasy. He noticed a young man washing cars, and a girl sitting beside him filing her fingernails. The only would-be customer was a mum with her pockmarked son inspecting a Nissan Pulsar.

A nasal voice came over the PA. 'Damien, telephone please.' William watched as a small, mushroom-shaped man emerged from a back shed and wandered into the office.

He moved closer to the office and looked in the window. He saw Damien Price on the telephone, shaking his head, sorting through a pile of papers on his desk. He studied his face. There were traces of Charlie – the curve of his nose, his flat forehead and compact ears. He could see a photo on his desk. The outline of two figures. As he got closer he made out this man and Charlie sitting on a jetty, fishing. Charlie was younger, his head rounder, his smile broader. Damien had his arm around him, and he was holding up a small fish.

There was another photo – a woman, but she was hidden behind a gluepot and stapler.

He rehearsed the words in his head.

You must be Damien?

He imagined shaking hands and Damien smiling and thanking him for being such a positive influence on his son. The older man would say, So, you're Guru Dutton, eh? Before long they'd be sitting in his office drinking instant coffee. He'd say, I've come to invite you to a gig. It's my band, but Charlie's going to get up. Damien would smile and look interested and say, I think I'm a bit old for all that, and he'd reply, It'd mean a lot to him. Then there'd be a pause. He didn't want to ask you, he'd continue. But I think, perhaps ...

But then from inside the office Damien slammed down the phone. He walked out, sliding the glass door behind him. Turning, he said, 'You after some help?'

William stared at him. 'No, thanks, just browsing.'

It was a backyard party. A friend of a friend of Greg's brother was getting engaged. Christmas decorations had been taken out a few months early, strung up through trees, fence posts and an old Hills Hoist with a ten-degree lean. There were a few card tables covered in pizza, No Frills dips, empty beer bottles and full ashtrays. The band had set up inside the shell of an old lean-to. They'd hung up their banner and put their amps out in full sun. Cords snaking everywhere, terminating at a mixing desk, itself plugged into an old power point that hung loose from the wooden frame of the lean-to. Groups of twenty- and thirty-something teachers and brokers, gardeners and dropouts stood about talking. There was a dog, and he was sniffing people's feet, dry-pissing on the skeleton of an old fruit tree and barking at a pair of pigeons.

William and Charlie sat together on the dead lawn. Charlie was playing an acoustic – the riff to 'Stairway to Heaven'.

'You're murdering it,' William said.

'It's hard.'

'Slowly … it's just a broken chord.'

William sat close to the boy. He took the fretboard and tried to show him the correct fingering. Charlie tried again, and William guided his hand. As they played, Pete Ordon came in a side gate. He looked around, but couldn't see anyone he recognised, so started to separate his six-pack of beers and pack them in ice.

'Pete,' a tall man said, approaching him and shaking his hand.

'Dan. How are you?'

As he talked to this man, Pete saw Charlie and William on the grass. He noticed them together, and their hands overlapping on the fretboard. He noticed William touch the boy's shoulder, and squeeze it, and he saw how they laughed and looked at each other. He noticed how they were like brothers, or perhaps something closer. Father and son? There was no sense of distance between them, physical or otherwise. From what he could see, William was not teaching, and Charlie certainly wasn't learning. It was an entirely different togetherness.

After he broke off his conversation he wandered over to them.

William looked up, saw him and leaned back with his hands on the dead grass. 'How are you, Pete?'

'Good. And you?'

'Fine.'

Pete looked at Charlie. 'Good to see you here, Mr Price. How's the BMX going?'

Charlie avoided looking at him. 'Fine.'

'No broken bones?'

'No.'

'And what's today … a bit of extracurricular?'

William noticed a sort of superior look on his old friend's face. He said, 'He's gonna play a few songs with us.'

'Good.'

William sat up, placing his hands in his lap. 'How's my replacement going?'

'Very organised. Had this lot playing at an assembly.' He indicated Charles.

'I heard,' William said. '"The Ash Grove"?'

'Yes.'

'I never got around to all that.'

'Well, he comes very well recommended.'

'By whom?' Charlie asked.

Pete just looked at him. Party or no party, *he* wasn't about to let the boy cross the line. 'Well, Charlie, Mr Dutton did up and leave us.'

'But he wants to come back.'

Pete looked at William. 'Really?'

'No.'

'He does.'

'See, that'd be a problem, Charlie,' Pete continued. 'We only need so many guitar teachers.'

'Well, get rid of Lewis.'

'Mr Lewis.'

'Everybody hates him.'

'I don't know about that.'

'I do. Everyone says so.'

'That's not what I hear.'

'From his students?'

Pete waited for William's support, but didn't receive it. 'Well, Charlie, you should make a petition.'

'I will.'

'Although, there's more to it, isn't there, son?'

'*Son?*'

William shook his head. 'No, it was my doing, Chuck. Like they say, you reap as you sow.'

Charlie grinned. 'You make your bed and you lie in it.'

'It takes two.'

'There's no business like show business.'

'Once bitten, twice shy.'

'A bird in the hand is worth two in the bush.'

They continued as Pete watched on. 'Well, good luck,' he said.

'You too,' William replied.

Pete walked off, looking for a familiar face. He found Greg and they started talking. As Charlie returned to his riff, William watched them. He noticed how they leaned into each other, shrugged, and seemed so serious. He saw them turn, look at him and Charlie and then look away.

He lay back on the grass and wondered. He'd been drinking other people's beer and now he'd half-emptied a bottle of someone's brandy. He looked up at the sky and felt the ground moving beneath him.

Christ, I'm drifting again, he realised, but then thought, So what?

He was happy to hear Charlie's bung notes and buzzing strings. He was glad to smell him, sense him. He sat up and took the guitar from him. As he played 'My Sweet Lord', he taught him where to sing the 'Hallelujahs' and 'Hare Krishnas'. After a while a few people joined in. He was happy, lost in the only world that seemed to make sense to him. But all the time there was the nagging feeling that he'd stepped out of reality and would have to soon return.

Then Charlie said, 'Hare Krishna? I thought you were Christian?'

'*Blessed Edmund …*'

'*Pray for us …*'

William returned the guitar and said, 'You know, since I'm not paid to be a role model any more, I may as well tell you: there is no God.'

Charlie grinned. 'Nobody believes in that bullshit.'

'Sinner!'

'And, since you're no longer my role model, what else would you like to admit?'

William looked at him, unsure. 'One question each. Complete truth.'

'Okay.'

'So … why do you hang around with a sod like me, when you should be off chasing girls?'

'I could ask you the same question.'

'But I asked you.'

Charlie thought for a moment, then said, 'Physically, I can see something in them.'

'Yes?'

'Coming from a boys' school, it's been difficult to find someone with … what I mean is, I've met some girls but then they're taking your picture with a phone, and messaging their mates.'

'You need someone you can relate to?'

'Right, my go. Same question.'

William thought for a moment and said, 'Same answer.'

Charlie was confused. 'But you must have plenty of friends.'

William looked up and Greg and Justin were standing above them. 'Come on,' Greg said.

They started with Charlie's 'String of Words'. Charlie sang the verse and William joined him for the chorus. There was only one microphone, so they sang together, their faces an inch or two apart. They tried to avoid each other's eyes but it was difficult, and they ended up smiling at each other, laughing.

Damien looked at his watch. It was after ten. He was angry, again. Still, he knew there was no point going over old ground. It was just a phase. He felt he was getting off lightly. Six, twelve months perhaps and Charlie would come good. He'd relearn the art of conversation (this time with actual thought-out words), mingle, appear to care about other people, lose his awkwardness, gain stature, strength and grace.

Perhaps.

A car pulled up further down the street. He stood behind his oleander and watched, and listened, as the engine idled. Loud, muffled music. A door opened and Charlie got out. He leaned into the car, said a few words then slammed the door.

Damien went inside. Turned up the television and sat in his recliner. Picked up the phone, held it to his mouth and waited. As Charlie came in he said, 'Okay, Rob, gotta go. See y' tomorrow.' And rang off.

'G'day,' Charlie said, standing in the doorway.

'Christ, you're sunburnt.'

'Am I?'

'How's Simon?'

'Good.'

'His dad still sick?' He stared at the television, then his son. 'What did you say it was?'

'Liver cancer.'

A long pause. 'Liver?'

'Yeah.'

'He in pain?'

'He wasn't there much. Anyway ... good night.'

'Night, son.'

Charlie went to his room, peeled off his shirt and smelt it. No smoke. Just the same, he took off his shorts, went into the bathroom and buried his clothes at the bottom of the wash basket. He returned to his room, found a pair of boxers in a pile on the floor and slipped them on. The birch tree was scraping his window, so he opened it, broke off the branch. Then sat on his bed, looking through his latest copy of *Rolling Stone*.

How depressing, he thought, looking at a picture of Keith Richards – sad, pathetic old man. Maybe I need a plan. Something to do when I'm too old to rock'n'roll. Write novels. Produce other people's music. Or die.

Damien was standing in his doorway. 'They go yellow.'

'Who?'

'People with liver problems.'

Charlie shrugged. 'He didn't look yellow.'

'No?'

Damien sat on the end of the bed. He produced the leaflet he'd found in Charlie's shirt pocket and pressed it flat on the sheets. 'Look what you missed.'

Charlie read it, then said, 'I didn't think you'd let me go.'

'How often do I say no?'

'It was just cos it was Mr Dutton.'

'What would I have against Mr Dutton?'

'Because ... I like to do stuff with him.'

Damien shrugged. 'So?' He looked at his son. 'I trust you,' he said, realising these might be the dumbest words he'd ever spoken. '*Can* I trust you?'

'Of course.'

'So?'

Charlie was studying the way his carpet had faded, and come apart. 'Mr Dutton, he's a top bloke,' he said. 'I mean, a good teacher, but not like the other idiots. You know?'

'I know.'

Charlie met his father's stare. 'Thanks,' he whispered. Then he pointed to William on the leaflet. 'That's him.'

Damien studied his face. 'I've seen him.'

'Where?'

'At work. He was looking for a car.'

'Are you sure it was him?'

'I reckon.'

Damien pushed the leaflet aside and said, 'Your mother was always on about Jesus this, Jesus that, eh?'

'And her rosary, remember her rosary?'

'I still got it.' In his bedside drawer, on top of a pile of freshly ironed handkerchiefs. 'Remember how she used to say, Life is a gift from God?'

'Did she?'

'Always. She said you repay it by doing what you're good at.' He stopped to wipe sleep from his eyes. 'She'd get out her Bible at bedtime and off she'd go – "The Pharaoh ruled over the Israelites." And there's me, tuning into the races.'

Charlie sat forward. He could remember her with her Bible. 'What would she say?'

'"Turn that rubbish off!" And I'd say, "If you turn yours off."'

Charlie took a deep breath and then asked, 'So, you think maybe that's what I'm good at?'

'Who knows? But you've gotta try everything. Otherwise it's off to Datsunland.'

'But you like cars.'

'Yeah, that's right – I like cars.'

There was a light breeze coming in the window and the sounds of cats in the undergrowth. Damien stomped on the floorboards, but they didn't stop. 'How did your concert go?'

Charlie's eyes lit up. 'Great. We played my song.'

'Ah, the *bullshit* song?'

'Yes, it's good, isn't it?'

'It is. The sort of thing people want to hear.'

'And we jammed on a few more. "Revolution". Want to hear?'

Before Damien could answer Charlie had his guitar across his legs. He bit his lip as he concentrated, and played the blues riff. Occasionally he'd look at his father and he'd nod approval.

Damien looked at the leaflet and the grainy, photocopied image of William Dutton. He was relieved.

In the moments after the noise subsides, he guessed, everything becomes clear. How the bits are just part of the whole, and how this drama of colour and movement is over before you know it's begun. How the things you say, and do, mostly, can't and won't change anything. Almost like it's all said, done, scripted, made, finished, and you're just waiting as the clock ticks, the hours unwind, down to minutes, and the moments (smelling of cut grass, and hair oil, and spring mornings) coming away from whatever it is you thought was holding life together. But nothing is. Just chance, accidents, good fortune, sometimes. As he heard Carol (in her last few hours) saying, There's no point worrying. Everything will be perfect … everything.

He looked at the boy and for the first time saw fine, black hair on his arms. He was surprised, but not concerned. Everything about his son was new – his proficiency with bar chords, the croak in his throat, the valley across his chest.

Yes, he thought, remembering awkward prayers. It's all part of the deal – love and six months' free registration. An eternity of agapanthus shedding their flowers.

William sat, lost, watching Langdon Hughes' LA report. There was a mental breakdown, an unwanted pregnancy and a writers' strike. Langdon had a habit of sitting forward, twisting his fingers together and smiling at his audience. William wondered why he appeared to be so happy. Was it surgical, well rehearsed? Was this a valid way of earning money? And who was watching?

He heard a knock on the door and muttered, 'Fuck off!' He waited but the knock returned. So he dragged himself up, walked across the room and opened the door.

It was John Mosby, principal of Lindisfarne College. 'G'day, William.'

William searched for a response. 'John.'

The older man wore a dark suit, white shirt and a red and green striped tie. He had a principal's face – shaved and buffed, unemotional, waiting to sit in judgement. His eyes were small peas in a big pudding. He was well fed. His teeth were even, with the slightest gap at the front. 'Can I come in?'

'Of course.'

William showed him in and cleared junk mail and soiled clothes from the lounge. He removed an empty Coke can from the coffee table and asked, 'A drink?'

'No, thanks.'

'Careful where you sit. There's a spring coming up there.'

Mosby checked before he sat down. William sat opposite him. 'How are you?'

'Fine.'

He could feel a tremor in his fingers and arms and hoped it wasn't noticeable in his voice. 'Everything going smoothly at Lindisfarne?'

'Yes.'

'I miss my little room. With my little window, and all that BO.'

Mosby tried to smile. 'You're probably wondering why I'm here.'

'Well, maybe it's because you want me back.'

No reply. A bad sign, surely, he guessed.

Mosby sat forward and rested his elbows on his knees. 'It's about one of your students.'

'Oh ... who's that?'

'A Year Nine, Charlie Price.' He waited for William's reaction.

'I taught him for a while.'

'I've heard you spend a lot of time with the boy.'

'A lot of time?'

'Time outside of school.'

'He's been to see my band. And he's played with us.'

The principal waited. 'And?'

'And?'

'He's been here?'

'Yes. He came to see my guitar collection.'

Mosby smiled. 'William, you know the rules.'

'What?'

'Did he have his parents' permission?'

'I suppose not.'

'So, whatever he says, a court will believe.'

William shook his head. 'Come on, John, he's not like that.'

'That's not the point. The thing is, you broke the rules.'

'Okay, perhaps I shouldn't have done it.'

'You certainly shouldn't have. You know who'll end up wearing it, when it comes home to roost.'

There was a long pause.

'And you socialise with him?' Mosby asked.

'I'm not breaking any laws.'

'To be honest, it might be good for him to see these things. But – ' and he raised and lowered his voice ' – you know as well as I, it's not about reality, it's perception.'

'What's supposed to have happened?'

The principal used his outstretched hand to make a point. 'I've seen this sort of thing happen before, William.'

'He hasn't got a mum. I help him; he's flourishing. Next thing you're saying I've – '

'I'm not saying anything.'

'Bullshit! You think ...' He trailed off. 'He's a smart, curious kid.'

'Good.'

'He loves music. The guitar. And not just the stuff he gets at Lindisfarne.'

Mosby stood up. 'Well, that's good. I didn't come for a fight, just a friendly word of advice. If the gossips take over, you know how it is, I'll have parents writing, questions from the board.'

William looked at his old boss. 'But what about the kid?'

'I've got eleven hundred kids, William. I don't want *Today Tonight* as well. You want people talking about you?'

'They won't.'

'They will. Keep going, they will. Then it won't be me, it'll be the cops at your door.'

William was caught in the middle of multiple truths.

'So,' Mosby continued, 'I've spoken to you, I've made the school's position clear.'

'Fine.'

'And I'm going to make a note of this, and date it, and sign it.'

All at once William remembered how much he hated schools, their bitumen yards, their fences, their drabness on warm spring days. 'Okay, John, you've made it clear.'

'I tell you, William, something like this would travel like wildfire. Some of those soccer mums, they'd have it around the school in hours.'

'Should I ask where you heard?'

'It doesn't matter.'

'Pete?'

'I've known it myself. You feel all chummy with a kid, and then you stop and realise ... something you've said.'

William lowered his head. 'Okay.' Then he shot up, walked to the door and held it open. 'All the best.'

'You too.'

'I take it you don't want to ask me back?'

'That's a separate issue, isn't it?'

An hour after William's talk with the principal, he entered the grounds of Lindisfarne College. His feet slipped on the gravel and he could smell pine oil around the chapel. He was still furious. He walked with fast, measured steps that left indents in the soft grass. Entering the music suite, he looked around for signs of life. A brass ensemble playing a chord full of slightly flat notes. Then he heard Pete's voice: 'What was that?'

'Bar nine,' someone replied.

'No, no.'

He walked into the rehearsal room and saw Pete standing in front of a group of seven or eight primary boys. 'Hello, Mr Ordon.'

'Mr Dutton. You wouldn't mind coming back in an hour or so?'

'Have you got a moment now?'

Pete put down his pencil and followed William out of the room. The door closed after them and William turned on him. 'So?'

'What?'

'Cut the bullshit.'

They stood facing each other.

'Why the fuck would you do that?' William said.

'What?'

He wiped his brow with his forearm. Pete looked at the food stains on his T-shirt, his unshaved face, slumped shoulders and bloodshot eyes. He could smell his breath. For a moment he wanted to help him, to be truthful, to return to what they had just a few weeks before. 'You look a mess,' he said.

'John said, "I'll be writing all this down, and dating and signing it."'

Pete didn't reply.

'He says, "I'll pick up the phone, and I'll call the cops."'

'Could you blame him?'

'You could've talked to me first.'

'I did.'

The students filed out of the rehearsal room carrying their instruments and music. 'Bell's about to go,' one said.

'Make sure you practise.'

The boys left. Pete decided it had to be said. 'What's going on with Charlie?'

'You don't get it, do you?'

'He asked to swap teachers.'

'So?'

'The way he looks at you. I'm not blind, William ... or stupid.'

They stopped as a cleaner passed through. Pete took him into his office. He sat him down and said, 'I read about this teacher who was deregistered. He took the boy for hockey, and used to drive him home ...'

'Fuck. Come on then, say it.'

'This stuff's always in the papers. People see it. That's what John means.'

William knew there was no point continuing. 'You think I'll get another job now?'

'Of course.'

There was a pause, then William stormed from the office. He walked from the music suite and stood on the grass in front of the windows dressed with teddy bears.

What was done was done. There was an order at Lindisfarne. It was reflected in the Neo-Gothic columns on the music suite. The smooth rendering on the walls. The rows of office windows in the administration block. There was no point imagining circles, or abstractions, or conceptual lines. It was about the solid, the real. The way things always had and would be done. Lindisfarne belonged to people who were happy navigating these lines. Who moved slowly, in small steps, or invented algorithms to move at a faster rate. People who saw the lines as something to be gotten up for in the morning. To dress in a suit for. To eat toast and drink No Frills tea for.

William sat on the grass overlooking the main oval. He watched a group of boys playing rugby. Some had their shoes off and nearly all of them had their shirts untucked. They tackled roughly and once they were down they rolled on each other, fighting for the ball.

He squinted and noticed Charlie among the group. He was standing back, eating a roll or sandwich and occasionally, when the ball came near him, he would approach it, push one of his mates, laugh, and then shout something across the oval.

A feeling came over him as he watched. A suspicion, a hunch that became solid, real – like the poplars moving in the wind on the edge of the oval as the distant city sweated fuel and light. His feeling concerned the boy, Charlie Price: a child, still, roasting in the glow of a long, hot childhood.

The mind I'd have, if I had my time again, he thought. The body I'd walk around in. The nose I'd turn up. The tongue I'd stick out. The songs I'd sing.

Someone pushed Charlie and he dropped his roll. He ran at the other boy, dragged him onto the ground, stood and placed his foot on his stomach. Then the other boy grabbed his leg and pulled him over.

They wrestled.

Charlie gathered his lunch and tried a final karate kick on the boy as he stood.

William felt completely empty. This wasn't his world, after all. His world was full of people he didn't like, who turned on him, daily, drawing blood, saying things to make him remember his unhappiness. His world was an hour wasted trying to requisition stationery he couldn't properly justify. His world was full of people who walked past him, but pretended to notice other things. Then there were the complaining parents he couldn't understand, the memos about lights left on and food left too long in the fridge. A world full of Post-it notes raining down on him, reminding him to cook, write, submit, clean, service and deliver.

'You idiot,' he whispered, watching the boys, feeling the walls of Lindisfarne closing in around him.

He noticed that the tall, thoughtful, stand-alone boy looked happy. It was his choice – to be there, in the thick of it, but apart from the others.

Charlie looked up, took a moment and then waved to him. He waved back. Charlie picked up his shoes and ran up the hill to him. 'You're back?'

'I just came to see Pete.'

They sat together. Charlie spread his feet on the grass. He stretched out his legs and William could see his long, arching bones. His knees were knobbly, still, and William watched as he wiped a fresh cut on his leg.

'Having fun?' he asked.

'Not really.'

'Sometimes you actually do kids' stuff?'

Charlie shrugged. 'It's killing time. What are my options? This place is so boring.'

William looked into his eyes. He noticed his cheeks, flushed, and a small, brown freckle he hadn't noticed before. 'Boring, but necessary,' he said.

'Why?'

'That becomes evident ... later. Another four years, then you can start living.'

'Haven't I started already?'

'Perhaps.'

William turned and whispered to him. 'There are these wonderful things called girls.'

'Wonderful?'

'You'll find yourself staring at them, hanging around them, trying to be funny.'

'Bullshit.'

'And then you'll get in a shit-hot band, make a record and earn millions.'

'I'll just join you guys.'

'We're just a bunch of old geriatrics. But you ...'

Charlie could see a change in his teacher: a stillness, a resignation that had replaced words with smiles, anger with acceptance. But this must have been good, because surely this man couldn't change? If he could, or did, then everything he'd come to sense and understand would mean nothing. Life would just be discount beans. He smiled and tried to reanimate his best friend. 'I'll be the front man, and you geris can be my backing band.'

William stood. 'And I'm sure you'll be shit-hot.'

'Where you going?'

'Home.'

Charlie stood beside him. 'I's gonna say, when you had your next jam, is it okay if I came along?'

William hesitated. 'There's nothing organised yet. But I'll let you know.'

Charlie took a few moments and stared at his favourite teacher. 'Mr Dutton, you okay?'

'Yeah.'

'Did you ask Mr Ordon about getting your job back?'

William almost laughed. 'He said they'll have to wait and see.'

'Maybe next year?'

'Maybe. See y' round, Charlie Price.'

'Mr Dutton ... sir.'

They waited, silently, as boys often did, because there was so little, really, that needed to be said.

'Oh, I almost forgot,' William said. He took a set of strings from his pocket and handed them to the boy. 'Fender. Phosphor bronze. Medium gauge.'

Charlie smiled and took them. 'Where did you get them?'

William indicated the music suite. 'Dickhead's office.'

'Back to your game, please, Mr Price,' a deep voice said.

William looked up to see John Mosby standing on a rise with his arms crossed. 'Mr Dutton was just on his way, weren't you?'

Three weeks went by and Charlie hadn't heard from him. So, one cool Saturday morning he went to his teacher's house and knocked on the door.

William answered. 'Charlie?'

'G'day ... I hadn't heard from you.'

'I've been busy.'

'You had a practice yet?'

'No.'

William bowed his head. He saw that the cracks in the concrete path around the house had widened. Weeds were already coming up. He looked at Charlie and he was still smiling, waiting. 'Can I come in?' he asked.

William looked at a fresh scar on the boy's cheek. He saw that his eyes were moist, and clear, and there was food dried on his chin.

Acknowledgements

'Dr Singh's Despair' (*Southerly* 68/1, August 2008)

'The Shot-put' (*Meanjin*, December 2008)

'Guarding the Pageant' (*Small City Tales of Strangeness and Beauty*, Wakefield Press anthology, February 2009)

'The Confirmation' (*Quadrant*, September 2009)

Riverland Stories ('The Photographer's Son', 'The Barmera Drive-in', 'The Pyap School', 'The Shack'). Published by the National Year of Reading 2012.

'The Photographer's Son' (*Quadrant*, November 2013)

'Datsunland' (*Griffith Review* 54, Novella Edition 'Earthly Delights', November 2016)

'The Shack' (*Southerly* 76/2, Long Paddock, January 2017)

Thanks to Alex Frayne for the cover image, Liz Nicholson for the cover design, as well as Michael Bollen, Michael Deves, Emily Hart and Ayesha Aggarwal at Wakefield Press.

HILL OF GRACE

Stephen Orr

1951. Among the coppiced carob trees and arum lilies of the Barossa Valley, old-school Lutheran William Miller lives a quiet life with his wife, Bluma, and son Nathan, making wine and baking bread. But William has a secret. He's been studying the Bible and he's found what a thousand others couldn't: the date of the Apocalypse.

William sets out to convince his neighbours that they need to join him in preparation for the End. The locals of Tanunda become divided. Did William really hear God's voice on the Hill of Grace? Or is he really deluded? The greatest test of all for William is whether Bluma and Nathan will support him. As the seasons pass in the Valley, as the vines flower and fruit and lose their leaves, William himself is forced to question his own beliefs and the price he's willing to pay for them.

The Barossa Valley of the 1950s is beautifully captured in this, Stephen Orr's second novel. His first novel, *Attempts to Draw Jesus*, was a runner up in the 2000 Vogel Award and published by Allen & Unwin.

'His prose lovingly packed with particulars, Orr's characters assume poignant life as modernity and old-time religion go head to head in a wonderful period portrait.' – Cath Kenneally

For more information please visit www.wakefieldpress.com.au

TIME'S LONG RUIN

Stephen Orr

Nine-year-old Henry Page is a club-footed, deep-thinking loner, spending his summer holidays reading, roaming the melting streets of his suburb, playing with his best friend Janice and her younger brother and sister. Then one day Janice asks Henry to spend the day at the beach with them. He declines, a decision that will stay with him forever.

Time's Long Ruin is based loosely on the disappearance of the Beaumont children from Glenelg beach on Australia Day, 1966. It is a novel about friendship, love and loss; a story about those left behind, and how they carry on: the searching, the disappointments, the plans and dreams that are only ever put on hold.

Winner, Unpublished manuscript award, Adelaide Festival

South Australian winner, 2012 National Year of Reading awards

'In *Time's Long Ruin* [Orr] has conjured up the suburban claustrophobia of the Fifties and added to it streaks of … darker pigments. His Thomas Street, Croydon – particularly on hot days, when no one has enough to do and everyone gets on each other's nerves – is Adelaide's very distinctive version of Winton's *Cloudstreet*, Malouf's *Edmondstone Street* and White's *Sarsaparilla*; but the quality and vividness of Orr's evocation of those stultifying times ensures he can hold his head high in such illustrious company. *Time's Long Ruin* is a compelling page-turner.' – Richard Walsh

For more information please visit www.wakefieldpress.com.au

DISSONANCE

Stephen Orr

Dissonance begins with piano practice. Fifteen-year-old Erwin Hergert is forced to tackle scales and studies for six hours a day by his mother, Madge, who is determined to produce Australia's first great pianist. To help Erwin focus, Madge has exiled her husband, Johann, to the back shed.

Madge takes Erwin to Hamburg to continue his studies. Erwin prospers in Germany with his new teacher until he meets a neighbour, sixteen-year-old Luise, and finds there's more to life than music.

Meanwhile, Germany is moving towards war. Late 1930s Hamburg forms the backdrop to an increasingly difficult love-triangle, as Erwin is torn between the piano, Luise, and the demands of his love and devotion to his mother. Soon the bombs, real and imagined, start falling. Marriage and parenthood give way to death, and tragedy. Before long Erwin and Madge are drawn into the horrors of a war that leaves little time for music.

Dissonance is a re-imagining of the 'Frankfurt years' of Rose and Percy Grainger. This is a novel about love in one of its most extreme and destructive forms, and how people attempt to survive the threat of possession.

'Compelling ... an engrossing novel. Orr is a vivid storyteller.' – Stella Clarke, *Weekend Australian*

'Our own Wakefield Press has produced a nicely bound and presented work which ranks as one of the finest pieces of Australian writing I've seen for a long time.' – Peter C. Pugsley, *Indaily*

For more information please visit www.wakefieldpress.com.au

THE HANDS

Stephen Orr

He didn't look like he could jump a bull, but she knew he could. It was all in the hands, he'd often explain. The will. The bloody mindedness.

On a cattle station that stretches beyond the horizon, seven people are trapped by their history and the need to make a living. Trevor Wilkie, the good father, holds it all together, promising his sons a future he no longer believes in himself. The boys, free to roam the world's biggest backyard, have nowhere to go.

Trevor's father, Murray, is the keeper of stories and the holder of the deed. Murray has no intention of giving up what his forefathers created. But the drought is winning ...

Longlisted for the 2016 Miles Franklin Literary Award

'Orr's ability to capture characters and the way they interact with each other is truly impressive. ... It's pretty darn perfect.' – Sue Terry, *Whispering Gums*

'*The Hands* has the scope of a Greek tragedy – not only in its focus on the violence underlying familial relationships. Ineluctable fate seems to press on a family forced into painful reflection. The encroaching desert is, like the Greek Moirai, remorseless ...' – Josephine Taylor, *Australian Book Review*

'The triumphant culmination of a five-book fascination with the dynamics of (family) groups as they function in extreme and often liminal situations ... Orr slides seamlessly in and out of his different characters' heads ... always moving the story efficiently along ...' – Katharine England, *Advertiser*

For more information please visit www.wakefieldpress.com.au

THE FIRST WEEK

Margaret Merrilees

Marian couldn't see the woman's eyes behind her glasses, and was filled with panic. That bosom was not for comfort. Not for Marian. She, Marian, was here so that this woman, this psychologist, could expose her failure to be a proper mother.

Her son's actions shatter Marian's life. As the days pass she is haunted by layers of grief rising like the salt of the degraded earth. Marian's everyday heroism, her earthy humour and innate honesty, sustain her as she confronts her own tragedy and sees beyond it to other moral dilemmas of white Australian life.

This novel has its roots in an ancient landscape – the dry farming country around Koikyennuruff (Stirling Ranges) in the south of Western Australia. It is the story of a journey from the country to the city and back again, a journey that will change Marian forever.

Winner of the Wakefield Press Unpublished Manuscript Award.
Shortlisted the Glenda Adams Award, NSW Premier's Awards.
Longlisted for the Dobbie Literary Award.
Shortlisted for the Barbara Jefferis Award.

'This moving and emotionally challenging debut novel shows an acute understanding of how prejudice against Aboriginal people influences perception of self and others ... [a] thought provoking stimulus for classroom discussion on racial prejudice and stereotypes.' – Margaret McEwan, *SCAN online journal for educators*

'... instantly gripping: picture-perfect in its capture of early bereavement, of distances and rapprochements between generations ... a writer of compassion, grace and insight.' – Cath Kenneally, author of *Jetty Road*, *Room Temperature*, and *Eaten Cold*

For more information please visit www.wakefieldpress.com.au

HERE WHERE WE LIVE

Cassie Flanagan Willanski

That's the thing about climate change, it comes home to you. In our case, literally – the fifth night after my husband's departure, while the children and I were sleeping in the front bedrooms, the old tree next door gave way and smashed through the kitchen roof at the back.

Brave and beautifully written, the stories that make up *Here Where We Live* chart the relationships white Australians have with the land and the Indigenous people they share it with.

A woman moves her three young children south in search of rain; a girl throws her glasses in the river to avoid bearing witness to uncomfortable truths; a boy involved in an act of desecration becomes a man with an identity crisis at an Indigenous healing ceremony; a pair of desperadoes take lessons in love from a woman and the ghost of her lifelong partner.

Winner of the Wakefield Press Unpublished Manuscript Award

'Each story in *Here Where We Live* provides much room for reflection about our own lives and our reactions to climate change and ... our attitudes to Aboriginal people. Equally importantly, each is beautifully written.' – Annette Marfording, *Rochford Street Review*

'This is a stunning, beautifully written and original work and I advise everyone to read it.' – Bill Holloway, *The Australian Legend*

'An original and engaging collection with many passages showing lyrical beauty and psychological depth.' – Gay Lynch, *Transnational Literature*

'I was moved and I was haunted.' – Brian Castro

For more information please visit www.wakefieldpress.com.au

Wakefield Press is an independent publishing and
distribution company based in Adelaide, South Australia.
We love good stories and publish beautiful books.
To see our full range of books, please visit our website at
www.wakefieldpress.com.au
where all titles are available for purchase.

Find us!

Twitter: www.twitter.com/wakefieldpress
Facebook: www.facebook.com/wakefield.press
Instagram: instagram.com/wakefieldpress

Printed in Australia
AUOC02n1601260517
286118AU00004B/4/P